FORBIDDEN STORM

A.R. VAGNETTI

FORBIDDEN STORM

First Edition

ISBN
Hardcover: 978-1-952152-04-7
Paperback: 978-1-952152-03-0
eBook: 978-1-952152-02-3

Edited by Sam Hendricks

BY A.R. VAGNETTI

FORGOTTEN STORM

FORBIDDEN STORM

ACKNOWLEDGEMENTS

None of my novels would be complete if I didn't thank several people who pushed… I mean inspired me along the way.

My undying gratitude goes to the love of my life, my husband. He boasts the patience of Job, a heart of gold, and is the best damn partner a woman could ask for. Thank you, babe, for always having my back, believing in my dreams even when I didn't, and doing the laundry.

Thanks goes to my biggest fan: my daughter Racheal. Your words of encouragement and excitement keep me going.

I'll share a little secret if you promise to keep it to yourself. The inspiration for Kurtis's character in the Storm Series is my personal trainer. His size and stature, and his devotion to family and friends, forged Kurtis's identity. So, thank you for being my eye candy even when I wanted to kick you in the shins for pushing me to my limits.

And as always, this book wouldn't be possible with my wonderful editors. Mary-Theresa Hussey at Reedsy, you helped take the first draft from disaster to some semblance of a novel.

My editor at Kyanite Publishing, Sam Hendricks: your attention to detail is amazing, but my favorite part is all the little uplifting notes you create in the margins. Their power made my heart soar and crushed my insecurities.

I'd also like to thank my awesome, amazing, and devoted beta readers! Jodi Baillie, without your critical eyes I would be lost. Mia Fendi, your support and encouragement never fail to inspire me.

And let's not forget the extremely talented Sophia LeRoux for once again creating a fantastic book cover!

Last but most important: I'd like to thank you, my readers, for taking a chance on an unknown author with Forgotten Storm, and for patiently waiting for Forbidden Storm. I hope you enjoy the ups and downs, twists and turns, heartbreak, and joy of Lucretia and Kurtis's journey as much as I enjoyed writing it.

A. R. Vagnetti

CHAPTER 1

Lucretia

Whatever gods control our fate and the universe have it in for me.

Despondent, I lean against the castle's inner courtyard wall. The swords strapped to my back press into my shoulder blades. The bitter cold of the pale stone seeps through my wool sweater. Even the fleece-lined leather pants and combat boots are no match for these freezing temperatures, and a shiver zings up my spine.

Here in the massive garden, the once fragrant flowers are lifeless, their roots dormant. Dozens of large trees stand barren, their enormous arms reaching toward the moonlit sky as if begging for the warmth of summer. Thick snow blankets the once vibrant green lawns, glittering like diamonds in the bright halo of light. Dead. Icy. Immersed in Canada's harsh winter. It mirrors my heart.

Out of habit, I fiddle with the end of my long braid which cascades down my chest as emotions bombard me. Guilt. Shame. Remorse. Daily I struggle with what I've done. Each cold glare or raised brow the queen shoots my direction lances fear through me. Nicki's a powerful empath. Does she sense my inner turmoil? I wake nightly dreading it could be my last.

As a warrior in the queen's Guardians, my duty is to protect humans from any rogue immortal species. Since the battle three months ago, I've jumped at the assignments farthest across the globe. Ones that keep me from the castle throughout the night and allow me to teleport straight to my room as dawn lightens the sky. Sleep. Repeat.

With her formal coronation days away, vampire leaders from every region assemble to support their queen. Other immortals inundate the outlying towns and villages. Those whose outward appearance passes for human roam freely. Those who don't, like the Centaur King or the Golem King, to name a few, stay hidden. I can't imagine what the humans living in those remote areas must think. The Nunavut Territory is the farthest north you can travel in North America. It's isolated, desolate, especially in winter, and with no roads in or out, a biplane is the only option for those who cannot teleport. Having an influx of so many must be confusing for them.

Thank goodness the immense security shield Icarus created centuries ago to surround the stronghold prevents other immortals with the ability to trace from just popping in whenever they desire. Unfortunately, that means the Guardians will be kept busy teleporting guests through the magical barrier on coronation night.

I rub my arms against the chill with a sigh as I recall the evening twelve years ago when Logan, the Guardian commander, knocked on my bedroom door and handed me a written copy of the prophecy before promptly assigning me to the teenage halfling's protection detail. He insisted I keep this duty secret from our king and my fellow warriors. After reading the decree, I understood why.

Our job was to protect the bringer of peace from her father, King Dimitri Giordano, his allies, and numerous enemies wanting him dead until her transition. It took two weeks before we finally found her, and we feared Dimitri would get to her first.

Until her twenty-fifth birthday, Nicole lived as a human, never suspecting Others existed. After her change, it surprised us how quickly she mastered her powerful abilities. She only trained for a few short months before challenging her father in mortal combat. The young halfling now rules over the largest immortal species on the planet—the Vampire Nation—and is the most youthful ruler in our history.

Impatient for their first look at the halfling, dignitaries and royalty from each species agreed to a temporary truce to attend the ceremony. With so many gathered in one place, security is our only priority. Which means I'm stuck in this enormous fortress with its ten square towers dominating the Canadian skyline every damn night.

"What are you doing out here all alone, Lucretia?"

The deep, seductive voice startles me from my internal chaos, and I straighten from the wall. The low rumble adds another complicated layer to my life.

From several feet away, he studies me until my blood boils and my pulse hammers in my ears. At six-eight, the big, sexy brute makes me wet with just a look. His intense sapphire eyes penetrate my soul. I itch to caress his broad shoulders and bulging biceps, run my fingers through his thick, short blond hair to discover if the strands are as soft as they appear, pierce the tender flesh of those full lips with my fangs and devour them, experience the darker scruff covering his strong jaw burning the inside of my thighs.

Dirty, wanton thoughts have consumed me more than I wish since peering into those blue depths on the battlefield, but dread fills my gut at his mere existence.

Kurtis Ruse is my one true mate, but he's forbidden—a shapeshifter. And not just any shifter, a future king, and the queen's closest friend. Based on the scowl he shoots my direction anytime we are in the same room, I'd bet my best dagger the bonding link is one-sided.

Even though the vampire within desires him with a craving akin to an addict, the incessant bond humming through my veins warns me the canine shifter might despise me. Nicki's triumph over King Dimitri birthed a semi-truce between our people, but vampire/shapeshifter history isn't a peaceful one.

It wouldn't matter if the link were mutual anyhow. Centuries ago our governing body, the Council of Unity, signed into law only immortals of the same species can complete a mating bond. Sex is permitted, given that pregnancy without the biological tie is extremely rare. Nicki exists because Dimitri had sex with a human, which is a big fat no-no, since keeping an immortal's inner beast under control during sex is almost impossible. For the safety of our races, we must keep humans ignorant of our existence.

But even with the laws in place, rumors ran amok of deformed offspring from such unlawful unions. It's all a load of dog shit. Their real fear is the unknown power a hybrid would possess. Can you imagine a vampire who was a slave to the pull of the full moon? Or a demon shifter? A centaur succubi? I shudder at the thought. We already fight the lure of bloodlust with our inner monster. I couldn't envision having to struggle with two internal beasts.

The council, along with every leader in the supernatural world, would view the child as an abomination, shifting the balance of power and nature. They would terminate the hybrid immediately, as well as the parents.

Harsh, but a necessary evil to continue to live in secrecy among humans.

The single reason the council spared Nicki's life was that she was born of a human with no otherworldly abilities. Not to mention, the High Priest Oracle foretold her future as the bringer of peace.

So, the 220-year-old, magnificent shifter prince devouring me with his scrutiny can never be mine. Sex with him, on the other hand—no, no, no. I could never control my inner vampire from completing the bond during sex. I'm only 142. I still struggle daily with my baser instincts and desires. Add in my physical and mental link to this male, and it would be all over. Regret sears my chest.

"It is no concern of yours, shifter." With quiet resolve, I harden my heart and lace my tone with a hatred I'm far from experiencing. I possess too many secrets to allow anyone close, especially the queen's best friend.

The frosty exterior that served me well since becoming a Guardian slides into place. Whatever disasters life threw at me, and I've had my fair share, I dealt with alone. But things keep piling up, and I'm gasping for air, barely keeping my head above water. I get an issue resolved, another boils to the surface—like the one standing before me.

"I'm making it my concern, vampire," he says in a low, angry rumble, stepping closer. The scorching fire from his body works to penetrate the ice around my heart. The tactical pants and snug-fitting wool t-shirt accentuate the bulges and curves of his impressive physique. Not a shiver ripples through him at the freezing temperatures. "You're hiding something. The stench of guilt radiates from you."

Ah, crap. Damn shifter senses are better than an empath's ability. *Go fuck yourself* rests on the tip of my tongue, but my inner vampire fights against uttering such foul language to its mate. The last thing I need is a tenacious male sniffing in my direction. Pun intended.

"Step off, Ruse. I will not hesitate to take you down, prince or not." An image of tackling him to the ground and stripping him naked spikes my heart rate. To have this powerful being pinned between my thighs, at my mercy, causes my nipples to harden.

The instant my mind recalls our first contact in the battle's aftermath three months ago, the mating bond zings through me and my inner vampire stirs in my chest. The magnificent prince sustained severe injuries, which forced him to shift back into human form. Deep lacerations flayed open the skin across his massive torso. Blood oozed from multiple stab wounds to his gut, and several broken bones protruded from his flesh. Sebastian, Logan's brother and second in command of the Guardians, ordered me to trace him to the castle.

My body still trembles remembering the scorching blaze of his bare skin when I drew him into my embrace. The intoxicating perfume of his blood, the impressive girth of his cock—even in its relaxed state, his incredible strength as he fought me, desperate to stay in the battle despite his numerous injuries.

When we materialized at the castle, he'd gripped my upper arms in a bone-crushing hold. Fury radiated from him in scalding waves. The piercing sapphire gaze glowed with outrage, and a low menacing growl vibrated the floor. For the first time in my immortal life, fear pulsed through my veins, warring with an instant surge of lust.

I shake my head and peer into those intense eyes as big fat snowflakes descend around us and longing gushes to the forefront once again.

"I'd like to see you try, female."

Kurtis's husky reply ignites my need, as does the aroma of his... desire? Damn it. This complicates things.

The enormous shifter's challenge is apparent as he steps into my personal space, his aggression warming my chilled body. Awareness tingles through my sensitive bits as his distinct scent of citrus and pine surrounds me. Against my will, my fangs descend, craving to sink into his neck and gulp down his nectar.

Will the prince's blood be sweet like honey or rich and spicy like the man himself? I suspect it's a potent combination of powerful magic. Next to his father, this male is the most formidable shapeshifter on the planet. The mere thought of his lifeblood flowing over my tongue, down my parched throat causes saliva to pool in my mouth and warmth to explode behind my irises. The amber glow dispels the surrounding shadows, showcasing my mate's masculine features to perfection.

"God, you're beautiful," he whispers. "Your eyes are molten lava."

"Leave, Ruse, before..."

"Before what, Lucretia?" Hearing my name in his deep, husky tone has my empty insides spasming. I adore that he doesn't shorten it to Lu the way everyone else does. "Before I have you writhing, moaning my name, begging for more?" Powerful hands grasp my biceps and pull me against his rock-hard body. Fire penetrates the leather, sinking straight to my core. God, he's so warm. I want to snuggle against his broad chest, and forget the world exists. "Or before I force you to reveal what those amber eyes hide?"

His words freeze the oxygen in my lungs. The lust stutters to a halt, replaced by anger and fear. Anger at myself for letting him distract me and fear he'll discover my secrets, putting lives at risk. Mate or not, I cannot allow him to uncover the truth. Everything I've sacrificed would be for nothing. His friendship with the queen would ensure it.

"You would do well to get your paws off me, shifter. I am not a fragile human you can bully." To demonstrate, I shove against his chest, knocking him back several feet with ease. Apprehension spears through me. Striking a member of royalty, no matter the species carries serious consequences. Kurtis recovers with a low growl and drops into a fighting stance, his pupils darkening with intent.

Damn he's impressive. I've witnessed his battle skills, and even though I am a vampire with exceptional speed and strength, with over a century of combat training, his abilities give me pause. I'm not sure I could best him in a fight, especially if he morphed into Loki, the two-hundred-pound, lethal Alaskan Malamute, with canines the size of my thumb.

Besides, the bond would never allow me to hurt him to any significant degree. In our history, a bonded mate has never destroyed another. But Kurtis isn't a vampire. His hatred for my kind could overshadow any desire he bears for me, although it doesn't seem to affect his friendship with Nicki. Is it because they were close when she was still human?

"Know this, bloodsucker." My jaw clenches at the slur. "You'll submit and whisper your secrets in my ear as I sink deep into you."

The threat stalls my heart. I press my shoulder blades against the icy wall. The swords dig into bone, allowing the pain to refocus my destructive thoughts. Kurtis's tenacity will be my doom. Best to retreat while I'm able. If I find myself pinned beneath this male for even a second, blood lust might consume me. Nobody can ever know the shapeshifter prince is my one true mate.

King Dimitri's lifeless body burned to ash months ago. My secrets are safe, but I must stay vigilant and guard my mind against the queen, Logan, and the prince. For if anyone discovers my betrayal, I'm as good as dead.

Kurtis advances. I hesitate, admiring his masculine beauty for as long as possible. When the warmth from his body heats my face, I trace away to the safety of my room feeling every bit a coward.

CHAPTER 2

Kurtis

Well, that fucking escalated out of control in seconds.

The objective was to befriend the exotic vampire, find out what secrets lurk behind those battle-weary eyes, and report back to Nicki. But the warrior fires every synapse in my brain. I revert to a Neanderthal type behavior; grunting and pounding my chest, demanding she obeys. I'm a goddamn Navy SEAL, a black belt in Krav Maga; where is the control?

Frustration gnaws at me as I recall the evening two weeks ago when Nicki showed up alone at my dojo, Red Dawn. Out at night without Logan was surprising, as he seldom leaves her side.

"Kurtis, I need your help," she said before flopping into an armchair facing my desk. The same desk where

I kissed her, although those days seemed like another lifetime.

"What can I do for you, Queen Giordano? Is your mate not meeting your needs?" I taunted, smirking at the saying etched on the front of her long-sleeved shirt. *'I'm not a princess, I don't need saving. I'm a queen, I've got this shit.'* "I'd be more than delighted to assist you in that department."

Her bark of laughter made me smile. In the few short years I'd known this fascinating, courageous woman, she didn't enjoy many opportunities to indulge in hilarity. Nicki was abused by her father as a teenager until Logan rescued her, only to lose her memories of her childhood, then be plagued by hideous nightmares which kept her on the run until she settled here in Newport, Oregon.

The night Nicki discovered vampires existed, she further learned who and what she was: a vampire halfling, prophesied in an ancient decree to deliver peace to the immortals. If those mind-boggling revelations weren't sufficient, she found out the individuals around her lied to incorporate themselves into her life. It crushed her heart. She questioned the motivations behind her friendships.

Yeah, not much room for amusement there.

"Never let him hear you say that, big guy, he'd blow a fucking gasket," she replied with a smile. "It's only through Sebastian's help I'm here alone. You'd think being an all-powerful vampire would grant me some advantages over my mate. Nope. Still as controlling and bossy as ever."

"Which I know from experience you enjoy, so quit whining." At my wink, Nicki rolled her eyes and grinned. A few moments later, the smile disappeared, and her expression took on the detached, calculated warrior I trained. Dread filled my gut as I watched her stroll around the desk before leaning against it to face me.

"You know I'm an empath, among my many diverse talents," she smirked, although the humor didn't penetrate the icy gray regard. "I need you to get close to Lu."

"What?" My spine tingled with trepidation. "Why?"

"Lucretia is an enigma wrapped up in a bacon mystery, Kurtis. Her emotions are all over the place, and I suspect a huge secret lurks beneath the surface. It's essential I find out what."

"Are you sure jealousy isn't rearing its ugly head, as the warrior was briefly married to your male?"

King Giordano forced Logan and Lucretia into marriage in the hope Nicki would turn against her mate. Since my friend possesses a history of acting irrationally when emotions get the better of her, I had to ask.

"Thanks for the reminder. It's true, Lu and I have not had the best relationship, for more reasons than the one you just mentioned." She crossed her arms, her expression altered from anger to concern. I trusted the little halfling with my life. Her intuition was one hell of a bullshit detector. "Beneath her cold exterior, guilt and fear smolder, and my instincts are shrieking she's betrayed me in some way, or is about to... I just fucking wish I could read minds instead of emotions."

Well, son of a bitch. "Did you speak to the Oracle?"

"Please, I went to him first, but as expected, the little blue weirdo gave me a non-committal answer about how the universe works."

Icarus was the Council of Unity's High Priest Oracle. His vision helped locate Nicki as a youngster. He also brought her back to life when she thrust a silver dagger through her heart to destroy her father and save her mate and friends.

"It's pissing me off I can't penetrate her mental shields." She pinched her forehead. "You're the only one I can trust with this. Logan and Sebastian are too close to her. She's been their most trusted warrior for a century. I don't want to voice my suspicions until I have concrete evidence."

"The commander would back you no matter what, Nicki. As your mate, he has no alternative."

"I realize that, but the big 'innocent until proven guilty' brute will conclude I'm being rash or seeking to prove Lu's guilty because of jealousy if I don't offer him proof." She settled her palm over mine, and the somber eyes darken. "Plus, his friendship with her is solid, it's gonna hurt him, and I need to be certain."

I'd never been capable of refusing this woman anything. She'd earned my esteem and devotion. I rose from my chair and planted my hand on her cheek while peering into the sparkling gray depths. "I once mentioned, in this office, I would always be here for you, and I meant every word. Let me see what I can find out." Nicki's smile had warmed my heart.

As I peer around the snow-covered courtyard of this twelve-acre castle, I shake my head at the irony. The woman I trust and care deeply for was demanding I spy on the female my beast craves. The attraction for Nicki was nothing compared to this all-consuming desire for Lu.

The fates were wicked in their mate choice. I always pictured I'd settle down into a tranquil, satisfying existence with a gentle, submissive shifter. A female to shift, run, and hunt alongside, to bear my children—not one against council law. My people will never tolerate a species we've been at war with for centuries as their queen, even with the tentative accord my father has with Nicki.

Not to mention, Lucretia Bramen is the farthest thing from gentle or submissive. The warrior is a cold-hearted, cunning bloodsucker. But it didn't matter. The second her lean body, encased in leather, appeared on the battlefield several months ago, my cock hardened. The bond pierced through my fast-thumping heart as sure as any sword.

Her alluring beauty astonished me. I envisioned those toned thighs wrapped around my waist; the long, black hair clutched in my fist, those lethal fangs sinking into my flesh. Even knowing it was taboo for my kind, I couldn't hold the tremors through my frame at the notion.

When those amber eyes zeroed in on mine, awareness shot straight to my groin. The beast demanded her beneath him. It was Nicki's sharp telepathic command ordering me to get my head in the game that held the animal in check.

I urge my mind from the past as snow crunches under my boots and seek the castle's warmth. Pausing inside the grand dining room, I dislodge the freezing flakes from my hair and shoulders. The sole reason the queen has no idea Lucretia's mine is because I've kept a steady rein on my emotions.

As part of my progeny training, and because of my friendship with Nicki, I'm the spokesperson for the Shifter Territory. This fortress has become my second home. My father respects the queen and the Moretti brothers, but despises the compound's remoteness. With no roads in or out or even an airstrip for miles, the sole access to the castle is teleportation. As convenient as the skill is, shifters fear it. No good can develop from scattering your molecules to the universe.

Needing time to settle my mind before heading to my suite, I meander around the most extended table ever created. The mahogany behemoth comfortably seats over a hundred guests. It's used for Guardian meetings every dusk, as well as parties. The stone arches, vaulted brick ceiling, and dozens of lit braziers add to the old-world atmosphere of the castle.

The ground floor also houses a small rustic kitchen Nicki threatens to modernize with gleaming stainless-steel appliances—much to Logan's horror—

and a media/game space for the Guardians to unwind. The queen's study, with an attached conference room for more private encounters, sits on the ground floor too. Oh, and let's not overlook the extraordinary: I'm itching to get my hands on, indoor training gym. Red Dawn is nothing to sneeze at, but this facility is the size of a damn football field. Unfortunately, it's a vamp only zone, and they prohibit outsiders.

The modern influence, besides plumbing or electricity in specific areas, are the electronic shutters which slam shut before dawn then disappear as the sun sinks below the horizon, although Nicki has no demand for such shelter. The rays caress her skin daily without the painful lick of fire. The bedrooms in each tower are the only ones missing the metal closures and are strictly for visiting immortals like myself.

A long hot shower sounds inviting, and I take the stone steps to the fourth floor three at a time. It boggles my mind the only areas with lavatories in these twelve acres of brick and rock are in the staff quarters and the tower suites. Although Nicki recently added one to her suite and insisted on a powder room off the main corridor. It's odd how the blood vamps consume gets reabsorbed by their bodies, which efficiently converts it to fuel their power. Bloodsuckers are above shitting like the rest of us lowly immortals.

As I enter my chamber, I'm grateful to whatever servant lit the fire in the spacious rock fireplace, but my mission weighs heavy on my shoulders. If Lucretia betrayed her queen, it won't matter she's my fated female; Logan will rip her heart from her chest.

A rough growl rumbles from my throat at the prospect of Lu harmed in any way, but fury shoots through me at my response. The soldier can never be mine. She's a fucking bloodsucker. Forbidden. This mission, along with Nicki's security, are my only priorities.

CHAPTER 3

Kurtis

In 220 years, I've never witnessed such a wide variety of species assembled in one place. During the battle there were vampires, werewolves, shifters, valkyrie, and dark fae. Those leaders or their high-ranking royals are here this evening—minus the dark fae king, Syn Grayflame and a certain gorgeous succubi queen: the Vampire Nation declared them enemies after siding with Dimitri.

Many of the species survived in complete secrecy until now. The twitter of diverse languages from witches, banshee, elves, and dwarfs bounce off the stone walls. Even the elusive centaur king stands majestic in the back corner. They all showed up for a peek at the prophesied halfling who killed her father and mated the legendary Logan Moretti.

Polished braziers encircling each of the fourteen limestone columns immerse the hall in a dancing glow of orange. The colossal walk-in fireplace blankets everything in warm radiance. The gem runes on the domed ceiling dance in the flickering light while stone effigies of vampire warriors glare down upon the porcelain floor.

A crimson rug runs from the throne to the heavy double doors with identical but smaller rugs lining either side. Banners with adorned plumes dangle from the walls and between each one stands a colossal candelabra. They spotlight murals depicting powerful creatures. The half-moon gleams through the floor to ceiling stained-glass windows which illustrate in gory detail significant battles throughout vampire history.

Centered in front of the colorful panes, atop an elevated platform, rests a lavish mahogany throne. Two similar, but undecorated seats rest on either side. The armchair on the left is for Logan, announcing he's the queen's right-hand man; a consort in the vampire culture. The one on the other side belongs to Logan's brother, Sebastian. Tonight, Nicki will promote him to Guardian Commander. Anytime the queen's in this room, the Moretti brothers will flank their ruler.

Rows of decorated, but uncomfortable wooden benches face the throne. Dozens of immortals either sit or mill around, remaining close to their claimed seat. Those of higher standing have the privilege of witnessing the ceremony from the lavish balconies lining both sides of the chamber.

I peer up, nod to my father sitting next to Queen Svaldana, and note the spot reserved for her daughter Alexandria is empty. I can't figure out why Nicki's best friend hasn't stepped foot in this castle since the werewolf king's funeral. She'd better have a damn good excuse because I know her absence wounds Nicki even if she won't admit it out loud.

"Quite the gathering."

The sweet melodious voice pulls me from scrutinizing the milling throng. My regard falls to the stunning creature next to me.

"Yes, Priestess Tanagra, it is."

Kleora Tanagra is a land nymph and the ruler of her people. The mysterious creatures isolated themselves from society centuries ago, but after King Giordano's death, the rarely glimpsed sprite petitioned for a seat on the Council of Unity.

No glittering dress adorns the little beauty. Kleora dressed for battle. Supple brown leather pants hug her dainty but shapely hips and thighs. A braided leaf design runs through the skin, circling down each leg before disappearing into knee-high boots with the same pattern up the face. A green peasant blouse with a keyhole opening matches her emerald eyes, and the intricate leather corset of interwoven buckles showcases her ample breasts. Chestnut hair gleams in the candlelight and falls to her midriff.

"Observed your fill, young prince?"

"Apologies, priestess." I chuckle at being caught staring like an adolescent pup. "Your beauty stole my senses."

Her delicate pointy ears twitch as she laughs outright. "I expect it's because you have never seen a nymph."

"You are correct, my lady, and after seeing you, your absence deprived us of remarkable splendor for far too long."

She offers a dainty snort. "Your father has instructed you well, young Ruse. I hope you endeavor to be as talented a king as you are at flirting."

Laughing, I wink at her and kiss her strong, graceful hand. It's rumored this fragile-looking woman is lethal with a bow. "But flirting is so much more entertaining."

"Careful, shifter or I will have you beneath me before your next breath."

Her candor takes me by surprise until I see amusement in the sparkling depths. "A position most men would submit their souls for I'm sure," I respond.

"Ah. But's it's not their souls I'm after," she parries. "Although, I suspect the young vampire glaring daggers at us right now might object. Shall we present her a show?" The Priestess whispers and moves closer, her breasts brush my arm.

Lu's delicious, addictive scent invades my senses. A primal stir shifts in my solar plexus and ignites a possessive need I refuse to acknowledge. The itch to twist and observe my female is almost too exceptional to resist. Instead, I maintain my regard on the five-foot minx before me.

"I'm uncertain who you mean, my lady. All others pale compared to your beauty," I flirt back, knowing full well Lu can hear me. The fire from my female's scrutiny flows across the vast room like a dark, humid heat, searing my neck.

"Ah, if that were true, young prince, the things I could teach you would blow your mind." Her seductive whisper fuels the deep odor of fury. I grin with pleasure. Lu is not as immune as she touts.

"My apologies," Logan interrupts with a nod before gently taking Kleora's palm. "Priestess Tanagra, the queen would love to meet with you before the ceremony."

The mighty fighter, decked out in combat boots, leather trousers, and two large broadswords strapped to his bare torso, is an intimidating sight. If I'm not mistaken, several battle paintings on the walls around this immense chamber depict his powerful frame.

"Of course, my lord." Kleora nods before turning an apprehensive stare to mine. "Until we meet again, my young strapping shifter."

"I look forward to it, Priestess."

Why is the petite nymph uneasy about seeing the queen? Nicki is the most potent immortal on the planet, but the nymph's earthy magic shimmers around her like a protective veil.

Shaking my head, I dismiss Kleora from my mind and zero in on Lu. My chest tightens at her fierce countenance. Clad in battle attire similar to Logan's, but with a black, long-sleeved t-shirt covering her torso and two smaller swords crisscrossing her back, she's the most striking woman in the place. Her height isn't the only thing setting her apart from the females, and several males; she exudes the alert grace of a predator. Her watchful visage causes my creature to rise to the allure of the challenge she presents.

The amber glare stirs my lust. It's disconcerting the way my body is in harmony with her every shift of sinewy muscle, each draw of breath. The raw, primitive compulsion to chase her down has my beast shifting in anticipation, even as desire—hot and pure—boils my innards.

Christ. Get control.

I'm expected to gain Lu's confidence, but I can't if she's pinned to the floor with my head buried between her thighs... not precisely a trust-building move.

Need her. Claim her.

"Oh, shut the hell up." I admonish the beast in a harsh whisper while shoving him deeper.

Since the moment of my first shift at eighteen, my inner animal spirit has been my constant companion. It's guided me with raw passions and impulses during the most profound moments in my life. He's a part of me. The wild, untamed element that flourishes in the heart of battle, whose natural instincts make us the ideal killing machine.

When I hit immortality at twenty-five, the beast's demand for sex grew exponentially. I devoted years of training to master his carnal proclivities. But when we encountered our mate for the first time, my seasons of discipline flew to the wind. I've redoubled my attempts to hold him in check around her.

Like tonight. Once my heart rate settles, and my erection no longer strains against my zipper, I refocus on the biggest challenge of my life.

CHAPTER 4

Lucretia

Visions of hacking the nymph's pointed ears from her head ease my soul as I stroll around the grand throne room, scrutinizing the guests. My trained gaze searches for any bulges indicating a weapon we missed, a nervous eye darting towards the exit or anything out of place. In all fairness, everything seems out of place. I've never seen many of the creatures here tonight. While a few make me shudder in revulsion, others make me marvel at their majestic grace, like the Centaur King. The chestnut flanks of his body twitch with each hoof stomp, the dominant male physique and flawless features boggle the mind.

The shifter across the room, on the other hand, produces quivers for an entirely different reason. Watching him flirt with the attractive priestess, hearing every word, caused my inner vampire to yearn to tear her limb from limb for daring to touch what's mine.

Kurtis is not ours. Nor will he ever be.

I conclude my rounds quickly before beelining it to the exit. His presence, even in a crowded room, is messing with my emotional discipline. I've worked years to hone the frigid indifference in this male-dominated occupation and in a few days, the shifter prince has wreaked havoc on my shield.

Out in the darkened passageway, I take a second to fill my lungs with the lavender-scented air permeating the castle since the queen's arrival. In my mind, she's already my queen. Tonight is purely a formality for immortal society.

"Lu. Have you completed your rounds in the throne room?" Logan's rich voice startles me, so drawn up in my concerns, I didn't even hear his approach.

"Yes, Sir. Everything seems in order." I tip my head and peer into the restless atomic green stare of the man I revere. To be honest, one I've had a crush on since my initial interview.

Bare-chested, the black Moretti tattoo swirls around his right bicep, up over his shoulder to curve across an impressive pectoral. The enormous broad swords strapped to his torso intimidate. His dark hair, drawn back at his nape, highlights his trim goatee to perfection. The subtle, eerie light from his orbs sets off the scar slicing through his left eyebrow; the thin line adds to his dangerous allure.

I envy my queen for fate choosing this incredible vampire as her mate. When Dimitri forced Logan to marry me and consummate the union, with him and the Guardians as witnesses, humiliation and fury blazed through me. But, the pleasure-pain of his size stretching me produced a powerful orgasm I struggled to keep concealed from those around us. No doubt, my commander felt my muscles convulse, just as I experienced his scalding seed saturate my insides. If it weren't for the hundreds of observers, it would have been the best sex I'd had in forever. But I'm no buffoon. I knew he pictured Nicole, and I didn't fault him.

I've been around the Moretti brothers long enough to recognize they are both sexual dominants. In fact, Sebastian unashamedly owns several BDSM clubs across the globe. There was a time I fantasized about exploring such a lifestyle, until a vampire from my past drilled it into me that only the low and depraved performed such acts—that craving pain with pleasure was wrong, perverted. To this day, even though I've mastered those black thoughts, I can't stop day-dreaming about encountering a partner who shares my dark passions. Then I meditate to purge myself of the shame and humiliation, like *he* taught me.

"I must profess, I get an uneasy sense about this ceremony," Logan states, rubbing the back of his neck as if it burned or itched.

"What other option did we possess, Sir? The world demanded to see her crowned." I'm unnerved by his misgivings. The fierce warrior's instincts served him well his six hundred years. It's saved him, and me, many times.

"We could have teleconferenced the occasion. But my mate insisted, and I quote, 'what a bullshit cowardly approach.'" Logan's attempt at mimicking Nicki's character has my lips squeezing together to keep from snickering. He grunts at my expression.

"Sounds like her, my lord."

"Indeed, Lu. It does. Her fierce attitude is one reason I love her so much."

"A warrior covers every exit, commander. We carefully searched each guest upon arrival. Icarus's no teleporting spell is functioning; the entire contingent of Guardians are here tonight," I declare, working to soothe his mind. "If anything goes down, we are ready."

"Thank you, Lu." The warmth from Logan's palm sears my shoulder. "Accepting you as a Guardian was the wisest decision I made. It eases my burden to know you protect what is mine."

Oh, if he only realized. "With my life, my lord." I present a slight bow even as guilt crawls up my abdomen.

The constriction on my chest lessens somewhat when Logan nods then strides away. The commander recruited me despite the fact the Guardians never had a female warrior in their history.

Vampire culture evolved with the times, along with the mortals, but throughout the centuries we remained a patriarchal nation. Females have their place: look beautiful, plan grand festivities, and service their males.

I'm an anomaly. As far back as I recall, I craved to be a soldier, to fight with swords, daggers, my bare hands. Corsets, frilly dresses, and tea parties would never be my destiny.

I stiffen as Kurtis's aroma ignites my senses: raw and masculine. Before I can halt them, my fangs descend, throbbing to plunge into his flesh. Saliva pools in my mouth, anticipating the flavor of his blood. The overwhelming vision of his nude body appears in my mind. I inhale deeply, glory in my primal reaction for a moment longer, before cramming it to the background and ordering my canines to recede. My visceral response to his mere scent is disturbing.

"Lucretia." I love the sound of my name on his lips. "Might I have a word with you?"

My eyebrow lifts. He's asking? Since when? A desperate impulse to rush down the hall away from the tantalizing presence has my muscles straining, but as a prince, he outranks me. In this public venue, I must keep it formal.

I enjoy my head attached to my neck.

With a courteous smile plastered on my face, I spin to meet the bright blue stare. "Of course, my lord." Attired in a black, pinstriped three-piece suite, Kurtis looks as if he strode out of GQ magazine for health and fitness fanatics. His wardrobe must be tailor-made to fit such a tall, muscular frame.

"I ah... I want to apologize for my remarks in the garden the other night."

Whoa. What? "You need not apologize to me, my lord. You are a prince." What the hell is he doing? I glance anxiously at a female banshee ogling Kurtis like candy. He doesn't even acknowledge the little beauty.

"Well then, as a prince, I should obtain better manners, don't you think?"

His deep husky tone, fused with the provocative grin, does weird things to my stomach. I gulp. Loudly. As much as I ache for this male, instinct demands I step back. Aggression and anger I can handle. This, not-so-subtle flirtation makes my head spin.

"Is there someplace we might talk in private, Lucretia?"

Oh, no. Being alone with Kurtis is a bad, bad idea. "The ceremony is about to begin, my lord," I stall. "Perhaps you should...."

"I won't bite." Crap. The lopsided grin melts my insides. "Hard anyway."

"No?" I overlook my breathy voice. "But I do." Good grief, I'm flirting with the next shapeshifter king. What the hell is wrong with me?

Kurtis's low grunt has my nipples tightening. Heat sears my breasts as he steps closer, his bulk blocks the hallway from view. I retreat as he advances until hard stone meets my back.

"Do you wish to bite me, Lucretia?"

God. Yes. "No." *Yeah, way to sound convincing.* I'd like nothing better than to slip my incisors into the hardness bulging behind his zipper. My heart rate spikes, along with my breathing.

"Your scent is intoxicating," he admits between clenched teeth like he's angry I smell good.

Well, I could say the same. His citrus and pine aroma cloud rational thought, causing my fangs to extend once more.

"Why is the notion of those sinking into me so damn… appealing?"

I'm not certain if it's me he's asking or himself, but the words ignite a fire behind my eyes and between my legs. The subdued light illuminates his face.

This is not a safe idea, but a part of me demands this moment. Maybe if I experience those lips on mine just once I could get over this preoccupation with him. He could be a terrible kisser. Yes, that's it. I need to test this theory. If he's a lousy kisser, I'll set him from my mind.

A big, steady hand clasps the back of my neck as he leans in and plants the other on the stone mere inches from my head. Warmth, blended with his masculine scent, envelops me and I'm lost. Wild horses couldn't yank me away from the searing burn of his embrace. For the first time in my existence, I'm fragile. Small. Protected. He draws out the feminine side I've struggled hard to suppress.

"My lord." My sigh is packed with longing and need, but I don't care. This male entrances me.

"Christ, Lucretia." The deep groan hardens my nipples even further as he leans his forehead against mine.

He doesn't shorten my name like everyone else, and I love it. From him, it's a sensuous caress. A slight inhale, and his fresh minty breath fills my nostrils. I tip my head to provide him better access, but the tantalizing lips hover just out of reach. My frustrated growl rumbles in the meager space between our bodies, and I drive my claws into the stone behind me to keep them from digging into his ass.

"Lu?"

My name has us both tensing. The familiar voice penetrates the haze of lust as effectively as a fifty-caliber bullet to the brain. My fangs retract in an instant, and the amber glow dissipates.

It can't be. Please don't let it be him.

Kurtis tilts his head. No doubt noting the immediate transformation in my demeanor. "Private conversation, pal," he says with a growl before straightening away.

The absence of his warmth leaves me weak, and I allow the immortal to shelter me from my past about to kick me in the face.

"Step aside, shifter." The low polished tone has my knees buckling, and I clutch the wall for support.

"Do you know this *vampire*?" Kurtis asks over his shoulder, never taking his fierce scrutiny from the male standing before him.

"Of course she does." The Italian accent thickens with impatience.

Everything inside me withers. The confidence and control I've worked a century to achieve suddenly die a quiet death. On unsteady legs, I stride around Kurtis to face the one man from my past who possesses the power to destroy my future.

CHAPTER 5

Lucretia

"Hello, Trezzo." I would never admit it, but I'm grateful for the warmth and energy of my mate at my back, even if it's purely an illusion. Kurtis is as dangerous as the vampire before me, more so because of the bond. "Been a long time." I'm amazed at how steady my voice sounds since my tummy is doing somersaults. I focus on slowing my breathing and heart rate.

Show no weakness.

"You look as beautiful as I remember," Trezzo murmurs before depositing an intimate kiss on the inside of my wrist.

Like most vampires, he is exquisite. You'd never guess the youthful-looking stud is seven hundred years old. Originally from Venice, Italy, his golden hair and blue eyes give him the appearance of a Viking. A Viking in a black tux.

A century ago, his blond locks hung loose to his shoulders. Now he maintains the sides buzzed short and the top slicked back from his forehead. His once clean-shaven jaw showcases a trim scruff.

Deep-set sapphires take their time devouring my physique. The nostrils on his straight, masculine nose flare, inhaling my scent. An appreciative smile curls his full lips.

"Discharge the young pup. We have matters to discuss."

Old habits die hard. I immediately open my mouth to obey but catch the words. A low rumble vibrates my back and my vampire hisses.

"Trezzo," I admonish, astounded at my audacity. "This is Kurtis Ruse, the shapeshifter prince. Rethink your arrogant tone."

Wow. What the hell's gotten into me? First, I flirted with the shifter progeny, and now I'm insulting my mentor. I owe this creature *everything.* He welcomed me in when I couldn't manage my bloodlust. Became my tutor in all things vampire and schooled me in combat and swords. Without him, I'd never have become a Guardian.

A raised brow is the single hint that Trezzo's stunned by my aggressive manner. "Apologies, my lord," he offers with a slight nod. "I am Trezzo Massaro, ruler of the Italian territory, and it appears I have been in

Italy far too long." Hard blue steel pin mine, and I swallow.

Yikes. My mentor has climbed the ranks since I last saw him. He obviously moved back to his home country right after I enlisted.

"How do you know Ms. Bramen?" I exhale with relief at the proper use of my name. I don't particularly care to endure Trezzo questioning his familiarity.

"Lu and I go way back. I was her trainer and mentor before she belonged to the Guardians. Isn't that correct, my dear?" Trezzo's scrutiny darkens. A sure sign he's not thrilled. With Kurtis or me?

"Yes. We are old acquaintances," I concede in a rough mumble, before drawing my braid over my shoulder to fidget with the end. A nervous gesture Trezzo tried unsuccessfully to break me from for years. It's what his presence does. It strips my poise.

The blue eyes narrow on my fidgeting fingers. My arms drop to my sides.

"We were so much more, my treasure." His knuckles glide smoothly down my cheek before he swings his intense scrutiny to Kurtis. "Would you permit us a minute, my lord? Lu and I have some catching up to do." Trezzo grips my shoulder to steer me away when a substantial hand clamps around his wrist, making it look dainty and fragile.

"Actually, I mind."

The low, threatening tone paralyzes my insides. A hasty glance up reveals the shifter's smile is as dark and dangerous as his voice. Why is he furious? He bears no feelings for me. Why should he care with whom I talk?

I open my mouth to break the stare-off when Liam Scott saunters over and plants a friendly palm on Kurtis's shoulder.

"Hey, buddy. Everything okay?" The wolf's worried expression flicks to mine, and I offer a subtle shake of my head.

Recently crowned werewolf king after his father's death, Liam is what we used to call a *tall drink of water.* A few inches shorter than the shifter prince, their complexions are in complete contrast. The king's skin tone has deepened from years in the sun working his ranch, with thick dark hair and mysterious, sultry eyes. And while his frame is massive by mortal standards, he's nowhere near my mate's stature. Very few males are.

I like the young king. And I don't claim that about many individuals, especially werewolves, but his easy-going nature relaxes those around him. The gentleness and sincerity in those chocolate-colored depths draw you in, comfort you.

Not much older than me, the 150-year-old immortal is considered youthful for a king in werewolf hierarchy. The vampires are the only species whose reigning ruler crowns the oldest son on his hundredth birthday before stepping down.

Vampire law states: a king, or queen now, must produce an heir before the end of their first three hundred years. If no successor is conceived, the Council of Unity appoints the next highest-ranking leader. If the offspring dies or the appointed refuses the responsibility, the current ruler can continue another three centuries. Since Dimitri's descendants never survived long enough to take control, and no one was stupid enough to go against him, his sovereignty lasted nine hundred years. Eight damn centuries too long.

Liam Scott carries tremendous responsibility. From his duties to the Werewolf Provinces, to managing the Leloo Blues Bar in Oregon, to controlling his enormous cattle ranch in Montana. His father, Jimmy, would be proud.

The grandfather clock against the wall chimes the hour. Responsibilities require my attention, and it's time to disperse the angst flowing between these two powerful creatures. My heart stutters wondering if, in the heat of the moment, Trezzo would blurt out my secrets. Sure as shit, the shifter prince would rush to the queen. The best course of action here is to separate them.

"Why don't you all take your seats. The coronation is about to begin." With a slight shift, I shrug off Massaro's grip.

"Yeah, it's why I came out here." Liam's frowning scrutiny roams my face as he addresses his friend. "I've saved you a seat, my man."

Why is the werewolf king glowering at me? Like he's not positive who or what I am?

Kurtis drops Trezzo's wrist, then wipes his palm on his slacks as if repulsed by the vampire's odor on his skin. Hell's bells. He just insulted a vampire leader. We all see it but avert our eyes and pretend it didn't happen.

With Dimitri dead, my former mentor is held as an elder in our nation, but in the immortal realm, Kurtis and Liam outrank him. My mentor's wise enough to let it pass. One quality he possesses in abundance: patience.

"Find me after the ceremony, Lu," he demands before bending to brush his lips across my cheek. Liam places a restraining grip on Kurtis's arm. "I look forward to getting reacquainted, *mio amore*. It has been a lengthy separation."

I cringe inwardly at the endearment. Even though we were once intimate, I have sincere doubts about Trezzo's capacity to love. Control. Yes. Love? Questionable.

With a terse nod to the shifter and werewolf, he saunters through the double doors with grace and arrogance.

"What is he to you?" Kurtis turns his deadly blue stare my direction, and my hackles rise.

He has no right to interrogate me. My jaw tightens as I peer around the hall. Thankfully, it's empty.

I abandon the formal bullshit. "None of your goddamn business, shifter," I reply before turning my back on him. Before I've taken a stride, his generous hand wraps my bicep, spinning me into his muscular chest. My palms hit the rigid steel of his abs, slamming lust through my torso in an instant.

Kurtis appears ready to offer a harsh statement, so I'm startled when he lowers his forehead to mine. Uncertain how to counter the change in him, I freeze. His moods swings are giving me a severe case of whiplash.

"The concept of you with someone else snaps my control."

What the hell do I say to that? I feel the same? Do I confess I craved to murder the land nymph earlier for putting her hand on his arm?

This needs to cease. We possess no future. Not merely because we're different species and against the law, but my past secrets rise between us like the Great Wall of China. And with Trezzo back in my life, my world could explode into a million deadly fragments. I will not allow my sins to poison him. He's the next king, an enforcer of laws, and I've broken more than I care to admit.

I smooth my expression and call forth the comfort of my icy mask. "I don't know." My tone's unemotional, heartless. "Perhaps you need to get laid. The priestess seemed enthusiastic. You should seek her out. Now take your damn paws off me, shifter." The vamp within squirms with unease as I thrust against Kurtis's abs, slamming him into Liam before striding down the hall.

Butterflies dance in my gut at the ominous growl behind me, but I don't stop. The sole thing saving my ass from the enormous shifter prowling after me is the werewolf king. I pick up his low rumble as he persuades his friend to let me leave.

"Come on, Kurtis. We are here for Nicki."

Yes. Go, Kurtis. Go to the woman who holds your loyalty. Who not only earned it, but deserves it.

CHAPTER 6

Kurtis

"What the hell's wrong with you?" Liam demands in a hushed tone as he ushers us to our seats in the gallery.

Good fucking question.

When the polished, Italian vampire pressed his lips to Lu's cheek, I'd nearly let the beast ramming against my rib cage loose. It demanded the bastard's head for touching its female. If it hadn't been for Liam's steadying presence, my ass would be chilling in a silvered prison below.

"I don't know," I whisper on an exhale.

I had genuine respect for Jimmy, and his son is like him in many ways, but different. My friend is easier going, enjoys life and women to the fullest. He flies through the ladies like a shifter goes through clothes, but there's never any commitment. He relishes them and moves on.

One day, his fated female will appear like a sucker punch to his balls and force him to his knees. I hope the fates treat him kinder than they have me with their choice.

"What is Lu to you?" Liam asks in a hushed murmur.

"My assignment." It's a half-truth, but I refuse to place the werewolf king in an unacceptable position. He sits on the Council of Unity.

"Assignment?" he questions with a glower.

When the towering double doors close with a reverberating boom, a ripple of unease shifts throughout the crowd. I immediately pinpoint Lu's location as she turns to blockade the entrance with her fellow Guardian.

The impressive warriors, attired in black leather and naked chests, line the entire throne room, upper and lower levels, each with massive broadswords on their backs. The potent display of energy causes my nerves to tighten. An expectant hush settles over the throng as they anxiously await Queen Giordano and the mighty Moretti brothers' appearance.

"Nicki believes Lucretia is harboring secrets. She's tasked me with finding out what."

"Fascinating. But what is she to you, Kurtis?" he demands again.

"I just told you, my assignment."

"So, there's nothing more between you?"

What is he getting at? "No," I lie.

"Perfect. So, you wouldn't care if I asked her out then?"

I scowl at his dark regard riveted on Lu.

Son of a bitch. Not only do I need to worry about the Italian bastard, but I must fret about my closest friend, the player?

"Stay the fuck away from her, wolf," I whisper fiercely, drawing my father's attention two seats down.

Liam tears his focus from Lucretia; his keen eyes cloud with apprehension and bewilderment. "She's yours?"

Damn it. Do I continue to deny it and grant the werewolf a green light to pursue her? Or do I reveal the truth and trust my friend?

"Yes." My low rumble is a buzz between us.

Liam's face morphs to shock, then confusion, then what appears to be acceptance. "You're serious."

"Unfortunately."

"Does Nicki know?" he inquires in a hushed murmur.

"No. I would never place her in such a position."

Several long minutes pass, and I'm having significant doubts about admitting the truth to Liam. He's my buddy, but also a king with a spot on the council.

"Okay," he finally responds. "How can I help?"

My shoulders relax at my friend's easy acceptance before my eyes seek the beautiful thorn in my side once more. She's widened her legs into a fighting posture, palms loosely clasped in front, ready to draw the deadly swords strapped to her back in a blink. The watchful amber gaze tunes in to every movement and shift in the place.

The warrior is tantalizing to observe, and I would love the opportunity to spar with her, to pit my skills against her training. It's ironic because she reminds me so much of Nicki; always the fighter, constantly in control. Lu projects this hard, couldn't-give-a-shit attitude, even though underneath I've glimpsed the gentle, vulnerable woman with eyes begging for affection. Those beautiful orbs express a yearning to trust, but with so many buried secrets, they remain guarded.

I must break through those walls. Earn her confidence.

"Find out all you can about Trezzo Massaro," I reply. "The fucker smells wrong." I hated the way he stole Lu's spirit with his mere presence.

"You mean besides the fact he's acquainted with Lu?" Liam smirks. My irritated gaze swings to him, and the smile evaporates. "I agree. His odor is familiar. I didn't adore the slimy bastard any better than you did," he admits with a glare. "I maintain connections in Italy. I'll find out what I can."

A loud trumpet blares, and everyone turns in their seats with excitement as Lu and another Guardian sweep the monumental doors wide to reveal Icarus, the High Priest Oracle. Dressed in a blinding white toga-like garment with a crimson and gold broach at his shoulder, I'm surprised when his regard stalls on Lu. The blue tattoos on his body and face pulse with each rise and fall of breath and a frown mars his forehead.

He blinks several times then proceeds down the red carpet. The long robe hides his feet, giving the illusion he's floating above the floor. Once he reaches the stage, he levitates to the top, and a gasp fills the room.

"What a showoff," Liam snorts with a grin.

Icarus will perform the coronation, which brings everything around full circle. His visions helped us find Nicki as a child. His potent dark magic brought her back to life after she sacrificed it for her mate and people. Tonight, he's crowning her the queen of all vampires.

A powerful energy surge envelops the area. It blankets the crowd with such strength it's almost suffocating. Every Guardian around the beautiful hall drops to one knee in unison. Their swords unsheathe with a metal ring of harmony before they strike the tips into the floor with a thundering explosion. A grunting chant shakes the throne room as Nicole strides through the doors.

A proud smile lifts my lips. She'd threatened to stroll down the aisle in jeans and boots, but it looks like her mate's demands won. Dressed in a full-length, blood-red gown with a three-foot train, she personifies royalty and grace. The bodice of the dress is a tight, black leather corset with a complex arrangement of buckles. Logan's design choice, no doubt. It showcases her generous breasts, and with her hair swept up in an intricate cascade of auburn curls, it leaves her lean, sun-kissed shoulders and arms on clear display. A large teardrop ruby falls from a delicate gold chain to settle at her cleavage.

Power brightens Nicki's sparkling gray regard as they scan the throne room, defying anyone to challenge her. When they meet mine, I wink, and a naughty smile teases her lips for a brief second.

My perplexity is short-lived when she lifts her gown slightly and takes her first step down the carpet. I almost laugh out loud. The black toe of a biker boot peeks beneath the hem. On her left, her mate's furious but resigned stare discovers her secret.

No doubt she spurned him on purpose. If there is one thing Nicki excels at, it's pressing the commander's buttons to obtain the response she covets: the Dom. I foresee a pink backside in her immediate future.

If Nicole's power display didn't stop you, Logan's legendary presence at her left would. The grace and supremacy in his movements defy gravity. The twin broadswords strapped to his back, plus the hardened green grandeur of his eyes, demands reverence. A respect he's earned through centuries filled with war and bloodshed.

On her right, Sebastian strides with quiet confidence. His presence is as daunting as his brother's. A deadly blue glow sweeps the chamber. Both males tower over Nicki, their black battle attire contrasting with her feminine garments. There isn't a being on the planet dumb enough to stand against these three at once.

I peer back at Lu. Dread churns in my gut. Could she be scheming against her queen? Determination sets my jaw, and I reaffirm my pledge to understand her lies, to discover her secrets.

Fear ignites at the potential choice in my near future. Could the woman I trust and value above all others force me to betray my fated female? This enigmatic, alluring vampire has gotten under my skin, consuming my every waking thought.

It's ironic. The two most significant women in my life are fucking vampires.

CHAPTER 7

Lucretia

On bended knee at the entrance, electrical charges ignite along my nerve endings at the power circulating through the vast room. Between Icarus, the Moretti brothers, and Nicki, it's overwhelming. My fist clenches tighter around my sword hilt embedded in the floor.

Earlier, the Oracle's peculiar look almost caused me to step out of formation. What had it meant? This is the second occasion in my career I've been this close to the small priest. He never appeared at the castle during Dimitri's reign, as far I know, but I never ranked high enough to run security at the Council of Unity meeting. Those were Logan's responsibilities as the king's personal guard.

Looking back, the first time I encountered him was after the famous battle when he performed a sinister, dark spell reviving Nicole from the dead. Even then he'd taken a second to assess me. His puzzled frown an indication he wasn't sure what to think. Can he read minds, predict the future? God, I hope the hell not.

No one perceives the complete scope of Icarus's strength, but the couple of moments I've been in his presence, his extraordinary energy was beyond measure.

I thrust my curiosity aside and rise in unison with my fellow warriors when Nicki reaches the stage.

Vincent and I—the young, good-looking Guardian on duty next to me—close the massive doors. The ominous boom triggers many beings to shift anxiously in their seats. A smirk lifts his lips at their unease. The hazel eyes sparkle with humor as we turn our backs to the exit and face the area.

Icarus raises his palms when Logan and Sebastian kneel on one knee facing Nicki. But before a word leaves his mouth, Trezzo steps into the aisle.

The Guardians tense. The Moretti brothers leap to their feet, draw their massive blades, and before anyone can blink, the sharpened tips press against Trezzo's neck.

Nicole turns regally and fixes him with her luminous gray glare. Her expression is cold. Indifferent. But fury ripples through the place. My fingers twitch to remove my weapons, but the last thing we need in an area crowded with immortals already twitchy is a panic.

"State the reason for your intrusion, vampire, before I take your head," Logan threatens in a deep, ominous growl, his huge fangs on bright display. The aggression is magnificent unless you're on the receiving end, which I hope never to be.

"I object to this coronation and declare my right to the throne," Trezzo states coolly, his shrewd observation never leaving Nicki's.

What in holy hell is he doing? He possesses no claim to the throne. He can't possibly believe because he's the Italian leader and a vampire elder he has justification? Only a fool would challenge the halfling, and Massaro's no fool.

"What right?" Nicki asks, her tone soft, menacing.

"My true name is Zachariah Giordano, Dimitri's first-born son, and your half-brother."

What the fuck?

"Bullshit!" Logan growls, pressing harder. Blood trickles down Trezzo's collar. "Dimitri's heir died six hundred years ago. Decapitated."

"No, my lord," Trezzo disputes. His bitterness rings loud and clear. "My father attempted to assassinate me a week before the coronation on my hundredth birthday."

A collective gasp fills the place, many species nodding and murmuring. Even I've heard the stories about Dimitri killing his first-born to maintain his throne. Knowing the departed king as I did, I believe every one of them.

Logan's glowing eyes narrow on Trezzo, his sword never trembles under the prolonged weight outstretched.

"Icarus," Nicki summons and the priest steps forward. "Is there a process to dispute or confirm his challenge, *scientifically*?"

Crap. Meaning she already perceives whether Trez is lying or speaking the truth but wants irrefutable proof. Only those close to Nicole know about her internal lie detector. She must perceive the authenticity, or he would be dead. If what he states is correct, his claim to the throne overrides Nicki's.

Damn it. How did I not detect it? We spent twenty-six years together. Not once did I catch a hint of Dimitri's blood in his veins. It makes perfect sense now why he never allowed me to drink from him, even during sex.

Hurt fills my gut. I trusted Trezzo with all my secrets. How could he not entrust me with this in return? He must hold a vile hatred for his father, yet he pressed me to become a king's Guardian. Why?

"We can run a genetic DNA analysis, but it will take several weeks for results," Icarus responds.

"We have Dimitri's blood for comparison?"

"Yes, my lady." Icarus's remarkable blue irises flick to mine, and my heart stutters.

Hell's bells. He knows. I swallow, silently pleading with the priest not to expose my secret to all these people.

Nicki's lids close for a brief second before she twists to mount the last few steps to the dais. Logan and

Sebastian's swords never withdraw from Trezzo's neck, awaiting her command. If she orders it, they will sever his head in a nanosecond.

Right about now, I'm hoping to see his brain go bouncing down the aisle. My secrets would perish with him, and only the priest would hold my destiny.

Even with all my issues stabbing at me from numerous angles, my heart goes out to Nicole and Logan. Both suffered through so much to get to this stage. How frustrating, how disheartening to have it ripped away at the last moment.

"Why did you wait so long to come forward, Mr. Massaro? What could you hope to gain by the timing of this surprise announcement?" Nicki asks. She peers down her nose, studies him like a bug she's about to crush beneath her boot. "You're lucky you still retain your head."

"My father tried to kill me once, my lady, and nearly succeeded. It took two centuries to repair. I had no intention of facing him again until I had accumulated sufficient strength to overthrow him." Trezzo lowers his eyes since lowering his chin would cause the deadly swords to pierce his neck. "I am in your debt for lifting the burden from me." He fires a furious look at Logan. "For the past three months, I requested an audience with you. Your mate informed me you were not overseeing any vampire issues until after your coronation. I apologize, but this was my one opportunity to reclaim the birthright taken from me."

A low murmur spans through the crowd. Nicki raises her hand. Instant silence. She's earned respect from every clan and species. Trezzo has not. His challenge to the throne is through a possible genetic link. Unless you reside in Italy, most of the individuals here never even heard the name he's lived under for centuries. No one cares about, fears, or respects Trezzo Massaro the way they do the prophesied halfling—the powerful vampire who took down the legendary King Dimitri.

"Let me be clear, Mr. Massaro," Nicole states with regal composure. "If the tests prove you are lying, I'll rip your heart out and crush it beneath my boot. But, if your claim is legitimate, the Council of Unity will determine your future. And mine."

Deep, angry growls erupt from the surrounding Guardians, including myself. The powerful rumble permeates the grand hall. It expands like thunder from a gathering storm until the windows rattle and the porcelain floor trembles. Trezzo's Adam's apple bobs and his stare widens.

"For your safety, and those of my guests, a Guardian will escort you home until the DNA results come in. The defensive shield around this castle prevents you from tracing in or out." The steel glow intensifies. "Anyone loyal to you will be banished."

"Yes, my lady. Might I have my neck back?" Trezzo requests with a glower at the brothers.

"For now." At her words, the Moretti's sheathe their swords before backing slowly to Nicole's side, their fierce scrutiny never leaving the Italian leader.

"Ladies and gentlemen." The assertive note in Nicki's voice draws everyone's attention. "Even though this suspends the coronation, it doesn't mean we can't proceed on to the party. You've all traveled a long way to be here, so if you would continue to the great dining hall, there's food, music, and dancing," Nicki announces, her smile overly bright. The crowd cheers before filing out of the pews and balconies toward the exit.

As Vincent and I swing the doors open at Logan's nod, I glance up at the mezzanine, but Kurtis and Liam already vacated their seats.

Once the last visitor and Guardian disappear through the exit, my partner and I close them and hold guard just as the shifter prince and werewolf king enter from a side door.

"Lu. Place guards at every entrance to the throne." Bastian takes command of security even though his promotion never transpired. "Vincent, escort Mr. Massaro home."

"It is Giordano, Sir," Trezzo dares to dispute as the massive Guardian roughly grabs his bicep.

"Until the DNA results are read, you will remain Trezzo Massaro," Sebastian grits out before nodding to Vincent. As the two disappear, Bastian's bleak glower lands on mine.

"On it, my lord," I say before scurrying out the door like my butt's on fire.

Has the hour come for me to go into hiding? What Icarus knows won't get me executed, but they would excommunicate me from the Guardians and maybe vampire society altogether. My mate would peer at me with contempt. Well, more than he already does. I rub my chest to alleviate the ache building.

One factor becomes crystal clear as I make my rounds, Trezzo is the real threat here. Not only to Nicole, but to my head staying connected to my neck.

I console myself with the knowledge Trez has no proof of anything. It's his word against mine. Yes, he's a vampire leader, an elder in our society, but Nicki trusts him about as freely as she does me. The ball of tension between my shoulder blades loosens somewhat.

If Icarus is revealing my tie to Dimitri, or Kurtis is blabbing about my prior relationship with Trezzo, it could be time for Plan B.

CHAPTER 8

Kurtis

"What the fuck just happened?" Nicki demands before plunking down on the throne. She hikes up the crimson gown and flings her leg over the arm, her biker boots on stark display. Surrounded by her most trusted companions, the composed, elegant queen disappears.

"He has to be lying," I interject thrusting my fingers through my hair in agitation.

"I felt no lie, Kurtis. Either it's the truth, or he believes it thoroughly enough I can't tell."

"I am sorry, my love," Logan murmurs as he crouches before her, clamping her fists in his. "Tonight, was to be your night. The culmination of all you have endured."

"We've endured, mate." She smiles.

"No matter the result, baby," he whispers before depositing a tender kiss on the inside of her wrist. "We have each other."

"Always," she confirms before pressing her lips to his.

What a fool I was all those months ago to believe I could compete with their bond. I never stood a chance. For the first time, I'm glad things worked out the way they did. She battled through purgatory to make it back to him. No force in the universe can split these two apart.

"Icarus?" Nicki grabs the Oracle's attention as Logan moves to her side in a watchful posture. "Do you possess Dimitri's blood, or were you bluffing?"

"I never bluff, my lady."

My lips twitch at the priest's indignant manner.

Nicki rolls her eyes. "Of course not. What I was thinking?"

Sebastian turns to the Oracle. "Do you mean to use Nicki's blood for comparison?"

"No, my lord. King Giordano's blood no longer passes through her veins. Logan's does."

"As it should be," the fierce warrior states arrogantly, his chest-puffing. It produces an unladylike snort from his mate, but I see the relief in her eyes. Logan poured almost every drop of his essence directly into her heart to restore her life.

When the priest adds nothing further, I growl in exasperation. "How do you have Dimitri's DNA then, Icarus?"

"Do you keep samples from past kings in the Vampire Nation?" Liam asks with fascination.

"It is not my truth to tell, young prince. And no, Your Highness, I do not."

"What do you mean it's not your truth to tell?" Nicki demands, leaning forward. "Don't play with me, priest. I'm in no mood for your riddle games."

"I cannot say, my lady." Icarus' character remains composed under Nicole's furious regard.

"Icarus, I demand you tell me how you retained Dimitri's blood." Nicki jumps to her feet, the gunmetal depths glowing brilliantly.

"It is not my truth to tell," he repeats. His irises churn, battling with hers.

"Then whose is it?" Logan demands.

"Mine." A soft voice whispers, shooting dread through my spine.

Lucretia steps through a passage behind the throne, her jaw clamped tight as she kneels on the first step before her ruler.

"Rise. Explain yourself, Lu." The apprehension in my gut reflects in Logan's expression.

She stands, fastens her fists behind her waist, spine ramrod straight, the perfect soldier with boiling amber focused on her queen. "Dimitri's blood—he was—" She stumbles over the words, her fingers fidget before she draws a heavy breath. "Dimitri was my maker."

Good. God.

This is the mystery she's been carrying? Lucretia is a turned vampire by King Giordano? I peer at the three leaders on the platform suspended in shock, their mouths hanging wide. How could she keep this hidden for so long? Shouldn't the vampires have perceived their connection?

"What the fuck, Lu?" Bastian is the first to crack through the dazed silence. "You were mortal?"

"No, my lord. A shifter."

What?!

"Is such an action possible?" Nicki exclaims. "Can one immortal turn another?"

"Many attempted it throughout our history, my lady, but none survived. Until now," Icarus proclaims.

What the hell? My beast tried to advise me she was unique, but I couldn't identify how. Like Nicki, I understood such a thing wasn't feasible. The fact she's my mate makes perfect sense.

"Can you shift?" My imagination runs wild with what animal form she takes.

"No," she whispers sadly. "Not since he changed me."

"Were you a canine, feline, or multi shifter?" I study her with fascination. My father is a feline shifter, a lion, but my mother was multi. Because of her genes, the spirit creature that claimed me was canine.

"Feline. A black panther, to be specific."

I grin. Of course, how perfect.

"And you didn't consider divulging this information when you applied to be a Guardian?" Logan asks in a low, threatening tone. My scrutiny sharpens on his.

"You wouldn't have approved me if I had," Lu responds with a determined lift in her chin.

"Let's slow this Tilt-A-Whirl ride down," Nicki interjects. She steps down from the dais and saunters up to Lu. "First off, did he turn you against your will?"

My fists clench dreading the answer.

"Yes."

The quiet response is almost my undoing. My lids close at the unexpected pain piercing my chest.

"You served under him for years, did he recognize you were his progeny?"

"No. Not that I know of. The sole hint I ever received was a slight lift of an eyebrow when Logan presented me as the newest Guardian."

Nicki nods. "How did it happen?"

Lu balks.

"Answer me."

"He assaulted me in an alley one night. Beat me until I was practically dead. Raped me, turned me, then vanished."

"Sounds like my father," Nicki whispers with regret.

The picture her words produce has the beast ripping to be let loose. A deep, animalistic growl erupts from my chest. My breath turns ragged, the sound bouncing off the walls. All eyes swivel my direction, startled by my reaction. Their bodies tense, bracing to run or trace for cover. While the blast from my transformation in such close quarters wouldn't kill them, it would hurt like hell.

Logan thrusts Nicki at his back, even though she's perhaps the one non-shifter in the room who could take the energy surge. Fury rides the beast's every pulse as I resist the progression.

When I think he's under control, Liam roughly grabs a gaping Lucretia by the arm and shoves her behind him. As a werewolf, he can absorb the power of my shift without discomfort. The beast zeros in on his hands, touching what's ours. Upper and lower canines shoot through my gums, my vision sharpens, and a rumbling howl reverberates around the chamber.

The beast's aggression triggers Liam's wolf. His dark orbs flash to a brilliant sky blue, and a menacing growl flows from his chest. He drops into a fighting posture; arms spread out in front of the one object the beast salivates for—aches for—its mate.

Lu steps from behind the wolf. My beast follows her every move, hungering to sink its teeth in and mark her. Muscles strain, bracing to pounce if she seeks escape.

Instead of fleeing, she edges closer. With each step away from Liam, the beast calms, and the ragged breathing slows. "Kurtis," she whispers, and the melody of my name on her lips for the first time is like a warm ocean breeze sweeping over me.

My gaze travels her body, seeking proof she's undamaged. A strong hand boldly lands on my suit jacket over my bicep, and my upper and lower canines recede. An unusual stillness invades my system. With a single stroke, Lucretia tamed the beast within.

I swallow, blinking at her several times before I'm capable of providing a slight nod the crisis has passed. Her concerned smile warms me. I wish nothing more than to haul her over my shoulder and take her far from this castle and the threats awaiting her.

"Kurtis." Nicki snaps. My regard immediately climbs to hers. "Are you under control?"

"Yes," I acknowledge, hoping it's true.

"What the hell just happened?" Nicki pins me with a stare of betrayal.

"The brutality of her confession shocked the beast." It's close enough to the truth. I hope she doesn't detect the underlying subterfuge.

Steele gray eyes narrow for a moment before turning to her Guardian. "Lu. No one recognizes my father's brutality more than me, but how the hell did you manage the bloodlust without a sire?"

Damn it. This situation is about to fly from bad to worse if the lithe warrior admits her relationship to the Italian bastard.

"I didn't. At first," she discloses, facing her queen with courage. "I wouldn't have survived if not for... Trezzo Massaro."

Nicki stares at her for several tense heartbeats. "Well, well, well. This cluster gets better and better," she scoffs. "Not only have you lied to the Nation about being a shifter turned vampire by none other than Dimitri, for practically a fucking century, now we learn you're linked to the biggest threat to my throne." She steps into Lu's space. "Not to mention whatever the hell is progressing between the two of you." The gray depths challenge the amber. "What else is in your bag of secrets, Lu?"

"Easy, love," Logan soothes. "Hear her out."

"I'd like to understand how Icarus knew Dimitri turned her when the rest of you didn't," Liam interjects with a sweep of his hand towards the priest, his dark inquiry smoldering, the wolf under control.

The focus shifts from Lu to Icarus, who clears his throat and straightens a nonexistent wrinkle in his robe. "I sensed his essence the minute I saw her."

"And you didn't think to fucking share with the rest of us?"

I cringe at Nicole's caustic tone. No one speaks to the High Priest Oracle in such a sacrilegious manner, but for whatever reason, he allows the halfling the liberty. Oracles are the conduits for the gods and quite rare. In fact, only two Oracles are believed to exist.

"Only so much one can...."

"Yes. Yes. I know," Nicki interrupts. "If I had a dollar for every time you said, 'Only so much one can reveal, my lady,' I could've bought another Oracle."

"Maybe we use Lu's connection with Trezzo," Bastian offers, ever the strategist. "They have history. She could get close to him, discover his intentions for the Vampire Nation. If he is anything like his father, we cannot allow him to become king."

"Why in holy hell would I trust her now?"

Logan runs his palm down Nicki's arm. "Lucretia has been a steadfast Guardian for ninety-four years.

Yes. She should have been forthright about her lineage, but what Dimitri did was not her fault. You of all people should understand that, my love."

Nicki was correct. Logan's devotion to the warrior could blind him to the truth.

"And Massaro?" she asks quietly.

"Until today, he was never a threat. She had no reason to reveal an old relationship. Give her the opportunity now to prove her fealty to you."

"What if he's exactly like Dimitri?" I ask. "You prepared to stick her in harm's way?"

"This is vampire business, Kurtis. You don't hold a voice."

"Well, I guess my opinion counts for shit too." Liam frowns in agitation. "For what it's worth, I agree with Kurtis. Based on their interaction before the ceremony, he will demand more than friendship."

Not fucking happening.

"You have a better suggestion, asshat?" Nicki argues defensively, reverting to their sibling-like name-calling.

"Technically, since Icarus didn't crown you this evening, I outrank everyone in this room. Besides the priest." Liam's demeanor changes. No longer is he the pseudo big brother, or the good-natured drinking buddy. Before us stands the proud werewolf king, bracing to insert his authority and state his argument. The tentative peace between the species is on the line if Trezzo takes control. I glimpse the father in the son, and the reminder constricts my heart.

The anger melts from Nicki's expression, and sorrow enters her eyes, recognizing the resemblance as well. "Okay, Your Highness," she taunts. "What's your plan?"

"Stop dictating other people's lives and just ask her." He hesitates, pointing at Lu. "She's standing right there. Ask if she's willing to endanger her life. Let her choose."

"You're right. As you so graciously pointed out, I'm not her queen. I can't order her to do anything." Nicki nods to Liam with respect. The intense gray scrutiny swings back to my mate. "Are you inclined to place your life in jeopardy for me? For your people, Lu?"

"Yes, my lady," she responds without hesitancy.

I draw a sharp breath, ready to blurt out, '*Not happening*,' when Lu's powerful fingers reach behind her and squeeze my hand in a bone-breaking grip. It takes everything not to flinch. The silent petition to keep my mouth shut clamps my lips. But if the Italian prick touches her, I'll fucking castrate him.

Nicki's glance bounces between the warrior and me, distrust in her contemplation.

"And if he discovers you're a double spy?" I can't help but ask as she releases her grip. I flex my crushed fingers. "What then?"

"He won't. He trusts me."

"You don't know that."

"Enough, Kurtis," Nicole barks. Her stare burns with anger. "Lu has agreed to discover whatever she can about Trezzo's intentions. His character. His plans for our Nation." With the grace inherent to vampires, Nicki resumes the throne in peril and peers down at my mate. "There might be a means to persuade him you're on his side, and I no longer trust you."

I scoff. More truth than lie in that statement.

"What do you have in mind, Nicole?" Logan asks, slipping into his seat next to her.

"At the celebration tonight, I'll expose your association with Mr. Massaro and publicly remove you from my personal guard detail."

Lu's eyes widen, but she doesn't argue.

"And my other Guardian duties?"

"You'll be appointed a shadow, further reinforcing my distrust."

Ah. Now Nicki gets to her original scheme, making it public under the disguise of finding out more about Trezzo. I peer down at my mate to gauge her reaction. She nods, her jaw clenched tight.

"Kurtis will partner you on your assignments."

Lu's head rears back. "A non-vampire?"

"Yes. It is the first step I'd planned on taking anyway at my initial council meeting. Pairing up my warriors with leaders from other species as a show of transparency and trust."

If that isn't the biggest bullshit I've ever heard, I'm not sure what is. How the hell can she keep a straight face? By the Moretti brother's reactions, they are none too pleased with her announcement.

"Nicole. I do not believe your proposal is a prudent course of action," Logan counters softly, working hard to be diplomatic.

"I concur," Bastian interjects.

"Oh, don't get your panties in a wad, boys," she responds sarcastically. I can practically see the steam rising from her mate's ears. I'd laugh if the situation weren't serious. "We won't send them out on any super secret squirrel stuff."

Logan growls low. "Make it happen, Bastian," he orders, never taking his menacing stare from his smirking mate. "Everyone out. I need to have words with the queen."

She pouts up at him. "Just words?"

CHAPTER 9

Lucretia

It's been three long nights since my revelation and the subsequent public humiliation at the after-party, but still no communication from Trezzo. For my subterfuge to be convincing, my former mentor needs to establish first contact.

That night, Nicki not only demoted me, she also surprised me with a one-week suspension from my other obligations. I've been spinning my wheels in this damn castle, and it's driving me insane. My fellow Guardians eye me with disdain and suspicion, not privy to the ploy. I have never been more grateful to enjoy my own suite. With over a hundred warriors coming and going, the lone privacy I receive is within the stone walls of my chamber.

My abused thighs protest as I take the stairs two at a time. With nothing but working out and sparring to occupy me, my body has taken the brunt of my displeasure. Well, it can just deal. It's the sole means at my disposal to keep thoughts of Kurtis and my present predicament at bay.

The prince disappeared after the celebration. I presume he traveled home to British Colombia or Oregon until his babysitting duties commence. The demotion I'm dealing with, and I'm handling the suspension by taking it day by day and beating my body into exhaustion, but having to spend every night with Kurtis petrifies me. How will I manage my yearning for him or this terrifying thirst for his blood?

Based on his beast's reaction, I'd bet my private suite I'm his fated female. I took a tremendous risk facing his enraged inner beast. If he hadn't responded to my gentle coaxing, his huge body would have morphed into his animal form, blown me across the room, and triggered Liam's wolf.

During the great battle, numerous immortals were injured when the werewolves and shifters transformed.

My nipples harden, remembering my mate's earthy growl. The impressive canines made me crave things I shouldn't. The primitive wildness in his sapphire eyes fired my instinct to run, but the conclusion would've been me on my hands and knees with his cock buried deep, and those choppers piercing the muscle between my neck and shoulder as he marked me. The image clenches my core, but the aftermath would be a humiliating trial, with the outcome not in my favor.

I was indeed a shifter once, but the second Dimitri turned me, my animal spirit disappeared. The vampire gene consumed her. The only residual sign left triggers on the full moon with a deep-seated need to run through the forest, to hunt. It develops into an unpleasant tingle along my spine. But no matter how hard I've concentrated through the decades, the energy lies dormant.

I have been a vampire for 121 years. I doubt the council wishes for the public to glean the knowledge an immortal can turn another. They'll keep my dirty little secret hush-hush. Which means if Kurtis and I were to complete the mating bond, they would try me as a vampire.

The members could most likely exonerate the prince, but the result would taint his reputation. I'll never allow that to happen.

The instinct latent in every nightwalker signals the arriving dawn with a tingling along the spine. Even during the bleak winter months this far north when the sunlight never breaches the horizon, the sleep claims us for short durations. Within minutes the metal shutters click into place, blocking the feeble twilight from my bedroom window.

After a brisk shower, I don my comfy red cami and boxer briefs before slipping beneath the scarlet silk sheets. I sigh as the muscles along my spine loosen and

I bury my head in the pillow, sliding my braid to my chest.

"I wonder what my mate is doing?" I mumble to the blackness, recalling the warmth from his body when he cornered me in the hall. His size excites and intimidates me. The deep, commanding voice sets butterfly wings flapping in my gut, and not for the first time, I'm curious what he's like in bed. Kurtis is such an Alpha. I can't imagine him being anything but in complete control. He would naturally exert his dominance over any female.

"I want it to be me." My forlorn whisper swirls around my brain and even to my ears, it's pitiful. But his absence these last few days disturbed me more than I believed possible. I need to see him for just a moment. Maybe it will grant me the fortitude to get through these next few nights until our first assignment together.

"Just a peek," I pledge before slowing my breath to undertake the deep meditative state required to transport my consciousness to an individual target: Kurtis.

Remote viewing is a unique ability among immortals, only a handful across the world report experiencing the skill. I've never reported mine. My philosophy has always been what the council doesn't know can't hurt me.

Besides, I seldom employ it. Prolonged or frequent use is dangerous, scrambling the brain and baking your internal organs. After a remote viewing, weakness invades my body and it takes several hours to recover—

precarious moments when I'm vulnerable. Since it's morning anyhow, with no obligations to occupy my time, why the hell not? I can no longer ignore this overwhelming demand to see the sexy shifter.

I force my heart rate to slow as I picture Kurtis's masculine features. The penetrating cerulean stare, the generous lips I crave against mine, the firm jaw with the perfect blond scruff.

One by one, stiff, tender muscles soften, and I sink further into the mattress. When my pulse thumps at thirty second intervals in harmony with each inhale and exhale, my spirit mind splits, traveling through hundreds of miles to what I seek.

A beautiful log cabin facing an enormous lake and hemmed in by majestic Ponderosa Pines slowly appears. Birds chirp and whistle as the sun begins its ascent into a sky laden with pinks, oranges, and blues. A bright green lawn welcomes you to the front steps of a screened-in porch. The intricate woodwork on the railing and stonework on the chimney gives the substantial house a rustic, homey charm.

From the outside alone, I've fallen in love with it, but where is Kurtis? The ability should take me right to his position. Slowly I float around the deck towards the waterfront, marveling at the spectacular architecture. The rounded edges of the massive logs create a magnificent design on every corner. A dark green metal roof blends in perfectly with the surrounding forest.

The lawn continues to the shoreline, but my feet leave no footprints. I don't sense the sun's warming rays or the coolness of the dense grass. I'm a ghost unable to interact with the environment or those in it.

As I admire the glittering lake, I'm astounded to realize Kurtis's cabin is the sole dwelling. He has total privacy. Wow. What must it be like to enjoy this much space all to yourself?

Several minutes pass with no Kurtis in sight, and I close my eyes to drift back to my body when movement in the water catches my attention. Massive, powerful arms streak through the dark blue surface with extraordinary grace and velocity, heading straight towards the house. No wonder I touched down in the front yard. My ability doesn't release me to land in water.

I ogle my mate when he arrives at the long wooden dock and hoists himself out with fluency, and I nearly pop back into my brain at the perfect symmetry of his nude body. Desire boils to the surface, and I'm riveted to the muscular perfection of his chest and abs, the well-defined V pointing the way to his impressive cock, even after a swim in the chilly water.

My mouth drops when he strolls up the dock with the menacing grace of a predator, and I almost bolt, forgetting for a moment he can't see me.

Like a silent drooling wraith, I follow his delectable ass into the house, absorbed by the ripple and shift of muscles. We cross an expansive great room with dark masculine furnishings, a splendid rock fireplace dominating one corner and floor-to-ceiling windows displaying the majestic beauty of the lake and forest beyond. I scarcely take notice of the gourmet kitchen with gleaming stainless-steel appliances as he heads into a bedroom. An enormous four-poster bed of deep mahogany is the focal point in this spacious area with vaulted ceilings.

Good grief. That is not a typical size for a king mattress. You could sleep eight people on it with room to spare.

Swiveling my stare back to my mate, I gape at the perfection of his muscular frame, right down to the two dimples above a sculpted ass. No tan lines spoil his flawless bronzed skin. Which means he probably swims naked more times than not. And why wouldn't he? No one around for miles. Not that shifters or werewolves care overmuch about nudity.

A series of images above a dresser catches my eye. It's a group of six guys, all dressed in military fatigues. They're suspended in time, laughing, or joking in a relaxed, alert way soldiers pull off with ease. Centered in the pictures is my mate. He stands heads above the other men who are undoubtedly human. This must be his SEAL team. How did he remain among this tight group of mortals without them discovering what he was?

The last image looks older than the rest. These soldiers kneel amid a dense jungle. The weapons slung over their arms are from an earlier period. Was Kurtis a soldier during the Vietnam war too? Closer scrutiny reveals the name on his uniform reads *Tillman.* Fascinating.

When he heads through a doorway, I follow, not wishing to miss an inch or second in his presence. Even in remote viewing, he fires every synapse in my brain. My nipples harden, and my clit throbs at the exquisite spectacle of my mate.

The few occasions I've done this in the past, I was never cognizant of my body, but I can't discount my responses to him. My fingertips graze my aching breasts, and I freeze. Holy crap. I shake my head in bewilderment at this strange development even as I sprint to keep up with Kurtis's long strides.

This is naughty and an invasion of his privacy, but there's no way in hell I'm walking away from watching this incredible specimen shower. What he doesn't know won't hurt him.

Kurtis reaches through the glass doors and turns on the spray. Everything fades as I slowly admire the shift and flex of his powerful thigh muscles. If he were a mere human, the strength and power in his body would cause me to take a second glance, but as an immortal, this shifter is a remarkable force.

He steps into the deluge, and I slip in, not wanting to miss anything. My core is on fire, and my panting breath should concern me, but the trembling in my clit supersedes everything else. Hunger claws deep and grabs hold.

Fascinated, I watch as he lathers his chest and arms, the movements a slow, sensual dance to my heightened state. I groan in torment, craving to touch the impressive physique, experience those massive biceps wrapping me in his embrace as they bend me to his will. Those huge hands stroking and caressing every inch. When he twists to rinse, I nearly lose it.

Yikes! His erection is enormous. It's thick and long with a large bulbous head I'm uncertain I could wrap my lips around. But oh, please let me try.

Back in my room, my fingers pinch hardened nipples imagining Kurtis's teeth biting down on them.

"Fuck!" Kurtis explodes, shifting to punch the tiled wall, and I lift my rapt attention away from his mouth-watering girth.

Both palms plant on the tile, his head drops low between his arms. The hot, powerful spray pounds over broad shoulders, down a strong back and muscular cheeks. I envy the water. Thick steam rises around us, creating an intimate scene.

What provoked such a reaction?

My raging desire escalates when he reaches down and grips his rigid cock. No force in the universe could pry me away from the slow, sensual movements of his fist sliding along his erection. My hand travels beneath my shorts into my slick folds, stroking in rhythm with his. I'm astonished by my ability to move, to feel as if I'm in the shower with him.

Kurtis takes his time exploring his hardness, applying a slight squeeze to the head with each upward stroke. A firestorm builds inside me watching my mate pleasure himself. Desperate cravings claw to be let loose.

A low groan escapes his throat, a sound of need, and his pace changes. Faster and harder he pumps; quicker and stronger my fingers work my clit. My skin is moist with sweat, my body on fire. My thighs drop open, craving this powerful being between them.

I've never observed a man masturbate before, and it's incredible. An orgasm builds, begging to be let loose, but I squeeze the advancing inferno back. The need to watch my mate bring himself off overrides my own pleasure.

When his stance widens, and the muscles in his legs tense, I realize he's close. Sensation after sensation bombards me and before I know it, I'm kneeling at his feet. More than anything, I want to get him off, experience my fingers and lips wrapped around his hardened length. Saliva pools in greedy anticipation. My scalp tingles, imagining his fist buried in my hair as he fucks my mouth.

Kurtis throws his head back and bellows, "Lucretia!"

The sound of my name escaping as he climaxes pitches me straight over the edge, and I cry out as my world explodes. Electricity shoots through every single nerve in my core, clenching it tight, spearing through my body. It's powerful, consuming, like a raging forest fire exploding into tiny fragments. I've never come apart so completely in all my years.

When the last little zings recede to a slow pulse, my lids drift open. I need one final look at my mate before I'm forced to merge back and let the sleep claim me. The piercing blue eyes stare down at me with a dark, savage lust. Shock freezes me in place.

"Did you enjoy that, sweetheart? Because I sure as fuck did."

CHAPTER 10

Lucretia

On a shocked gasp, I bolt upright in bed. "Oh shit."

No way Kurtis saw me. It's ludicrous. And yet, his heavy-lidded stare bored into mine, his cock still hard in his grasp.

I always believed, only my spirit left my body. Not even an apparition should be discernible to my remote target, but something of me was visible in the shower. Based on his husky comment, he perceived my presence the whole damn time.

How do I face him now? My cheeks blaze with humiliation, and I squeeze my eyes shut. It was wrong to violate his privacy like that.

The desire dies in an instant as great lethargy tugs viciously on my muscles. This viewing session lasted way too long. I collapse back on the pillow with a groan and fight the dark abyss attempting to sink its claws into my scrambled brain. My insides hurt and pain lances through my gut. If my spirit had remained a minute later, I'd be trying to heal a ruptured spleen.

I urge my feeble mind to focus, breathing deep and even, and allow my body to repair itself. It takes longer than usual—an obvious sign I've not fed since the coronation.

My phone buzzes on the nightstand, and I feel every bit of my 142 years as I reach for it and bring it to my face. The words blur, and I blink several times to focus on the text.

Cute trick, vampire, but the next time you come it will be by my hands, lips, and tongue buried in ur sweet pussy.

Oh. My. God.

Even in my exhausted state, his comments shorten my breath, kindling a renewed hunger. Not only did he discover me spying on him in a decidedly private moment, but he also heard me when I exploded. Son of... Did I moan his name? I can't remember. And how did he get my number? If I had one theory, I'd say Nicki.

No way in hell I'm answering his text. I should delete it in case Nicole monitors the Guardian's phones as Dimitri did. But my mind balks at the prospect of making it disappear forever with the push of a button.

When it buzzes again, I almost drop it.

3 more nights and ur all mine.

No idea how I'll disguise my mortification, and the smug jackass will smirk at my discomfort. I could just pretend nothing transpired. If Mr. Royalty is crass enough to bring it up, I'll act like I don't know what he's talking about.

Yeah, and you're an idiot.

* * *

"Lu, you are back on rotation starting tomorrow night," Sebastian announces as he strolls into the indoor gym. He looks as devastatingly handsome as usual in his combat gear, his black hair damp from a recent shower.

"Um. Okay." I pant and continue pounding the punching bag with bare fists and feet. It's a rare opportunity to gain the entire place to myself, especially in winter.

"Please, hold back your enthusiasm," he smirks before capturing the bag to keep it steady.

The muscles in his arms stretch the black t-shirt. The Moretti tattoo snakes down his right bicep. Thank goodness they stopped the custom requiring Guardians to ink their family crests on their bodies. One, because it's painful as hell. On a rapidly healing immortal, they lace the ink with salt, so the stain becomes permanent. Second, I'm uncertain how I would've talked my way around not having a family emblem. Not that it matters now.

"The way you have sulked around this castle for the past week, I figured it would thrill you to get back to duty."

Yeah, I was. Until my mate caught me spying on him.

While he masturbated.

Thinking of me.

I still question whether he put on such an incredible, erotic show because he realized I was observing or if I encountered him in an unguarded moment, and he simply perceived my presence towards the end. The main issue: how did he see or hear me? There's one being in this castle I can inquire about remote viewing, but hogs will sail out my butt before I approach the strange Oracle.

Either way, it was sensual, naughty, erotic as hell, and I cherished each second. The vision of Kurtis stroking his massive erection, while hot water pounded his hardened muscles and steam billowed around him, has my core throbbing all over again.

"I haven't been sulking," I snap out with a glower and attack the bag with a solid roundhouse kick to dissipate the evocative images. Sebastian absorbs the impact, his cobalt eyes laughing. "I'm not looking forward to having a shifter shadow," I admit with a pout.

"Too bad." His lack of compassion ignites my displeasure, and I punch harder, which results in his sensual lips lifting at the edges. "You brought this on yourself, Lu, by not being straightforward with Logan and me."

"You understand it was close to impossible for me, a female, to be accepted as a King's Guardian? I wouldn't have stood a chance if I declared I was a former shifter." Bitterness rings through in every syllable.

"You do not know that," he snarls in exasperation. "We welcomed you because of your combat skills and strategic analysis results. Period."

"Yes. Because you and Logan presumed I was a natural-born vampire," I argue before striding away from the bag and seizing a towel off a nearby bench. I grimace as my sports bra and yoga pants chafe my already sensitive bits.

On duty, I wouldn't dare speak to my commanding officer in such a manner, but I'm not officially back until tomorrow night and I need to vent. Sebastian was unlucky enough to be the first victim to step through the door.

"If you truly believe either of us would have disregarded you after discovering your history, then I do question your instinct and intelligence."

"What would you have done in my place?" I ask, my stare direct.

"I am not in your place, so we will never know." He evades and strides for the exit. "By the way," he says, piercing eyes glaring at me over his shoulder. "Pick Kurtis up at sunset tomorrow at the LeLoo. He will be ready for you." I open my mouth to argue but snap it tight when his gaze narrows. "I would do it myself, Lu, but a wayward valkyrie needs retrieving."

"Did you find out why she's avoiding us?"

"No. But I'm about to," he grins with evil intent.

Yikes. If the determination in Sebastian's expression is any indication, Alex is in serious trouble. He's an Alpha with control issues and not a male many disobey. If I know anything about the little redheaded spitfire, a tremendous battle of wills is about to take place. I wonder if Bastian is pursuing the valkyrie on Nicki's orders, or for his own reasons.

I spin back to my current victim, the boxing bag, when my cell phone buzzes on the bench before dropping to the matted floor with a dull thud.

Kurtis hasn't texted me once since the shower incident, and my heart rate quickens. Even though a small part dreads seeing him again, I quiver with anticipation. His charisma and sharp wit make me smile. The keen intelligence behind those beautiful sea-blue eyes challenges me. His citrus and pine aroma is as wild and masculine as the man himself, and blended with the tantalizing bouquet of his blood, he blasts all rational notions right out my head.

Everything about Kurtis calls to my inner vampire. She craves his domination, his claim. Her one driving force: complete the bond. Drinking from a mate during sex completes the link and fuses us until my dying breath.

In the next few weeks, it will be a miracle if I don't go batty. The daunting task of controlling myself each night almost has me banging my skull against the stone wall. Because it's not solely my passion I must resist, but Kurtis's as well.

This new arrangement is a disaster and could end up with me incarcerated in a silver prison for who knows how long. Even if it means fighting my inner vampire and his beast every step of the way to protect us both, then so be it.

Brave words, but can I stick to it? Doubt and fear pith my resolve. Because I understand, beyond any hesitation, the second his skin touches mine the defenses I've built up will crumble to dust in a windstorm.

A cursory glimpse at my phone shows the text is not from my mate.

We need to talk, Lu. Meet me along the northeast barrier in an hour.

Damn it. Is my number splashed across a billboard somewhere?

Well, I guess Nicki's plan is about to begin. Trezzo has finally established contact.

CHAPTER 11

Lucretia

After a hasty shower, I trace outside the magical barrier and amble across the frozen wilderness in full combat gear, my damp braid resting between my tense shoulder blades. The warm leather duster brushing the snow with each stride is a comforting sound. Even though I'm not on rotation tonight, I demanded the confidence booster my weapons and position offer when facing my former mentor.

For twenty-one years, Trezzo was my everything. A true friend when I needed him. A patient guide in all things vampire. He produced new documents to protect my shifter past. Thank God it was the pre-digital age. He was also a merciless taskmaster in training, but without him, I wouldn't be a Guardian.

As a lover, Trez demanded restraint, but in an extremely straitlaced kind of approach. I believe the term these days is *vanilla*. He did not tolerate kink, and missionary was his preferred position. To be fair, he was a patient sexual partner, consistently making certain I orgasmed, but every movement and reaction seemed calculated. He also insisted I never bite him, which I understand now. Sex with Trezzo was cold, manipulated, and he never surrendered control.

At first, it had been exciting to experience such an impressive, attractive vampire interested in an impoverished country bumpkin from the south. He was educated, worldly, with a hot Italian accent. I readily yielded to his centuries of wisdom and expertise, grateful he remained in America to be with me.

At first.

When I discovered during training that my desire raged with a little discomfort, I sought to communicate my desires to Trezzo. He was my lover, after all. Shouldn't we explore this together?

Striding beneath the canopy of timbers, the moonlight flickers between the branches and I shudder as I recall his reaction. Oh, he offered me pain alright, but there was no pleasure in it. It was strictly a punishment, meant to hurt and demean.

Afterward, he insisted I meditate to purge myself of such abominations. "Only the low and depraved crave such things," he'd scolded. I wasted more time on my knees meditating than I did in combat training.

Several feet ahead, I spot Trezzo patiently lounging on a downed tree with a cougar's grace, like the stillness before the attack. His penetrating scrutiny devours my body with every step, and fear tightens my throat. Dressed in his customary dark business suit, he seems unaffected by the harsh chill.

"Lucretia." Satisfaction rolls his consonants as he rises.

"Trezzo." My heart pounds in my breast hard enough to rattle my ribs, but my voice remains steady.

"It is wonderful to see you." He steps close and brushes cold lips across my cheek, lingering longer than necessary. "Shall we sit?" Even though he presented it as a question, it was all authority.

How simple it would be to settle back into old patterns and let him control everything, but I am not a vampire fledgling anymore. I am a Queen's Guardian. On suspension, but a Guardian none the less.

"No. Why didn't you ever inform me you were Dimitri's offspring?" I'm under strict orders to get close to him, but I don't wish to seem overly eager to fall into his arms. Trezzo would see right through such a maneuver.

"Would it have made a difference?"

The hushed question startles me. "Yes. You were the son of the man who transformed my entire world."

"Precisely." Eyeing my Guardian uniform with contempt, he asks, "Were you expecting a fight?"

"No."

"Then, why combat attire? I gathered they relieved you of your duties." Curiosity fills his regard.

Interesting. Nicki was correct, Trezzo had allies at the party. "We live in perilous times. I prefer to be prepared."

He nods. "I trained you well, no?"

"Yes. You did." My hands tremble, so I stick them behind my back in a comfortable soldier stance. Trezzo's stare intimidates me, but I refuse to let him understand how much. "Why?" At his bewildered glance, I elaborate. "Why did you encourage me to become one of Dimitri's Guardians?"

"I've always respected your intelligence, Lu." His face hardens. "I required an ally when the moment arrived to make my move. One I could trust."

Dread flips my stomach.

"You mean control."

"You say tomato, I say..."

"You summoned me, Trezzo. What is it you require?"

He raises his head, peers down his nose, and inhales. "Ah. Berries and cream. A scent I recall with fondness." He moves in tighter, and it takes everything not to step back. "You would do well to remember who you are speaking to, *principessa*." His calm tone is deceptive, and I can't contain the shiver racing up my spine.

I force the muscles in my back to loosen and let my strategic mind take over. "I'm no longer your princess, Trez," I state quietly, my head tilted with curiosity.

"By your scent, you have not selected a mate." Where was he going with this? "I've waited a long time for you, Lu. For your vampire to recognize me as hers." A cold finger slides down the surface of my neck. "Like mine has yours, but it seems your shifter side refuses to let go."

I stiffen. I'm his female? Since when? "What are you talking about? You never once declared I was your mate, and you damn well know the change extinguished my panther spirit."

His expression morphs from thoughtful to hard. "You have everyone fooled, do you not, *principessa*?" he drawls, his accent thickening.

I shake my head and back away. Nerves burst into overdrive at the danger I've placed myself in. Even with all my years of training, I could never assume to match the strength and power of a seven-hundred-year-old vampire. Only two beings in the castle have the ability to defeat him; one is livid with me, and the other hates my guts.

"I don't know what you're talking about."

"Yes, you do." He seizes my biceps in a punishing grip. "You are the cold, stoic, hard-ass female Guardian everyone avoids. The woman who reveals no fear or emotion." At my raised brow, he smirks. "I asked around. I appreciate, all too well, the mysteries you keep behind the facade."

I catch my gasp and resist the compulsion to flee. Trezzo returned for the throne, but he's also here for me. How foolish to presume I could manipulate him.

His observation darkens. "No, you're an exotic mix; lethal warrior, loving family member, and masochist. The first two I respect and applaud, the final one sets my blood on fire."

Shock overshadows the fury building at his painful grasp. "What do you mean? You said..."

"I did not understand your desire or mine back then. My intent was to curb it and you." His irises shimmer in the moonlight. "Now, I embrace my sadistic nature."

The grip intensifies. My body stills when he leans in and runs a fang along my jugular.

Oh shit.

CHAPTER 12

Lucretia

"Wait, Trez. Let's talk."

He shakes his head and continues his exploration along my neck. If he bites, his scent will be all over me. And while Logan or Nicki couldn't care less, Kurtis would lose it.

"You can't show up after nearly a century and expect me just to resume our relationship." When he straightens, I stifle a sigh of relief.

"Yes. I can." Amusement and dark determination spark in the luminous gaze. "I obtain the capacity to crush you, *mio amore*, and I am not above exploiting it to gain what I require."

Bastard. I realized this day would come. *Remember the mission, Lu.* "I understand why you seek the throne,

Trez. If what you claim is correct, by birthright it's yours," I bluff. "But, why me after all this time?"

A blond brow lifts. "Don't ask foolish questions, Lu. You know precisely why."

Do I? "Because you presume I'm your mate?" This vampire blackmailing me in my own territory holds all the damn cards.

Trezzo leans in close. "I would prefer to rule with my woman by my side than without. But either approach works."

Fuck you, asshole. "You supported me through an extremely challenging time in my life. I'd be dead if it weren't for you. I owe you everything, Trez. Or should I call you Zachariah?"

"Soon that will be my title once more, but I have been Trezzo for six hundred years, and the sound on your lips pleases me."

"You need not coerce me. I'm more than amenable to aid you and win back what Dimitri stole from you." I hedge, stepping around him to place a little distance between us. "But my vampire has not claimed you as hers." And she never will. "I'm not the same female I once was. Allow us space to learn one another again?"

The devil laughs, and my skin prickles.

Shit, shit, shit.

A freezing wind rustles right before powerful fingers close around my throat and I'm weightless. My back slams into the unforgiving, frozen ground, and he pins me down with a knee to my rib cage.

I had half a second to speculate if he planned on cracking my sternum when his fist smashes into my cheek. Pain ricochets through my skull, but instinct takes over, and I plow my boot into his neck. When he staggers to the side, I thrust him off me and flip over backward, barely escaping his next punch. In a blink, I draw my sword and sink into a battle stance.

Trezzo chuckles. His irises transform to inky black, so like Dimitri. "I've waited long enough. My patience is stretched thin. Besides, I seem to recall this was foreplay for you, *mio amore.*" Lust blazes from the depths, and it nauseates me.

"No, Trez. But I suspect it was for you." All along the sick bastard got off on hurting me during practice. "Don't do this," I plead in a last-ditch attempt to salvage my mission.

"You are no match for me, hybrid, although I would enjoy your shrieks of pain. I've discovered a certain aptitude for it." His malicious grin has fear racing along my neck. "Report back to Nicole and Logan that you are confident I will be a kind and honorable king, and I am nothing like my father. If you do not, it might interest the queen and the Morettis in learning you were turned by our father. That you're a shifter/vampire hybrid." Trezzo's lip curls in vengefulness, not realizing I already confessed as much. "An abomination. Not to mention, the other secrets you keep concealed. Offenses punishable by death."

I'm such a moron. All those years, I assumed he welcomed me under his wing, trained me, mentored me because he cared. All along he was manipulating me for his own agenda. And yes, he's obsessed with me, but quicker than you could blink he'd rip my heart from my chest if I got in his path. Trezzo is indeed like his father: willing to destroy whoever stands in his way and revel in their anguish.

Rage fills my spirit. Dimitri forced me to do atrocious things, and I will never tolerate another immortal being my puppet master, never be at the mercy of their sadistic whims.

Before I consider my actions, I hurl my sword like a hatchet, aiming for the bastard's heart. Trezzo catches the blade with ease.

With a tsk, he grips the hilt. "You are still an infant." A simple thought and he elevates the weapon, the point hovering a foot above my skull. "You have until the DNA results to champion my cause and grant me a detailed strategic analysis on my adversary." He moves with such speed I don't get a second to counter before my back collides into a giant timber. His powerful body crushes me against the unforgiving bark, his erection grinding into my hip. His fist wraps around my braid and snaps my head to the side—sharp pain lances through my scalp.

I shove against his unyielding chest, and his grip becomes punishing. "Why, Trez? If you obtain a legitimate claim to the throne, Nicki will have no alternative but to step down."

"You assume I would allow her the opportunity to challenge me down the road? My dear sister must meet the same fate as our father." He grates before his head rears back and sharp, lethal fangs descend past his lips.

No!

I writhe against his formidable strength, but there's no stopping the fangs sinking into my neck with such violence I cry out against the invasion. My palms ram against his chest, but it's as solid as the great oak digging into my back.

After several deep drags on my vein, he rips free. I grit my teeth against the agony, declining to grant him the pleasure of realizing how much he's hurting me, inside and out. But fear sparks in my gut as the oh-so-familiar ink swirls in the bottomless regard. They track the warm, red liquid streaming down my collar and into my shirt with sickening satisfaction.

"I love seeing blood on your body, your cries in my ears, *mio amore*. I have craved your scrumptious taste far too long. Our hour is near, and together, we will rule the immortal world." I tense when he leans in again, but he gently licks the wound sealed, his rough tongue devouring every drop. When a palm grips my breast, and his erection pumps against my hip, my mind flashes back to his father doing the same thing.

Dimitri forced Logan to drink from one side of my neck while he was on the other. I shudder, evoking the pain as the king's blackened nails pierced my nipple, his enormous hard-on rubbing against my hand.

Trezzo's breathing turns harsh, and the momentum against my hip increases. I resume my struggles. No fucking way is he getting off while dry humping me.

"Trezzo. Stop." But my demand inflames his lust. His head lifts and deadly fingers wrap around my throat.

The evil bastard scrutinizes every nuance of my expression as he squeezes in a savage grip. I dig at his wrist, but the more I resist, the quicker his hips grind against mine.

"That's it. Struggle, *cagna.* Fight me."

His panting breath sickens me, and I crave nothing more than to deny him, but after several excruciating minutes, my lungs demand air and darkness dances at the edge of my vision. While this won't kill me, I could pass out, and I wouldn't put it past him to molest me while unconscious.

Helplessness washes over me as I pound my fists against his shoulders. My dangling feet kick out in a futile attempt to injure him or distract him at the very least.

After several more minutes, his muscles tense, and he shudders against me. "Lu," he whispers hoarsely in my ear. "You still do it to me."

The vise around my throat eases, and I inhale blessed oxygen. The second the fucker steps away, I harness my energy and smash my fist into his jaw. He reels a step backward with a laugh, and I'm repulsed by the flush of desire in his cheeks and the dark spot staining his pants.

"Oh, I've missed you, Lu." He mops the blood from his lips with the back of his hand. "Make no mistake, *principessa*, no matter what transpires, you are mine." The smile evaporates. "Discover the halfling bitch's vulnerabilities or your secrets will meet the light of day."

"Do you honestly believe you can best her when your father couldn't? Not to mention, the Moretti brothers will eviscerate you before you're within a mile of her."

"That's where you come in, my dear. Find a means to lure her from Logan and the castle, and I will take care of the rest."

Before I respond, he traces away, and I sidestep to evade my falling sword.

What the hell do I do now? Tonight was about getting close to Trez. But do I need to at this stage? I'm confident the bloodwork will corroborate what I already know: Trezzo is Zachariah Giordano. But I've also determined what else he craves. Me.

Nicki is expecting a detailed report so a little fact-gathering from my contacts in Italy might be in order. Even though my gut tells me what kind of ruler Zachariah is—I can no longer think of him as Trez—I need to gather as much intel on him as possible.

And then what, Lu?

If I reveal Zach's true nature and his objectives, he'll expose my past, my secret, thereby sealing my fate. Only one option out of this predicament; good ole Zach must die.

The likelihood of me killing him is slim to none, but it won't matter. No fucking way is he going to blackmail me like Dimitri did for ages.

I refuse to sell my soul to the devil again to protect my twin.

CHAPTER 13

Kurtis

The ever-punctual Guardian—according to the dossier Bastian emailed—is an hour late. Not that I'm in a hurry to teleport. My insides roll when a bloodsucker traces me, and I fear it will scatter my molecules through the universe never to return. Although, I am looking forward to getting my arms around my mate, no matter the consequences.

I grin at the reason for her delay, and lean against the LeLoo Blues Bar's outside wall, observing the multitude of vehicles in the packed lot. And it's only 8 p.m. Inside, the low hum of country music penetrates the quiet.

I'd bet my cabin she's trying to avoid me for as long as possible, no doubt embarrassed at being caught spying. I still haven't decided whether to broach the subject. My mate's attitude when she arrives will determine my next move.

Remote viewing has been around for centuries, but until three days ago, I never believed it existed. And according to the rumors, the unknown target has no clue they are being observed, but I scented her the minute I stepped from the lake, and a tingle of awareness shot up my spine. With the morning sun striking the earth, my confused brain knew it was impossible.

Her strawberry and cream scent followed me through the cabin, and my cock hardened with every step. In the shower was when her form took shape. Her distinct perfume intensified, and my dick pulsed with a painful need to bury deep inside her. Her image wasn't stable, more of a shimmering apparition, but the amber stare glowed like lava as they raked my body. I'd trembled with the desire to look directly at her but forced myself to go along with the charade to discover how far she wanted to play.

She invaded my privacy. The only person I've ever allowed in my home, besides family, was Liam. I prefer the isolation of my retreat. The reason I bought the entire lake and the surrounding three hundred acres fifty years ago was to allow me the capability to shift and run in concealment without the risk of humans mistaking me for a wolf.

All I can think about was how intensely erotic it was to have my mate thinking she was observing me covertly. Not to mention, she risked a remote viewing to be with me. I've heard using the ability too often or too long has serious side effects.

No matter how adamantly Lucretia denies it, she wants me as much as I want her. And for the first time, I couldn't care less about her lineage or that our mating is against legislation. Lu will be mine, even if it's in secret, like my father and Queen Arra, until we get this archaic law changed.

I glance at my phone again. Lucretia's little reveal session at the coronation hopefully put an end to her secrets. With too much to overcome as it is, I'm not sure we could survive more lies or deception. I can't imagine the burden to keep such a secret for so long, unable to trust anyone. Even surrounded by hundreds of Guardians, she's lived a lonely existence, but I hope to change that.

Where the hell is she? I step away from the building to text her when she materializes before me, dressed in full battle gear minus her blades. Probably not a good idea to walk among humans with two large swords strapped to your back. By the heavy look of her long duster, she has a plethora of weapons hidden in its folds.

Even with her stance rigid, her deep amber eyes daring me to bring up the shower incident, she's magnificent. But the vulnerability beneath the defiant warrior decides for me.

My objective is to gain Lu's trust, but it's no longer for Nicki. The beast stirs in agreement as I shove away from the wall.

"You're late," I reprimand softly.

Her hard glare intensifies. "Grab your bag, shifter, and let's go."

I grasp the duffle at my feet, reach into her leather duster, and wrap an arm around her waist. Long dark lashes lower to my lips as I pull her tall, lean body against mine. Her height fits against me perfectly. The crown of her head brushes my chin, and I take a moment to enjoy the full breasts against my ribcage.

"I'm ready." In more ways than one. "Where to first?"

Strong, delicate hands clasp my shoulders, and I silently curse the thick jacket.

"A quick stop at your room at the castle to drop your things, then on to downtown Edmonton in Alberta, Canada."

The husky whisper has my dick twitching, but in the next heartbeat, it's replaced by nausea as Lu draws on the universe, controls our dimensions, and teleports us with pinpoint accuracy into the middle of my tower suite. My arm tightens on her waistline, bringing her closer until the queasiness eases. Will I ever get used to tracing?

"Are you alright?"

The velvety voice soothes me, and I drop the duffle to wrap both arms around her midriff. A flush spreads across her cheeks, and the deep amber regard slips to my mouth once more. I recall the brightness in her stare as she knelt before me in the shower, and my cock hardens in an instant.

"No," I groan. "Give me another minute." It's deceitful to pretend I'm still affected, but the need to keep her close overrides any decency.

"Of course." The low husky tone causes my canines to throb in my gums.

Millimeter by millimeter, I lower my head, my scrutiny never leaving hers. The slow progression allows her the opportunity to stop me, which goes against everything the beast demands.

A hair's breadth away, her nails digging into my shoulders through the jacket, her panting breath fanning my lips, a strange scent invades my nostrils and I pause. Skirting her luscious mouth, I bury my nose in her neck and inhale.

Rage ignites in my gut, and I shove her aside. "You reek of Massaro." My low, angry growl envelops the room, and Lu's eyes widen for a brief second before her jaw tightens.

"You might recall he is my mission."

Her mission. My mate anywhere near that son of a bitch intensifies my fury. "Just how dedicated are you? Did you fuck him, Lu?" I cringe as the harsh words contaminate the air between us.

Her chin lifts, regard narrow. "How I conduct my assignment is no concern of yours."

Damn it. My idiotic jealousy snuffed the warmth in her gaze and drew out the icy warrior she presents to everyone. I'm not everyone.

I'm used to having my orders obeyed; from the SEAL team I commanded, to my trainers and clients at the dojo, and from my people. To ignore my nature rubs me the wrong way, but Lu is not my soldier, a student, or a shifter. If I wish to keep the wall surrounding her from developing into a permanent fixture, I must curb my demand for control. For now.

"You're right." Her brow lifts. "It was a foolish assumption." I step closer. "Shall we go?" In other words, I'm asking her to ignore my stupidity and carry on with the assignment.

Lucretia tilts her head, contemplates me for several heartbeats before answering. "Yes," she whispers. Two steps and she's back in my arms. Without a sound, the room blackens and my stomach flip-flops.

* * *

This time we touch down in a darkened alleyway off Jasper Avenue and 100th street in the heart of downtown Edmonton. The bustling noise and aromas of city life assault my senses. I scan the alley for threats and allow the rolling in my belly to recover.

"What's the agenda here, boss lady?"

"We utilize our enhanced abilities to hunt for trouble. Rogues out of control, youngling's having fun but requiring a gentle reminder of the laws. Werewolves and vampires are the most problematic because of the bloodlust and pull of the moon." She shrugs. "If the infraction is nothing severe, the majority will back down when I disclose my credentials. I'll give them the proverbial slap on the wrist and a warning before sending them on their way."

"And if it's serious?"

"I teleport them to the Council of Unity's confinement area to stand trial."

No doubt, few go along voluntarily. "And if they resist?"

"Most likely hand-to-hand conflict with silver blades or throwing stars. We permit guns if they possess a silencer, but unless they're loaded with silver bullets, it won't have much effect. The objective is to subdue and teleport, but often it requires lethal force."

The slight pressure of my short swords under my jacket reassures me. "And the Guardians do this every night? In Canada or elsewhere?" I ask, intrigued.

The military mechanics of the various species is a subject my father and I haven't broached yet. My little mate can educate me during our time together. "I understand the different immortal territories operate their own exclusive units to enforce the laws. The shifters boast the Sentinels, the werewolves their Wardens, and the valkyrie the Protectors—to single out a few. But the vampire Guardians are the elite of the elite, right?" I ask as we tramp through the snow-lined streets.

Few humans walk around in these frigid conditions, and I'm relieved I chose leather pants for added warmth. As a shifter my body temp runs high, so I can endure the cold with ease, but this is downright freezing.

"You're correct. But it's not just because of our long, intensive training. Our strength, speed, and tracing abilities are unrivaled by most species." Presented as a straightforward fact without a hint of prideful boasting, even though she's earned a right to brag. "The queen's Guardians patrol Alberta, British Columbia, and everything west of Arizona up through Idaho. I suppose you could claim the western quarter of North America."

"That's a lot of real estate. What about the rest of the world?"

"Vampires reside in every region across this planet, just like the other species. Before the great battle, the Nation employed over 400 vampire Guardians. After, our numbers plummeted to a mere 200. Each district maintains its own division of guards to defend their territories, although, the queen's Guardians trace anywhere when requested. With Queen Giordano controlling the largest territory among the Others, we are stretched pretty thin."

"Not bad for a middle-class girl from Kentucky," I chuckle.

"Indeed."

We wander for several minutes in comfortable silence. Scanning. Listening. Its apparent Lu has something on her mind. She keeps glancing my direction readying to propose a question only to veer away before the words escape her inviting lips. I'm a patient man when circumstances call for it, so I wait.

After about half an hour and several blocks later, she finally speaks. “Can I ask you a personal question, my lord?”

“You can ask me anything, Lucretia. And it’s Kurtis.”

A puff of vapor saturates the air for a brief second when she exhales. “Why did you enlist in the human military and fight in their wars?”

The inquiry startles me. She obviously spotted the pictures in my bedroom during her secret invasion. Pain and guilt burn my throat as long-buried memories thrust to the forefront. That span in my history is a murky pit of anguish I keep hidden for my own sanity.

With a casual shrug, I look anywhere but at the prying stare of the warrior next to me. “I was a bored prince in need of some intrigue and action.”

Lu’s inquisitive gaze warms the side of my face. “I’m sorry. I didn’t mean to bring up bad memories.”

Fuck. Am I that transparent? “I’ll confess if you will,” I quip back with a smirk, hoping to lighten the mood.

I don’t even get a twitch. “Was there ever anything between you and Nicki?” she blurts out.

The rushed request means more than most folks would surmise, so I answer honestly. “At one point, I mistakenly believed we could end up together, but her destiny was always with Logan.”

“That must have hurt.” The soft reply has me peering down at her, but she averts her face, analyzing people, buildings, and alleyways.

I hesitate on the sidewalk. She stops ahead of me but doesn't turn around. "Lucretia. Look at me." After a brief hesitation, she twists, chin raised, expression blank. "What is it you're seeking?"

"It's not my business."

Oh, but it is. A pleasant hum builds in my rib cage, and I wait once more.

After a lengthy interval, she draws her braid over her shoulder and frets with the end. The warrior possesses a tell, and it's cute. "Did…" she falters, her stare glued to my boots. "Did you have sex with her?"

Warmth invades my spirit at the suppressed jealousy. "Look at me," I command again, and when she immediately obeys, my cock stirs. "No." The relief in the amber depths pleases me.

"My turn. I dealt with your query, now answer my earlier one."

Confusion creases her brow. "What question?"

"Did you fuck Trezzo?"

"Recently or in the past?" Her sarcastic tone clenches my jaw.

"You know damn well what I mean. Spit it out, or your pretty backside will feel my palm." *Okay, that kind of argument will infuriate the little warrior, idiot.*

Lu inhales deeply, and her scent intensifies. Amber eyes flicker. "I've had my fill of males threatening me."

A snarl wants loose, but I thrust it aside and take the beast by the proverbial horns. "Who threatened you?" My casual tone belies the savage fury coursing through me.

"It doesn't matter. To answer your question, no I did not," she admits with a huff of frosty air.

"Then why is his essence all over you?"

"I'll explain if you confess why you took up arms for the mortals."

My shoulders tense. I've lived long enough and been through numerous hells to mask my reaction. She couldn't perceive the pain lying down that highway, or how my impatience and naivety of youth destroyed a beautiful life, sullying a part of my soul.

I'm freed from responding when a woman's high-pitched scream rents the air. Our gazes collide for a split second before taking off in its direction. The terror in the cries rip through my cranium, and I press harder to keep up with Lu's extraordinary speed.

A mile down, we slide around the corner and stop dead. The long, narrow alley reeks of decaying rubbish and blood. Heavy darkness shrouds the area, and dirty snow line both sides. The dingy lights mounted along the buildings give off a dull, eerie radiance, and the tall abandoned structures inhibit the moon's rays from penetrating, but our enhanced vision plays out the scene with crystal clarity.

Four large werewolves surround a young woman. One male is thrusting between her open legs while another holds her arms bound above her head on the filthy ground. Long angry slashes mark her exposed chest and bite marks, still oozing blood, stain her thick thighs. Two already shifted, incapable of controlling their beasts in the frenzy. Each wolf weighs a solid hundred and fifty pounds.

Fury blasts through my gut and I reach inside my coat and seize the sword hilts the same second Lu throws a thin silver dagger. The sharpened blade impales the tall blonde restraining the woman in the eye. He reels back with an agonizing shriek.

Nice shot.

Feral eyes rotate in our direction as we advance into the darkened alley.

The enormous bastard between the human's thighs rises to his feet. He hikes his jeans up to his hips, not bothering to zip them closed. A violent kick to the woman's midsection sends her fragile body slamming into a shadowy corner—the deafening crack of ribs fuels my rage.

I peek at Lu. An evil smile lifts the edge of her lips right before she soars into the air, landing with a soft thud smack dab in the center of all four bastards.

Goddamnit!

In a blink I'm at her six, engaging the shifted wolves. My senses come alive. Anger, apprehension, and determination. My mate spins, kicks, and slashes with such velocity, her long duster flares out behind her with every turn in a choreographed display of artistry. She's fucking impressive, but I can't help the fear churning in my gut.

She plunged right into the midst of the fray. These young beasts are clumsy but strong. The shifted ones are even more dangerous. What would she have done if she'd been patrolling alone?

My beast stirs. My mate and I will enjoy words if we survive this conflict.

Within a few minutes, the tall blonde shifts and the power surge slams Lu against the side of the building with such force it caves in the bricks. She lands with a thud. Blood trickles from her lips.

My roar fills the alley as I slice through the wolf's heavy white fur at his neck. Before his head smacks the ground, I've spun to confront the next one. It would be easier if I shifted, but I need to remain in communication with Lucretia.

Instead of staying behind me, she strides to my side, flipping small daggers in each palm.

With one dead, the other two injured, the fourth inches from the exit, too damaged to change, a phone to his ear. Fuck. Backups on the way. A cursory glance at the body crumpled in the corner shows she's out cold or gone.

"You fuckwads will regret this," he pants as he holds together the gaping wound in his side from Lu's blades. The silver prevents him from regenerating.

"You've broken several laws, young pups. The queen doesn't take too kindly to injuring humans in her territory," Lu growls, the luminous amber glow lighting up the gloom. The enraged smile showcases those sexy fangs.

"You must be Lucretia," a deep, grating voice rumbles from the alley entrance.

My gaze swings to the fresh threat while keeping the young wolves in my periphery. He's a huge son of a bitch. My stature, maybe more, with the most exquisite hair I've ever encountered on a male. The heavy dark waves cascade to the corded bulk of his chest. The deep-set, blood-red eyes expose his lineage.

Demon. And a potent one. Even with ancient magic flowing from him, the male's dressed like a teenage biker: shredded jeans kids pay big bucks for, an ordinary gray t-shirt topped by a heavily zippered, black leather jacket, and biker boots with a scuffed metal buckle at each ankle.

"I've heard all about you," he continues with a sneer. "The only female Guardian in the history of the vampires. Who did you blow to get accepted?"

"You're about to surrender your head, demon," I underline the threat with a harsh, angry rumble, the beast breaking through loud and clear.

"Well, well, well, the shifter prince, Kurtis Ruse." His gleeful smile causes my inner animal to crash against my rib cage. It craves to hack into the demon's throat. "This is my lucky night."

CHAPTER 14

Kurtis

"I do not wish to fight you tonight, shifter." The massive demon saunters closer. "But, she does." His eerie red irises round on Lu. "Your age and lineage do not grant me control over you, Ruse, but the vampire is youthful enough to be receptive to my charms."

Shit.

"Don't look at him, Lucretia," I order too late. Her muscles relax as she peers into the demon's gaze with a vacant expression.

"The young always fall prey. She is luscious, is she not? Mayhap I will keep her as a sex slave when she has defeated you. There could be no greater thrill than for a vampire under my spell to suck me off whenever I choose," he chuckles.

The beast thrashes, and I clench my fists to keep it at bay. *Must protect Lu.* "Who are you, demon?"

"How unfortunate my reputation does not precede me. Allow me to enlighten you, Ruse." His crimson regard takes on a sinister glow, and he bows in a theatrical flourish. "King Jagorach Darath at your service."

My insides congeal. Until tonight, I assumed this creature was a mythical being. Rumors about him ran rampant throughout the ages, but the ones I recall most say he's a direct descendant of Lucifer himself and over two millennia old.

"Ah, by your expression, you *have* heard of me. That hardens my cock." His grin is pure malevolence.

"You have a fascination with your dick. What do you want, Darath?" I ask and clutch my sword tighter. I've no inkling what his fighting capabilities are, but I'm no fool. If I engage, it could mean my death and Lu's. Or worse.

"Many things, young pup. I would love to stick around and observe this beauty cut you into bits, but I have a realm to run. It is a shame, actually," he drawls, those flaming eyes traveling the length of my frame. "You are a strong, handsome devil. It would be entertaining to break you." His tongue slithers out and passes along his red lips. I shudder inwardly. "I wager you have never been with another male. There is virgin territory to explore." My teeth grind in revulsion. "But alas, duty calls. If you survive, please take a message to the halfling queen."

The polite request contradicts the demon's evil leer he transfers to Lu. She spins and trains a poisonous stare in my direction as she whirls her small daggers with wicked intent. Anxiety rolls in my gut. How can I keep her from killing me without injuring her?

"Let the Guardian go, and I'll gladly relay the information, King Darath." I address him by his title and pray his ego takes the bait.

"What fun would that be?" he asks with a deep, vicious laugh. "Tell the halfling the Vampire Nation will answer for their atrocities against the Demon Realm with her head on a platter, but not before I torture and fuck her delectable little body." He turns to leave the alley, but before he rounds the corner, the red glow pins Lu. "Kill him, Lucretia." His tall, bulky form disappears.

I don't even get a chance to talk reason before she charges. Her daggers thrust and swing for my throat. I block and evade, struggling not to hurt her, but damn she is skilled and quick. Not as powerful and fast as Nicki, but it still requires all my concentration to keep away from those deadly silver blades.

"Lucretia. Stop this." I command between swirling and dodging from her attacks.

"Can't." The word is but a squeak as if forced out against its will. Even though tears glitter, she advances with a ferocity becoming increasingly harder to defend against without causing her severe damage.

"Yes, you can." I insist. "You're my fated female, Lucretia. I cannot harm you." My desperation at our predicament rings loud and clear. The sole clue she understood my proclamation is a lone tear trailing down her cheek. Otherwise, her attacks intensify.

"Kill me."

Lu's faint plea through gritted teeth explodes the panic building in my gut. What if I knock her out? Could it loosen whatever hold Darath has on her mind? With her capability to heal and her strength, it will take a mighty blow to bring her down. What—what if I crush her skull? Can it mend? Hurting her to such a degree fills me with fear, and my past rears its hideous head.

I spin away from the dagger aiming for my heart and shove her in the back. Her forehead strikes the brick building with a resounding *thwack*, and I cringe. For a split second, she staggers, her head shaking. My soul aches, the beast strangely dormant.

Lu spins unsteadily, and I don't notice the blade until it sinks deep into my shoulder with a bone-jarring thump.

Fuck.

Even shaken, she'd embedded the dagger through cartilage and bone. White-hot pain radiates down my arm as the energy-zapping silver spreads. Before it can weaken me further, I yank the knife from my body with a rough groan. Muscles and tendons scream in protest. If I shifted, I would heal, but communication with my mate is paramount; it overrides every other demand.

Reflexes weakened, I comprehend too late Lu released another dagger. This time, her aim is true. The second blade plunges into the side of my neck, and I falter from the impact. The silver's powerful effects seep directly into my jugular, and it takes all my energy to remain on my feet.

"No!"

Lu's distressed cry keeps my muscles rigid. I blink at my mate's blurry image coming at me with yet another dagger, at the tears running unchecked down her cheeks, her arm raised for the final death blow to my heart.

"Please," she pleads.

The beast hears her and stirs to the forefront. With the last visage of strength, I swing my fist at her advancing form. The impact slams into her temple hard enough to shatter my knuckles. The sickening crunch of her skull fracturing is my undoing, and I roar in torment. Not from the pain, but from watching Lu's unconscious body slump to the alley floor. My fist's imprint in the side of her head quiets the beast, overcome by the violence we inflicted on our female.

With my energy deteriorating rapidly, I sink to my knees next to her. I need to get us out of here before some random human passes by, or the young woman in the corner wakes. For the first time, I notice the other werewolves disappeared.

I'm uncertain whether I should remove the blade from my neck and possibly bleed out or leave it and let the silver continue to weaken me until I sink into oblivion. With my good hand, I reach into my pocket for my phone and dial the one person who can be here in a millisecond.

"Hey Kurtis, how's your first night out on assignment?"

"I'm in trouble." I hiss.

"Where?" she demands in an urgent growl.

Shit, where am I? I glance up for a street sign, but everything blurs, and my vision blackens. "Not sure. Alley—downtown." I clamp my jaw shut and clench my teeth to remain conscious. In the background, a deep murmur comes through the line, but I can't make out what's being said.

Unable to hold my torso up any longer, I crash on my side next to Lu, keeping the phone pressed to my ear. I overlook the pain in my shoulder and fist to reach over and gather Lu's still form to my chest.

"About to ... pass ... out. Nicki... hurr...." Before I finish, I sense Nicki's presence above me.

"Excellent job, Bastian," I hear her express before she snatches the dagger from my neck. I grunt as hot liquid flows freely down the front of my collar, and the coppery stench mingles with the rancid trash and congealing werewolf blood around us.

Lavender tickles my nostrils before Nicki's supple hair caresses my shoulder. Her warm tongue slides across the wound, and my skin tightens as it mends.

"Do not ingest the blood, Nicole," Logan commands in a harsh voice.

"Immune, remember?"

"Silver," I breathe out.

"I know, big guy. We're gonna get you back to the castle and fixed up in no time," she responds pleasantly, although I sense her worry.

"Mortal ... corner."

"I'm sorry. She didn't make it. Sebastian is taking care of her body." Sadness burns through my heart at our failure to protect the delicate human. My friend senses my sorrow and passes a tender caress over my cheek. "She wouldn't have survived the transformation,

Kurtis. Logan needs to pick you up now and trace you to the castle. Let go of Lu so I can lift her."

When Nicki tries to dislodge my fierce grip around Lu's waist, the inner brute growls low and draws her closer.

"Kurtis." A soft brush through my hair and my beast calms. "Come on, hon. I promise to take care of her."

With reluctance, I relinquish my mate into the safekeeping of the only woman in the world I entrust with such a precious package. Strong, thick arms slide beneath my knees and shoulders, and I grunt against the pain. I can't image how ludicrous this looks. Logan is a large, powerful male, but my bulk is taller and broader.

I drag my heavy lids open and almost smile at the fuzzy picture of Nicki holding a woman as tall as some men with ease.

I will never live this down, crosses my mind before the blackness envelops my vision.

CHAPTER 15

Lucretia

"Why isn't she waking, Icarus?" The heated, frustrated tone can only belong to my queen.

"I cannot say, my lady. Head trauma is difficult to predict."

"If she doesn't wake soon, Kurtis will blow a fucking gasket. I've run low on excuses to keep him out of here."

Why would they hold him from me? And why can't I open my eyes or move? I concentrate on lifting my lead-filled lids, but they refuse to comply. Not even a fragment of light. What the hell is wrong with me? Am I the one with the head injury? But how?

I remember the wolves attacking then murdering the human. The big male crushed her sternum with a careless kick like she was rubbish to toss with the rest of the garbage. Then the exhilaration of engaging the bastards with my mate by my side. A gray mist cloaks everything after. What put me in this state?

"Mayhap Lord Ruse can rouse her enough to consume his blood."

"Why would his blood be any different from mine or Logan's?"

"I cannot say, my lady, but is it not worth the attempt?"

The queen sighs. "Of course it is. Let him in, Logan, before he goes ape-shit."

I renew my struggles, desperate to see my mate, to reassure myself he's not hurt. Panic bubbles below the surface when I realize my vampire lays dormant. She doesn't even stir when I summon her strength.

Whatever transpired tonight was traumatic enough to send her into hiding.

"Lucretia?"

His deep voice shoots tingles through my body. I want to shout, '*Yes. I am here.*'

"Tell me how bad, Icarus?"

I don't recognize the dark and guttural tone. A large, warm hand covers my own. I would know the hot grip anywhere, or the citrus, woodsy masculine scent.

An excruciating ache pounds in my left temple, and I take a second to examine my body mentally. Besides the fact I'm immobile and lying prone on a hard, cold table, and pain stabs through my cranium, I don't seem to be experiencing any other damage.

"We are uncertain why she has not awakened enough to drink from the queen."

"Is this the mind control or my doing?"

Why would he think my condition was his responsibility? And what mind control?

"I cannot say, my lord, but I trust your presence can draw her from the slumber, and your blood repair her injuries."

My vampire awakens with a purr. Oh no. If I ingest my mate's lifeblood, my need for him will heighten tenfold. I lust after it, but I don't want to make matters worse.

"Then what are we waiting for, open my vein for her."

"Are you certain, my lord?" the priest asks in a hushed whisper.

"Yes, Icarus. I'm the reason she's on this table." His large palm squeezes my fingers.

What? How? Maybe I was mistaken. If I were his female, his beast would never allow him to harm me.

"Kurtis?" The queen questions. "Your emotions are...."

"My love," Logan's deep rumble interrupts. "Some things are better left unsaid. For now."

"Your mate's right," the shifter responds in a rough whisper. "Let it go, Nicki."

After a lengthy pause, she huffs. "Whatever. Wake her ass up so we get some fucking answers."

Firm, gentle fingers clasp my chin and open my mouth. The prince's scent wafts through my nostrils a second before the nectar I've yearned for since the first moment I laid eyes on him flows over my tongue. My taste buds explode at the exotic richness.

Good. God. Almighty. After one drop, I'm addicted.

"Come on, angel. Swallow." Kurtis rumbles next to my ear.

Muscles convulse as I endeavor to obey while slightly roughened fingers massage my throat. A cool palm tilts my head backward, and pain shoots through my skull. I silently scream for the nourishing blood pooling in my mouth, but the muscles remain lax.

"Lucretia." Kurtis's voice alters. It's hard, commanding, and sexy. "Drink now."

The synapses in my brain fire at the command, and my vampire trembles with the tremendous desire to obey. Painful hunger drives me to swallow. The first huge gulp of pure adrenaline flows down my throat. Holy crap. Intense power shoots straight to my core with lightning speed, and a ragged sob vibrates through my chest.

"Yes," Kurtis exclaims. "Good girl."

It's ludicrous, but I preen at his praise and dutifully consume another mouthful.

"Mayhap we should leave them to it," Logan mumbles.

"But we need to talk to her," the queen says in confusion.

"My love. Do you recall what transpires when you drink my blood?"

"Oh. Yeah, okay, let's go."

As soon as the door closes with a soft thud, my lids snap wide. Kurtis's handsome features hover above me. His piercing blue regard darkens with passion, and a relieved smile lifts those luscious lips.

I latch onto the wrist suspended above my open mouth with my fangs and drive deep. His grin fades replaced by a sexy rumble. It vibrates throughout my body before settling on my tightened nipples.

Strength spreads to my limbs like a potent upper. The pain in my temple intensifies for a brief second as my skull mends.

"Damn. I never realized this would be—so erotic."

I almost laugh, but to do so would require dislodging my fangs. Not happening. Need more. I moan my agreement and grasp his wrist with both hands. My lids grow heavy with desire, but I battle to keep them on my mate's masculine perfection; irises the same hue of the sky at mid-day, hard jaw clenched with suppressed hunger. The picture of him in the shower as he stroked his massive erection rushes to the forefront and my core pulses with demand.

"I confess," he says, his tone rich and husky with desire as he regards me; his free hand coils in my hair. "I enjoyed you spying on me." My eyes widen. Did he read my mind? "Your shimmering image kneeling at my feet while I came was fucking amazing. Next time, it will be for real."

I whimper in agreement.

After two deeper pulls on his vein, I mentally assess my body. The shifter's powerful blood has restored my strength and mended my injuries. With regret, I slip my fangs out before sliding my tongue across the punctures, greedily enjoying the last few droplets before the wound closes. Kurtis's observation swirls with emotion, and thanks to his potent essence circulating through my veins, I perceive his rampaging desire as my own.

I surge up, trap my mate's hips between my spread thighs and clutch his neck. Before I can tug him down to me, he swoops in and takes possession of my lips.

Warm palms cradle my cheeks as he explores my mouth with a thoroughness that leaves me breathless. Kurtis's kiss sends a current of liquid fire straight to my nipples, causing them to stiffen into hard, painful peaks. I haul him tighter and brush them against the rigid muscles of his torso. A desperate keening rumbles from my chest as lightning zings right to my clit.

I work to scoot to the edge, to alleviate the throb between my thighs, but Kurtis is quicker; he grips my ass and yanks me to him. The enormous erection I've fantasized about since the battle rubs against my throbbing, wet center.

With his high-octane blood fueling my passion into a seething inferno in a matter of seconds, I shamelessly gyrate against his hardness. In moments, intense electrical currents flutter through my core. I break the kiss and throw my head back as a powerful orgasm shakes me to my soul.

"Oh God! Kurtis," I shout, a little startled with the velocity at which the detonation took hold.

"Lucretia," he exclaims between harsh gasps, as astounded as I by the speed of my climax. "You are incredible," he murmurs against my lips, cradling my face once more. He inhales, as if needing my scent as deep as possible, then presses his forehead to mine.

Several minutes pass before our breaths even out. A dark shadow flickers across the prince's encounter, and a heavy sadness forces its way to the surface. "I can't express how sorry I am. I hurt you."

I tip my head back to regard him with a frown. The small aftershocks ease as a nagging memory tries to intrude. "What do you mean?" I ask, not positive I want the answer.

A puzzled scowl mars his forehead. "Do you not remember what happened in the alley two nights ago?"

"Two nights ago?" Stunned speechless, my arms fall from the powerful shoulders to brace against the cold edge of the metal table.

"Yes," Kurtis whispers and drives a palm through his thick blonde hair in an agitated movement. "I've been out of my mind thinking I'd damaged you beyond repair." The torment in his voice confuses me, and my vampire stirs at his distress.

"You're the reason I'm on this table? Unconscious for… two days?"

He swallows. "Yes."

"I..." There must be a logical explanation. How could I be his mate if he hurt me? "Why?"

"I had no alternative," he evades, not answering the question.

"Why?" My fingers clutch the cool steel.

Sorrow fills his expression as he caresses my temple. "Because, angel, you sought to kill me."

CHAPTER 16

Lucretia

"What? Impossible. I could never harm you." *Careful what you reveal, Lu.* "I mean—why would I? Killing the next shifter king would cause my head to roll, and I prefer it where it is."

You're babbling. Shut the hell up.

Panic bubbles below the surface while the prince studies me.

"Advise me on what transpired," I urge, hoping to distract him from my blunder.

"What's the last thing you remember?"

I stay a sigh of relief.

"We would appreciate the answer as well," Logan announces as he, Nicki, and Icarus file back through the door.

"Yes." The halfling agrees. "Kurtis refused to grant us a breakdown of why he bashed your skull in until you were awake." She shoots me an annoyed glare, and I swallow.

"Um, the last thing I recall was engaging the werewolves," I explain before hopping off the table to face my queen and commander.

"That's it?" Kurtis asks in disbelief, and I nod. "The human girl didn't make it," he announces, and a dark shadow crosses his expression.

A similar darkness altered his features when I inquired about his reasons for participating in the mortal wars. Interesting. The prince hides an intense pain from his past. Does it involve a female? Or are the emotions behind his wall from the tragedies of war?

"Care to inform us now that sleeping beauty is awake?" Nicki asks.

With fascination, I observe my male as he recounts that night's events. Has he always been so... Alpha? I smile inwardly imagining him as a young boy, or a teenager, developing with such speed he didn't know what to do with his limbs.

"I assume the wounded werewolf holding the phone contacted the demon," he concludes.

"What demon?" Logan and I ask at the same time.

"King Jagorach Darath."

"I thought he was a myth," my commander responds, more to himself than Kurtis.

"Okay. I missed this class. Who the hell is this Darath guy?" Nicki asks, hands on her hips.

"He's the King of the Demon Realm, my love. Said to be Lucifer's direct descendant," Logan answers.

"Get the fuck out?" Nicole whispers in wide-eyed shock, and I share her disbelief even as a figure with long black hair and flaming red eyes flashes through my mind.

"He had a message for you, Nicki." The prince's grave tone has my insides churning.

"The Demon King, Son of Lucifer, had a message for me?" She swallows. "Whatever it is has gotta be awful." Sensing his mate's agitation, Logan pulls her into his side protectively. She clutches his waist, her anxious stare glued to Kurtis. "Spit it out."

"He claims the Vampire Nation will answer for their atrocities against the Demon Realm with your head on a platter, but not before he..."

"What?" Logan demands softly, his glare sparkling like emeralds under a full moon.

"Tortured and fucked you in every way imaginable," Kurtis mumbles as he rubs the back of his neck.

An intense, animalistic growl echoes off the stones. Brilliant green pins my mate. Oh boy, please don't slay the messenger. On instinct, I seize my mate's wrist readying to trace us out if necessary.

Nicki bravely confronts the angry predator, overlooks the ragged breathing, the enormous fangs, the deep grating rumble setting my nerves on edge, and clasps his face between her palms.

"My love," she soothes. "The only one who will fuck me is you. Put the beautiful vampire away for later and let's figure this out. Together."

Logan responds by dragging her against him and plunging those huge, white razors deep into her neck. A purely primitive display of ownership to settle his raging inner monster, and one I understand.

The queen moans low, and the three of us pivot in unison to provide them a smidgen of privacy.

A scalding hand grasps my own, as affected by Nicki and Logan's passion and love as me. Shivers ripple down my spine at the remembered orgasm this dynamic male drew from me moments ago.

After several long minutes of listening to Nicki's comforting murmurs and discreet sighs, I yearn to trace Kurtis to my room, climb his frame like a tree, and have my wicked way with him. If his quickened heart rate is any indication, he's suffering the same effects.

"All better," the queen finally announces, and we turn to find Logan's vampire back in check, but he holds his mate firmly tucked against his side.

Kurtis drops my hand. "I'm sorry, but I thought you should know."

"What crimes is he talking about?" Nicki asks.

"No clue," Logan answers. "But I would bet it involves your father."

"Bastard is still creating problems from the grave," she mutters through gritted teeth. "So. Let's recap my first month as the prophesied bringer of peace. One of my kind is after my throne. The Dark Fae King and the Succubi Queen are potentially plotting war against the Vampire Nation and calculating my death. And now we are at odds with the Demon Realm, whose ruler, the direct offspring of the devil," she air quotes, "craves my head on a platter, but not before he tortures and rapes me." She steps in front of Logan, who immediately plants his palms on her shoulders, keeping her against his torso and flings her arms wide. "Did I miss anything?"

"Nope," Kurtis responds quietly. "I think that about sums it up."

Guess now would not be a great occasion to let them in on Trezzo's ultimatum. It's my problem anyhow. Nicki and Logan have enough on their plate.

A sudden agony shoots through my skull, and I clutch my head as the bare round room tilts and spins. Nausea rips through my gut as agonizing pain lights up the nerve endings in my brain.

"Lucretia?" Kurtis grabs my elbow. "What's wrong?"

"Brain—on—fire!" My scream bounces off the walls, and I sink to one knee as an inferno bursts through my cranium, zapping all my newfound energy. It wouldn't surprise me if the side of my head just exploded sizzling coals all over the room.

"Icarus. What's happening to her?" Kurtis's bellow fuels the blaze.

I press both palms against my temples as scalding blue flames fill my vision, and my skull splits in two. The torment is excruciating, and when I think I can't stand anymore, another white-hot streak of silver lightning discharges. My scream pierces my eardrums, and I arch backward.

"Do something goddammit!" Kurtis roars as he gathers me into his embrace.

I cling to him, silently beseeching him to take the pain away, and bury my scalding forehead against his neck.

"Christ, she's burning up."

"Her mind is seeking to restore the missing memories," Icarus' melodious voice states above the fireworks exploding in my brain.

"What is she blocking?" Nicki asks my mate.

"The fact she attempted to kill me."

"What?" Nicki exclaims, and I can't fault her. If pain weren't stealing my speech, I'd declare the shifter insane for expressing such a thing. "Lu tried to kill you?"

"The demon controlled her," Kurtis informs them through clenched teeth.

"Can you relieve her suffering, Icarus?" Logan asks.

"I will try."

Cool, tender palms gently cover on my forehead and the back of my skull. Their chilly contact eases the agony somewhat, but I sincerely wish they were ice packs.

"Remember, my child." The ethereal tone whispers through my mind. I bury tighter to my mate, my arms like steel bands around his collar, my pathetic whimpers muffled against his skin.

Through the raging fire, a pinpoint grows. It coils and snakes through the flames, swelling larger and more extensive the closer it becomes. I latch onto it. In the blurry depths lies my salvation from this purgatory. Distantly, I hear the others talking, but nothing penetrates the firestorm inside me.

The more I fixate on what I now recognize is an image, the sharper it develops. The spinning and weaving slow. The flames dim. After a few minutes, the searing pain recedes, and the vision morphs into a scene.

It's Kurtis and me in the alley fighting the wolves. From this outside perspective, I'm enthralled by my mate's combat skills—the strength and speed in his strikes and kicks, the graceful symmetry in his movements. The concentration is lethal, and yet he always keeps me in his line of sight.

When a towering, dangerous-looking male with long dark hair and crimson orbs enters the alley, the scene slows through my mind with clarity. Horrified, I observe myself attack my mate, cringe at Kurtis's attempts to avoid my advances without injuring me. If I was undecided before about being his female, no more. His words confirmed it.

My body stiffens when the first blade slams into his shoulder. My vampire screams her outrage. By the time the second knife plunges into the tender meat of his neck, tears cascade down my face to soak Kurtis's shirt. It torments me to observe the mental war he wages with his beast. Given no alternative, he plows his fist into my temple.

The agony dissipates like a flash bomb, but it's nothing compared to the misery and shame my soul is now enduring. I tried to murder my mate. I poisoned him with my knives. Threw those silver daggers and drilled them into his flesh without regret or hesitation. Only one thought obsessed me: kill him. And right until the last second, the valiant shifter fought to protect me.

Wrapped in my mate's searing hold my actions repulse me. My vampire cowers in stunned silence, too disturbed to howl her failure and dishonor.

Quietly, I withdraw from Kurtis and stand on unsteady legs. When he rises and tries to grasp my shoulders, I stride back. I don't deserve his consoling or his embrace. I don't deserve him.

"I remember," I whisper before retreating another step.

"It wasn't your fault."

Tremors rack my frame, and I swipe at the evidence of my weakness running down my face. Where is my cold veil of indifference when I require it? Probably as ashamed of me as I am.

"Angel..."

"Don't call me that," I grate out and work to stem the stream of tears. I am the farthest thing from an angel. I sought to kill my one true mate. Every time those words whisper through me, disgust stabs through my heart. What if I'd succeeded? I couldn't continue knowing I destroyed the one thing in my world that means—everything.

Hell's bells. Yes, Kurtis is my mate, and the bond links me to him physically. In the last month, I've fallen hard for this forbidden shifter, which makes what I attempted even more reprehensible.

"Lu." Nicki steps around the prince to confront me. Too humiliated to look at my queen directly, I drop my lashes. After a weighty sigh, she swings to the room. "Could you all give us a minute? I need to talk to Lu. Woman to woman."

"Ah, Nicole..." Logan begins, but the halfling cuts him off with an upraised hand and deadpan stare.

"I got this," she says with a confidence I'm sure she's far from experiencing. Nicki and emotions, especially other's emotions, go together like bullets and babies.

Once everyone clears the place, the silence suffocates. Those penetrating gray eyes look right through me. She opens her mouth then closes it again with a grimace. I'd snort at her discomfort if I weren't so overwhelmed by my own concerns.

"They say talking about trauma helps. That and jogging. Two concepts which make me feel like crap."

She offers nothing further, and I suspect this is where I'm expected to wail out all my shame and humiliation on her shoulder. Never in a million years.

"As much as I appreciate this," I note with a wave between us, "I'm fine."

She winces before barking out a laugh. "Oh, Lu. We are more alike than you think." She places an awkward hand on my shoulder. "You know, Logan's training me to think before I act, so if I smack the shit out of you right now, rest assured I've thought about it and I'm confident in my decision."

"My lady?" Sometimes her sarcasm escapes me.

"I experience lies the way most individuals get brain freeze from eating ice cream too fast. So you just caused me a severe headache. Wait? Did they have ice cream back when you were a shifter?"

"I was born in 1877, not the stone age." Her countenance tightens as I return the mockery, beyond caring at this point.

"Anyway, the phrase, 'the devil made me do it,' fits this scenario for once." She extends a smirk at her own joke before her expression turns severe and my insides somersault. "You were being controlled by a powerful demon." She shudders. "What happened wasn't your fault. Kurtis doesn't blame you, and neither do I."

"My lady..."

"Don't interrupt me when I'm on a roll, Lu," she scolds.

"My apologies." I submit a brief nod. I understand what she is struggling to express, but I'm not certain my vampire, or I, concur.

"My recommendation is to suck it up or get it all out on the table. Preferably with someone who can offer you sensible guidance. Since it's not my forte, I suggest either Liam or Sebastian. Surprisingly, I've discovered they're both pretty good listeners."

I notice she didn't extend Kurtis's shoulder.

"All great advice, but I think I will go with option A and suck it up."

She snorts, nodding with understanding before turning toward the door. "Your choice." She hesitates, her hand on the knob, and peers over at me. "Take tomorrow night off."

"But I…"

"Are you going to argue with your queen?"

"No, my lady." *Shit.* "And thank you."

"When you're recovered, I expect a full report on Trezzo. I'm aware you met with him. And the less I know about what's happening between you and Kurtis the better, but you need distance from him right now. Trace to your room before I let the angry shifter inside. I'll deal with him."

Gladly. "Yes, my lady."

Nicki swings the door open, and a fevered glare pinpoints me in a heartbeat. The second I begin to teleport, his bellow fills my ears.

CHAPTER 17

Kurtis

The plush mattress in my tower room does nothing to ease my turbulent mind. I cram the silk sheets to my waist for the hundredth time. The embers in the fireplace are long dead, and the chilly air envelops my exposed chest but fails to dispel this simmering need for Lu.

Earlier I wandered around this entire castle hoping to run into my mate. Her scent teased my nostrils, tested my control, but I never glimpsed her dark hair or amber eyes.

Last night, Logan and Nicki grilled me for two hours about the incidents in the alley, the demon, and Lu's actions. Through it all, the one thing pounding away at my brain was Lucretia's reaction after her memories resurfaced.

It wrecked me to witness her in so much agony, my beast desperate to end it, but my heart softened when she clung to me with such trust. In her anguish, she unconsciously exposed her need, her vulnerability, and her faith in me to ease her suffering.

I clench my fist and drape my arm over my forehead. Could Lu bear more than a desire for me? She'd mentioned she couldn't hurt me. Does that mean

I'm her mate? If so, the resolve to change the law post-haste pounds through me. Although, my father and Arra petitioned the council numerous occasions over the years with no reliable results.

I flip back the covers with a sigh and roam to the balcony doors. The full moon's resplendent glow streaks across the stone floor like a welcoming beacon. Its potent magic pulls at my beast, whispering as if a lover to run free under its brilliant light. I fling the French doors wide and stride out onto the snow-covered terrace in just my boxer briefs.

Tonight, the glacial air doesn't come close to mitigating the burning demand for my angel. If I knew which bedroom in this vast castle was hers, nothing would block me from pounding down her door. I grasp the freezing stone railing and peer out over the treetops laden down with ice and fresh snow in this harsh Canadian wilderness.

If I'm Lu's mate, then her inner vampire is in turmoil over the attempt on my life, just as my beast was at injuring her. She needs me whether or not she admits it. We've not completed the bond, but with the moon full, heightening my senses, I might get a bead on her emotions.

My lids lower as I visualize those gorgeous amber eyes. How they brightened and sparkled when she erupted from a mere stroke. My cock hardens in an instant. The stone railing creaks under my grip.

A twig snaps three hundred yards to my left, leaves long-dead crunch from the nocturnal creatures scurrying through the forest. A wolf howls in the distance, quickly answered by another. The Guardian patrols around the perimeter are scarcely a wisp of sound. The demanding urge to turn and run crawls along my spine, but I thrust the pull aside even as it strains my muscles in preparedness.

Unlike werewolves, who are a slave to the moon's commands, shifters learn to master the lunar cycle's effect on their beast after their first transformation. Both species can shift at will, but on the night of the full moon, the wolves lose all control, especially if their mate is near.

Her scent plows into me. Four stories below, Lu steps out a side door to stand all alone in the icy snow. White plumes escape her lips as her arms hug her midsection. The thin yoga pants hugging her luscious ass, and the purple tank top, do nothing to protect her from the freezing temperatures.

I'm about to call out and demand she go back inside where it's warm when her body stills and her head slowly lifts. Deep amber irises collide with mine and my cock twitches.

"Come to me, Lucretia," I command in a harsh rasp.

Her gaze brightens as she examines me. Will she obey, or could the hunt begin? I'm relieved and disappointed when she crouches at the knees and soars into the air.

Without a sound, she settles on the balcony floor, her bare feet disappearing into the frigid snow. Desire ignites the golden regard as they devour my near-naked appearance, but it's the remorse and shame shadowing her face that crushes my heart.

I take my time devouring every nuance in her expression, each fidget and twitch of her athletic body. White clouds puff between us with each breath. Her succulent lips quiver in the frosty air.

"Come inside out of the cold."

"No."

The anguish in that one word is almost my undoing. A large stride and she's cradled in my embrace. She doesn't resist, just wraps her toned arms around my shoulders and buries her face in my neck. Before the doors swing shut, muffled cries shake her frame. The sound squeezes my lungs, and I tuck her tighter to my chest.

With a tender kiss on her cheek, I settle on the bed against the headboard and hold her close. The soft weeping from this proud warrior pierces my soul.

"Hush, angel," I whisper in her ear as I rock her gently. "It wasn't your fault."

"I—I almost—killed you." She grates out between hiccups. She lifts her head, and I peer into the beautiful, tear-filled eyes in wonder. "I forced you to injure me."

"Lucretia. I don't blame you. You were manipulated against your will," I declare, kissing the moistness from her rosy cheeks. I unravel the band at the end of her braid, toss it on the nightstand, and pass my fingers through the mounds of dark hair until the silky curls settle around stiff shoulders.

"What are we going to do with this?" she whispers brokenly as I mop the last of the tears.

"I don't know," I answer, grasping what she means. "All I know is I want you. All I think about is being buried deep inside you. How I crave to hear you scream my name again as you come apart under my touch."

Her moan is all the encouragement I require, and I grasp her skull and ravage her mouth. God, she tastes good. Everything about my mate sets me on fire. Her fingers shove into my hair as she presses those hardened nipples against my chest.

I need to caress and devour every inch of the velvety skin. The fragrant aroma of her desire is driving me wild.

Lifting on one knee, I lay her lithe body across the bed. The amber glow and the sight of her fangs stiffen my cock further.

Without hesitation, Lu opens her long, lean legs and wraps them around my hips. I press my throbbing erection against her core. Jesus. Her slick warmth penetrates the thin yoga pants right through my boxer briefs.

It's curious, the way I wish to embrace her with tenderness but fuck her like an animal. I've experienced the conflict once before in my life. With a growl, I force the dark past down deep. It has no place here with Lu.

She senses my inner struggle because, in the next instant, she reaches down between us and seizes my cock in a punishing grip. I groan low at the pleasure-pain she inflicts. My mate's challenge is apparent in the glowing stare. She's urging me to take control.

A feral smile spreads my lips, and Lu's breath hitches. There's no finer gift than her trust and submission.

I straddle her hips and in one swift move, rip her tank top in half, exposing perfect round breasts with puckered rosy nipples. These were made to drive a man crazy with the need to touch and devour.

I slip off the bed, taking her yoga pants with me. Holy Christ. The smooth mound and bare glistening lips almost have me tumbling to my knees and burying my face between her thighs. Saliva pools in my mouth at her sweet aroma.

Lu arches her back, her eyes imploring. Before tonight is through, she will beg for permission to come. Excitement surges at finally having my female right where I want her. World War III could start outside, and I wouldn't give a damn.

"Spread your legs," I command, and she obeys without a qualm. "Good girl." I praise and stroll around to the other side of the bed by her head. Molten lava follows my strides. I reach for her shoulders and slide her to the edge. Lush, dark tresses cascade down to brush the floor, her graceful neck slightly arched.

I finally do what I've been dying to do for over a month: I stroke my female, marveling at the smoothness of the skin covering such fine muscle. Lu sighs with pleasure as my fingers trail across her collarbone, around the fullness of her breasts, before cupping them and rolling the nipples. Her back arches on a gasp and she reaches up to caress my thighs.

“Keep your arms at your sides.”

“I want to touch you,” she protests.

At the slap to her glistening pussy, Lu gasps and her legs snap shut. I pause, breath trapped in my lungs, waiting for a sign I misread her signal. We both know physical domination over my mate is an illusion. If this isn’t what she prefers, our play will be over in seconds when her fist connects with my jaw.

By the pure nature of being an Alpha, I am dominant. Sexually and otherwise. One day soon, I’ll command legions of shifters and rule my people. I demand control in all matters, chiefly in the bedroom. If Lu fights me for sexual dominance, I might need to reevaluate my strategy, but she *will* submit and enjoy every second.

CHAPTER 18

Kurtis

After several tense heartbeats, Lucretia's legs fall wide, and she dutifully places her arms back on the comforter, fisting it.

My heart soars. "Good girl. Before tonight is through, angel, every inch of your skin will belong to me. Every opening thoroughly fucked and pleasured. Your cries and whimpers for more are for me alone." I kneel and stare hard into the amber depths. "You. Are. Mine." She swallows at my aggression, and her tongue darts out to moisten plump lips. "Say it, Lucretia."

When she wavers, I slap her drenched pussy a little harsher. She moans low, her lids closing in ecstasy.

"I won't ask again."

"Tonight, I belong to you, Kurtis."

The second my name escapes her lips I lean in and devour them in a searing kiss. Her flavor imprints on my senses for all eternity as her tongue duels with mine. The muffled groans fuel my appetite. When my tongue catches on a fang, I pause and slowly caress its length.

It's remarkable. I've hated vampires my entire life, been at war with them for centuries. Killed my fair share in battle, yet here I am, getting off on tonguing Lu's deadly fang. An intense yearning to experience them buried in my flesh ignites straight to my groin. Lu groans as I graze the other one. Her legs tremble with the effort to hold them open. Her strong, delicate fists clench and unclench the blanket to keep them at her sides.

While I savor her mouth, I stretch a palm down her soft chest, over her exquisite breasts trembling with each breath, the flat muscular abdomen, to the core of my mate. While my tongue continues to run along her fangs, I slip a finger between the silken folds.

Christ, she's wet.

Lu's back arches and I inhale her sharp cry of pleasure, welcoming it as my own. When one leg tries to close, I surrender the kiss and whack her soaked labia twice more. Hard. Her eyes light up. Her whole body shudders with the need for release.

"Do not come until I give you permission, angel. Do you understand?"

"Yes," she sighs.

I slap her folds again. "Yes, what?"

"Yes, Sir." Radiant amber meets mine.

"Lucretia. You're stunning."

Uncertainty shadows her face, dulling the blaze. "Are you not—you're okay with this? It doesn't disgust you?"

Her timid question surprises me. It exposes a vulnerability she's kept suppressed. "Angel. Nothing about you disgusts me. Far from it." I sweep my lips across hers. "Your need pleases me. You please me."

To demonstrate, I rub the swollen bundle between her folds in tight, fast circles, and she nearly arches off the bed, keening and writhing with the effort to heed my earlier command. Before she reaches the point of no return, I withdraw my fingers and run them up her exquisite body. She whimpers in protest but doesn't move. I step back and remove my boxer briefs.

The vivid glow devours my cock. It twitches in response to the pink tongue she swirls around a fang. Does she seek to bite me there? My erection hardens further at the idea of her sucking me off while my blood nourishes her.

With my legs on either side of her shoulders, I position my engorged head at her mouth. Her scrutiny brightens greedily.

"Do you want to taste me?"

"God. Yes." She grunts.

I roll and pinch a nipple, and she sucks in a sharp breath.

"Yes, what?"

"Yes, Sir. I need to savor you."

"Keep the fangs retracted." I chuckle at her pout.

My smile disappears when Lucretia leans up and wraps those supple lips around the throbbing head. Warmth engulfs me, burns every nerve, and I lean over to allow her better access.

With her neck angled, it opens her throat, and she greedily swallows half of me down. I draw back and gently prod again. Jesus. I plant a palm on the mattress by her torso as her tongue swirls the crown with each slow retreat, lips and throat soften for each thrust. Lu growls, and it vibrates through my shaft, tightening my balls.

The intense thrill of fucking Lu's mouth is beyond measure. Not knowing how much she can take, I start with manageable, shallow thrusts until the vampire quickly modifies the rhythm. Sharp nails dig into my ass for better leverage, and I couldn't care less she disobeyed me. Before long, her powerful grip is dragging me deeply, and I plant both hands at her sides, undulating my hips. By the feral growls vibrating her throat, she is enjoying herself. I've never been this thoroughly consumed. My balls draw tighter as they brush her forehead, and pressure builds at the base.

Part of me wants to explode, but the desire to bury deep in her pussy has me resisting her grip and slipping from her greedy lips. Lu whimpers in protest and tries to pull me in again.

"Enough, Lucretia." She obediently lowers her arms to the bedspread. Pleasure shoots through me. This is what my female requires. I never imagined in my wildest dreams this mighty warrior was a sexual submissive.

I edge around the bed, seize her ankles, and flip her over on her stomach. A slight tug slides her body to me until her thighs rest on the rim of the mattress.

"Stretch both arms toward the other side and draw your knees under you." She complies and her delectable ass lifts until her drenched opening is level with my pulsing cock.

The folds glisten with her need, and I deny myself no longer. I fall to one knee and latch onto her sweetness with ferocity. Christ. Her sweet strawberries and cream essence set my taste buds on fire as I torment and ravish her beautiful pussy and ass with my lips and tongue. Lu's keening turns frantic, and she presses back into my face.

"Please, Kurtis."

Her begging pleases me, and I pinch her clit. "Come, angel."

Lu explodes, her scream muffled in the bedspread. I delve a finger inside, her muscles squeeze and ripple around it as I lap at pure fucking bliss, drawing out her orgasm. A second digit joins the first as I gently bite down on her swollen bundle.

"Kurtis! God!" She shatters again, clamping down on my thrusting fingers.

Before the pulsing eases, my cock replaces my drenched fingers with one deep plunge into her spasming core. Damn, she's tight. Lu stretches to accommodate my girth, and I pause, allowing her a second to adjust before I clutch her hips and set a vigorous pace.

After several minutes, I realize I'm not going to last long in her quivering sheath, it's too fucking incredible, and I haven't had sex since I laid eyes on her months ago.

Lucretia whines in protest when I glide out and wriggles her perfect ass to entice me back. A resounding slap of flesh on flesh echoes through the room. The sting in my palm and the pink imprint sets me on fire.

"Kurtis," she whimpers in bliss and clutches the comforter.

"You like that, angel?"

"Yes, Sir." Her prompt response almost has me thrusting deep once more.

"Do you want more?"

"Yes, Sir."

I smack the other cheek. My female craves a stinging pain with her pleasure and complete submission. So many things I envision doing to this delectable body, the pinnacles of ecstasy I yearn to take her.

The trust placed at my feet humbles me. I will do everything in my power to never betray it. Nicki's request to snoop on my female flashes through my mind, but I shove it aside to focus on the here and now. Besides, Lu aired her secrets coronation night. The need to spy is over.

By the time I stop, both cheeks are bright red, her juices flow down her spread thighs, and her moans are constant. I pass my thumb down her drenched opening, soaking it, before sinking my cock balls deep in her tight wetness once more. Lu cries out, grasps the comforter, and grinds her beautiful rosy ass backward, urging me deeper.

With one hand on her hip, I control the velocity while my thumb pad massages her puckered hole in slow circles. The beast calls for the flesh between her neck and shoulder. My canines extend, overwhelmed with the urge to subdue and claim. I grit my teeth and ignore his insistent demands, slipping my thumb into her snug opening while maintaining a hard-fast pace.

"Oh, God, that's... your finger there is amazing."

"You like that?"

She groans her answer and clenches me tight. "Need your blood, mate." Her slip confirms my earlier suspicion. I am Lu's one true mate. Emotion spears through my chest. The desire to nourish and tend what's mine consumes me.

I slide out and flip her on her back, and before she can blink, I'm sheathed again, her long, toned legs wrap around my waistline. But the bright amber ogle my canines with trepidation.

"Kurtis. You cannot mark me." The brightness dims with sorrow. "There would be no disguising it."

My creature rages to fuck the consequences, make her ours. Claim her. Bite her. I squeeze my eyes shut. She's correct. Marking her puts my mate in jeopardy. With extreme effort, I cram the beast under and force my canines to subside.

"You're right," I acknowledge through clenched teeth. "But you can, Lucr..." Before I finish, those deadly incisors plunge into my neck with a sharp sting. The first tug on my vein and she convulses, milking my cock to join her. Unable to contain it any longer, I grasp her skull to keep her fangs from dislodging and throw my head back, bellowing her name as I shatter in a million different directions.

A satisfied growl rumbles from my chest as the first half of the bond completes. I am now bound to Lucretia for all eternity. She can sense my emotions from anywhere, experience my pleasure as her own. But sadness overshadows the joy in knowing the link is merely one-sided.

A vampire bite during mating heals like it never was, but a shifter or werewolf's mark is discernible to all immortals. Forever. If I'd granted the beast its way, my father would have no option but to adhere to the Council of Unity's judgment. My birthright would be in peril with the possibility of prison time.

Lu's fate would be much worse. The council members would either throw Lucretia in a silver cell below ground for who knows how long, excommunicate her from the Vampire Nation or demand her death. I will never allow that to happen.

Once she closes the punctures with her warm tongue, Lu reaches up and captures my face. Her stare penetrates my soul. "I may not carry your mark, Kurtis, but tonight I am yours, and you are *mine*." The possessive growl causes my cock still entombed in her tightness to stiffen.

I will do everything in my power to safeguard my female from my beast, from the council, and even from her past. I am truly my father's son. Like him, I must keep our relationship secret and never allow the monster to claim its mate.

CHAPTER 19

Lucretia

Kurtis is the most gorgeous man I've ever encountered, and that's saying a lot since male vampires surround me constantly. Strong, genuine, and a fiercely demanding lover. The sole male in over a hundred years to provide me what I've lacked, and who sought my submission as much as I craved to give it.

Warm water pounds over my head and I grin. The burn on my ass, the sensitivity in my nipples and core faded, but the erotic memory seared my brain like a hot branding iron. Butterflies dance in my gut at the prospect of being in his presence in a few hours for rotation.

I'd lost count how many times and unique ways Kurtis dominated my mind and body last night, or should I say early this morning. He was a male true to his word. His lips, tongue, fingers, and glorious cock didn't neglect a single inch of me.

When he finally allowed me to explore his magnificent frame, I licked, sucked, and nipped every valley and hard, sculpted muscle, obsessed by the citrus and pine flavor of his blood and skin. The power and heat emanating from him drew me like a moth to fire. It was the most incredible sex I'd ever experienced. Right until the first rays of dawn scorched the flesh on my back as I dozed on his chest.

I chuckle and massage shampoo into my hair, reliving his panicked expression, how he vaulted from the bed, flung the silk comforter over my naked form, and practically ripped the heavy drapes from the wall trying to pull them closed.

Thank God it's winter. The full force of a summer sun would've set any exposed skin on fire. My smile evaporates as I rinse the suds under the hot spray. Apparently, last night was the first time Kurtis was intimate with a vampire. The shifter's spent his whole life at war with us. If I remember rightly, his favorite saying for my kind is *bloodsuckers*. And yet, he's never looked at me like I was something less.

Pride fills my heart, knowing the fates gifted me such a dynamic, virile, and beautiful male. But they're probably laughing their asses off because he can never be mine.

I don't know how I discovered the courage to stay him from marking me when my vampire was desperate for his bite. And apprehensive. I've heard rumors, even back when I was a young shifter, about how painful it is when those massive canines plunge into muscle, pinning your body as they fuck you. Tendons and sinew snap, and their saliva scars the flesh, leaving behind a permanent imprint on another immortal. Werewolves are no different.

Tears burn my eyes, and I scrub my skin harder. Never will I bear my mate's mark. After we are together, I'll need to scour his essence from my body. One sniff and a Guardian would scent him all over me and realize the truth.

Not that enjoying sex with another species is against the law, it's merely forbidden if they perform a complete mating resulting in the prospect of offspring. Nevertheless, my fellow warriors would peer down their noses, and being the only female... I've worked too hard to gain their respect to destroy it now. Not to mention Nicole would throw a conniption fit. Her distrust of me will never be okay with any relationship with her best friend.

Last night can never happen again. My body hums remembering the way Kurtis dominated me, showed me tremendous pleasure mixed with pain. Never having that again sends an ache spiraling through my chest. But with my vampire craving his mark, I'm not confident I could resist what we both desperately want. I must protect my mate from his baser impulses and mine.

Our lives depend on it.

As I step out of the shower, my phone dings with an incoming email. Reading over the report from my contact in Italy, anger burns through me. It looks like Trezzo's been a busy boy over the last century.

* * *

"Lu. I need you and Kurtis to patrol Seattle," Sebastian orders from the head of the immense table in the dining hall. He'd arrived back at the castle right at twilight in a foul mood. Evidently, his quest for Alex hadn't progressed smoothly. "Edmonton is a bubbling pot of demon control, so I am sending seasoned teams to scout the entire city. If you happen across any organized groups of immortals, consider them dangerous and call for backup immediately. There is significant probability pockets of werewolves and shifters are under demon influence."

"Take pictures of them if you can. It would be invaluable for Liam and me to catalog which clans they infiltrated," Kurtis interjects.

Bastian throws a picture of King Darath down the table, and ice slithers through my veins.

"If you encounter this male, do not establish eye contact. Trace away and call Logan or me. I order anyone under two hundred years not to engage. An elder can manipulate your minds, and we suspect those opposed to Queen Giordano are conspiring with the Demon Realm to usurp her reign. It's rumored King

Darath covets the vampire regions and has come out of centuries of seclusion to make his move."

A nagging memory tickles the back of my mind that's not altogether true, but I can't ferret out how or why I recognize that.

Bastian continues, directing teams to various sectors but I tune him out. I've learned what I need. It's all I can manage not to squirm in my seat at the smoldering stare a pair of baby blues keep shooting my direction. They undress me with raw, unadulterated lust. My insides clench and unclench so many times in response, I fear I'll collapse on the floor climaxing convulsively.

Bastian wraps up the briefing and the hundred-plus Guardian's file out just as Nicki and Logan stroll in, pursued closely by Icarus. It's weird, during King Dimitri's regime I never saw the Oracle, but since the halfling took over, he's developed into a permanent fixture at the castle.

The queen motions Kurtis, Liam, and me over. What the hell is going on now? My stomach flutters when Nicki turns her penetrating regard on Sebastian. "What happened, Bastian? Is Alex here?"

A rough growl rumbles from the commander's chest. "I never encountered her. She is either deep undercover on an assignment for the Valkyrie Regency or in hiding. I am heading back to Astoria, Oregon, tonight. According to my source, it was her last known whereabouts."

"I think it's a much bigger shit show than we assumed." Nicki runs an agitated hand through her auburn tresses, and Bastian stiffens. "Icarus believes King Darath controls Alex's mind."

"What?" His quiet response agitates me more than if he'd bellowed. "Control like he had over Lu?"

"Yes, my lord," the Oracle answers.

"If that's the case, as much as I want my best friend here, it's too risky. He could have programmed her to assassinate me, and the last thing I wish is to harm her in any way."

"If he directed her to kill you, why hasn't she come back already?" I ask. "We would've had no inkling what her end game was until it was too late."

"Yes, my child," Icarus responds. "I would agree with your assessment; however, the young valkyrie is strong. She is resisting the psychic command and has stayed away to protect the queen."

"What kind of toll would such resistance produce on her brain?" Bastian asks.

"In the short term, a headache for a few days. Long term, the side effects could be severe. Complete memory failure is the greatest worry."

"Once I locate her, how do I eliminate his control? Please tell me I need not bash her skull in as the prince did Lu?" Bastian's Italian skin pales.

In my periphery, Kurtis winces at the reminder.

"It will depend on how long she has been under his sway, my lord," the priest replies. "Lord Ruse resolved the mind-meld fairly swiftly. The influence on

Lucretia's brain had not taken a significant grip. Alexandria is immortal, but her healing capabilities are nowhere near the degree of a vampire. I would recommend not bashing in her head."

"Is it all doom and gloom, Icarus?" Nicki demands in irritation, the concern for her friend written all over her face. "Good news would be a fucking relief."

"Yes, my lady, there is a silver lining. If she completes the mating bond with her fated male, he alone can free her from the demon's control. Once mated the psychic link should release. If Alexandra has suffered memory loss, her mate must thrall her to help restore her memories."

"Great," Nicki responds dejected. "Any idea who that might be?"

"Wait a minute," Logan's deep voice interjects. "Only demons and vampires can thrall."

"Correct, my lord," Icarus replies delicately. "Her mate is a vampire."

"Brilliant," Nicki mumbles. "She'd sooner cast a vamp into the sun then mate him."

"Back to Nicki's question," Liam insists. "Do we even know who the unlucky bastard is?"

"Yes." Bastian sighs and we swing in his direction.

"Who?" we all demand.

"Oh, no," Nicole whispers, staring at Bastian with dread-filled eyes.

"I believe I am."

Shock grips our group into utter silence.

Hell's bells. The gods hate Sebastian as much as they despise me. Shifter hatred for us is immense, but the valkyrie and vampires… their animosity is legendary.

"Brother." My former commander steps forward, concern deepening his tone. "What causes you to presume you are her mate?"

A muscle pulses in Bastian's jaw. "Because the fiery redhead is mine."

"Nicole feared as much." Logan clasps Sebastian's shoulder. "I'm sorry."

"This goes no further than this room," Nicki commands, her gray glow encompassing our little circle. "Understood?"

We all nod our agreement.

"Sebastian?" The fierce halfling steps over to him and tips her head to look him square in the eyes.

"Yes, my queen?"

"What I'm about to propose is against council law and could place your freedom or life at risk. No one in this group would think less of you if you declined."

"No matter the outcome with Trezzo, in my heart, you are not merely my queen, but family. Command what you will. *Darei la mia vita per la tua.*"

Nicki smiles. "My Italian's a little rusty."

"I would give my life for yours."

"While I appreciate that, I'm not suggesting you sacrifice your existence for mine. Yet. I'm asking you to put it in jeopardy for Alex." She hesitates, draws a deep breath before continuing. "I realize you have an aversion to a mate, to commitment in general if we're honest, but push your reservations aside. Find her, Bastian, and break King Darath's control."

"Are you condoning a mating between different species, Nicki?" Kurtis asks softly, his body tense.

Hope ignites in my heart. Or perhaps it's coming from the prince. I've never had a mate before, so separating his emotions versus mine is challenging.

"Are you certain that's a good solution, Nic?" Liam questions.

The queen spins her determined gaze on the werewolf king. "To save someone I love? Yes." Her fierce expression swivels to Kurtis. "To prevent a situation where I'd have to choose between killing her or being killed? In a fucking heartbeat." She strides back to Bastian and spreads her hand over his heart. "Just as you pledged your life for mine, know this; if the council demands retribution for mating Alex, I will protect both your lives at all cost."

"As will I," Logan adds, stepping next to his mate.

"I do not give a shit about the law," Sebastian growls. "The little spitfire is my one true mate, and although the burden grates along my nerves like sandpaper, I swear not to cease until I locate her, sever the link with the demon, and deliver her back to you."

"Be warned, my lord." Icarus steps forward. "Darath may have programmed her to slay anyone who seeks to intervene."

A feral smile teases Bastian's lips, and the blue orbs flare. "That's foreplay for me, priest."

A rosy blush creeps over the Oracle's cheeks, and I bite the inside of my cheek to keep from cracking a grin. Oh boy. Alexandra will have her hands full with this fierce, dominant warrior. Or maybe the reverse. Bastian expects his orders followed in all area, but one detail I've learned about Alex over the years, she doesn't possess a submissive bone in her body. She's wild, sarcastic, and in love with love. Sebastian better guard himself, demon mind control or not.

"I will figure out this shit show, but there's no version that ends well," Nicki murmurs.

"Perhaps you should consult with Queen Svaldana, Nicole," Logan advises.

"Pfft. Like she consulted with me? Arra knows her daughter is MIA. Her lie is the reason I initiated an investigation into Alex's whereabouts in the first place."

"If Bastian mates with Alex, it could potentially start a war with the Valkyrie Regency." I hate stating the reasons Kurtis and I will never fully mate.

Nicki shrugs. "Eh. One war, two wars, same same."

CHAPTER 20

Lucretia

A warm palm grips my elbow, impeding my progress down the darkened corridor towards the stairs.

"Lucretia. Meet me in my suite."

I swallow at the desire swirling in the blue depths and electricity sparks where his scalding skin touches mine. Dressed in black jeans and a gray long-sleeve Henley, he towers over me. Sexy beast.

"I need to snag a few items before we head out to Seattle."

I peer around, satisfied we are alone. "Why don't you call me Lu like everyone else?" I ask, curiosity getting the better of me.

"Because I don't want to be like everyone else to you."

Aw, crap. Why does he always say the perfect thing? "I have to gear up as well. Let's meet at the bottom of the stairs?" I suggest, ignoring his remark because being alone with him in his chamber, with a bed, is a dreadful idea. It would severely test my shaky resolve to hold him at arm's length.

He blinks slowly. Like a predator, yet with lazy indulgence. "My room. Ten minutes."

I remain perfectly still. My lungs compress. "Listen, Kurtis." I pause, scanning the hallway again. "Whatever you assume will happen here, can't. Last night was a mistake."

"A mistake?" He leans in, his sparkling cobalt scrutiny an inch away. "I've been inside you, Lucretia. You've moaned my name. You will again."

"No." Regret mingles with hunger. "I've worked extremely hard to secure my position here. A relationship with you would jeopardize everything. For me, and you."

As an Alpha, Kurtis wouldn't stand by and let his mate walk into danger. Like in the alley; his inclination was to protect me, keep me visible. He didn't trust in my fighting skills to defend myself. My career is dangerous, and now that we've had sex, his possessive instincts will intensify, as will mine. The wise thing would be to get Bastian to assign me a different partner, but anxiety fills me at the prospect of not spending time with him.

"What we had was one night of intense passion. That's all," I insist, curbing the urge to step back.

He closes the meager space between us, his breath stirring my lips. "Prove you don't want this, that you aren't craving more."

An inferno arcs through my sex. Kurtis is fire and storm, and a part of me, the submissive element I've denied for years, wishes to experience the thrill and ride the burn of pain he's offering, even if forbidden.

His nostrils flare, no doubt scenting my arousal. "Say it."

"I can't deny I want you," I confess. "However, I have a job to do, and if this progresses, it will get in the way—make me weak."

"Why would you suppose a relationship between us would weaken you?"

My dark desires cripple me, and he draws them out in full force. Not to mention, I'm a freaking Guardian. I don't need an Alpha male hovering over me, undermining my authority.

At the outset of my career, several Guardians sought to do just that. Thought they needed to protect the little female. I made certain they understood their mistake, but it's something I struggle against nightly.

"An affair between us can never happen. I've mated you, and I enforce the laws. As do you."

"There's no refuting that, right now. But nothing's stopping you and I from enjoying each other. If keeping this secret allows you the control you require for your position, I'm on board. For now. In private, however, you are all mine. To play with as I see fit. To give you precisely what you seek, Lucretia."

My insides tremble, and I gnaw my lip. Can I do this? Enjoy him sexually and keep my emotions submerged? Hold the bonded vampire at bay? Will I be able to conceal my desire when surrounded by my peers?

My heart rate speeds up at letting him have his way, the thrill of keeping it secret. Fierce warrior by night. Sexual submissive by day. I'm a natural risk-taker, but also a masochist with illicit desires I've sought to suppress for ages. Kurtis not only acknowledges them, he demands them.

"Just sex?"

"It's not just sex between us, angel. We are much more." He smiles and smooths his knuckles down my cheek. "Say yes."

No. "Yes." *No.*

In an instant, I'm enfolded in his embrace, and his lips are devouring mine. Warnings clang in the back of my brain. This is a colossal mistake, but I don't care. I want more. He makes me feel alive. Whole. Feminine. Kurtis gives me a sense of completeness. Sparks explode in my blood as his talented mouth continues to devour and concur. Whether or not he realizes it, the kiss states a claim. Deep down, I bask in it.

He releases my lips, and I can't help the whimper. Pure male satisfaction curves his tantalizing mouth, and my knees weaken. "My room, ten minutes."

I obediently lower my lids, committed totally to our game. Lust zings through my frame, and I shiver. "Yes, Sir."

He grunts his approval and turns for the door. Before he's taken a step, both our cell phones ding, it's a group text from Bastian to our little gang of odd members.

Meeting in conference, ASAP!

Kurtis growls with annoyance but nods towards the exit. "A rain check, for now, angel. Duty calls."

I follow my mate to the castle's secure conference room, and marvel at the hold this shifter has on me. It can't be shaken, and it travels deep enough to strike bone. He possesses me, declares me as his, even without the mark. For the first time, I'm perfectly okay with being claimed by a male. I just wish it wasn't temporary.

We enter the area, and Liam, Sebastian, Logan, and Nicki sit at the long black table. Numerous monitors are staged on the wall at one end. With no windows, the stone walls bare, the room is nondescript to those viewing in on a teleconference. Bastian clicks away on a keyboard, and the screens blink to life. The striking cerulean of the displays reminds me of Kurtis's eyes.

Jesus. Now I'm comparing computer monitors to my mate's eyes? Before you know it, I'll be singing love ditties in the shower.

I shake my head at the ridiculous thought and grab my seat next to Bastian on Nicki's left nodding to Logan on her right. The sexy prince lowers his broad frame into the chair on my other side, and it creaks under his weight.

Directly across the gleaming surface, Liam's bleak contemplation rakes over my face, and a muscle flexes in his firm jaw. It looks like he hasn't slept in a week. His thick, brown hair stands on end as if he'd run his fingers through it again and again, and several days of growth darken his chin. Liam is what Alex would refer to as tall, dark, and yummy. By the brooding inspection the whiskey-colored irises keep shooting my way, something is eating him, and it appears to focus on me. Maybe he doesn't think I'm good enough for his best friend.

Ding, ding, ding. Give the werewolf a prize.

"My man, you look like hell." Kurtis chuckles as they fist bump over the table. "Late night with the ladies again?"

"Something like that," Liam responds quietly, his penetrating regard never moving from my face. I lift a brow in challenge, and he shifts away.

"Icarus contacted the council a few minutes ago. The Nation's lab completed the DNA analysis. We're all gathering for the final report." The queen's expression is a controlled blank, but the lines around her mouth reveal her apprehension. "The other members are standing by to teleconference. Kurtis, you must step off-camera when we begin. Lu, take a position at the door."

Dread fills my gut even as I nod my agreement.

"Lu," Logan turns his turbulent emerald regard my direction. "Before we start, I require your perceptions of Trezzo as a king if the results are in his favor. How was the reunion?" Tension, fueled by fury, radiates from my former commander in waves.

Oh boy. Here we go.

"No doubt in my mind he's Dimitri's son, and if you'd asked me that question a century ago, I would have declared he'd be a tough but fair ruler. After our little chat last week, I realize Trezzo is not the male I expected. The vampire elder has already proven he'll be as brutal and ruthless a leader as his father."

"Backs up what his constituents in Italy relayed," Liam adds.

The vampires around the table turn surprised expressions to the werewolf king. Before the queen can investigate why the wolf was looking into Trez, Kurtis interjects. "I asked Liam to find out all he could about Massaro. He has affiliations in that country."

Anger ignites in my chest. This is the exact reason I argued against permitting a relationship with him, even a sexual one. The shifter didn't entrust me enough to do my duty. He had to dig into vampire matters himself. I fire him a glare, but his gaze remains locked on Nicki.

"As do I," I grate out between clenched teeth, returning my focus to the queen. "In fact, my contact emailed me just this evening with more information. When Trezzo discovered Dimitri's death and that his halfling daughter assumed the throne, he went ballistic. Raped and executed several female and male consorts. For years before that, his constituents endured the brunt of his violent sexual tendencies, but none were brave enough to oppose him and come forward. They feared Dimitri would never support their claim."

What I don't reveal is they all had similar looks to my own—tall, slim, long dark hair. No doubt Trezzo envisioned they were me as he humiliated and debased them publicly, forced them to endure his perverse sexual appetite. And according to my source, he once raped and murdered a guard because his name was Lu. Not to mention the asshole is blackmailing me into mating him.

If Trez doesn't possess proof my twin, Viessa, exists, it's his word against mine. With him being the Italian ruler and possible king, the odds are not in my favor, although with the way his reputation has deteriorated over the years, I might persuade the council he's lying.

In that crazy, fucked-up brain, Trezzo truly believes I'm his one true mate. Which is utter bullshit. If I were, he would never have walked away after I joined the Guardians. He would have demanded we complete the bond and remain together. God forbid if he finds out I've already mated Kurtis. Quicker than you could sneeze, the psycho would wage war with the Shifter Territory to rip the prince to shreds. Not to mention what he'd do to me. Death would be preferable.

"I believe Trezzo intends for the Vampire Nation to dismantle the Council of Unity and be the ruling authority over all Immortals. Unlike Dimitri though, he has no interest in controlling humans. No high-powered connections. Yet."

Nicki's gaze sharpens. "Precisely what I speculated. Great job, Lu. Is there anything else he's after?"

Oh, shit. How do I respond without lying? I shift uneasily in my chair. I've discovered that honesty is not always the best approach in my life, but I do so now. "Yes, my lady. Me."

"Excuse me?" Kurtis's manner turns lethal. His intense regard pierces the side of my skull, but I refuse to acknowledge him.

"What do you mean?" Liam chimes in, the coffee-colored gaze stone cold.

Confusion clouds Nicki's expression as she leans back in her armchair, her observation bouncing between the three of us until a frown deepens the path between her brows. I swallow.

Before I can come up with a suitable excuse that doesn't reveal Vi, Icarus strolls into the room. The blue tattooed priest, draped in his customary white toga, perches behind my chair, prepared to assume my seat for the council meeting.

"We will move back to this exchange later," Bastian warns. "For now, the other representatives are ready. Kurtis, Lu, please take your places."

"This conversation isn't over," my mate whispers in my ear as we rise.

A shiver ripples across my skin as his cool breath caresses my neck. Old habits die hard, and as I lean against the door, I stretch my braid over my shoulder to fret with the end.

Putting aside the prince's threat, for now, I glance around the area at the individuals who played prominent roles in my life over the years. This meeting could transform our futures. The tentative peace the werewolves, shifters, and valkyrie fought for with the Vampire Nation is in jeopardy. And I still haven't figured out Liam's peculiar reactions to me.

A dark unknown future stretches before us. One in which my mate and I could be on opposites sides of a war.

CHAPTER 21

Kurtis

Each council member not present pops up on different screens. When my dad's familiar mug comes into focus, I wish I could relieve the grim determination in the sapphire depths. The single feature, undeniably marking me as his son is our eye color. The king passed his dark, exotic good looks to my younger siblings. I inherited the golden tresses and lighter skin of our mother, who died giving birth to my baby sister Rhianna.

Those deep-set eyes scour the room, searching for me. The Shifter Territory has suffered a lengthy and devastating war with the vampires, and he's worried about me living at the castle with no means to leave unless a vampire traces me. The temporary truce since

Nicki took over was a welcome respite for my father and our people. The prospect of it ripped to shreds weighs heavily on both our shoulders.

The second Syn Grayflame's white shroud of hair, pointed ears, pale skin, and silvery gaze take shape on the screen, my jaw clenches. It's all I can do to control the growl.

Logan holds no restraint. His deep, menacing rumble spreads through the room as the emerald orbs flicker.

It chaps my hide the Dark Fae King still occupies a spot on this council after siding with Dimitri in the great battle. Since he broke no laws against the organization directly, he's permitted to maintain his seat and vote. The glittering silver pinpoint Nicki and a sneer lifts the edge of his thin lips.

Fucking bastard.

When the sensual Jilaya Oresha appears, I can't help but appreciate her alluring beauty. Everything about her comes together to make a male want to plunge deep into her flesh; from the luxurious scarlet hair tumbling down her waist, to the lush ruby mouth and porcelain skin, down to the hypnotic light blue gaze. The Succubus Queen is as provocative as she is lethal.

When Priestess Kleora's form develops, the newest council member, I glance at my female. Translucent amber watches me with a brooding intensity, still infuriated I recruited Liam to investigate Trezzo. Well, she can be pissed all she wants. I will do everything in my power to safeguard what's mine. I have no wish to step on her toes or undermine her authority as a Guardian, although technically, I suppose that's precisely what I did. But she can't expect me to sit back and not act when there is a direct threat to her existence.

"Thank you all for gathering on such short notice," Icarus begins the meeting. The strange Celtic designs on his face, down his arms, and covering the hands now clasped on the table surge with light. "Before I reveal the DNA results, I advise the members of the mission and objectives of this council. We all agreed to unite, set forth laws, enforce the order to bring about a resolution to the centuries of conflict between the many clans." The azure irises shift and churn. "No matter who controls the Vampire Nation, we must adhere to those dictates."

Logan grasps Nicki fingers under the table, and I grit my teeth in irritation. Nowhere in the damn prophecy does it state Nicole is not the queen. It affirms she will prevail and create peace.

"We understand our obligations and responsibilities, Icarus." My father's assertive tone towards the priest is proof the results weigh on him. "I would further remind everyone of the revelation you foretold. Mayhap you should read it anew for our newest member."

"It's not unheard of for an Oracle's visions or ancient prophecies to alter, King Ruse." Jilaya's sexy rasp tenses every male shoulder. "The unpredictable actions of males and females dictate the possibility exists."

"Yes, my lady," Icarus responds. "Need I remind you, in three millennia, my insights were never false."

Shit. The Oracle is three thousand years old?

"That's a bold proclamation, priest." Kleora blinks with raised brows.

"No, Your Highness. It is a fact."

I snort. There is no boasting in his manner, purely an assuredness that lessens the knot between my shoulders.

"Yes, yes, Priest, we all understand how great and mighty you are. Could we please hear the prophesy and thus learn the results?" Syn demands in exasperation.

"Of course." Icarus nods before withdrawing an ancient scroll from the hidden folds of his garment, somehow knowing he would require it for the meeting. How strange it must be to see the past, present, and future. How does he keep it all straight?

Even though I've read through a copy of the foretelling many times over, I pay close attention to the reading in case there was some little nuance I missed.

"*Nine August The Year of Our Lord 1482,*" Icarus begins in a soft musical voice. He holds the scroll open in front of him, but his stare never lowers to the parchment. "*During the reign of King Dimitri Tobias Giordano, a female Halfling will be born of his seed. Half-human—half-vampire. The first and last to exist. During the transition, the halfling will require blood. But only the blood of her one true mate will save her.*"

Logan smirks at his mate, and she answers with an eye-roll.

"After her transition, she will gain King Dimitri's powers while maintaining her human capabilities: Immunity to the sun's deadly rays, the ability to eat and digest regular food."

I nearly laugh out loud when Nicole blows on her knuckles and brushes them across her collarbone as if to say, 'Yup, I'm a badass.'

"As the first vampire queen, she, her one true mate, and The Council of Unity will destroy those who oppose peace. She will bring unity to the other species and give birth to the first vampire king with the ability to walk in the sunlight, thus ending the vampire curse of eternal darkness.

"Should the halfling become with child before her transition into immortality, her change will not occur, and she will live an average human lifespan, ensuring King Giordano's reign for another three hundred years. Under his rule, war will continue among the Others.

"The Council of Unity will cease to exist. King Dimitri will lead the vampire race into open conflict with the humans. A catastrophic, hundred-year war will begin. Hundreds of thousands of humans and Others will perish, some species to the point of extinction. Devastation will ravage the planet.

"Beware. The halfling's life essence is linked to King Dimitri. If one dies, the other dies."

Icarus rolls up the manuscript and gently rests it on the table in front of him. "We all witnessed Queen

Giordano fulfill part of the prophecy by slaying her father and delivering us from the ruin the last half mentions." With that, he resumes his seat.

Nicki rises to her feet and addresses the council. "No matter the results, I felt it prudent, we should all obtain knowledge of who might be the next ruler. This involves all immortals, not just our Nation. At my behest, my team has done a comprehensive investigation into Trezzo Massaro, A.K.A. Zachariah Giordano, in a limited amount of time. What we've uncovered is chilling." She nods to Bastian. "Sebastian is emailing you a dossier. Please study it before you cast your final vote. Most of you desire peace, with Massaro that ship will sink."

Once Nicole lowers back into her chair, we wait several anxious minutes as the representatives read over the report. When everyone's focus returns to the priest, Icarus waves towards Bastian. "You may open and deliver the DNA findings to the members, commander." At Bastian's reluctant acknowledgment, icy chills spread through my chest.

"As you notice, the results prove Trezzo Massaro is Zachariah Giordano, Dimitri's son and heir."

CHAPTER 22

Kurtis

Even suspecting the answer, devastation hits hard. The trauma Nicki endured and survived, the years of secrecy and acts of treason Logan, Sebastian, and Lu performed to keep Dimitri off her trail, the months of intense training to prepare her to defeat her father—it was all for nothing. I can't imagine the emotional turmoil she's suffering, although her stoic expression doesn't reveal a thing.

"I suppose there's a first time for everything, Icarus." Her soft tone stills the council members. "It appears you were mistaken."

The priest's sorrowful countenance tightens my chest, but he surprises Nicki and everyone in the meeting by settling his blue tattooed palm on her cheek. "You are who we meant you to be, child."

What the hell does he mean?

"We should put forth a motion to recognize Zachariah Giordano's right to the vampire throne," Syn demands, the silver gaze shimmering with exuberance.

"I second the motion," Jilaya agrees, forever Syn's lapdog, so no fucking surprise there.

"What exactly are we voting on?" Liam asks. "Just so we're clear."

"A yes confirms Zachariah's lineage and claim to the sovereignty." Queen Arra responds with sympathy. "A no vote rejects his challenge."

I'd punch the wall if I thought it would do any good. Most of these immortals want Nicki to remain the ruler, but they will not turn a blind eye to the evidence submitted.

Icarus stands, his expression rigid with suppressed anger. This meeting is the first time I've witnessed such powerful emotions from the Oracle. He's always so even keel. When he brought Nicki's lifeless body back to life, not a flicker of distress crossed his tattooed face, but for some reason, this event displeases him.

Couldn't agree more, little priest.

"All those in attendance please verbalize your response as I announce your name." He turns toward Nicole. "Since this vote applies to the eligibility of your reign and place on this council, my lady, we cannot allow you to respond."

"Understood." The acceptance in the gray gaze pierces my spirit.

Nicki was the first woman I let close to me after the shitstorm three decades before, where my overzealousness took an innocent life. The halfling opened my heart. We established our friendship on mutual trust and respect.

Wish I could say the same about my mate. Lu's wariness and insecurities plowed a vast chasm between us and I have no inkling the lengths she'll go to shield herself. If I don't bridge the divide, scale the thick wall riddled with the secrets of her past, it will finish our fragile start before it's begun.

Nicki's gaze drifts to mine. I nod and hope she scans my emotions. No matter the result, the immortals within these walls will do anything to reinstate her and fulfill her destiny.

The thin smile doesn't penetrate the sorrow in the smoky depths. *'Thank you for your friendship, Kurtis.'* The pleasant voice fills my brain. *'I agree; this isn't over.'*

I grin with admiration. Whatever life threw at this female, she faced it head-on, shook her fist at fate and declared, 'You want to fuck with me, take a number and get in line.'

"King Scott, your vote please?"

"No." The wolf answers without a qualm, his gloomy stare riveted on the woman he regards as a sister. She smirks at his steadfast support.

"King Ruse, what say you?"

"Yes." The low growl reveals it's not the answer he wished to present. I understood my father would adhere to the letter of the law and not disregard the evidence as Liam so willfully did, yet I'm still stunned by his choice.

"Queen Arra Svaldana?"

"After reading through the report on Mr. Giordano, my gut tells me to return a no, but, I must comply with the by-laws. Yes."

"King Syn Grayflame, what..."

"Yeeeessss," he interrupts, excitement sparkling in the silver depths.

My fists clench. God, I despise that bastard. I want to rip his pointed ears from his skull and shove them up his ass.

"Queen Oresha?"

After a brief hesitation, piercing contemplation riveted on Nicki's fierce expression, she responds. "No."

A gasp saturates the room.

"Jilaya!" Grayflame's nostrils flare, the silver gaze hardens.

Nicki examines the succubus ruler with curiosity. When the queen's eyes widen, it's evident the powerful halfling spoke to her across the miles. Oresha continues her deep regard.

"She cast her tally, my lord," Icarus says to Syn before proceeding on to the last vote besides his. "Priestess Tanagra, what say you?"

"As I am new here, I can only go by the evidence presented. I vote yes."

"The yeses have it 4 to 2, no need for my choice. We recognize Zachariah Giordano as the lawful inheritor to the vampire throne. Since the Vampire Nation has been without a legitimate ruler for several months, resulting in unrest throughout the territories, his coronation must take place as soon as feasible."

This can't be happening. My gaze flicks toward the door to study Lu. Fear radiates from my mate in waves. It's past time I discover what Trezzo, or Zach, or fuckwad, demanded. The slick Italian asshole will never get his hands on my woman. I'll tear him to shreds and damn the consequences.

"Pack your bags, halfling," Grayflame taunts from the middle screen. "Your short reign is over."

"Hey Syn, you know what's really fun?" Nicki responds with a wicked grin. "Kicking your ass. No clue what your beef is with me," she holds up a palm when the dark fae opens his mouth to reply, "And I don't give a fuck, but one day you and I will come to blows," she threatens as she rises to her feet, the radiance in her irises blinding. "Trust me when I say there's no force in hell to save your sorry, shriveled ass next time."

His eyes narrow. "Guard what's precious, little halfling," he warns before the monitor blackens.

"Jilaya." Nicole turns her stormy gaze on the gorgeous queen. "Why did you endorse me? You sided with Dimitri and Syn during the battle."

"I choose whatever position benefits me." She frowns. "Don't make me regret my decision, vampire."

The screen darkens, and Nicki blinks several times before turning to Kleora. "I understand your choice, Priestess. I carry no animosity towards you or your people. You did what you felt was appropriate."

"Thank you. I hold a great deal of respect for you. If you need me, please ask."

The second her face dissolves, Nicki pins Arra with a livid glare. "Where is Alex?" she demands, planting her palms on the table. "Don't you dare say she's on assignment."

"Watch your tone, halfling," my father growls, forever the small valkyrie's defender.

To abate the tension, I stride in front of the camera and my dad visibly relaxes.

"Nicole." Arra runs a shaking hand down her neck. "First, let me apologize for my vote. I hope you recognize I had to follow the law. Second, Alex's whereabouts are not your concern."

"That's where you're mistaken," Nicki growls. "Everyone in this room cares about your daughter." She peeks at Bastian, but his menacing regard never deviates from Arra's image. "Tell me where she is."

"While it warms my heart, my youngest has many friends; I cannot divulge her whereabouts. Most of all to a vampire."

"Arra," my dad admonishes in a soft tenor.

"I mean no offense, Queen—er—Nicole," Arra says with a superficial nod, her demeanor not contrite in the least. "It's difficult to let go after centuries of prejudice and war, but my daughter is better off without vampires in her life." When her dark glare shifts to Bastian, his brow lifts in surprise.

With the lethal grace ingrained in all immortals of considerable age, the commander rises and challenges his mate's mother. "Thank you for confirming my suspicions, Queen Svaldana." Smug satisfaction radiates from the brilliant blue gaze. "Until this moment, I was uncertain if I was her fated one."

"You stay away from my daughter, vampire, or you'll encounter a silver dagger through your heart."

"Arra!" my father barks.

"Make no mistake, Your Highness." A soft cobalt light illuminates the screen. "I will find her."

Nicki steps forward, a frown marring her forehead. "Let's put our cards on the table, shall we? I consider you an ally. Am I incorrect in that assumption?"

The pretty valkyrie blinks. "No. You garner the utmost respect, Nicole, however, the sole reason the Valkyrie Regency aligned with the Vampire Nation is because of our complete loyalty in the Oracle and prophecy."

"Fair enough," Nicki concedes with a dismissive wave. "But I'll let you in on a little-known secret about me." She pauses, reaches for a jumbo coffee mug that reads; *'Me? Sarcastic? Never.'* and takes several loud slurps. I bite the inside of my cheek to control the grin, while Arra frowns with annoyance. "When someone lies to me, pain shoots through my skull." She sets the cup back on the table before fixing Arra with a direct stare. "You have no idea where Alex is, do you?"

The queen hesitates. Her conflicted black eyes dart among the leaders and warriors in the office, snagging on mine. Dark circles shadow the flawless skin. The once vibrant and shiny blonde locks fall limp and dull around her face, but she presses her lips together, declining to respond.

"No." My father answers after several tense minutes, his expression laden with desperation. "We do not."

The queen's lids close and a lone tear courses down her cheek. My dad responds to her obvious pain with a low rumble, his stare wavering from deep blue to the golden hue of his lion.

"Thank you, Cipher, for your honesty. Now I'll be brutally honest with both of you. Icarus believes Alex is under King Jagorach Darath's control with orders to assassinate me, but the little fighter you raised is resisting. Hence the reason she's MIA."

"What?!" Arra erupts, and lightning streaks the night sky outside the window behind her. "I will eviscerate that demon spawn!" she exclaims before her chin drops to her chest, fists pressed against her temples. The deafening boom of thunder does nothing to drown out the ear-piercing scream.

"Sunshine." My old man's rough, soothing endearment somehow snags the queen's attention through the racket.

Devastation shadows the dark eyes that focus on my father's image before her. This small, fierce valkyrie is my dad's life. The one female he would do anything for, except claim with his bite. The apple doesn't fall too far from the tree.

"Cipher... gods..." she stutters with grief.

"We will find her," he vows in a comforting tone before pinning Sebastian with a glower. "Jagorach and I were once allies. Let me reach out to him."

"Great idea, Dad," I interject. "But Arra, if Dad's unsuccessful you need to understand, only one individual in this room can locate Alex and eliminate the demon's psychological link." I step next to Bastian and marvel at how these vampires not only earned my respect but my friendship. "Let your hatred go, for Alexandria's sake."

Arra inhales a deep, slow breath and studies Sebastian. "I would be beholden if you found my daughter, Mr. Moretti, however, your reputation with women precedes you. If you mate with Alex, the Valkyrie Regency will consider it an act of war and petition the council for your head." My father's jaw clenches, but he offers nothing further.

Logan's arms cross over his chest, and he smirks at his brother. Sebastian's gaze is blue steel, his deadly grin legendary. Over the centuries, those who survived his blade in battle did so purely because he allowed it, but numerous recounting always asserted; his smile was a thing of beauty, right before he took your head.

"Be very careful, Arra," he warns in a soft tone, and my father's shoulders tense.

Nicki slams her palm on the table, snagging everyone's attention. "You threaten Sebastian, you threaten me, and I don't take kindly to threats, Your Highness." She crosses her arms over her chest, mimicking Logan's stance. "Besides, I'm no longer queen. You wish to wage war against my stepbrother, be my fucking guest."

The valkyrie swallows and I watch the battle she wages within herself. "If you return my daughter, alive, and *unmated*, the valkyries will aid you in reclaiming the throne," she negotiates.

"Yeah, no offense, but I don't need your help." Nicki's smirk is like a loaded gun.

CHAPTER 23

Lucretia

The last few weeks have been surreal. Right after the council meeting, Nicki traced Kurtis away before I could say goodbye. Sebastian took off for parts unknown in pursuit of Alex after tracing Liam home to handle his many commitments, and where Icarus goes when he's not around, I couldn't guess.

Between Logan, Nicole, myself, and a small contingent of Guardians defecting, it required an entire week to gather up our belongings, secure all sensitive intel we didn't wish to fall into Trezzo's hands, and wipe all the hard drives after an extensive backup to our own.

We moved into Nicki's former cottage on the outskirts of Newport, Oregon and set up her studio in the garage as a makeshift war room. The Guardians loyal to the queen camped out in the clearing where the great battle ensued, setting up massive blackout tents to shield them from the sun. Each warrior took an enormous risk siding with Nicki. Zachariah could track them down and condemn them for treason for deserting their duties. The only exit strategy for a Guardian is death. It stuns me the battle with Dimitri was a mere four months ago. With everything that's transpired, it seems like another lifetime.

Forced to bunk in Alex's old bedroom, it flabbergasted me how much stuff the valkyrie loaded into the walk-in closet and lavatory. The female possesses more clothes and makeup than Macy's. I can't imagine what she's doing for outfits, but it doesn't appear as if she took a stitch with her. She just packed up the essentials and strode out.

At least the valkyrie's bed is super comfortable, even if the bedspread has purple unicorns splattered down the center and the stares from supermodels and actors hanging around the room ogle me all day.

The worst part is rooming across the hallway from Logan and Nicki. Wow. What a real eye-opener. The freaking thin walls do nothing to mute their intense passion, and my skin crawls with the need for my mate. Endless lust rages, and it takes extreme meditation not to trace to Kurtis's cabin and demand he fucks me. With multiple orgasms.

The Bluetooth headphones I invested in didn't dampen a damn thing. I tried country music, new age spa—and hell, even acid rock—nothing helps. It's not like I can waltz out in the middle of the day and crash on the couch in her studio/garage. This isn't winter in Canada, the sun blazes above the horizon, and the skylights in the roof make it hopeless. If I had someplace dark and protected, I would trace there in a heartbeat.

In a desperate move one early morning, I smuggled into the warrior's tent and passed out on the floor in between bunks. That lasted until I woke up at sundown to discover a humongous male spooning me, his enormous erection cradled between my ass cheeks. The Guardian didn't have a second to react before I booted him to the other end of the canvas. That was the last occasion I used the tents as an escape.

I flop on my side for the zillionth time, the sheets tangling at my feet. I should be sound asleep, but my damn mind refuses to shut off. The switch from virtually no sun to standard dawn and dusk is messing with my equilibrium.

And, okay, I miss my shifter. The heavy rumble of his speech. His intoxicating odor. The way he commands a space with his size and power. Kurtis's bearing saps all the oxygen in the room and animates the nerves in my body—and poof, I'm on fire.

Since our situation has changed and we're no longer living under the same roof or working on assignments, figuring out a strategy to be together in secret has been freaking impossible. The only moment Nicole lets me out of her sight is when she's far too preoccupied with Logan during the day, and during those daytime periods, shifter business and managing Red Dawn engage Kurtis.

Thank God they organized a meeting for later tonight. Hopefully, Nicki and Logan have been doing more than screwing in their suite and developed a game plan to obtain her throne. I require a mission to occupy my mind before I go batty.

Over the weeks, my mate kept in contact through text. As much as I'd prefer to hear his sexy voice, I sure as hell didn't want Nicki or Logan overhearing our discussions. The texts quickly firestormed into sexting. Our desire for each other intensifies the longer we're apart. He commands, I obey, and while getting myself off relieves the pressure, my body craves my mate's strong touch on my skin. His big beautiful cock in my flesh. His blood cascading down my throat.

Since our night together, consuming from anyone else nauseates. As a result, my strength has rapidly diminished. Before long, I will need to either seek my mate or overlook my protesting stomach and go to one of my fellow Guardians. It still bewilders me how little the shifter prince knows about vampire physiology.

He's no doubt relying on me to communicate my needs, so, furious wouldn't hit close to characterizing the huge soldier if he found out I sipped from anyone. Those baby blues would gleam with anger and retribution. My butt cheeks clench imagining his palm stinging my backside.

Hmmm.

At Nicki's low, needy rumble, I flop over on my tummy and jam the pillow over my head.

For days after the council vote, the couple locked themselves in their bedroom. Brilliant lightning streaked the sky, accompanied by earth-shaking claps of thunder, but no rain kissed the ground. My heart reached out to them. Like the valkyries, the storms spoke of her tempestuous emotions even if she never would.

One afternoon about a week ago, the haunting notes from the piano and Nicki's throaty voice invaded my slumber. The song reflected her identity; a reminder to keep fighting the voices in her mind telling her she's not enough, or she doesn't measure up. When feeling weak, to lean on *his* strength. Listen, when he declares she's loved, strong, and more than sufficient. My soul resonated with each phrase, and I wept as I understood at that moment, she was correct. Nicki and I were more alike than I ever imagined.

Underneath the tough facade, we both experience moments of inadequacy, where we believe we fall short. The words revealed how the sole factor protecting her from falling apart is everything he thinks of her. In him, she finds her strength, her purpose. That evening I downloaded "You Say" by Lauren Daigle, as an incentive to get up every single night and declare I am enough, I am worthy, this is the truth.

Over the preceding month, Zachariah texted or tried calling many times, but Nicki's orders were clear; "Don't respond. Let the bastard stew." I'm uncertain it's a wise approach. Blatantly ignoring him will enrage the vampire, which causes the back of my neck to burn with anxiety. If I know my mentor, he's working his resources to locate my twin to use as leverage.

My phone pings and I spring up to snatch it off the nightstand. *Come to me at dusk. Meeting isn't until ten. I require ur sweet pussy clamped around my cock, Lucretia*—even in a text he uses my full name—*and you need to feed.*

Excitement flares in my stomach, and my insides soften anticipating the coming invasion. I glance at the time. Damn it. It's only two o'clock, and twilight is a good four hours away.

With a huff, I plop down on the bed, a mischievous plan springs forth, and before I reconsider, I text back, a devilish grin spreading my lips.

I've already fed.

When several minutes pass with no response, the glee fades, replaced by nervous butterflies flapping violently in my empty stomach. Should I declare it was a joke, or wait and see what develops? I wish him juiced up, not furious.

My fingers tremble as they hover over the keys with indecision. After more moments of questioning my common sense, my dark side wins out, and I gently place the phone back on its charger. Anxious excitement tightens my abdomen, and I bolt upright again. I require a strenuous workout to distract me, but since that option's not available in our present living situation, I head to the shower on wobbling limbs, giggling like a schoolgirl.

* * *

A yellow glow still illuminates the border around the blanket I tack up over my window when a vehicle skids to a halt out front. Anxiously, I yank on jeans, force a sweater over my head, and snatch my boots by the dresser. Kurtis never texted me back, and my apprehension level is at DefCon two.

Unable to set foot outside my room with all the damn bay windows in this dwelling, I listen at the door while frantically braiding my hair. The second the front entry opens, citrus and pine fill my nostrils and saliva pools in my mouth.

Holy crap. The prince is here. For me or another reason?

“What are you doing here, Kurtis?” Nicki asks. “The meeting’s not until ten.”

“We need to talk. Privately.”

Oh boy. By the rough tone, he’s pissed. The bedroom door opposite mine opens.

“Do not step outside that entrance, Nicole,” Logan orders. “Ten goddamn minutes the sun will be below the horizon and I can leave with you.”

“I’ll be right back, *Dad.*”

I cringe at the sound of the soft click. It’s almost worse than if she’d slammed it.

“Nicole!” Logan bellows and I hop away from my door. “If anything happens to her, shifter, I will rip your fucking head off.” My vampire stirs at the threat to my mate, but I’m sensible enough to ignore her.

After the car doors thud shut and the rich, powerful engine fades, I slowly open the wood to peek out. Harsh iridescent light challenges the sun’s harmful rays in the corridor, and I regard the enraged warrior standing three feet away in a pair of jeans.

The impressive muscles in his chest and arms flex and ripple with the clenching and unclenching of his fists. The Moretti tattoo snaking around his bicep and upper pectoral undulates with each harsh breath, and the low growls set my nerves on edge. Ever since Nicki's momentary death, the fierce warrior keeps his female within sight at all times.

"Logan," I whisper to settle the beast. "Your mate is the most powerful vampire in the world, and Kurtis would give his life to defend her."

"She could not wait ten minutes." Alarm rides the angry rumble.

I imagine his inner vamp is crashing around inside him, urging him to stride out into the waning sunlight and go after what's his. I want to offer him comfort, but the last glimmers of the deadly sun still illuminate the carpet. Besides, I'm not positive my touch will do anything except agitate him further. A diversion is in order.

"Can I ask you a question?" When the harsh green light turns my direction, I squint against the intensity. "Do males ever learn to trust their mate's ability to defend themselves?"

Logan regards me for several long minutes before the radiance diminishes. "You inquire like you are experienced with such a predicament."

Well crap. Leave it to the commander to cut right to the chase. "Just curious." I shrug and lean against the door frame. "I'm a female soldier. Unless my mate turns out to be another warrior, I need to discern if a male can handle his woman having such a dangerous occupation."

Logan's regard narrows, and it takes everything not to glance away. Powerful arms cross his naked chest as he too leans against his jam. "If we were fated, I would take you over my knee right now for lying. We both know who your mate is; he just walked out the door with mine."

I purse my lips and wisely keep my mouth shut.

"Your fate is sealed, Lu. We are not like mortals. We do not choose our mates, and the bond is not a contractual document we can nullify. A physical connection links us until the day we perish." He smiles, his muscles relaxing. "And often, beyond."

"A mate is a weakness. A distraction I can't afford. Not to mention against the law." I confess quietly, fixating on the shadows creeping over the carpet at my feet.

"You could not be more mistaken, Lu. A mate is our greatest strength. And yes, no matter the species, the protective instinct runs deep, but there is no higher purpose in existence than to protect what is yours. No greater joy having that in return. Legal or not." His eyes dart back to the entrance. "Right now, I would argue love offers an individual power, often at the cost of their sanity."

I smile even as Logan's words batter the wall around my heart. Tiny cracks fissure the cold, indifferent shield. Dimitri's action left me worthless. The rape and destruction of my inner animal crushed my spirit. Trezzo, because that's who he was to me back then, devoted years teaching me to trust no one. He instilled the belief that to be effective, I needed to bury my dark passions and focus entirely on becoming a stronger warrior than my male counterparts. He warned me the thirst for pain with pleasure was demented, wrong, and would weaken me in the minds of my peers.

"I am a woman. I fought harder than most men, pushed myself beyond my limits for over twenty years to become a Guardian." My chin lifts with pride. Most female vampires boast a superior, princess attitude and would never conceive of lowering themselves to the grunt work of a warrior. "How does one let go of all they believe?" I beg, frantic for my former commander to offer me the answers my heart is demanding.

"Only you can determine that, Lu. I have met thousands upon thousands of people in my six centuries, and few touched me. You meet a certain individual, your mate, and it transforms your life. Forever. The thing you must ask yourself: is he worth the risk, and the precious gift of your trust?"

The bigger question: am I worthy of his? The words Nicki sang the other day pop into my mind, and I recognize it's easier stated than achieved.

We both tense when the familiar rumble turns down the drive just as the sun's rays quit the sky. I peer at Logan and uneasiness tightens my shoulders at the feral determination in his grin.

"Vacate the premises, Lu. To quote my mate: shit is about to get real."

I almost feel sorry for Nicki, until I see the storm in my mate's expression as he stalks through the front door, straight for me.

CHAPTER 24

Lucretia

I retreat inside my room as Kurtis charges in and kicks the door shut with his boot. What do I do now? I've enraged the shifter. He advances, his ground-eating stride like the stalking of a cougar, graceful and calculated. It makes the large bedroom seem cramped. My breathing takes on a shuddering, erratic tempo, and my insides melt at the enormous, threatening canines on vivid display. Fear and lust pool in my belly as the blue eyes darken to the fiery chestnut of his animal. My mate is on the verge of a shift and only controlling it by sheer will.

His fury is... intimidating and sexy as hell. I squeak with apprehension when he seizes me around the waist and drags me against his solid body. Jesus.

Even his muscles are fuller, straining against the gray t-shirt and jeans.

I could toss him from me with ease, but any aggressive moves would trigger his change. It's evident what he's after when he jams his nose against my collar and sniffs. My mate is seeking confirmation I lied.

"Kurtis, I…"

"Silence." The one word is rough and guttural. Harsh breath warms my neck and shoulder. If he bites, will I shove him away, or welcome it?

Our ragged breathing fills the deafening stillness in the house, and for a split second, I wonder how Nicki is fairing with Logan.

"Trace us to my cabin. Now." At the authority in his growled command, I hastily nod and grasp the powerful shoulders in preparation. Even though my instincts scream, this is a bad, bad idea, I scatter our molecules to the universe and visualize Kurtis's beautiful living room. No way in purgatory I'm tracing to the bedroom. Not until he's cooled down. I want the animal—hell, I lust after the beast—but I need Kurtis, the man, in control.

Several moments later, we land beside the towering rock fireplace in the great room. The shifter releases me and clutches the thick wooden mantel for support to recapture his equilibrium.

I edge back, and his eyes snap open. The glare halts me mid-step. It's like being next to a wild predator;

no significant movements and keep your arms inside the vehicle at all times. My wariness eases somewhat to realize his irises reverted to their vivid blue.

"You lied. Why?"

"I meant it as a joke," I whisper lamely with a shrug. "I wanted to tease you."

"To what outcome, Lucretia?"

"I—I don't know." Another lie. I knew exactly what I was doing.

"Stop lying to me," he growls and advances a step. I swallow but hold my ground. "Tell me, and the truth better leave those lips."

"Or what?" For Pete's sake, I was playing. He doesn't need to get so worked up about it. But isn't that precisely what I wanted? To make him angry enough he'd spank me. To toss me over his lap and paddle my ass with his wide palm until the sweet burn floods my body. Just thinking about it ramps up my heart rate.

"If it's a spanking you're after, it won't work."

"Why the hell not?" I blurt out, exposing my real intent, and my lids lower to the beautiful hardwood.

Filter idiot.

"This is my fault." His quiet response stuns me, and I jerk my gaze to his. "I should have set ground rules. It wasn't fair to expect you to know what is acceptable and what isn't."

"What do you mean?" This twist in the conversation has completely thrown me. There are rules?

"Rule number one. I'll *never* strike you in anger."

"Again. Why not?" How else is he going to offer me the pain I fancy if he doesn't set his hands on me?

"Angel, I'll grant you precisely what you need, what we both seek, but with desire and control. Never anger. It's the only way this will work."

I inhale deeply. It never dawned on me there was another alternative. My mind reflects on my brutal younger years and compares it to our first night together. My breath hitches as realization dawns. With all those other males, they got off on punishing me, my enjoyment never their intent and the pain they inflicted was in anger or downright maliciousness. At no point was I in control. Nothing I'd said or done would have stopped them. Trezzo a perfect illustration.

With Kurtis, it was different. He offered me precisely what I craved, and yes, it turned him on, but he was always in command. My pleasure was his objective, and with a single word, he would have ceased.

"I've known no other way," I confess.

His expression softens. "That changes now. Rule number two: If you push me hard enough, you'll experience consequences to your actions, which is what you solicit. But no matter how furious I am, or how many buttons you press, I'll walk away until I'm back in control before I ever raise a hand to you. Are we clear?"

Warmth spreads through my breast, and my walls crumble a little further. Hell's bells this is freaking me out beyond anything I've encountered. I need him with a deep, consuming yearning that frightens me to the core. He scrambles my brain and shatters every judgment about myself. My desires. It's not just because of the bond. It's him.

Our hurdles are numerous, ones that could tear us apart. At some point, Zach will force me to choose between living under his thumb or death. Mine or my twin's.

How much longer can I keep Vi hidden from him? From the council? The sadistic bastard won't stop until he controls me. Rules me. And based on our interaction outside the castle, it will be a painful, brutal existence.

I've already put Kurtis's life on the line by mating him. One factor ensures security for everyone I care about: Zachariah's death.

* * *

My mate's large hands span my midriff, and I dismiss Zach from my mind as fire ignites in my core. His scent electrifies my senses; hunger cramps my gut.

"Rule number three. I only demand your submission sexually." Warm fingers grip my chin, lifting my face until I've no choice but to peer into his keen regard. "You are a proud, fierce warrior. A factor I find sexy as hell, but I won't lie. Your position is dangerous, and my first impulse is to throw you behind me and protect this delectable body from harm. I can extend one guarantee: I'm working on it. Unless you purposely place yourself in harm's way, then all bets are off." His charming smile sends tingles throughout my frame, and I shiver.

No longer able to withhold myself from this male, I close the narrow gap, step into his forbidden storm, and wrap my arms around his fit waist. My mate is presenting me with everything. A world I've only fantasized about exploring. It may be for a night, a week, or a month. I don't care. I want what he's proposing for however long it lasts. I choose him.

"Last and final rule, angel, then we'll proceed to your punishment." My insides hiccup, not merely at the heavy rumble but at the term *punishment.* "I think it goes without saying, you will never feed from anyone but me unless your survival depends on it. Do you understand? I'll not tolerate your lips on another male."

I stare into cobalt depths. "Yes, Sir." Good grief, my tone is gruff. I crave this prince, his beast. "Now, are we finished with the regulations? I'm starving." I inspect the pulse in his neck with desperation.

His deep chuckle makes me purr. When he grips my waist, lifting me until my face is level with his, my legs automatically wrap around his middle. He backs to the couch and sinks onto the cushion, keeping my core against his firmness.

"Allow me to nourish my female."

I like the sound of that—his female. I sift my fingers through the short blond strands and grip fistfuls before yanking his neck to the side. In the next pulse, my fangs sink deep into his jugular with deadly precision. Kurtis groans and the scorching hands grasp my ass, steering my core up and down his hardened length. My eyes roll back in my head at the glorious friction, the sweet heady nectar flowing down my throat, easing the fiery thirst. I didn't understand how ravenous I was until the first drop exploded through my taste buds.

"Damn. You *are* starving. Why the hell did you delay in coming to me?" Frustration rides desire, I whimper in response and hold on tighter, apprehensive he will end the feeding before I'm ready.

"Easy, angel," he murmurs stroking my back in soothing circles. "Take what you need."

Ten minutes later, the cramping in my tummy has vanished, replaced by revitalizing energy coursing through my system. His thick, solid shaft drives the stiff denim against my throbbing clit and spirals of fervor build, clenching my empty core.

I slip my fangs from his generous vein and gently lick the punctures closed, reveling in the salty goodness of his skin. He rises while I continue to suckle his neck, his firm arms wrapped around my waist.

We enter the bedroom. When I was in this room before I wasn't actually here, and I didn't take the time to investigate everything. My sole focus was on Kurtis's naked posterior.

It's a masculine space. The large furniture is dark, but not overpowering. Thick wall-to-wall tan carpet softens the enormous log walls. The bed is still as mammoth as I recall, and the fluffy comforter gives the area a generous splash of color with black and red Celtic swirls. Centered on the opposite side is a smaller version of the rock fireplace in the living room. Massive glass doors open to the rear deck overlooking the moonlit lake.

Kurtis stops at the foot of the bed, and I slide my legs to the floor. Anticipation spikes my heart rate, while my chest expands and falls rapidly.

He takes several strides back; his stare devours me from the top of my head to the tips of my shoes and up again. "Remove your clothes." The voice melts my insides. It projects a savage 'don't fuck with me' vibe.

Never taking my gaze from the forceful cobalt, I wrench my sweater off, and before my braid thuds against my spine, I'm toeing off my boots and socks and unzipping my pants. His keen regard follows me with a detached remoteness that gets my juices flowing.

I shimmy the jeans over my hips and thighs before kicking them to the side. After my shower earlier, I chose my lingerie in anticipation we'd finally get time alone tonight. Not knowing his predilections, I went with a vivid blue lace thong and barely decent, lacy bra I imagined matched his eyes.

The in-depth inspection travels my near nakedness in a slow, languid manner utter devoid of expression. I have no indication if he appreciates what he sees or not. Before I realize it, my braid is in my grasp, and I'm fiddling with the end.

Kurtis's lips twitch. "You. Are. Exceptional. While the lingerie is beautiful, I want those perfect breasts on full display. Keep the thong." He strolls over to a magnificent wooden armoire with intricate designs and small wolf heads carved into each corner at the top. I unclasp the front closure and toss the garment on top of my other clothes.

By the look of the furniture, I expected to discover a flat-screen TV or an impressive sound system behind the double doors. Instead, I gasp in surprise and wonder at what he reveals. Crops, whips, floggers, narrow and wide leather paddles, a few with studs or laden with holes to elicit more pain, and belts, ranging in thicknesses, line the interior of the large doors. Toys, most still in their packages, and an extensive assortment of restraints lay organized on the open shelves in the middle.

Holy moly! Jackpot.

CHAPTER 25

Lucretia

"Do you understand why you are being punished?" Kurtis stands with his arms crossed; the black t-shirt stretched over his bulging biceps showcase all those *devices* meant to bring me off in ways I can't imagine. The art of speech has escaped my brain. I offer a jerky nod.

He glowers. "Tell me."

"Because I lied," I bite out sheepishly.

"Good girl." My prize, his inviting grin. "Now, as a reward, I want you to choose which instrument you covet." He steps to the side, and I regard the display with trepidation.

Oh, no. He wants me to select? If I'm honest in my preference, I'll expose how hardcore I am, the degree of pain I require. If I go with a more novice or mediocre device, it sets a precedent. Either will bring me to climax, but mediocrity won't grant me the complete surrender and euphoric state I seek.

My palms sweat as I shuffle over to the cabinet on unsteady legs. Azure irises roam my body. The one I want snags my attention, and I bite my lip. We may only possess a limited time together before circumstances rip us apart. I desire everything this male has to offer, but I'm petrified my level of need will drive him away.

My fingers tremble as I reach for the medium width leather paddle with the gold studs and settle it on Kurtis's open palm. Apprehension grips my innards as I attempt to interpret his emotions as he inspects my choice, but he's locked down tighter than Fort Knox.

His gaze gradually lifts, and my breath stalls in my lungs as he examines me intently for what seems like an eternity. My palms sweat, and I rub them on my bare thighs, the heightened tempo of my heart pounds in my ears. A part of me wants to snatch the offensive paddle, throw it in the back of the cabinet, and pick a less revealing device. It's too late.

All the scoldings from Trez rotate through my mind like a tornado. I'm terrified my choice accomplished the one thing I assumed outside forces would do: rip us apart.

“Excellent. One of my favorites.” The lopsided grin releases the pent-up breath lodged in my lungs.

Jesus. By always believing I’m sick and twisted, I am my own worst enemy. *Calm yourself, Lu. Slow your breathing.*

“Now go face the end of the bed.”

I don’t hesitate. In fact, I force myself not to rush, but then I sense Kurtis’s presence at my back and my heart rate triples in speed. The rustle of his shirt being removed clenches my fists, and I fight the compulsion to peek at his imposing body, but the desire to obey wins.

When his scorching blaze penetrates my spine, it soothes the trembling in my muscles. “You have the most incredible ass Lucretia, and I’m going to enjoy giving it the attention it deserves.” Gentle fingers loosen the band securing the end of my braid before spreading the silky strands across my bare back. “Anytime we are together like this, I want your hair down,” he instructs and leans forward. “The braid is the warrior. In here, I expect the submissive.” His nose and lips bury themselves in my mane, and he sucks in a heavy breath before striding back and taking his glorious heat with him. “Bend over. Place your hands on the mattress.”

The controlled Dom voice causes the flutters in my belly to multiply into a chaotic flapping that tightens my abdomen as I settle my palms into the plush comforter. This is about to happen. I'm more anxious and turned on than I've ever been in my existence.

"Angel? What is your safe word?"

Oh crap. My rapid breath trembles from parted lips. I have no clue. His fierce, wild animal leaps into my brain. "Loki," I pant.

His rough chuckle makes me grin. "Okay. Loki it is." Hotness sears my back as he leans over me to press his mouth to my ear. "Do not lift your hands from the bed. This finishes when I stop, or you deliver your safe word. Understood?"

"Yes."

I squeak in surprise when his massive palm connects with my ass, and I almost lose my hold on the bedspread. The sharp sting has me gulping down a startled whimper.

"Yes, what?"

"Yes, Sir." Did that breathy, needy reply come from me? I'm fixed to combust, and he hasn't even worked the paddle yet. Arousal soaks my thong.

"The number of strikes depends on the transgression, and since I consider dishonesty a serious offense, your punishment will be severe."

My eyes widen at his harsh tone. Oh shit. Kurtis is the real deal. A true sadist. Based on the array of toys, this isn't his first rodeo.

When a full minute passes and nothing develops, my brows furrow. Maybe he explored the studded paddle more closely and changed his mind. I twist my neck to peek behind me when the initial blow smacks my lower ass with such force I tense to rise, to evade the sting darting through my butt cheek. At the last second, his order sears my brain, and I clutch the comforter to hold in place.

Hell's fucking bells!

Tears prick my eyes at the severity of the burn. Maybe this was a mistake. Perhaps I'm not ready for this level of pain. Kurtis pauses, and the hurt slowly subsides, replaced by the addictive, fiery inferno.

The paddle smacks my ass again mid-center. I absorb the ache a little easier. A third slap to one cheek, pursued by a fourth on the other. The discomfort is no longer unbearable. Instead, the strikes spread a delicious, sizzling firestorm through my anus, straight to my clit, and finally up to my nipples, coaxing them to pebble into hard throbbing points.

I moan, urging him on and my mate doesn't disappoint. The climax inducing blows continue one after the other, alternating cheeks, varying between the bottom, middle, and top of my ass until I slip into the euphoric bliss only this can offer. The intense rhythm sets up a complex vibration in my center, building, and building until the eruption is inescapable. There's no way I could check it even if he ordered it.

I grip the comforter harder and cry out Kurtis's name as I shatter. Sensations skyrocket through the nerves in my convulsing core, and I hold on to the bedspread for dear life to keep from dissolving to the floor. My mate steps forward, tears open his fly, rips my pretty lace thong in two and slams deep. My slick insides object at the forceful intrusion before stretching to accommodate his massive girth, and the intense pleasure-pain has me exploding once more as the shifter pounds into my responsive flesh with brute force.

A scalding grip latches on to the muscle between my shoulder and neck where I crave his bite and utilizes it as leverage to pound deeper. Sweat plasters my hair to my neck and back, and with every thrust, the coarse fabric of his jeans and the cool metal zipper scrape the ultra-sensitive skin. It produces ripples of electricity swirling through my body. I shove back, demanding more, and the pressure builds anew.

"Fuck, Lucretia," Kurtis growls as his other hand moves along my waist to grasp a breast. His thumb and forefinger twist and pinch a nipple. "Come again, angel."

At his command, I plummet over the precipice once more. My convulsing insides spasm around his thickness as he'd demanded in his text. And my reward is my mate's rough shout as his scalding seed saturates my core.

Holy. Fucking. Wow.

As the tremors begin to settle into a sluggish vibration, my knees finally give out. Before I face-plant on the carpet, Kurtis withdraws, hoists me into his arms, and cradles me against his sweat-slicked chest. I'm drained. I can't even raise my limbs to wrap them around his neck. He flips back the bedspread before gently turning me over onto my stomach on top of the crisp sheets.

My body sinks deep into the supple mattress as I listen to his footfalls head for the bathroom. Water flows. A cabinet opens and closes before he's padding across the carpet; his weight dips the bed next to me.

I flinch and suck in a gasp when rough fingers caress my tender backside, spreading a cool cream over both cheeks.

"I realize you heal rapidly, but this will further speed the process."

"I don't want the burn to fade yet," I whine.

Kurtis chuckles. "You'll feel this for a day at least, I guarantee."

When satisfied, he drapes a cold washcloth over my ass and stretches out on his side next to me. I angle my head to peer at the male who just gave me exactly what I've yearned for my whole life. He measured the strokes, worked the paddle along my skin to intensify and expand the delicious fire. I'm overwhelmed with emotions, spent beyond my wildest dreams, but a live wire of energy at the same time.

Kurtis gently brushes my damp hair from my face and neck. "You okay?" The concern he was too rough clouds his expression.

I clasp his elbow and jerk it out from under him. The second he's prone on his back, I cover his chest with mine, mindful to keep the wet cloth in place.

There was a point I considered that the gods or fate hated me for offering me this shifter as a mate. But I was mistaken. Kurtis is a true gift. The most erotic, seductive, and fierce male, a lowly warrior could hope to capture.

"I'm better than okay." I caress his sculpted chest, marveling at its perfection and strength, up over his massive shoulders that provide comfort and security, to the ruggedly handsome face. His eyes darken with an affection I prefer not to consider, so I lean up and glide my lips over his to keep the words from escaping.

My mate gently enfolds me in his warm embrace and for the first-time hope stirs in my gut. Hope for a real future. That's what I choose to believe at this moment. The world outside can wither and die for all

I care. I refuse to let anything spoil the next few hours.

"Are you okay?" I ask back. Did he enjoy doling out his discipline as much as I relished being on the receiving end?

His enormous hands reach up and clasp both sides of my face. The strength in them never fails to impress me. With slight pressure, he could squash my skull like a melon. "You were perfect, angel. Watching you come alive as your ass turned pink, then a brilliant red was better than any fantasy I'd conjured. The second you exploded from it, I couldn't sink my cock inside you quick enough."

"So... you liked it?" I tease.

"No. I loved it, and I'm looking forward to the next time I need to discipline you. Only I get to choose the means." The devilish grin gets my juices flowing all over again, not to mention the hard erection pressing into my hip.

"Hmmm," I murmur as I slowly drift down his body. "But what if I'm a very good girl?" I claim between kisses, bites, and licks across his rib cage and down his ripped abdomen.

"Are you a good girl, Lucretia?" he counters with a low moan, his fingers fisting in my long strands.

"Oh no, Sir," I taunt before working my tongue up his pulsing shaft. Its silk encased in granite and thick enough my fingers don't reach around it. "I'm a very," I lick and suck the sensitive flesh on his scrotum. The grip in my hair tightens, the amber glow from my eyes lights my path. "Very." I lap at the moisture glistening at the slit on top of the bulbous crown, and his hips lift off the mattress. "Bad girl."

"Prove it." He commands with a rough growl before guiding my lips over his length. I eagerly obey.

CHAPTER 26

Kurtis

"I can't get enough of your sweet taste," I murmur before placing a lingering kiss on Lu's neck when her sweater falls back into place.

What we shared was fucking incredible. Fate could not have chosen a more suitable mate. The intensity level she requires sets me on fire, and I crave to provide more of what she demands—take her body to heights she's never experienced. I'm addicted to the slap of leather on her flesh, her skin reddening, her little sighs as she welcomes every strike and pleads for more.

"And I yours, but we must leave, or we *will* be late."

I sense her mental withdraw as she takes a step backward. Maybe she's correct. It's time to get our game faces on for this meeting. I haven't overlooked her revelation before the DNA results. Zach wants her. A hasty glance at the clock on the bedside table reveals we possess half an hour before we're needed. I think my mate needs to answer a few questions.

"We have several minutes." With a hand low on her back, I steer us into the living room. Lu in my room is too damn tempting. I indicate with a wave she takes a seat on the couch. The ever-mistrustful warrior eyes me warily. "Have a seat, Lucretia." Earlier I declared I didn't wish to dominate her outside of sexual situations, but she is as stubborn as she is cautious.

"No. We should go."

"Sit, or I'll tan your already sore ass, then we will be late."

Her gaze narrows, but she strides over to the couch and perches on the edge. The slight wince causes my cock to jerk in satisfaction.

"What does Zach want from you?" I lower onto the wide, square coffee table facing her, wishing I possessed Nicki's ability to discern a lie. It would come in useful with my secretive mate.

After a sharp inhale, she murmurs. "To own me."

My beast stirs. "To own you how?"

Her anxious glance agitates my nerves. "Oh, he sought to cloak it in a nice flowery package about how he wants me to rule by his side, but the grim reality is Zach prefers to break me."

Fury vibrates through my chest. "I'll never allow that to happen, Lucretia."

"Nor will I, mate, because I aim to kill him."

Her confession to committing murder should trouble me. Instead, it soothes the beast. "What's your strategy?"

Her eyes widen. "You're not going to berate me and talk me out of it?"

"If I'm honest, Zach's death would resolve many issues." Chatting about assassination makes me antsy, and I rise to prowl in front of the fireplace. Lu's conflicted scrutiny follows. "It would allow Nicki back on the throne which would fall in line with the prophecy and protect the Vampire Nation from collapsing under yet another tyrant. Negate a potential war between my people and yours that would save hundreds of lives." I halt and stare directly at her. "Most importantly, it would dispose of a threat to you."

It's so frustrating being powerless to sense Lu's reactions. Without my bite, I only perceive her baser emotions: lust or rage.

Lu stands with grace, her unbound hair tumbling like a magnificent dark curtain around her face and shoulders. “I don’t want you engaged in my chaos.”

Her response tightens my jaw. “You’re my mate. I’m involved whether you like it or not.”

“My life is toxic, Kurtis. You should steer clear of me.”

“Lucretia.” Instinct warns she’s about to trace away to that meeting without me. And with my vehicle still at Nicki’s, I’d need to call someone from the team to come get me. I grasp her biceps and draw her to my chest. “What does Zachariah have on you? It must be significant if you’re prepared to murder him for it.”

“I will deal with Trez—Zach, like I’ve dealt with everything else. This is my headache. Let me handle it. I’m not a frail human who requires a knight to come to her rescue.” Her anger calms my own.

“Everyone needs help, angel. It has nothing to do with whom or what you are. We all need to band as one to achieve our goals, to fulfill the prophecy. You aren’t relying on me to do anything. I’m watching out for you because...” the words die in my throat, realizing if I uttered them, she would run. “I’m watching out for you because you’re my mate. We are a team. In this, whatever this is, together. You are no longer alone.”

A light sparks in the amber depths. “I’ve been on my own my whole life. It’s the only way I comprehend.”

"What about when you were younger? Your parents?" It hits me I know nothing personal about my vampire's history besides what was in the dossier Bastian provided. One thing I'm confident about; Lu's holding back more than what she confessed already.

Nicki believes Lu betrayed her, or will. What would provoke her to turn on her own queen? The woman she's watched over all her life. Does it have anything to do with Dimitri? Zach?

She steps from my embrace. "Immortal hunters massacred my parents while out on a run when I was thirteen." Her tone alters. It's cold. Remote. She wanders over to the floor to ceiling windows facing the moonlit lake, her back ramrod straight, her hands clasped at her waist.

"Who raised you? Weren't you part of a shifter pack?" Needing her close, I follow in her wake, but pause a foot from the delectable body calling to me. Our gazes clash in the window before hers dart away to refocus on the twinkling water.

"My parents were loners. I reared my... myself."

"At thirteen, in what I'm guessing was the late 1800s?"

"Yes." Her shoulders tense. "You want to know me, Kurtis? Here it is. I turned to prostitution to support myself. To survive. In New Orleans, it wasn't difficult to obtain employment in a brothel. Young girls were in high demand. The younger, the better.

Whores became my family. The customers my educators in all things sexual, no matter how deviant."

Christ. She was just a child. My heart constricts at what she endured at the mercy of sick, perverted men. No wonder she claimed she knew no other means but anger with punishment. My stomach drops, recalling what I did to her, how I struck her with that studded paddle until her bottom burned crimson.

Fuck.

"Stop it." Her whispered plea reaches through my loathing and hatred. She turns, but I can't bear to look at her, too repulsed by my actions. The muscles in my back tense with shame and my beast recoils. Someone should take me out and shoot me for using her in such a manner after everything she's suffered as a youngling, and from Dimitri.

"We should go," I state abruptly before she cites the reassurance shimmering in the amber depths. I don't deserve them. "Before we're late."

Lu's irises spark for a split second before the frigid mask I loathe falls into place. With a brief nod, she reaches for my wrist.

"Lu. I'm sorry." I blurt out. I get the impression I've failed her by my reaction, and I am uncertain why. Did she expect me to be okay with what she revealed?

The weight crushing my chest is oppressive. What kind of damage could that do to a young girl's mind? Are her experiences as a child what guided her need for pain? Or is it truly what she enjoys? The big question ripping fear through my gut: would she ever use her safe word if it became too extreme, or would she grit her teeth and take it because it's what they taught her? What they demanded?

"For what?" she asks.

"For letting this progress too far."

Her lids close for a brief second before they refocus on my chin. The icy, emotionless depths scare me. But before I utter another sound, she scatters our molecules to the wind and sends us spiraling through space.

* * *

"Someone better come up with a plan other than the one my mate is proposing because it is not fucking happening," Logan growls at the occupants gathered in the makeshift war room in Nicole's garage/studio. His fingers stab through his hair in frustration for the hundredth time.

"Logan," Nicole sighs. "It's our only play."

"Care to enlighten the rest of us?" Liam leans forward at my left to glance down the table.

We've sat, paced, and strategized for the past two hours, hashing out a viable scheme to get Nicki back on the throne. I'm boggled by the circumstances which brought us to this point. We are among the most influential leaders and warriors in the world, yet our current situation requires this secret gathering. It still amazes me a werewolf king, a shifter prince, the legendary Moretti brothers, a prophesied halfling, a sexy lethal Guardian, and a divine Oracle are sitting down to plot strategy to dethrone Zach. This clandestine meeting is proof of our desperation to bring peace to our race, and the strength of our friendship.

"We do this by the book for the '*great and powerful*' council to sign off on it." Nicki stands, her somber expression contrasting with her sarcastic Wizard of Oz comment. "I've scoured the laws and discovered anyone with a legitimate claim to the throne, the prophecy being my claim, can challenge a sitting king in open combat. Now, I admit this law is archaic, and someone should have obliterated it from the records a long time ago, but it's our good fortune it wasn't. A mistake I will rectify once I'm in command again."

"Combat?" I inquire as dread drops into my gut like a lead weight. "To the death combat?"

"Duh."

"The exact reason she is not fucking doing it," the angry vampire repeats, luminescence flickering in the emerald depths.

"Then propose another plan, Alaric." Uh oh. Nicki uttering Logan's given name is not a good sign.

"I have a solution," Lu announces from across the wood surface, ripping the focus away from the passion swirling between Nicki and Logan.

The second Lucretia and I appeared, she couldn't abandon my wrist fast enough before putting the room and the table between us. I let her leave, too caught up in my anger and self-loathing. Not to mention Nicole was contemplating me like a predator about to strike.

When I'd absconded with her earlier, it was to pick her brain about vampire basics. I've never been with one before, and I wished to understand their physiological needs. She reported little, instead devoting most of the drive trying to talk me out of getting embroiled with Lu.

Peering along the table, I'm confident I will not like what my mate is about to propose. The cold indifference still blankets her expression, and the fact she never makes eye contact with me reveals deeper emotions boiling below the surface. I just wish I perceived what they were.

"Oh, really?" Nicki drawls. Mistrustful eyes zero on Lucretia. "Do tell."

"I determined many facts under Darath's mind control..."

"You had an insight into the demon king, and you are only informing us now?" Logan's quiet manner has everyone tensing.

Lu swallows in trepidation, and it's all I can manage not to snarl at him to back the fuck off. I grit my teeth and ignore my beast's defensive impulses.

"Only bits and pieces. I've been sifting through the images in my brain, struggling to create a sense of it all and I think I finally figured out King Darath's motivations," Lu responds with a slight lift in her chin. "He seeks to annihilate the ruler of the Vampire Nation no matter who it is, but if it's Dimitri's offspring more the better. He suffered a tragedy at King Giordano's hands and demands retribution. It consumes him. I don't believe it has anything to do with you directly, Nicole." Nicki's mouth tightens at Lu's familiarity. "I propose we align with Darath, Icarus lowers the shield, and we present him with what he craves. The council has not revealed Zachariah's true lineage yet. We can capitalize on that and let the demon take care of our dilemma."

"Which in turn solves your problem, doesn't it, Lu?" Nicki eyeballs my woman with cynicism.

"My lady?" The cold warrior raises a brow.

My gut clenches, recalling our discussion about murdering Trezzo or Zachariah or whatever the hell we're expected to call the bastard now. Lucretia just presented a resolution to accomplish that goal and keep her hands clean with calm resolve. I don't know whether to be proud or troubled.

"By eliminating our headache, you're conveniently getting rid of the one individual I believe holds all your mysteries," Nicole accuses, her tone dangerous. My mate's demeanor never alters.

"What mysteries?" Liam asks, and I kick him under the table.

"I merely submit a strategic plan. Do with it what you please." Lu's sharp regard flicks to mine for a brief second before confronting her queen with rebellion. She doesn't fidget or appear to draw breath. With her hair unbound and spilling down her back she's powerless to fiddle with her braid, a sure giveaway to her emotions.

The silence stretches between the two women who mean the world to me as they stare each other down.

"Lu's theory holds merit," Sebastian interjects from the monitor mounted on the wall. Big fat snowflakes fall outside the window behind him from wherever the hell he is in his hunt for Alex. "The chatter is King Darath is plotting to lay siege to the compound within the week. He has witches working night and day to break Icarus' barrier spell."

"A futile exercise," the priest interjects.

"All right." Nicki concedes. "I concur, but the safer strategy would be to draw him out. The less damage the demons do to my castle, the better. The place has grown on me. Not to mention, I'd like to spare as many of my Guardians' lives as possible."

"Agreed," Logan nods. "I'm assuming you have a suggestion on how to make that happen?"

"No." Nicki's gray glare bores into Lu's amber depths. "But Lucretia does."

CHAPTER 27

Lucretia

"What the hell do you mean?" Kurtis asks around clenched teeth, his anger a living, breathing entity.

Devastation spreads through my soul, remembering his withdrawal at the cabin. After the most profound sexual experience ever, a deep intimate connection, his disgust at my confession was palpable. It crushed me. I opened myself to him, well, as much as someone with dangerous secrets can. I was a fool to assume my mate would sympathize or understand, or... accept, damn it.

Zachariah always warned me, my past and appetites were revolting and reprehensible. The brief stir of hope I'd discovered a partner who cared enough to overlook the lengths I went to survive, and who enjoyed my darker side, died a violent death. Never will I surrender to my needs again, nor trust anyone with my heart.

What heart? The one broke and bleeding on the floor?

"Lu already admitted Zach wants her, let's exploit that," Nicki explains.

"How?" I thrust my hurt down deep, as I've always done and concentrate on my duties and combat; two factors in my life that never fail me.

"Contact him. Tell him you want a meeting. Since he can't trace out..." she raises a brow at Icarus. "Right?"

"Correct, my lady."

"And you're not stupid enough to travel in alone, request to meet on the perimeter."

"Then what?" Kurtis demands, his fists clenching around the arms of his chair.

"The priest will lower the shield, and we strike," she responds with an implied "duh" and her famous eye roll.

"I loathe putting a damper on your parade, Nicole," Logan pipes up. "But Zachariah can perceive an immortal a mile away."

"Why don't we just drop the barrier now and slay the fucker?" The werewolf king asks.

"I'm trying to avoid killing my own people, Liam."

"Fair enough," he acknowledges. "So, Lu lures him to the shield's edge, signals us, and Icarus lowers the cover. Then what? She grabs him and traces him to a specific location?"

"I can't," I admit with reluctance. "Zach's a seven-hundred-year-old vampire, and far too powerful."

"Damn it." Nicole grumbles.

"I could accompany Lucretia," the priest says in a hushed murmur. The immortals in the room turn a questioning stare in his direction. "Cloaked. He would not sense me."

"You can do that?" I ask in awe. Why am I always astounded by the little priest's talents?

"Yes, my child."

"Between the two of you, do you expect you will be able to restrain and trace him?" Logan inquires.

I peer at Icarus for verification because I have no freaking clue.

"Yes."

"Excellent." Nicki beams. Happy once more, she reaches for the perpetual coffee mug at her elbow.

"No. Not happening. What's keeping him from just killing her outright?" Kurtis asks in a rough growl.

I fix him with a glower. Rage snuffs out my indifference. "You don't have a say, shifter." You lost the right when you turned away from me. A profound rumble blankets the table, and I'm uncertain if it's from him or me. "This is my job, back the fuck off." Hot, rapid fury lights the synapses in my brain, eclipsing the throb in my chest. The room and the immortals in it evaporate as I direct my wrath at the one being who's hurt me more with his disgust than if he'd stabbed me in the back.

"That's where you're wrong, angel," Kurtis says in a deliberately mild tone, but as he leans forward, upper fangs score his bottom lip. My insides flutter at the feral intent in his furious regard. "I believe we had an agreement."

Red fills my vision. Oh no, he doesn't. He can't bring up his addendum to rule number three now. Besides his betrayal negated all the rules. "I didn't agree to a motherfucking thing."

"Lucretia." Sebastian admonishes from the screen. "You neglect your rank. Watch your tone, or I will dismiss you from this task force."

What the hell is it with the males in my life? They are forever commanding me to do their bidding. Well, I'm sick and tired of it. "If you pull me off this team, commander, who will call Zach out? You? The prince?" I smile viciously, not giving a shit about anything in my fury. "I'm your only option."

"She's right," Liam mutters. "As much as I hate the idea, Lu's all we got."

"We could go back to plan A; mortal combat." Nicki sneers around her mug.

The shifter prince rises to his feet with such controlled rage it claims attention. The deadly regard fixates on my mine. He's about to go all Alpha male. I tense, bracing to stand and confront him head-on when Nicole intervenes.

"Kurtis." Her bark snags his attention, like always.

Jealousy ignites in my gut. Does he still love her? White-hot pain lances through my spirit. *Why do you care? Your affair with Kurtis died back at his cabin.*

"You need to cool down, or it will be you I separate from this team. Are we clear?" she commands.

Several heartbeats pass. A muscle pulses in his clenched jaw, tension saturates the place. A myriad of emotions flicker in the cobalt eyes glaring my direction, but I dismiss them, turn my gaze to the halfling, and harden my heart.

"Understood." His response is clipped, but he drops back into his seat.

Such influence Nicki wields over my mate. I am relieved she stalled his outburst, but also disappointed in him she could. After living in such proximity with Logan and my queen these past weeks, I realize she has similar needs to my own during sex. Would Kurtis think negatively of his best friend if he knew? Or is it just me?

I'd wager my life he enjoyed our play. He claimed as much. Did the disgust and shame stem from the knowledge I was a prostitute? Or because his actions sickened him after the fact. It's as I foresaw: a mate is a liability. To my heart. To my job. His performance tonight, whether or not intentional, caused me to look weak.

I ignore his constant glower and concentrate on Nicole. "Once he responds, and we meet, where should we trace him?"

"I... ah," Nicki shifts a margin away from Logan. Uh oh. Whatever she's about to recommend is going to provoke the warrior. Again.

Damn Alpha males.

Logan's body, so in harmony with his mate's tenses, his head slowly pivots, the emerald orbs laser-focused on his mate.

Despite the intense fervor from Logan's regard, Nicki keeps her gaze fastened on mine. "Before your rendezvous, I will take the initial step to implement your idea and... face King Darath."

Logan smiles, but there's nothing humorous or pleasant in it. "If you imagine you are meeting him alone, guess again, my love."

Nicole swallows, and I think it's part dread, part anger. "Pfft." Eye roll. "God help us if I suggest the prophesied, all-powerful halfling do anything remotely dangerous."

Wow. She's either brave or stupid. I can't put my finger on which one. The rest of us hold our breath as Logan rises to his feet, a fresh spark kindling in his stare.

"I forbid you to go alone," he states in a sharp growl, his massive body tense.

Oh boy. Did he just meet her?

"You forbid me?" A steel light illuminates his face, and her fangs descend.

His jaw hardens, not backing down an inch. "As your consort, I'm advising you to take Bastian and me with you. As your mate, I will not tolerate you putting yourself in peril by going alone. You do not understand the sphere of Jagorach's power."

Jesus. Kurtis and Logan are two peas in a pod with the whole, 'I won't allow you to purposefully place yourself in harm's way,' bullshit. Although in this case, my throat itches with the desire to agree with my former commander, but I wouldn't dare choose sides in this battle of wills. She already hates my guts.

When there doesn't seem to be an end to the stare-off, Liam bravely coughs in his fist. "Logan's right, Nicki. Take them and Kurtis. They are the only ones on this team old enough to fight against the demon's mind control. You don't even know if you can."

Irritation rides Nicki's deep sigh, but her shoulders relax in what I hope is resignation. "Fine." She flicks her gaze to the prince, and after a few seconds, he nods.

"Thank you, my love," Logan whispers.

"Oh, I didn't do it for you." She steps into his space, going toe-to-toe with the deadliest Guardian in history. "I did it because it's a good strategy. I'm still fucking pissed at you."

The grin is tender and full of sensual promise as he cradles her livid face. "You can show me how pissed later," he suggests before planting a blistering kiss on her mouth.

Their love and passion do strange things to my gut, and I can't help peeking at Kurtis beneath my lashes. The huge shifter stands, his furious glare burning a hole in my forehead. Crap. Alpha males are such a pain in the ass.

Before he can give another irritating command I won't adhere to, I yank my phone from my rear pocket and trace from the room, not even sure where I'm going. I require time alone before I deliver the text that will place me dead center in Zachariah Giordano's crosshairs.

CHAPTER 28

Lucretia

Surprise hits me when I materialize on Kurtis's dock. Even furious and hurt, I'm drawn to him. The light from the half-moon sparkles along the undulating water, and a refreshing breeze feathers through my hair as I stroll to the wooden bench at the end. While freezing temperatures and heavy snow still blankets the forest surrounding the castle, spring is right around the corner here in Oregon.

As much as I detest the cold—I miss my home. The diversion of my fellow Guardians. I'm not the most social vampire but being enveloped by their boisterousness and camaraderie distracted me from my inner turmoil.

A doe and her fawn snag my attention on the other side of the lake as they step from the tree's security and brave the open to appease their thirst. Their beautiful dark eyes dart with nervous energy. Black noses twitch, scenting the air. Big ears twist in all directions listening for sounds of a predator. I hold still, afraid any slight movement will startle them away. With only the eerie cry of a loon and these magnificent creatures for company, sadness weighs heavy on my heart.

This rugged wilderness is splendid, but without Kurtis's commanding presence, lonely. And while the tranquil lapping of the waves soothes, and a momentary peace invades my blood at the serenity, it provides my mind time to dwell on my failures.

I foolishly believed when I presented my plan that it would eliminate the need for me to have any contact with my mentor again. I could avoid risking my life to kill him. Zach trained me, but the vampire has harnessed tremendous power and strength over the centuries. It would be ridiculous to take him on in a one-on-one battle.

The cast-iron ball between my shoulders eases knowing Icarus will be there with me. It's peculiar, but his presence calms me. Is it because the priest never becomes angry or riled? He accepts life's shitstorm in stride with a confidence I envy. On the flip side, having him there is a gamble. If Zach believes we are alone, he may well blurt out all my sins. The Oracle would run to the council.

After several hours of resting on the cold, hard bench, pondering my madness, I sigh and force my mind clear of everything but my task. Fear is an extravagance I can't afford. With steady hands, I shoot a quick text to the male who was once my savior but is now my greatest adversary.

'Ok, u win. Can we meet?'

I'm startled when my phone dings an immediate response. *'Glad to hear it. What changed your mind?'*

'She's been a vampire for a minute and yet she treats me like I'm less than dirt. I won't tolerate the child telling me when and where to piss.' My fingers hover over the keys as I hesitate. *'As much as I loathe to admit it, you were right. My sick, perverse desires need what you alone can provide.'* When several minutes pass with no reply, anxiety pounds through my skull. Perhaps I overplayed my hand.

Disgusted with myself, I lay the phone on the bench next to me like it's a ticking bomb. If I can't lure Zach to the boundary, we will be forced to assault the castle, slay my fellow Guardians, and demolish the only home I've known for almost a century.

There is another prospect. I could employ my remote viewing capability. Pinpoint the bastard's exact position. The complication is, if I don't detect him quickly, the process would deplete my energy and possibly burst my innards, making tracing impossible. Over seventy Guardians still reside at the castle, and who knows which ones are loyal to the former queen or their current ruler. Our team requires my sword.

Kurtis, Nicki, and Logan must face the demon king. Drawing Zachariah out is the most reliable solution. Besides, Nicole would go ape shit if she discovered I'd kept one more secret from them.

Zach will contact me. His obsession with owning me would demand no less.

Another hour passes and an uncomfortable prickle skates along my neck at the impending dawn. In about fifteen minutes, I must seek refuge, but going back to the cottage holds no appeal, and staying here isn't an option either. Kurtis could arrive home any minute.

A bone-weary sigh escapes as I glance across the rippling waves. The deer vanished.

Even though he infuriates me beyond belief, I can't shake this overwhelming necessity for my mate. The pressure of my burdens crushes my chest, enduring my challenges alone grows tiresome. For the first time, the inclination to relieve all my issues on my mate's strong, capable shoulders is tempting.

"A stupid dream," I mutter as I rise and snatch my phone, nearly dropping it into the water when it rings. Thinking it's Zach, I answer without noticing the caller ID.

"Angel. Where are you?"

Kurtis's deep seductive voice has me collapsing back onto the bench and a repressed sob bursts from my chest before I can stop it. All my righteous anger earlier dissolves away.

"Lucretia." His manner shifts to the commanding Dom I crave with every molecule. "Tell me where you are."

I scrunch my eyes shut and force the words from my lips that will seal my bleak, lonely fate. "Thank you, Kurtis, for giving me... what I needed even though it's... wrong. I'm sorry my past is not pure and worthy." My voice is hoarse, laden by emotions I don't want to identify, but I'm proud it didn't wobble as a lone tear tracks down my cheek.

"Angel," he murmurs in a gentle tone. "Nothing we did was wrong. It was all kinds of right. Your needs match my own. I couldn't give a rat's ass about your history."

"I completed the bond on my end, remember? I felt your emotions. It disgusted you I was a prostitute." Humiliation burns my cheeks.

"That's not what disgusted me. Allow me a chance to explain. Where are you?"

"There's no point. My entire world is crashing down around me. Let it go, Kurtis. Let me go."

"Never." The vow is a rough, promising growl sending shivers racing along my arms. "You are mine. I can aid you. Allow me do my job and shelter you."

Heaven help me, he does not understand how much I want what he's offering. "I never lived until I found you. And for that, I will be eternally grateful. You are my mate, and every vampiric instinct demands I protect you. Even from myself."

"No." Panic enters his voice. "Don't fucking hang up."

"Goodbye, Kurtis." Tears fall fast and furious down my face.

"Lucr..."

With the push of a button, I interrupt his bellow. Grief envelopes me, and I clutch at the ache in my chest, brushing the moisture from my cheeks with loathing.

I rise slowly in defeat, feeling every bit of my 142 years. With one last glance around the beautiful lake, I shove my phone into my pocket just as a pair of headlights paralyze me in their beam.

Kurtis leaps from the enormous, red Super Duty and we both freeze. My insides constrict over the desperation in his expression, but he makes no action toward me. The shifter waits for me to come to him. Wants me to trust him.

I swallow knowing I am about to disappoint the one creature who means more than my own life. "I'm sorry," I whisper brokenly, and his face shuts down. The eyes harden.

"I never took you for a coward, Lu."

His fury is dark, dangerous, raw, and primal in a way that has me biting my lip. And the use of my nickname sends pain exploding through my heart. I've always been Lucretia or angel. Never Lu.

"I'm not a coward. You must understand, this is for your safety."

"Why?" Kurtis demands across the gaping distance. "What is it you've done you think I need protection from?"

I shake my head. "It's better you don't know." I couldn't bear for him to look at me with disgust and horror. And he would.

"Don't do this. Don't treat me as if my strength is inconsequential. Trust me to be competent to handle it. Trust us, Lucretia."

How can he not see the prospect of losing him scares the shit out of me? I'd rather face a thousand centaurs then condemn us to this misery. Grief chokes the air from my lungs, stills my heart. I've reached a now or never moment. If I trace away, Kurtis will not pursue me. Isn't that what I want? No. But it's what I must do.

"I can't trust you." Would he betray me to Nicki? With no way of knowing, fear keeps me from spilling my guts. I am a coward after all.

"You're a fool then, and I'm tired of bashing my head against your walls." He slams the truck door and walks toward the cabin with long angry strides. "You want to go it alone? Fine." He pauses at the porch steps and fixes me with a closed-off expression, but in those seething sapphires, I glimpse the beast he holds back, and my vampire shudders in response. "Have it your way."

Even though it's warranted, I'm ruined by the coldness in his gaze. It sits like hot steel in my gut, burning me from the inside out. My eyes follow him as he climbs the steps without a backward glance, and I linger to engrave this male I've fallen in love with to memory just as the first rays of dawn sets my skin on fire.

CHAPTER 29

Kurtis

Exhausted, I fall into bed just as the sun peaks over the treetops, striking the water with a beautiful explosion of sparkles. My cock is hard as stone, and my body wound as tight as a spring. It's been two weeks, and I still can't get Lu's yielding and responsive flesh beneath my palms from my mind, or her cries as she came from my ears.

After the night on my front lawn, I insisted on teleconferencing from home for any future gatherings, fearing I'd throw Lu over my shoulder, tie her to my bed, and demand she confess her sins.

Thank God a multitude of duties to my people and king consume every waking moment. I never realized how many complaints my father dealt with day-to-day, not to mention the endless, tedious meetings with shifter leaders in each territory. From as far up as Alaska, across the wildness of Yukon, down picturesque British Colombia, over to South Dakota, Wyoming, Nebraska, and finally Colorado. As much as I hate teleportation, it sure would come in handy. I've been on a plane more in the last two weeks than in my entire life.

None of it stopped my thoughts from turning to Lu every spare minute, replaying the rare instances where she let down her shield and trusted me.

Like in the alley, when she relied on me to guard her six, or when she clung to my neck in pain as she broke through the demon's mind control. In my tower room, in a vulnerable episode, she even allowed me to console her as she wept, revealing her shame and horror at trying to kill her mate.

Just when I think we've advanced a couple of steps, she pulls away, forces us to take a huge leap backward. Like when I found her on my dock to contact her former mentor, it spoke of an inner need her stubborn ass refused to acknowledge. And a small part of me understands Lu's reluctance to trust me. Once again, I'm trapped between two vampires.

During the meeting, while Nicki engaged in her little battle of wills with Logan, her husky voice filled my head, pleading with me to go with the Oracle and report back anything of significance.

The second Lu traced away from the war room before I could stop her, Nicole took the priest and me aside. "Icarus. Can you cloak anyone besides yourself?" she asked in a hushed tone.

"Of course, my lady."

"Right. What was I thinking?" She winked my direction. "I want Kurtis to go with you and the Guardian when you meet with the Italian nut job."

The little priest tilted his head with curiosity. "May I ask why?"

"You may ask." The deadpan response almost had me choking on the hot coffee I'd just swallowed.

The sheet rubbing against my sensitive groin bounces me to the present, and I growl in frustration. Why Lucretia refuses to acknowledge our bond, especially to herself, I'll never understand, because no matter what she's done, deep down, I want to believe she had good reasons. Like her explanation for becoming a prostitute. Christ, she was a young, defenseless shifter in the wild west with no clan to give her shelter. It breaks my heart that circumstances forced her to sell her body to survive. I would never think less of her for it.

I drop my arm across my forehead and wonder, for the hundredth time, what she's doing. If I possessed her remote viewing ability, I'd have her image before me in a heartbeat. A part of me wishes I'd ignored her concerns the night we were together and marked her as mine because it drives me crazy she perceives my emotions, but I get nothing. And, the longer we're apart, the more agitated my beast becomes, clawing at my brain to go to her, no matter the cost.

Just as I doze off, my phone chirps on the bedside table.

'Zach made contact, meeting set for tonight, midnight. Why does everything always happen at the witching hour? Just saying. Pls be here, NOT teleconferenced in, at 11. Depending how things go, we will meet with the demon the following night. UGH. Texting that gives me chills. Get rest. Meeting in war room. Still makes me LOL my studio is now a war room. Love u big guy.'

Whoa, she must be anxious. Nicole is not big on emotions. *'I'll be there. U okay?'*

'Geez, can't I say I love u without everyone thinking I'm going into meltdown?'

'Haha, love u 2. U talk to Lu?' I wince even as I hit send.

'Duh, she lives here.'

'I meant, how is she?'

'A moody bitch. Btw if she's feeding from u now, u need to juice her up before the big game, if u get my meaning.

'Maybe u could talk to her, calm her down.' Christ. What am I, in high school?

'Just so you know, I rarely have that effect on people.'

'Good point. Never mind. See u at 11.'

I rub at the burning ache in my chest. My mate is ravenous. While I am pleased she followed my orders and didn't feed from anyone else, at the same time, I'm furious. Her insecurity, secrecy, and pride forced her to stay away, to go hungry. Again. Lu needs to be at full strength to face Zach.

Decision made, I leap from the bed, draw the drapes closed, making sure not even a single ray of light shines through, pull on jeans, and text my stubborn ass female.

'U need to feed before the meeting. Prepped bedroom, can u trace here?' No response. *'Not a request. Either you come here or I will come 2 u.'*

'Give me a few.'

I exhale. The vamp is beyond hungry if she is willing to teleport during the day. Is it too dangerous? She's weak from lack of blood, and the sleep must weigh heavy on her at this hour.

I really need to do more research on the ins and outs of vampires. No matter our issues, only my blood will strengthen my mate. I would kill anyone who dared to touch what's mine.

My bare feet sink into the plush carpet as I pace at the end of the bed. Her naked, pink bottom fills my vision. I stab my fingers through my hair for the tenth time and will my erection away. Today is about feeding my female and preparing her for the battle to come. Nothing more. Lu needs to take the first step. I won't force her no matter how much my beast demands it.

One second I'm alone, the next the breathtaking creature stands before me. Faded blue jeans hug her lean hips. Pink flip flops highlight her blood-red nail polish. An oversized pink hoodie with the words, *I just can't adult today*, hugs her breasts. The long, dark hair rests in a haphazard bun on top of her head.

Fuck me. She was already in bed. Naked? My cock stiffens to the point of pain.

"You don't have to do this."

The comment irritates me. "How else will you nourish yourself?"

She shrugs. "Blood bank."

The fact she didn't say another male eases my temper somewhat. In two strides, one hand wraps around her neck, and the other encompasses her trim waist. "Is that what you want?"

She swallows at my aggression, but her chin lifts with steel resolve. "No."

"What do you need, angel?" I shiver when her scrutiny drops to the pulse hammering in my throat.

"You."

The whisper is my only warning before she strikes. The erotic sting of her fangs, combined with her strong arms wrapping around my neck, has my beast puffing its chest in satisfaction.

I palm her ass and lift until those lean, muscular thighs envelop my waist, before striding to the lounger in the corner. No way in hell I'm getting near the bed. Each deep pull on my vein is like a direct tug on my cock.

A few minutes ago, I vowed Lucretia should make the first move, and even though I want to rip her clothes from her luscious body and devour every inch of her, I force my fists to grip the cushion and my hips to remain in place.

Lu stills the second my touch leaves her ass. But instead of pulling away, stiff fingers grab fistfuls of my hair, and she draws deep on my vein, grinding her core against my throbbing hardness.

I'm consumed with images of sinking inside her tightness while she feeds, reveling in the convulsions gripping my length when she shatters. Suckle the perfect breasts. Ravage her sweet pussy and ass with my tongue.

No. No. No. Lu needs to come to me without hunger driving her.

After several more minutes of my life essence flowing down her throat, sweat beading my forehead and my fingers cramped from my death grip on the chair, her fangs finally retract. I can barely manage to keep the groan submerged when her warm tongue slides along my skin to close the punctures.

"I taste your desire. Your claim on me," she pants in my ear.

"Do I have a claim on you?" I ask.

Lu leans back, studying my expression. A small drop of blood smears her lower lip. My blood. "Since the second I saw you," she admits, and hope fills my chest. "Why did you join the human wars?" She blurts out, nodding towards the pictures on the wall.

The last thing I want is to talk about my past, but if I'm asking for her trust, shouldn't it go both ways? Maybe it's time I opened up about what happened.

Unconsciously, I swipe the blood off her lip, ready to bare my soul, my deepest darkest regrets to the scrumptious woman straddling my hips.

"I've embroiled myself in the human battles since the civil war."

"How did you hide the fact you weren't aging?"

I shrug. "Long stretches between wars, new identities."

"The immortal conflicts were not enough for you?"

Her sad smile stirs the remembered nightmares of my past. "Each human fight I involved myself in had a purpose. For myself. For the country. The civil war determined what kind of society this would be. The northern victory preserved the United States as one nation and ended the institution of slavery that had divided it from its beginning. This is my home. I felt compelled to help in any way I could.

A hundred years later, I rejoined the military right after they established the navy SEALS in 1962. Their grit, perseverance, and skill intrigued me. I've been a union officer, a marine, and Navy SEAL. The human military is where I discovered my passion for Krav Maga and..."

The screeching of twisted metal. Glass imploding. Blood.

"What happened?" Lu asks, reading my emotions.

"My impatience and selfishness killed my fiancé." At Lu's shocked gasp, I stand abruptly and gently place her feet on the carpet, the need for space overwhelming. Gruesome images bombard me as I stride to the fireplace and grip the wooden mantle.

"I needed one more hour of flight training to procure my pilot's license. My fiancé, Jasmine, was my instructor. I was leaving for the Middle East the next day, so I convinced her to take us up, even with a bitch of a storm brewing on the horizon."

Blood. Shattered bone. Death.

My grip on the mantle splinters the wood as I transport back to the horrific night that changed my life.

"About twenty minutes after take-off, the aircraft entered a zone of strong turbulence. Lightning struck the plane, causing a fire on the right wing which separated, along with part of the left wing. We crashed in flames into mountainous terrain. A large tree branch impaled Jas through the chest. She died instantly, but it took me a week to extract her body and haul us both out of there."

Without a word, Lu steps up behind me and wraps her arms around my waist. "I'm so sorry, Kurtis. That must have been horrifying."

Bitterness creeps up my throat at her sympathy. "All I thought about was myself, how I wanted to become the first Navy SEAL pilot. I should never have insisted we go up in such a storm. My need for glory killed her."

"What was her rank?" Lu asks, and I frown.

"She was a Naval Aviation Instructor."

"So, she trained pilots? She was your trainer?"

"Yes. What are you getting at?"

When she hesitates, I turn.

"Kurtis. She was in charge—your commander, NOT your fiancé. If she felt conditions were unsafe, she should have denied your request." She lays her palm on my cheek, her expressive eyes sad but determined.

A simple statement said by many, but coming from Lu, a seasoned soldier, it somehow frees a small portion of the guilt that's weighed me down for decades.

In a move so fast it's a blur, Lucretia grips my wrist, slides my thumb between pink lips to suck the smeared droplet I wiped from her mouth earlier. Amber swirls as she studies me with the intensity of a deadly hawk as she suckles and nibbles the flesh of my pad.

Lust shoots through my being with the swiftness of a locomotive, dissipating the past in a millisecond. Her warm tongue hardens my cock with a painful demand and jacks my heart rate. She slips my thumb from her mouth in a slow sensual glide. Lava flickers in her gaze.

"Do my needs disgust you?"

"No."

"Does my past?"

"No."

"Then, why?"

"The men who used a child in such a way disgusted me," I confess, my sole focus on the female before me as I let the tragedy of the long-ago slither back to the dark, dusty corner where it belongs. "I was ashamed of how I treated you after you revealed your initiation into sex. I feared your experiences tainted your perspective."

She frowns, confusion shadowing her expression. "I admit, my initial few times were... unfortunate." Understatement of the fucking century no doubt. "But I didn't uncover my darker needs until after my turning. Quite by accident, I discovered a little pain heightened my pleasure."

My cock twitches at her confession, and my lungs expand. "Then who taught you it was wrong?" Her face shuts down, and she backs away before I can stop her. A growl bubbles in my chest and I grit my teeth against the beast demanding the soft femininity of its mate back in our arms.

I advance on her. "Who, Lucretia?"

She retreats until her thighs hit the bed, and her butt plops on the mattress. When trembling fingers rub her forehead, the anger vanishes in an instant. My vampire is fighting a losing battle: sleep.

"I should go," she whispers, trying to keep her lids open.

"Stay with me," I command, forgetting my earlier vow to let her take the first step. "Provide me the opportunity to watch over you while you rest."

She exhales a shaky breath and slips her feet from her flip-flops. "Okay," she mumbles, dark lashes drooping. "But no more questions."

"Copy that. Will you allow me to undress you and put you to bed?"

"Okay," she whispers again without opening her eyes.

To be honest, I've never been around a vampire while they slept, and I'm not sure what to expect. I reach out to lift her, but she collapses back on the comforter. A little panicked, I press my fingers to her throat, and the pulse is shockingly slow. I scrutinize the barely discernible rise and fall of her chest. Is this coma-like state normal for a vamp?

With quick, efficient movements, I remove her clothes. I can't help admiring my female's beauty, the unbelievable suppleness of her skin, the perfection of the curves and valleys. The distinctive strawberry and cream scent stir my senses as I nestle her lax body under the sheets.

I brush a gentle kiss on her lips and wonder if she's aware of my presence, even as satisfaction warms my heart. She may not entrust me with her secrets, but she trusts me enough to watch over her during her most vulnerable time. That has to account for something.

Since I've not slept in days, I kick my jeans off and climb in next to her, arranging her delectable body snug against mine, her head on my chest.

I work the band around her bun loose and massage her scalp until her silken strands flow down her back.

Lu sighs and snuggles closer. This is my life's purpose. To protect, nourish, and care for my mate. Mentally, physically, and sexually. Now, if I could get her on board, nothing else in the world would matter.

"I will not fail you, angel," I whisper to the sleeping vampire in my arms.

CHAPTER 30

Kurtis

Pitch blackness leaves me disoriented when scalding, soft lips and roaming hands wake me. I don't usually sleep with the drapes closed so I have no means of discerning what time it is. Not that I care when Lu's warm tongue swirls around my nipple before gently biting down.

"Mmmm, Lucretia." She climbs over me to give the other one the same treatment. Lust pools hot in my gut, straight to my pulsing dick.

"You taste like citrus and the wilds of the forest," she whispers before sucking and licking a path down my abdomen.

I flip on the bedside lamp, the desire to observe my mate pleasure me too hard to resist. Beautiful golden orbs flick my direction, their wicked intent plainly evident. With hair skewed from slumber, her body lush and warm, she grins and her fangs descend. I groan imagining them sinking into my cock.

"I'm still hungry." Her grin widens, and I hope she means for more than blood. The compulsion to capture her by her glorious mane and fuck her exquisite mouth has the beast growling.

"I am all yours, angel. Do with me whatever you desire."

"Whatever I desire?" She wavers in her pursuit of my thickening cock, the lust in the amber pins mine. "That's a dangerous statement, shifter."

"I live on the wild side," I tease. "I'm not afraid."

Her face turns serious. "You should be."

I presume she's speaking about more than a sexual encounter, but I let it go for now. "Nothing between us is off-limits, but I have a couple of rules."

"More rules?"

I laugh at her dramatic eye roll. "Yes. One: I do not share. It'll only be you and me in the bedroom. Are we clear?"

"A safe bet, because I would slaughter any woman who tried to touch you."

"Ditto. Rule number two: Never lie or withhold your desires from me. If I propose or undertake anything you enjoy or detest, communicate it to me, and I'll do the same. Understood?"

"Yes, Sir," she whispers, her lashes lowering demurely. "Now may I proceed?"

I grin. "By all means."

She slides down my body and grasps my firmness in her fist before tasting her way up the span from balls to tip. "Do you like that?" she challenges in a gruff murmur.

"Absolutely," I grunt and smooth the hair from her face.

"What about this?" she asks before dropping her head and boldly taking both testicles into her hot, moist mouth. I spread my thighs to allow her room as her tongue swirls across and around them while she suckles. She strokes my cock in a strong-upward jerk.

"Fuck yes." Her warmth consuming me is incredible, and I fist the sheets to keep from seizing control. Lush lips travel my inner thigh, a fang scraping along the interior from my knee to groin.

When those lethal fangs suddenly sink into my femoral artery, I nearly shoot my load, but Lu's rough grip at the base of my shaft keeps me from erupting. With each deep drag, my hips buck and my balls tighten. I never imagined having a vampire feed from me would be this erotic or addictive. I would gladly nourish her every damn night.

The grasp on my cock eases, and the strong, delicate touch introduces a slow glide in time with each tug on my vein. The two sensations become one, and I imagine all the numerous veins available to sustain my mate.

The second her tongue licks the punctures closed, I bolt upright and grip her waistline, flip her around, and settle back with her glistening pussy over my face. "I want to feast on your sweetness while you do the same," I declare and latch onto her pink, wet folds.

"Oooh, fun," she giggles before leaning down and engulfing me with her oh-so-talented mouth.

This is sensory overload. Her sucking, licking, and gentle biting tries to distract me from the incredible scent and flavor of my mate. My tongue flicks her clit repeatedly, sucks hard, nibbles, and bites my way to her opening before burrowing between the clenching folds. The pinkly puckered hole receives equal consideration, and by her moans reverberating down my cock, I need not inquire if she's enjoying it. If there's one thing I've discovered about my female, her ass is her highest erogenous zone.

I release a deep, vibrating growl of approval when my head hits the back of her throat and her fingers fondle my testicles, rubbing the sensitive spot just below. I slip my forefinger, glossy with her juices, in her tight anus, gently thrusting it rhythmically while ravaging her slick folds. Lu rides me, pushing and pulling to counteract my finger. My arm clamps around her midriff to hold her still.

"God, Kurtis."

I ease another digit inside and delve my tongue deeper into her pussy, mirroring the action of my fingers. Her glorious scent and essence blanket me, coating my lips and chin. I would gladly spend the next millennia right here, feasting on my mate's juices.

"Kurtis," she pants. "I need—I need to—"

"Come, angel," I command, penetrating her with my tongue once more. I release her waist to rub the swollen bundle beneath my chin. Lucretia explodes. Wave after wave of clenching earthquakes, her cries muffled around my girth. Before the tremors cease, I introduce a third finger, preparing the delectable ass for what's coming. Lu keens low against my cock, renewing her administrations with vigor and I'm so close it's all I can manage to keep from spending my seed down her throat.

She whines in protest when I withdraw my fingers and hoist her mouth from my length. "Lay on your belly with a pillow under your hips," I direct and set her crossways on the sheets.

Lu licks her swollen lips in anticipation before snatching a cushion and doing as commanded. My mate lying prone on my bed with her sweet, delectable ass propped up begs for a good spanking.

I stride over to the armoire and select a large butt plug with a purple jewel at the end. Next, I capture a broad paddle the width of her cute behind. Amber liquid follows me with intense curiosity as I arrange the toys on the mattress beside her. Climbing on the bed, I straddle her hips and cage her in with my elbows bordering her shoulders.

"Has anyone ever fucked your deliciously sweet ass, Lucretia?" I breathe in her ear as her muscular cheeks rub against my hardness.

"No."

"Do you want me to fuck you…" I lean on one hand to run the head of my cock between the cleft, swirling her anus with my pre-cum. "Here?"

"Yes," she sighs, and I smack her bottom hard. My throbbing length twitches at the resulting sting in my palm.

"Yes, what?"

"Yes, Sir. Please."

I vibrate with the desire to possess every entry. "We need to prepare you a little first. Lift your hips."

I slide down her thighs until I'm resting on her bare feet. She wiggles her toes enticingly before lifting her butt into a downward dog position. Unable to help myself, I lean forward, spread her cheeks wide, and devour her, wetting her tight opening.

Lu keens low, pushing against my face. "I love your mouth there."

I ease back. "Then you're going to love this." I dip the tip of the plug into the juices soaking her core before drawing it up to her puckered entrance. With a slight nudge, her muscles release to accommodate the toy. Her sharp inhale has me glancing up at the mass of hair shrouding her face.

"You okay, angel?"

"It burns."

"You wish me to stop?"

"Fuck no."

Her low guttural growl eggs me on, and I press forward. It descends a little further. With a round cheek gripped in my palm, I slide it back and surge deeper. "Relax your muscles, Lucretia."

The second the constriction around the toy eases, I plunge until it's seated all the way.

"Hell's bells, it hurts, but you're right, I love it." Her honesty pleases me, and I lean over and kiss her shoulder. "Please, don't stop," she whimpers.

I reach up and gently push her hair to the side to observe her face. "I have no intention of stopping, angel. Just giving your body a second to adjust. I'm much bigger than this toy, so I need your walls relaxed a bit."

"Oh." She beams, and my heart softens.

I step off the bed and snatch my chosen paddle. "Do not move." Without preamble, I smack her ass dead center, striking the plug.

"God," she gasps, her fingers clutching the sheets.

"You enjoy that?" I inquire.

"Y... Yeah...yes...yes, Sir." Her eyes practically roll back in her head.

It's the green light I demanded. Smack, smack, smack. With each strike I make certain the heavy middle hits the purple jewel. In no time, her cheeks pinken and soon turn an erotic bright crimson. Lu frantically gyrates her pelvis and gauging by her harsh moaning, my woman is close. I love how she gets off on being spanked. My lust turns into a raging inferno insisting I command her mind and body to my will, bring her to heights of ecstasy she's never experienced.

"Hold still, Lucretia." Immediately she freezes. Just to make sure she'll obey; I swat her several more times. Her thighs tense, but she stays immobile. "Good girl." I abandon the paddle and pass my fingers along the crease in her magnificent red behind. She whimpers but doesn't move. "Relax, angel." The second the stricture on the plug lessons, I slide it from her. "Place your hips on the pillow." When she complies, I straddle her hips and plunge my engorged cock into her saturated core, thrusting deep to coat the length with evidence of her arousal before withdrawing and positioning it at her tight entrance. A slight push and the head slips into the well-prepared opening, but it grips like a delectable vice. I shove a little harder, and Lu instinctively relaxes the muscles until I slip deeper, inch by delicious inch until my balls rest against her cheeks.

"Ready?" At her nod, I glide out before surging forward. It's so tight, and I grit my teeth to keep from bursting. Buried once more, I ease my torso over her back, the fever from her reddened butt warming my groin. While my thighs grip hers, I support most of my weight on one hand. With the other, I fist her long locks, wrap it around my wrist, and undulate my hips in a gradual smooth rhythm to allow her channel more time to accept my girth.

"Kurtis?" Her voice swells with wonder.

"Yes, angel?"

"More. Harder. Deeper."

With a low growl, I give my mate what she calls for, tug her hair, so her neck arches backward, and ride her in earnest. Lu takes it all, arching back and forcing me further. Supporting herself on one elbow, she reaches behind and clutches my ass; her nails dig deep. When her needy sobs become frenzied, my canines extend and pressure tightens my balls. The beast demands her flesh. To mark her. Own her. Possess her.

My snarl is a violent demand, and Lu submits to my call, tipping her head to the side to expose her vulnerable neck.

The punishing hunger to claim what's mine hammers through me with each thrust. At the base of my brain, a notion seeks to encroach. There's a reason biting her is a terrible idea, but sensation after sensation obliterates any coherent thought. My one driving force is pleasuring my mate and completing our bond.

I rear back to strike, all four canines salivating with the demand for her flesh when Zach's image flashes through my frontal lobe. It hits me like a baseball bat to the temple. If she goes into the meeting tonight with my mark, the fucker will execute her outright. Must protect what's mine. My bad decisions destroyed one woman; I'll never allow it to happen again.

Through sheer force, I override the beast's insistent pleas and order my canines to recede. Gently, I ease my torso over her back, freeing her hair. With the bulk of my upper body on my elbows, our bodies fuse. Lu's slimmer, more delicate frame is concealed by mine as I continue to pump my hips in a slow, sensual rhythm.

"As much as I crave to complete our bond, angel, I can't mark you. It would place your life in further danger." I kiss the spot my beast requires, the tender flesh between her neck and shoulder. She moans and shoves against me.

"I'm close, Kurtis," she pants and weaves our fingers together by her head. "Make me forget everything but this."

I heed my mate's demands and reach down between her hips and the pillow. My rough pads find her swollen bundle and press down in sluggish sensual circles. She clenches tight in response, and I can hold back no longer.

"Come with me, angel," I command before we shatter as one into a million beautiful fragments. The muscles in her anus milk me like a vice I never wish to escape. Buried deep in my mate, our panting breaths mingle, our heartbeats race.

Tonight alters everything. My soul connected with hers, and I will never let her go. She is my other half. Lu sighs as I rain gentle kisses along her neck and shoulders.

"Are you okay?"

"More than okay," she murmurs. "I love you inside me, your weight on top of me, and your scent surrounding me."

At her heartfelt words, my cock twitches to life once more. "Ready for round two?" I propose.

"As much as I yearn to devote all night exploring each other, we have a meeting."

I growl at the reminder and glimpse the clock on the nightstand, stunned to observe it's already ten p.m. I've never slept so soundly or for that long in—ever.

"Loosen your muscles, angel," I advise as I lean away slightly. As soon as the addictive constriction eases, I withdraw from the tight, warm cocoon. She sighs and flops her head down on the mattress, her arms hanging limply over the side.

"That was the most incredible thing I've ever experienced. Who knew there were so many nerves and pleasure points back there?"

I chuckle and whack the redness already fading from her ass. "Shower woman. Now."

"I can't move."

"You better, cause I'm not done with you."

I laugh outright when her head pops up, and a huge grin spreads her lips.

CHAPTER 31

Lucretia

"Okay, go over the plan one more time," Logan demands.

"For Pete's sake," Nicki huffs. "How many times do you need to hear the same thing?"

"We call it perfecting your strategy, my love. You should try it."

Oh, brother. Nicki's sarcasm is rubbing off on the commander. But a repeat is probably a good idea anyway because my mind keeps wandering back to Kurtis's confession.

My throat tightens from unshed tears at the horror he endured in that forest, but also the pain he still carries with him because of it. His fiancé was in charge, his instructor. If the woman had put her foot down and grounded him, she'd still be alive.

'Then she'd be the one enjoying his enormous cock in her ass,' my vampire whines.

I rub the back of my neck at such selfish thoughts, but I can't stop my nipples hardening when I remember how his size hurt just enough to give me the pleasure/pain scenario I crave. The ultimate was having his tongue there. Holy mother of God. It was erotic and naughty. Not as taboo if I were human, or an immortal who ate food, but still.

"Lu?"

I lick my lips, tasting his silken hardness in my mouth. I really want to sink my fangs into the bulging vein wrapping his length and suck him until he comes, but I should probably make sure he's okay with it first.

"Lu?"

"Oh, sorry. I ah—I was thinking about what I would say to Zachariah tomorrow night." A believable lie. I flick another glance at my mate, but the knowing smirk on his face makes me think I didn't pull it off. At all.

"And what exactly will that be?" Sebastian asks, having traced in from parts unknown in his search for Alex.

I shrug. "To convince him I hate Nicki enough I'm willing to betray her and submit to him." A low rumble vibrates from Liam and Kurtis. From my mate I expect it, but from the werewolf? He and I better sit down at some point and engage in a serious discussion about his connection to me.

I ignore them both and turn my focus back on Logan and Nicole. "With our past, it shouldn't take too much convincing. I just need to draw him close to the shield, have Icarus open it, and we grab him."

"Who's history, Lu? Yours and mine, or yours and good ol' Zach's?" Nicki inquires with a raised brow.

"Both, my lady."

"Where are we tracing him?" The Oracle questions. His demeanor is always calm and confident.

"The second you get in touch with me, the task force will meet here." She points to a spot on the map spread across the table. It highlights the vampire castle. To the southeast, at the edge of an enormous circle indicating the shield, a large clearing is visible. "Everyone except Liam; sorry, bro, you are too young to face the devil spawn. Lu, the minute we have Zach, trace away. Do not look at King Darath.

"Satellite images show the demons set up camp in this open glade," Bastian informs us and enlarges the area on the monitor mounted on the wall. I gasp at the number of tents filling the snow-covered meadow. Good Lord, there must be hundreds of demon warriors waiting to lay siege to our home.

"We will meet on the camp's southeast perimeter," Nicki explains for the third time, pointing to the big X on the map. I guess X does mark the spot. Although in this case, it doesn't reveal a golden treasure, instead, it takes them directly to the son of Satan.

Fear settles in my gut, and I stare at my mate over the table. '*Whatever you do, Kurtis, stay alive.*' Startled sapphires shift to mine. '*Don't respond, telepathy is one-sided right now. Do not engage King Darath.*' He offers a subtle nod of understanding before his scrutiny darkens to traverse my face, down my neck, before stalling on my breasts encased in leather. My core clenches with need.

'*Would you object to having my fangs in your cock*?' I ask and press my lips together to hold back a smile when he shifts in his seat. He shakes his head slightly, and I want to crawl the width of the table and do just that, not caring about the others. Feeling emboldened, I tease him further. '*I can't get the sensation of your tongue on my ass out of my mind.*'

Kurtis's jaw tightens, and his fingers clutch the arms of his chair. Damn. Now I hate the fact the telepathy is one-sided. I'd love to experience his sexy growl in my head.

"Oh, for God's sake," Nicki barks. Her angry glower zeros in on me. "I can hear you, you know."

Holy shit!

Warmth spreads through my face as I drop my chin to my chest, hoping my hair hides the embarr-assment highlighting my cheeks like a neon sign. At Kurtis's chuckle, I glare at him beneath my lashes.

He fucking knew?

Since telepathy is only possible between bloodlines or mates, unless you're Nicole apparently, I guess the cat's out of the bag. The halfling now knows, if she didn't already suspect, I've mated the prince. I shrug mentally, I'll worry about that later.

"Any more questions?" Logan asks, jerking me from the mental foreplay with my mate. We all shake our heads, so he glances at his brother. "Any luck finding Alex?"

A deep sigh escapes and fatigue lines his face. "I was close enough a few times to catch her sweet, vanilla scent, but the fiery little valkyrie is slippery. Make sure your negotiating points with Darath include him releasing his mind control on Alexandria."

"Of course," Nicole pipes in indignantly. "She's at the top of the list, Bastian. By the way, how are you going to get her to complete the bond with you? She loathes vampires."

Sebastian's sapphire eyes darken. "About as much as I hate the idea of a mate. We will cross that gorge when I find her." Nicki nods, knowing Bastian's our only play to retrieve her best friend.

"Okay, kids. I think a little R&R is in order before shit gets real tomorrow night," the halfling announces, rubbing her palms together. "I'm ordering you all to the LeLoo for singing and dancing. If I don't perform soon, I'll go postal."

CHAPTER 32

Kurtis

"Okay, I can honestly say, I'm freaking the fuck out to meet this spawn from hell," Nicki confesses in a harsh whisper after our quartet materializes at the edge of the demon encampment.

Thick snow blankets the forest floor, and frigid air penetrates the fleece lining my leather jacket. I force a little shifter energy to warm my body and regard the hundreds of tents set up in probably the lone clearing in a thousand miles. Brilliant orange from campfires dots the landscape. The scene reminds me of my father's battle encampments when I was a child. In two centuries the weapons changed, but the implementation for laying siege to a castle remains constant when you can't draw the attention of the human world.

"What's the plan? We waltz right through the camp and hope we're not slaughtered?" I ask in a low hiss.

"Don't get your panties in a bunch. Give me a second. I should be able to pinpoint the king's location. I'm sure he's projecting some strong emotional vibes."

The Moretti's move to her sides and I take a position at her six. With so many demons in one place, my skin tingles with their energy, and unease slithers up my spine.

"Make it quick before we're spotted," I murmur while scanning the encampment for any movement in our direction. Logan and Bastian do the same.

Crouched low, soundless in the darkness, as hundreds of gigantic trees camouflage our presence against the brilliant light from the half-moon, we exhale into our cupped palms to keep white plumes from marking our location.

The weight of my swords at my back comforts me, but even with the Moretti brother's legendary strength and speed, my power and fighting skills, and Nicki's multitude of abilities, we don't stand a chance in hell against so many.

"Got him," she whispers. Logan and Bastian grasp her tense shoulders as she clutches my wrist in a death grip. I inhale as she scatters our molecules straight to the demon king. It's hard to explain why I always hold my breath when tracing. I guess I foolishly believe I can somehow control it if something goes wrong.

I expected us to land inside the king's tent, so I'm startled when we appear at the opposite edge of the clearing. I clutch Nicki's shoulder to regain my bearings. God, I hate teleporting.

'*You okay, big guy?*' Nicki asks in my brain, and I nod as nausea eases and my vision clears.

Over the top of her head, the mysterious and elusive demon king slowly turns to face us. I do a quick survey of the area for any guards waiting to attack.

He's dressed for battle. The tall, muscular frame is encased in thick black leather from his broad shoulders to the big boots on his feet. I hate to admit it, but the creature is an impressive being. Those blood-red irises keep my nerves on edge, so I edge in tighter to Nicki.

"The prophesied halfling," he says, his voice low and gruff. "You are incredibly brave or extremely stupid."

"I've heard a lot about you, King Darath. All of it nauseating by the way."

"I love it when my reputation precedes me." His smile tightens the muscles along my spine. "What do you hope to gain, vampire? Even with the powerful Moretti brothers and the shifter prodigy, you are no match for my army. Or me."

"I have no wish to tango with you, demon. I'm here to offer you a proposition."

His dark eyebrow arches. "Intriguing." The grin widens, showcasing massive fangs. "What could you possibly bargain with besides your delectable body?" Logan growls low at the comment. Jagorach doesn't even glance his way. The eerie red regard travels Nicki's frame before flicking my direction. "You are no longer queen, my dear. You are of no use to me, but if you offer up the shifter, I might be interested in hearing you out."

Nicki laughs, and I frown down at her. "Oh man," she says, wiping a pretend tear from her eye. "I would pay big bucks to see that. Although, if I know Kurtis, it would be more of a WWF fight then an actual sexual encounter."

Damn straight.

"How disappointing," he pouts, and my jaw clenches. His gaze shifts back to Nicki. "Then you possess nothing I want, little one."

"Oh, but I do." She steps forward. The three of us go to proceed with her, but our limbs are frozen in place. I glance down at my feet, wondering why they aren't obeying my brain's commands. My head and arms move. Why won't my damn legs get with the program?

"Goddamnit, Nicole," Logan bellows, his muscles bulging in an attempt to free himself.

"This is a bad plan, Nicki," Bastian snarls.

"Calm down, boys. I need a minute with the king without you hovering over me."

"Your powers are impressive, child." Jagorach steps towards her and our growls surround us like a blanket. "And quite the entourage you have there. Please tell me you enjoyed all three at once."

Ignoring his sexual comment, Nicki inquires, "Do you know who the current vampire king is, Darath?"

"I may be good looking, but do not think for a second I am stupid," he says with a frown. "Trezzo Massaro, the Italian region's leader."

"Why do you possess such a hard-on to kill the vampire ruler no matter who's on the throne?" Nicki asks her head tilted to the side in curiosity. "A month ago, you wanted me dead."

When my big toe twitches, I inhale a sharp breath and concentrate all my energy into moving the next one. If I can get function back in my feet, I might break free.

"No, wait." She holds up a finger. "Let me guess. It has something to do with my dearly departed father." She takes another step closer, and my left foot moves a millimeter.

At the mention of King Giordano, Jagorach's eyes burn a deep red. "Dimitri massacred my family ten years ago." He advances, and Nicki maintains her ground. "When you killed him, you ripped my revenge from my fingertips."

Darath's fury pulses through the air, tightening around us. Logan glances at me. I subtly point to my foot, moving it another millimeter. He nods, bunching his thigh muscles, and his boot shifts forward. Bastian's big shit kicker slides an inch to the left.

"When his daughter was next in line, I nearly danced with glee," he continues, his smile pure evil. "If I cannot kill the father, why not the heir and future queen? Unfortunately, you fucked that up as well. I find killing you when you are no longer on the throne holds no appeal. Besides," he waves a hand in my direction. "You aligned with shifters, werewolves, and if my intel is correct, the fierce little valkyries. As much as I want my revenge, I have no desire to wage war with half of the immortal world. My only option is this Massaro."

"Uh-huh, that's all very interesting, and I totally understand where you're coming from."

For Christ's sake, her sarcasm will get us all killed. Anger builds, heating through my body, and I call on my beast for help to break Nicki's hold.

She steps into the imposing king's space, craning her neck to look up at him before boldly placing her palm on his chest. I don't know whose growl is louder, Logan's or Bastian's.

Darath's rage diminishes, and his lips twitch with amusement. "You are saucy, halfling. I like that about you."

"Well, you're gonna love me in a second." Her smirk widens his grin.

"I think I love you already. Ditch the vampire. You and I could enjoy some real fun."

"Trust me when I say, you couldn't handle me."

I snort. "Truer words were never spoken, Darath."

"Amen to that," Bastian chimes.

Logan's silence is disconcerting. The furious blaze remains laser-focused on Nicki's palm centered on the king's massive chest.

"What if I told you I could offer you, not only the current vampire king but Dimitri's son?"

Darath's grin disappears. His eyes narrow with suspicion. "Are you informing me Trezzo Massaro is your stepbrother?"

"That's exactly what I'm telling you. Why else would the council grant him the throne? He had a legitimate claim."

"If I find you lied to me, young halfling, I will rip you to shreds, and everyone you care about."

"Not before I drain you dry, demon spawn," Logan growls, his huge fangs on full display.

Jagorach glances down at our feet. "I think your hold is slipping, my dear."

"It's good to give them a sense of achievement," Nicki remarks with a glance over her shoulder at our trio, her grin wicked. The king roars with laughter.

Fury, hot and swift, sizzles through me. If she were my mate, I would take her over my knee and tan her hide. By the near-feral look on Logan's face, it's precisely what he's contemplating.

"Let's not add to my mate's rage." She turns back to Darath, wisely removing her palm from his torso before retreating a step. "I believe we can help each other."

His expression sobers, and he crosses his arms over his broad chest. "You have my attention."

"Through a DNA test, the council has proved Trezzo Massaro is actually Zachariah Giordano and getting rid of Dimitri's son satisfies your revenge and puts me back on the throne, which according to the prophecy is where I'm needed." Nicki saunters over to us, flicks a nervous gaze at her mate's livid face, and twirls to challenge King Darath. "I can bring the evil little shit to you, but I have stipulations."

"It would disappoint me if you did not."

"I've heard you boast a hard-on for my territory..."

"My dear, I always enjoy a hard-on, especially for your territory," he interrupts with a devilish smile. Green fire flickers in Logan's enraged stare.

Nicki laughs. "Stop enraging my mate, Darath or our alliance will be over before it begins."

The king smirks. "My apologies, little halfling, do proceed."

"In exchange for eliminating our mutual enemy, I'll grant you the Arizona territory." Darath's gaze sharpens with interest. "With the stipulation that you sign a peace treaty between our people and allow all vampires living in the region to either leave or continue to stay with the promise no harm will come to them." Bastian's hand brushes Nicki's arm. She glances at him and he nods.

"I want California," he counters. "I love the beach."

"Arizona or no deal, and you and your men can freeze to death in the Canadian wilderness waiting on a shield that will never fall."

"You drive a hard bargain, beautiful, but you have an accord."

"Awesome," she exclaims, and Logan reaches into the inner pocket of his long black duster and produces the peace treaty. "You'll find I'm like a girl scout, King Darath; always prepared."

I clench my jaw with impatience, mentally willing this meeting to end. I want time with my mate before the sleep claims her. She faces Zachariah tomorrow, and she needs to relax and forget all this shit until then. The minute this fiasco is over, and Zach is dead; she'll wear my mark. Damn the consequences.

Once Darath and Nicole sign the treaty, she steps back into our protective half-circle. "I'll contact you the second we acquire him, so be ready."

"And how exactly are you going to contact me?"

Nicki's head tilts, and Jagorach's eyes widen. "What a new sensation," he whispers, his red gaze glued on Nicki. "I am always in other's minds. It has been a long time since I had mine invaded. You are amazing."

"Yeah, I get that a lot," she says with a teasing smile and reaches back to grab hold of my wrist. "Oh, one more thing." Her tone alters, becoming the deadly warrior I trained. "Release your mind control over the valkyrie Alexandria Svaldana, or I will burn this treaty and you to the ground."

He examines her for several long seconds. I tense, expecting at any moment for the legion of demons behind us to attack. Would Nicki wage war against the Demon Realm over one valkyrie? What am I thinking? In a heartbeat. She'd sacrifice anything for her friends.

"I don't take kindly to threats, but since you have captured my interest and can deliver my greatest desire to me, I will allow it this once." Jagorach's deep tone grates along my skin like steel wool. After a brief pause, he nods. "Done." My muscles relax. "I can honestly say, I am relieved I did not kill you. In all my millennia, I have never encountered a creature as delectable as you."

"Flatterer. Before I go, do you mind if I ask you a personal question?"

"Enquire away."

"Are you actually the spawn of... you know, Satan?"

Jagorach's sudden bark of laughter sends chills up my spine, but it's nothing compared to the ominous sound of hundreds of boots crunching through the snow. A battalion of red-eyed demons advance in our direction and real terror spreads through my chest.

Jagorach leans forward with an amused grin, raises his hand and crosses two fingers. "Lucifer and I are like that."

CHAPTER 33

Lucretia

Kurtis's fear reaches through the miles to stab into my flesh, and I spring from the couch in Nicki's living room; the book I'd been attempting to read thuds to the floor. What the hell? I squeeze my lids shut to block the pounding in my ears, and mentally search for my mate. What would provoke a severe reaction in such a fierce soldier? Were they forced to engage the demons? I will move mountains to defend him, demon king or not.

Before I acquire a bead on his exact whereabouts, the front door slams open. I whirl to confront the threat. My heart stops. The gentle radiance of the porch lights silhouette Zach encased in a black three-piece suit, his tall frame eclipsing the entrance. Shock cements my feet to the floor. How the hell did he get past the shield? This is not good.

I'm about to trace away when his sky-blue eyes land on mine and he whispers the one thing to seal my fate.

"I have your sister."

I gasp. No. It's a lie. I spoke to the caretaker an hour ago, and he assured me Viessa was fine. My gaze flicks to my swords resting against the potbelly stove.

"Fight me, call out to the foul-smelling dog in the garage or trace away, and your twin will pay the price."

Ah. Now I understand why he's keeping his voice low; he doesn't wish to tangle with an enraged werewolf.

Zach lounges in the doorway with casual grace; one hand rests in the pocket of his slacks, the other is open and relaxed by his side. I once regarded this vampire as the finest male I'd ever encountered. Tall and handsome, always attired in dapper clothing, even in jeans and a t-shirt, and in complete control. I now recognize it was a facade to disguise the psychotic evil underneath.

"Bullshit. Prove it." I pray he's bluffing.

He pulls a cell phone from his pocket, punches a few keys, and when he swings the screen my direction, my heart plummets. My twin's image, with a black eye and busted lip, blinks to life. With his arm outstretched to take the selfie, Zach's cheek presses against hers with a shit-eating grin.

Fuck. Fuck. Fuck.

The same smile appears as he re-pockets the phone. "Invite us in, Lu."

Us?

It's then I spot the Guardians outside bordering the entry. Son of a bitch. My vampire screams at me to slam the dense wood in his arrogant face, but with Viessa's life hanging in the balance, my hands are tied.

"Come in."

He ambles through the doorway, the two warriors close on his heels. They gently shut the front door, and I inch a little closer to my weapons.

"Did you truly believe I would fall for the bitch's trap? I have not survived seven centuries and ascended the ranks in vampire society under a fictitious identity because I am foolish." His expression tightens. "The second I received your text, I knew it was a ruse. And until I found your sister to use as leverage, there was no way I was getting close to you, and certainly not on your terms."

"How did you locate her? I talked to the director an hour ago."

"I give you credit. It was not straightforward. I had to call in several markers and extend numerous favors. A matter I am not too thrilled about." He brandishes a finger at me with displeasure. "When I arrived, the facility manager was simple-minded and easy to manipulate. Face it, Lu, there is no escaping me. I am your future." He holds out his palm, beckoning me.

Bile churns in my stomach and terror clogs my throat. Maybe he's right. Perhaps my destiny is to suffer at the hands of this male for my transgressions. Deep down, I understood defeating Zach on my own was precarious, but facing this trio would indeed result in my death.

I have faith. If anything happens to me, the prince would protect and care for Vi if for no other reason than she's my flesh and blood.

Kurtis.

My heart constricts. If I leave will he assume I up and disappeared because of my secrets, or could my mate have confidence in our delicate bond and realize something happened? As much as I yearn for it to be the latter, it places him and Viessa in jeopardy. If I engage these vampires here, the evidence of our battle will clue Kurtis in real quick that I didn't go voluntarily, and the beast would cross heaven and hell to retrieve its mate.

Not to mention, Liam would haul ass in here at the initial sound of trouble. I refuse to put his life on the line. His existence has purpose, meaning. Mine does not, and I deserve what's coming.

"With one phone call, my guards will whip your sister." The long, tapered fingers wiggle at me. "In a blink, I could have you bound and gagged, Lu. However, I prefer you to walk into my embrace willingly."

"Willingly?" I laugh with bitterness. "Nothing is willing about this, Zachariah." Pure venom laces my remarks as I advance another step towards him.

"Semantics," he says with a dismissive shrug. "Hmmm, the closer you get, the harder I become. Interesting. Your body is mine, and it will soon hum with the sweet torment of my touch, *mio amore*, crave it even. The things I plan for us are glorious."

My strides falter several feet away. Nausea rolls in my gut and fear clouds my vision. I've faced numerous enemies as a Guardian, had many close scrapes with death, but taking the final steps to deliver me within inches of my ultimate test seems as though it spans miles, or perhaps I just wish it stretched that far. Zach's intense indigo regard follow every tread, his patience unnerving.

"Why me?" If I stall long enough, Kurtis and the others could appear and together we could eliminate our mutual enemy.

"A fair question," he drawls evenly before placing both hands in his pockets as if we're old friends enjoying a nice chat. "The second I detected you in that alley, I understood the gods aligned with my objective. I had hunted for you and your sister since the moment I learned of your existence."

What in purgatory is he talking about? I blink several times as I mentally search for an explanation.

"You still do not recognize who you are, or the raw power your twin possesses in her scattered brain. *Mio pazzo padre* was too shortsighted to perceive your *lignaggio*."

My lineage? "What do my parents have to do with your crazy father, or you?"

"Your shifter *madre* was your parent, *mio amore*, but the shopkeeper was not your papa," he declares with a quiet chuckle. "It astonishes me you never figured it out."

"What the fuck are you talking about, Trez?" Irritation and anger melt away a chunk of the fear, and I regress to his old nickname. I know who my parents were.

Zach's smile evaporates. His eyes harden to steel. "Watch your mouth. No bride of mine—and the future queen—talks in such a fashion."

Okay. The vamp has officially fallen off the deep end. One second his demeanor is calm and composed, and with a single curse word, his anger erupts and the delusional asshole is back.

"Enough of this. Step into my embrace or your sister suffers. I will not ask again."

Like he's asking? Acceptance weighs heavy on my shoulders as I surrender, my feet dragging with reluctance until I finally walk into his outstretched arms. I've sacrificed much to keep my sister safe. My felony was a secret, right up until Dimitri found her and used her as leverage, adding to my crimes. A cold arm wraps around my waist, and brutal fingers grip my skull. I shudder with revulsion. My life has run full circle, from the father to the son.

It's now or never to seek Kurtis's aid or dissuade his pursuit. My spirit pleads to confess my love, but my vampire rages against such a selfish act. It would place our mate in peril. The prince is a powerful shapeshifter, even more so with an enraged mated beast who would stop at nothing to protect what's his, but Zach has five centuries on the shifter and with enough Guardians at his side to rip my male to shreds.

So what do I do? Break his heart by fooling him into believing I rejected him? With mere seconds to decide, I squeeze my lids shut and crush my world. My heart. My soul

'*Kurtis. I'm leaving.*' Fuck. The pain in my chest spreads. I grit my teeth against the agony hacking at my sternum, ripping the beating muscle to shreds before stomping it to a gory pulp. Tears threaten, and I blink them away, infusing cold steel into my voice. '*I need to be with another vampire. I was mistaken.*

Zach's not the male I imagined. He can provide what you cannot. Don't come after me.'

His rage penetrates my skin like sparks from a fire, and I'm relieved he cannot return my communication. I pray he accepts the lie, even as my selfish side hopes he'll trust in me enough to realize I would never purposely hurt him.

Zach scatters our molecules and severs my connection to Kurtis. Before we re-materialize, determination stiffens my spine. Just because I've agreed to leave with him, doesn't mean I'll submit without a fight. With my last breath, I will protect my mate, my sister, and my queen.

CHAPTER 34

Kurtis

"Damn it, Kurtis. Don't ever fucking struggle when we're teleporting. You could've killed us," Nicki roars the second we emerge in her living room. But her comments do not penetrate the tidal wave of violence and anguish flooding through muscles and tendons like a rampaging river, and my frame morphs; my fangs elongate.

"He is shifting!" Logan shouts and wraps his arms around his mate.

The three vampires disappear to God knows where just as the bones in my body fracture. My vision sharpens, and my clothes rip apart with the detonation of energy. The metamorphoses are no longer painful, it's like a satisfying stretch after sitting for too long, but the misery in my chest forces my head back in a howl of madness and torment to the demolished room.

Need to run. Must get away. Her scent is all over this house. My gaze swivels to the closed front door, and I snarl in frustration, baring my canines. The window it is. I leap over the overturned couch, skid along the piano's slick lid leaving deep grooves in my wake, and dive headfirst through the bay windows.

Pain bursts through my skull as glass shatters in all directions. My paws barely connect with the porch before I'm shoving off again and vaulting over the railing to the dirt driveway. After a vigorous shake to discard the fragments lodged in my fur, I notice Liam exiting the garage. The Moretti's and Nicole try to block my path.

"What happened, big guy?" Nicki asks, worry filling her expression. "Please don't take off. Talk to me."

In animal form, I can only huff or growl a response. Besides, talking about my mate's betrayal is the last thing I wish to do right now. I need to get the hell out of here and run until I'm too exhausted to think.

"Let him leave, Nic," Liam says. "He requires this. He'll tell us when he's ready."

Only another shifter would understand this primordial desire to escape and lick my wounds in private, to drive out my aggression and hurt.

"Please go with him," Nicki begs. "His emotions are all over the place, and he shouldn't be alone."

The king glances at me and I nod, pawing at the ground with restlessness. "Sure," he answers as he undresses. "Head back inside. I'll contact you later."

The second they depart, Liam shifts into an enormous blue-eyed, white wolf, and we sprint at full speed across the drive, plunging into the forest. The inky blackness is no hindrance for our enhanced sight as the massive paws of my closest friend pounds the ground next to mine. His exhilaration at letting our beasts loose soothes me. My malamute form and Liam's wolf are comparable in stature, but it's the streamlined features inherent to all wolves versus my broad head and stocky structure that sets us apart.

Mile after mile we traverse the dense woodlands, vaulting over fallen timbers and full streams. The forest's damp floor never penetrates our thick coats. Rabbits and squirrels scatter at our approach, but tonight isn't about hunting, it's about escaping my ravaged soul.

I press harder until my lungs burn from exertion and my muscles weaken with fatigue. Twenty miles later, when I barely clear the next log, I force myself to ease the pace. Liam matches me stride for stride. The rapid-fire beat of his heart and heavy pants proves he's as exhausted as I am but was prepared to continue as far as I needed.

I scent another stream so I veer left, slow to a lazy trot, and grant my body a chance to normalize.

What just happened? She'd dropped her guard, trusted me enough to sleep the daylight hours away in my arms. And what took place earlier tonight was nothing short of spectacular. Lu relaxed. She seemed content. I would've wagered my land she loved me. The words never escaped her lips, nor mine, but it was in every caress, each kiss. It sparkled in the brilliant amber depths.

How could she say I can't give her what she requires? Or she desires to be with a vampire? And not just any bloodsucker, fucking Zachariah Giordano. I'd offer her the world if she asked. I may not drink her blood like a vamp, but I sure as hell can sink my canines into her flesh if it's a bite she craves.

We approach the stream, and I stroll right in, letting the chilly liquid flow over my paws to cool my elevated temperature. Liam does the same, dropping his massive head to lap at the refreshing water.

If anything, Lu cannot provide what my species expect. A companion who can shift and run beside me, wild and free. Roll in the dirt, hunt, and chase prey. And the ultimate raw reality: to fuck and claim my mate in beast form. I'd gladly forsake all of it to make her mine because those things pale compared to what I experience when in her presence. Her beauty steals my breath, the softness of her voice soothes my inner creature, and a single touch from her silky skin sets me on fire. Behind the frigid exterior rests a vulnerable, passionate female whose insecurities shape her decisions. Right or wrong.

I trot out of the current and transfer back into human form, the desire to confide in my friend paramount. I ease my bare ass on the rough bark of a fallen log and wait for Liam to change. As shifters, nakedness means nothing. The fact two grown males are sitting nude amid the thick forest might appear odd to a mortal or vampire—to us, it's quite normal.

"What's going on, bro?" Liam questions as he sinks to the ground a few feet from me, his back to a giant pine tree.

"She left me." I'm not certain how else to explain it.

"What? When?"

"Right before we showed up at Nicki's, she spoke to me telepathically and announced we were through. Said she needed a vamp, namely Zach."

"Are you kidding me? She dumped you for the Italian fuck?" Anger ignites in his dark regard, and pain lances through me to hear the words out loud. "But how? I sensed her in the house. Did she trace through the shield and join him?"

Good question. “I don’t know, but I no longer sense her. I presume she’s inside the barrier.”

“Damn it. I shouldn’t have worn headphones while recording. I’m sorry, Kurtis, I was so absorbed with finalizing an original song I neglected to pick up a new scent or sound. Are you sure she left willingly?”

While I am pleased to discover Liam is back to singing after his long hiatus following Jimmy’s death, my insides liquefy. Why didn’t my mind go there first? “You think he took her? Icarus said Zachariah couldn’t teleport outside the defensive shield. If that wasn’t the case, and he showed up to abduct her, it doesn’t explain her comments.”

“Maybe the dude has leverage over her? We all believe the Guardian still harbors secrets. What if he’s blackmailing her?”

Liam’s faith in my female shames me. Why didn’t I trust in her? In us. The second I heard her voice say I couldn’t give her what she needed, my brain rebelled. It was the antithesis of what I’ve learned about Lu regarding her emotional and visceral responses to me. I should never have assumed she’d change her mind on a whim and trash our bond. Our link is infinite. She would never throw it away willingly.

“Christ, Liam. I’m such an idiot. That sick bastard took her, doing God knows what to my woman.” My beast rages, my breaths turn harsh. “We need to return and inform the others. Whether Logan and Nicki like it, Icarus needs to lower the damn shield. I will burn the castle to the ground to get her back."

The werewolf king jumps to his feet and I join him. "You got it, bro." We clasp forearms. "Let's go rescue your female and annihilate the bloodsucker."

CHAPTER 35

Lucretia

I watch Zach warily as he circles me, his smoky stare devouring and scrutinizing my snug jeans, Saints t-shirt, and tennis shoes. The four of us materialized in the middle of what looks like a playroom, but with this twisted vampire as the master, it's more of a torture chamber. The two Guardians promptly disappear.

By the heaviness in my chest and the thick, moist stone walls enclosing three sides, I can tell we are in the castle's underground dungeon. The fourth barrier is twelve feet of heavy silver bars broken by the open cell door in the corner. A wide bed with an intricate iron headboard and footboard centers against the rear wall. Large linked chains hang from the ceiling above my head, and along one whole surface, various torture devices gleam in the flickering lights from torches placed around the room. Fear pools in my gut like a thousand slithering snakes.

Based on the unusual layout of the cell, Zach's been a busy little vamp. "Where's my sister, Zach? I demand to see her."

"Indeed."

With casual grace, he strolls over to a wooden console and plucks a remote off the top. A monitor mounted above it comes to life, and I gasp at my own image huddled in the corner of a cage similar to this one.

Viessa's once vibrant mane falls limp and ratted around her shoulders. Dark circles hollow out her vacant stare. Based on the black eye and the purple bruise on her cheek, someone roughed her up, but why isn't she healing?

I observe with increasing trepidation as my mirror image presses the side of her face against the stones and murmurs unintelligibly in a low, raspy voice. She stretches her palm across the surface as if caressing a lover. In a snap, her demeanor changes; she strikes the wall with her fist, shrieking at the top of her lungs, "She's not me! She's not me!"

"Oh, Vi." I choke back a sob. My twin's psychosis has deteriorated. "What did you do to her?" I ask, never taking my gaze from the monitor.

"Nothing. When I retrieved her from the institute she was in this state, and according to the physician, the damages are self-inflicted," he answers before pressing the power button. "I don't think you were getting your money's worth from that facility."

An urge to smash my fist into his arrogant face has them clenching. "Like you give a fuck."

Before I even realize he's moved, my cheek explodes in pain, and for a brief second, I'm weightless until my spine impacts the stone wall with a deafening crunch. My left side slams into the unforgiving concrete floor. Agony radiates up every vertebra and through my arm as I attempt to sit up, but my limb refuses to cooperate. The fall dislocated my shoulder.

"The vile language will cease this minute," Zach says in a low growl. "Do you understand?"

I push up into a seated position with my good arm and brace my throbbing back against the damp wall. With a violent jerk, I pop the joint in place and send healing energy into my spine and cheek before rising to my feet.

I narrow my gaze at the male I once worshipped and respected above all others. The Trez I once knew taught me how to survive, how to fight, but I don't recognize the evil being before me. There's a crazed malevolence in his contemplation I never noted before. Or maybe I ignored it.

Most immortals possess a darker side. For my species, it's our inner vampire. The predator we battle against daily to remain, for lack of a stronger word, human. For shifters and werewolves, it's their beast. Somewhere along the way, Zachariah lost command of his hunter, authorized the sinister part of him to dominate his thoughts and ambitions. Exactly like his father. Toward the end, Dimitri was as crazy as my sister. Although, he mastered the ability to mask his psychosis right up until his demise.

"Do you understand, Lu?" Zach repeats, taking a step towards me.

I lower my lids to present the illusion I'm submitting. In my heart, no matter how long he tortures me, I won't allow him to break me. My body, mind, and soul belong to Kurtis. He is my master in the bedroom, my mate by bond, and the love of my life by choice.

I raise my head, and amber illuminates the demented depths before me. "Fuck. You."

This time when he comes at me, I'm ready. I twist to the side, and his fist smashes into the stone behind me. His bellow is deafening as he swings for me again. I crouch and slam both palms into his rib cage with such force it sends him careening into the console. The wood splits in two, and the monitor shatters against the floor.

Rage clouds my mind, and adrenaline energizes my body, but it's Kurtis's powerful blood that fuels my strength. I hope it can sustain me long enough to immobilize Zach, get the hell out of here, find my sister, and trace us to safety.

Before he gains his feet, I'm on him, my fist crashing into his nose with a loud, satisfying crunch. Where are my damn swords when I need them?

Leaning against the potbelly stove where you abandoned them, idiot.

I swing at him anew, but meaty hands seize me from behind, wrenching my arms with such force my shoulder dislocates again with a resounding pop, driving to my knees. Fear isn't an emotion I can afford, and yet, peering up at the two bare-chested Guardians restraining me, it compresses the air from my lungs and chills my vampire. Any chance of escape just blew to smithereens with their appearance.

Zach gains his feet, his injuries repaired. I gulp at the icy, dangerous gleam in his gaze. "It appears I trained you too well," he grits out, wiping the blood from his nose before grasping my chin in a painful grip. "You will submit, Lu, but I am going to enjoy breaking you first."

He strolls to a bench at the foot of the bed and brushes dust from his Armani suit before reclining on the seat, one leg crossed over the other. "Sedric, please fetch my special restraints on the wall."

Sedric had been Dimitri's lapdog, and now it appears he's the son's little bitch.

Apprehension gnaws at my belly when I glimpse the leather cuffs. Inside the wide manacles pointed silver protrusions cause terror to constrict my lungs, and my muscles to seize. Nothing I've endured in my life could equip me for the torment I'm about to confront.

Zachariah's demented leer sends tremors through my frame. "Animalistic, aren't they? Those are just the beginning my sweet, sweet warrior. When this is over, with a snap of my fingers, you will kneel and suck my cock without question."

Okay. Don't panic. Keep Zach talking. "You stated you'd allow my sister to leave if I joined you. Are you a male of your word?"

His dramatic sigh sends dread slithering through my intestines. "I never mentioned I would let her go. She is too valuable to me. I said no harm would come to her. And if the shield continues to hold, she remains protected."

What the…? "What does Vi have to do with the barrier?"

The knowing smile causes my skin to tingle with apprehension. "When your sister is coherent, she is quite powerful."

I gape at him. "What trickery is this? Viessa possesses no powers."

His shit-eating grin spreads as he leans back and drapes his arms along the edge of the bed. I blink and attempt to swallow past the sawdust taking up residence in my mouth.

"I find it staggering a woman as intelligent as yourself is so ignorant."

"You're lying."

The blue in Zach's regard swirls with a black madness. When he nods to Sedric, I struggle against the brute holding me down. "Remember, my dear." Zach leans forward, elbows on his knees. "The boys will get a turn at you, so I advise you to play nice."

My body stills. "You would share me?" Unheard of if I was indeed his mate.

"Well, now, that depends on you. I fancy seeing you impaled in every orifice at the same time, but that's down the road. When you're ready and begging for it."

Christ. "What happened to the cool, detached lover who demanded straight vanilla sex?"

"He no longer exists. My passions run high and in multiple directions." He waves at Sedric. "As a matter of fact, this one has become my favorite plaything. I think his need for pain outmatches yours, *mio amore.* Plus, I cannot get enough of his tight little anus and greedy mouth."

When the warrior appears to preen under Zach's praise, bile clogs my throat.

"Yes. Master has a much bigger prick than his father."

The strong grip restraining me strengthens, and my resolve intensifies. No one will violate me again. Zach will need to knock me out or kill me, and I suspect he wants me conscious and alive so he can get off on my cries of pain. Terror tightens my gut. What'll happen when he discovers I'm already mated?

The second the sharp points puncture my skin, I grit my teeth to keep from crying out. My vampire thrashes in a fury against the blood seeping from under the leather to stain my hands, the silver ensuring the gaping wounds don't heal.

When Thaddeus lifts me to my feet, I raise my leg and slam my shoe into Sedric's kneecap, crushing it. His growl is my only warning before a substantial meaty fist connects with the side of my face. Pain shoots through my socket, and my cheekbone shatters. Thaddeus' cruel grip on my biceps holds me upright against his torso, and I'm disgusted by the erection pressed against my lower back. I could hold my own for a time with Zach, but I don't stand a chance against all three.

I shake my head to clear the darkness encroaching and struggle in earnest as the bastards raise my arms to the chains attached to the ceiling. Sedric grips my midriff and hoists me off the ground.

Thaddeus attaches each cuff, then leans in and licks the side of my face.

Before I can slam my skull into his nose, Sedric drops me. The spikes dive deep, and I cry out as pain rips through my wrists, down my forearms, and into my dislocated shoulder. Fresh blood streams down my biceps before disappearing inside my white t-shirt, staining it red.

Everything in me demands I struggle to break free, but thrashing would simply produce further damage to my already shredded wrists. I close my eyes and inhale several sharp breaths to steady my inner trembling and order my muscles to relax. The meditative process Zach taught me long ago helps push past the worst of the injuries to gain command over my powers and send healing cells to my eye and cheek.

When I lift my lids, my former mentor stands before me with a sneer. "Meditation will only benefit you so far." Cruel fingers clutch my jaw. "Submit. Tell me where the halfling bitch is hiding out."

Hiding out? So, he possesses no inkling they reside at the cottage? I wonder if Icarus designed a cloaking spell for Nicole, no doubt at the insistence of Logan. I'd laugh in triumph if my situation weren't so dire. Instead, I do one better and spit in his face. I watch in sick fascination as it glides down his cheek, amazed I could even produce enough saliva.

A solid blow to my solar plexus has me gasping for air. I grip the chains tighter while my body swings mercilessly, my feet twisting and turning, seeking purchase on the floor just out of reach. Silver rips into tendons, and a hoarse groan fills the room. Mine.

"You will notice my tolerance isn't what it used to be, *mio amore*," he declares, producing a white handkerchief from his pocket to mop the spit from his face. Painful fingers dig into my waist from behind to halt my swinging.

"Is this truly what you want, Trez?" I wheeze out the familiar name of our past as a busted rib punctures my lung. "To be exactly like your father?" My teeth clench against the unrelenting agony in my wrists as I mend the bone and lung. How long before this weakens my capacity to heal?

His glare narrows and he produces a short blade from his belt. "You should know better, *principessa*." When he slices my neck open, warm blood gushes down my body to drip on the concrete below my dangling feet. Before I can close the vein, Thaddeus lowers his head and suckles the wound with surprising gentleness, his hardness slowly undulating against my ass. I allow him to heal the slice, preserving my energy for later.

"My father let his perverse fascination for his own daughter cloud his judgment." That's the pot calling the kettle black. "My love for you is special," he adds defensively, reading my expression. “First, you are not my flesh and blood, and second, deep down where you refuse to look, you still love me—crave me to dominate you, to take command. Things would have been different if I had understood your desires, and my own back then, instead of shunning them.” He pockets the knife.

I stare into the face of madness. He’s lost touch with reality. “You can’t be serious?”

He saunters over to a counter against the wall, picks an object up, and traces back. “I have never been more sincere about anything in my existence, besides recapturing the throne and ruling the immortal world. You will be my mate.” Certainty lives in the swirling ink swallowing the blue of his irises. “But first, give me the halfling’s vulnerabilities. When is she alone? What strengths does she possess?”

No way in purgatory I’m betraying Nicki again. “Trez. What happened to you? You’ve lost your damn mind.”

His face hardens. “I believe I cautioned you about your foul mouth.”

When he raises his hand, I finally discover the item he retrieved, and my heart drops. It’s a thin glass syringe loaded with what looks like... liquid silver.

Oh, God.

He nods to Sedric. “Cut her clothes from her body. It’s time for the true fun to begin.”

CHAPTER 36

Kurtis

"Icarus, open the fucking barrier," I demand for the fifth time. The beast fights my control as I pace behind the little priest kneeling in the snow, his tattooed arms raised above his head, palms resting on a transparent surface. "She's suffering. Need to get to her." I'm not positive how I sense Lu's pain since she doesn't bear my mark; the damn shield is between us, but I do, and it's intense.

"I know, my lord," he hisses. "I discern it as well, but this new cover has many intricate layers. It is quite impressive."

"You've been at it for three days, Icarus, are you certain you can break it?" Nicki questions, blowing on her fists to warm them. She's covered in full leather battle gear with a red beanie on her head that reads; '*Giving a fuck doesn't really go with my outfit.*'

When Liam and I arrived back at the cottage, Nicole, Logan, and the priest were waiting outside the war room with a change of clothes for me and Liam's discarded clothing. Once dressed, I disclosed everything, including the fact Lu was my fated female, and I was her one true mate.

"I suspected as much, but she doesn't wear your mark, Kurtis."

"For her own protection," I admitted as my fingers raked through my hair. "There's no time to waste. We need to lower the shield and storm the castle. Now."

"I would love to, but we have a slight problem. Someone has altered it, and Icarus is having trouble bringing it down."

Three nights later here we sit, stewing in the demon encampment, the evil bastards eyeballing our group with hostility. Sebastian's been in constant contact via phone to check on our progress, vowing to arrive the second the shield is down.

Three damn nights my mate's been a captive, no doubt being tortured based on her pain levels spiking and dropping. I'm going out of my mind.

Please stay alive, angel.

If I lose her, my beast will consume my humanity in order to shelter me from the agony, and my animal's baser instincts and needs are all I'd become. Given no choice, my father would be forced to lock me up or end my life. Once a shifter or werewolf finds their mate, whether they complete the bond or not, they will wither and die without the physical and mental stimuli from their other half.

"How do you plan on pinpointing where the young Giordano is in this massive castle?" King Darath asks, his nearly seven-foot frame towering over Nicki. Leave it to Jagorach to call a seven-hundred-year-old vampire young.

"Once the barrier is down, Nicole can isolate his position in seconds." Pride resonates in Logan's tone.

"Hmm. Impressive." The demon's crimson scrutiny travels the length of Nicki's body, before smirking at her hat.

"I advise you to keep your eyes to yourself, Darath, or you could discover them missing," Logan threatens with a growl.

"Just admiring your mate, Moretti. No need to get pissy." The king smiles innocently.

"Boys. Behave." Nicki grabs my arm and ushers me several paces away from the kneeling priest. "Give him space. Your growling and pacing are not helping."

"I must get to her." The beast rides the gravel in my tone.

"I feel you, and we will." Her cool fingers grasp my own. "But you better fight your animal and channel your inner soldier because that's who Lu needs when we storm in there: the badass SEAL who trained me, *capisce*?"

I nod in agreement, shifting the AR-15 loaded with silver bullets at my back. While they won't kill a vampire, it'll slow them down. Nicki insisted on these measures to minimize Guardian deaths. She's right; to save Lucretia, I must remain in control. She could require my blood.

"One further detail and you're gonna hate it, but Darath gets first dibs at my stepbrother. Don't shake your head at me, big guy. That was the deal. You concentrate on your female and allow him his long-overdue revenge."

I grit my teeth and scowl down at her. The beast demands retribution, needs to slay the being responsible for injuring our mate. How can she ask me to permit another male what should be my right?

Nicki grips me harder. "Promise me, Kurtis."

"That was before the motherfucker abducted my female and is doing God knows what to her. Don't demand such a vow, Nicole. He dies at my hands. My beast demands no less."

She sighs. "I understand, but if we do not grant Jagorach his vengeance, he'll tear up our peace treaty and wage war against the Vampire Nation, and probably the Shifter Territory for stealing from him what I promised. Is that what you want?"

A low growl rumbles through my chest and Logan darts a pointed glance in our direction. "Of course not." Damn it. "The best I can offer is I'll try."

"Better than nothing. But fair warning, I will suspend your ass in place if I must."

"Copy that."

When she strolls back to her mate, I peer over at Liam pacing the boundary. His face appears drawn and haggard, with three days of growth covering his jaw. The normally perfect black hair sticks up in odd angles from working his fingers through it repeatedly.

What is going on with him? While I appreciate him having my back, his zeal to save Lu and his protective instincts towards my mate teeters the line. I've noticed the way he regards her with a brooding look, or how he's quick to defend her against Nicki. I need a diversion, and I think it's about time my friend and I had a little chat.

With angry strides, I step into his path. He halts and squints up at me. Before he masks it, I recognize the haunted expression in the tormented chocolate stare; it matches my own.

"What the hell is going on with you, Liam? This," I indicate the apparent line he's cut through the snow from pacing, "is more than a concern for my mate."

"I don't know, Kurtis." His brows draw together. "I sense her pain. How is that possible?"

My eyes widen in shock, and I stumble back a step. “Lucretia’s pain?” What the hell?

Liam’s gaze falls to his feet, and he fists his hair. “Yes,” he hisses. “Her emotions are all over the place, but her agony is my own.”

I seize him by his wool shirt and slam him against a nearby tree. My deep animalistic growl blankets the forest, and I sense our team’s concerned stares. “Did you fucking touch her?” If she drank from him, I’ll kill him.

“No! God no. I would never betray you, and neither would she. You’re her mate, Kurtis.”

“Then what the hell, Liam?”

“I can’t explain it,” he says helplessly. “I—I just don’t—understand.”

I release him with a shove and step away, needing distance. “Do you love her?” It stings to ask, but how else could he develop such a link?

“I...” When he falters, my fists clench with the demand to punch something, namely him. I scowl at his bleak, tormented expression. “I can’t define it or nail it down to an exact emotion. I just hold a connection with Lu I don’t understand.”

“When this is over, if you come near my female, I will kill you. Clear?”

“But...” he hesitates before his face shuts down and he nods. “Yup. I get it. I’m sorry, man. Don’t know what else to say.”

My head spins with the knowledge my best friend is in love with my mate. How long has he felt this way? Does Lu suspect?

Beyond fucked doesn't do justice in this situation. Deep sadness mingles with the unrelenting rage. I trusted Liam, confided in him, enjoyed his company, and all along, he had the hots for my female. The thought of him with a hard-on around her screws with my brain. I need as far away from him as possible before I do something stupid, like kill him.

"Nicki," I whisper, and in a blink, she's by my side. She throws Liam a disappointed scowl, and he swallows before lowering his head in shame. "Get me the hell out of here."

"Sure. I'll come for you when the shield drops."

She locks both arms around my waist and teleports me away from the friend who shattered my trust.

What bothers me most is why my beast remained quiet during Liam's confession. He should've been raging to tear the werewolf limb from limb. Instead, he seemed to accept his declaration of love for our mate.

CHAPTER 37

Lucretia

I resist the burning desire to reach out mentally to Kurtis, not that it would do me any good with the shield. My strength abandoned me after the first full day of torture. In its place, agony rolls through bone and muscle in waves, stripping my vision, or maybe it's because my eyes swelled shut.

Zach fractured my left femur, along with my right forearm. Sedric and Thaddeus broke most of my ribs from the repeated impacts of their fists. My former lover took great delight in flaying open my backside with the cat-o-nine.

The good news? They carried me from the dank, musty dungeon to the dining hall. The bad news? I'm strapped to the long ass table. Silver chains restrain my raw bleeding wrists above my head and around each ankle, displaying me out buffet style with my naked, blood-soaked body shivering in the frigid castle air.

The three of them took numerous turns pinching, twisting, and biting both breasts and my clit. I no longer retain any sensation in them. They rammed their enormous fangs into my flesh, but the assholes never drank. With all the silver in my system, I'd hoped one of them would take a nice deep drag on a vein. Sedric and Zach were brutal in their administrations, but Thaddeus was almost gentle, his warm tongue healing the wounds left behind by the others. His glance was filled with regret.

I begged him on numerous occasions to let me go, but he feared his king more.

My eyes nearly bled as they forced me to watch them perform sex acts with each other down in the dungeon. I was surprised when Zachariah wasn't always the one fucking but enjoyed being taken as well. Although he never allowed Sedric that privilege, only Thaddeus. The little fucker reveled in his submissive bitch role, sometimes being plowed from both ends at the same time.

They haven't raped me yet, so I suppose I should be grateful for small favors. I expect it's all part of my conditioning. No concept of how long I've lain on this cold hard table with the rough wood digging into the open wounds on my back and ass. Days? Weeks? It seems like ages.

Kurtis obviously took me at my word and washed his hands of me. Although I'd like to believe the shield is blocking him from storming the castle. The longer he's a no show, the more I fear the defensive barrier isn't the obstacle. Since Nicki failed to present Zach to the demon king, I wonder if the demons killed my friends or drove them to retreat. Pain stabs through my heart at the knowledge they might be dead.

I still can't wrap my brain around the fact my sister has some unknown powers I knew nothing about. How was she lucid long enough to master it? As Ricky Ricardo always says; she has a lot of explaining to do.

Jesus.

I rasp out a hysterical laugh. My cracked ribs scream in protest, and my abused lips burst open again. My mind is genuinely gone if I'm quoting old TV shows.

The silver flowing through my veins has rendered the healing energy nonexistent, making each injury excruciatingly apparent, and all abilities vacated my weak, battered body not long after it entered my system. Not to mention, my inner vampire abandoned me after the first day, retreating to a shadowy corner in my mind to endure in silence. I'm alone, with no one to turn to, and my soul burns with the knowledge.

Deep down a manic scream bubbles toward the surface, but I couldn't bellow my rage and heartache to the rafters if I wanted. My voice deserted me yesterday after shrieking for hours during torture. My weakness shames me, but I quickly understood it was a futile exercise to hold it all in, to not give Zach the sick pleasure. After one entire day of unrelenting pain, I caved—screamed and cursed my damn head off, but I never uttered a word against Nicki or our team. So, there's that.

I've reached my breaking point though, and the bastard knows it. My only recourse is to submit or endure this endless torment and hope he eventually throws in the towel and kills me. The male I once called my mentor, my lover, my friend, brought me close to death many times over the last few days, only to brutally snatch the escape from my grasp mere seconds before death's door finally closed with a sip of his blood. Not enough to repair my wounds or lessen my misery, but enough to keep me alive.

I perceive his evil presence at my feet long before he touches me. Cold fingers graze my ankle above the chains in lazy circles before sliding up my shin and along my inner thigh. I stiffen waiting for the onslaught and pain shoots from my broken femur in protest.

After hours and hours of mental and physical abuse, the dam breaks and tears trickle from the slits in my swollen flesh to drench my hair. Submitting to him and betraying my friends stabs through my heart, the agony worse than the days of torture, but I'm out of options. I can't wait for a rescue that might never arrive, and if I perish, it will leave Viessa alone with no one to defend her.

The icy fingers gliding up my deadened mound are nothing like my mate's rough, scorching heat. They linger over my quivering belly before circling each breast and nipple. The touch is tender, exploring, and such a dichotomy from the previous few days.

The odor of his blood hits my nostrils a second before warm liquid spreads over my eyelids with a soft brush. Instantly, the swelling and tenderness reduce, and I blink against the brilliant light above the table.

"Trez?" I question, my throat clogged with tears.

"Hush, *principessa.* Open your eyes. I have brought you a gift."

I squint against the garish illumination, but when I angle my head everything inside me congeals with fear. Viessa stands meekly by my torturer. My breathing quickens and pain arrows through my ribs.

He adorned her in a designer gown of dark amber. The shimmering fabric matches the hollow and vacant gaze. Her black mane hangs in a shining mass of curls down her back.

"Vi?" I croak out, but she doesn't even glance in my direction.

"See," Zach says, his grin doing nothing to soothe me. "As promised, we took excellent care of your twin." He steps behind her and gently brushes her hair to one side. His intense stare never leaves my face. Despite the excruciating agony flowing through my frame, I struggle against my restraints.

"Don't touch her!" I try to bellow my fury, but it comes out as a hoarse squeak.

"Submit, *mio amore* and I will not." His long fingers graze her neck before delving into the bodice and groping her breast. My sister's expression doesn't even blanch.

The amber glow, absent these past days, flickers to life as I thrash against the silver chains; my brain swells with adrenaline and hate.

Zach shoves Viessa forward, and her palms slap on top of the table by my chest.

"Vi. Please snap out of it." The tears flow freely. Her stare shifts to mine and... nothing. There's not even a flicker of my twin visible. She's gone. Buried in the pandemonium of her mind.

He throws her skirt up over her back and fondles her naked backside. "I will enjoy fucking your *pazzo* sister while you watch."

"Okay," I whisper in defeat as my body stills. "You win, Zachariah. I surrender." I'm hoping he'll heal me before he rapes me, but knowing him, that's a pipe dream.

"Magnificent," he beams before gently replacing my sister's skirt and helping her to rise. He could have presented her at any time and I would've submitted. He deliberately waited, prolonged my suffering to savor every second. No matter what transpires from this point on, I vow to destroy the bastard; by silver through his heart or decapitation, he will perish at my hands.

Zach snaps his fingers and a Guardian steps forward. The big brute lifts my sister in his arms. I protest, but Zachariah holds up a finger. "He is just going to hold on to her. I want Vi with us as a perpetual reminder for you to behave. The second you do not, I will let the warrior enjoy her."

Sedric and Thaddeus emerge from a door with gloves on and dispose of the chains around my ankles. I weep when the burning silver disappears. My panicked mind searches a pathway out of this nightmare.

When Zachariah seeks to mate with me, and it fails, he'll realize I've bonded with another. The bastard will go ballistic and rape my sister anyway. Damn it, what do I do?

God. If you truly exist, please help me figure a way to save Vi without betraying my friends.

Caught up in pleading with a being I'm not certain even hears me, my brain doesn't register when Sedric and Thaddeus grip each ankle, or when Zach climbs on the table between my spread legs. I frown at him in confusion, not assimilating what's happening until he unzips his slacks and strokes his cock in preparation.

Revulsion, panic, and horror seize my tendons.

Kurtis! I scream mentally, in a last-ditch effort, refusing to acknowledge it won't make a difference. *Help me!*

CHAPTER 38

Kurtis

'Icarus thinks he's almost figured it out. I'm coming to get you. Be ready.'

I shake off the disorientation at Nicki's voice in my brain, secure two swords in the harness at my back, sling the AR-15 strap over my shoulder, and thrust a dagger in each boot.

Nicki traced me home last night, but with fear and anger for company, it proved to be a dreadful idea. All I could envision was Lucretia being tortured, and my friend's strange connection to my mate.

At first light, I'd shifted and run for miles to obliterate the images of Lu suffering atrocities my brain refuses to contemplate, and it's driving me insane. I keep reminding myself my woman is a formidable warrior, capable of enduring more than most males. She will survive. She must. Once Lu's back in my arms, she is never leaving my side again. I now understand Logan's obsession with Nicki after losing her. I'll cherish and love the stubborn female for the rest of our lives and prove to her she is worthy of all I can give her.

Nicole materializes before me, her pinpoint accuracy amazing me once again. Not long ago, she struggled with tracing, emerging blocks from her destination with a shrug and a sheepish grin.

Tonight, her expression is grim but determined. She's dressed in full leather once more with a Glock 19 strapped to each thigh, a sword resting against her spine, and her thick auburn hair pulled back in a high ponytail. She reminds me of a cross between Lara Croft in the *Tomb Raider* movies and Selene in *Underworld*.

"Ready, big guy?"

"I was ready four goddamn days ago," I reply with a low growl.

"When we pass through the shield, we will be bombarded with Lu's emotions. Since the demons have never been inside the castle, I need to concentrate on teleporting you, King Darath, and his handful of fighters to Zach's exact spot. Don't fucking shift, or you'll slaughter us all. You feel me?"

"Copy that. Just get me to Lucretia."

Two seconds later, we're back at the encampment. Jagorach, a dozen of his finest soldiers, and our small task force form a semi-circle around the kneeling priest. His blue tattoos light up the night sky, casting an eerie glow across the snow. Nicki and I take our positions next to the Moretti brothers, and I block out Liam's tortured face. My sole focus is getting to Lu, and I don't care who I go through to do it.

When I sense my father come up behind me, surprise and relief have me spinning to him. He takes one glimpse at my expression and wraps me in his embrace. My father's warmth and strength fortify my own.

"No matter what, son, you have my support. Laws be damned," he whispers in my ear before easing away and clutching my shoulders. "Let's go rescue your female."

I raise a brow. "How did you..."

"Boy," he interrupts. "I've been in love with a forbidden mate for over a century. I recognized the signs in my own flesh and blood. Your brother and sister support whatever decision you make. As will I."

"Thanks, Dad." Hot tears prick the back of my eyes at the unconditional devotion and loyalty from my family.

"How did you get here?" I think to ask.

"Jagorach brought me." He chuckles at my stunned expression. "As I mentioned, the demon king and I have a history. He's a wicked son of a bitch, but underneath lies a good heart. One which has suffered much."

"If you say so," I mumble.

"It is time." Icarus gasps minutes later, and the once invisible shield shimmers and comes to life. The walls expand several hundred feet into the star-riddled sky before curving at the top and disappearing. I'm amazed anew at the Oracle's power. "Step through, but hold on the other side," he commands in a strained voice as the blue irises swim, his pulsing tattoos blinding in their intensity. "Quickly."

We move around the Oracle and traipse through the force field. The second my body passes through the surface, Lu's pain and emotions stab into my brain like a thousand silver daggers. I stumble to one knee at the magnitude of her suffering and grip fistfuls of snow to keep from shifting.

"Holy fuck," Nicki whispers next to me, and Logan grips her bicep to hold her upright.

My father's big palm comes down on my shoulder as I gain my feet. "Thrust it aside, son." I wrangle control over my beast to obey.

Icarus moves to face us all, his irises absorbed in cobalt energy, his tattoos dimmed to a low hypnotic pulse. "Fair warning. Tonight will expose many factors, but for every action, no matter how abhorrent, there is always a reason."

What is he talking about?

"We don't have time for your riddles, Icarus." Nicki scowls in exasperation. "Help with transport or get the hell out of the way."

"Yes, my lady." He bows and ambles over to the demons. "I will take King Darath and his crew."

"Thank you," Nicole sighs with relief. I didn't realize she was apprehensive about teleporting so many. "Everyone, give me a second to locate the douchebag and Lu."

I examine her intently, impatience crawling over my skin like a thousand tiny spiders. The demand to get to my mate batters my skull with the force of a sledgehammer. Another ten seconds pass, and I clench my fists.

Lu's scream rips through my cranium.

"Fuck! Now, Nicki," I bellow just as she seizes my wrist in a crushing grip.

"Dining hall," she barks out before tracing us across the miles.

CHAPTER 39

Lucretia

"I agreed to submit. Heal me, so that I can participate in our mating." It's a stupid attempt to stall the inevitable and convince him I'm willing.

"Not a chance, Lu," he sneers before leaning over my torso, prick in hand. "Our bonding benefits our race. With you by my side, we will restore the Vampire Nation to its former greatness, control the weak Council of Unity, and other factions will fear us once more." Crazy swirls in his contemplation.

A Guardian traces into the area. "Sire, they breached the blockade."

"What?" Zach leaps from the table, zips his trousers, and motions for the warrior holding my sister to come forward.

My body awakens with Kurtis's energy. He's inside the shield. Thank you, God! I struggle against my bonds despite the pain as my spirit swells with hope. Sedric and Thaddeus tighten down on my ankles.

"Viessa. Place a barrier around this table immediately, or Lucretia dies."

Zach's urgency startles my sister. The blank cloud lifts as she observes him draw a broadsword from Thaddeus' back. Cold steel presses against my neck, and I freeze.

Why the hell is he asking Vi to produce a cover? Is this the power he was talking about?

Her golden regard meets mine, and my lips part at the fiery determination in their depths. Pale fingers tap the vampire holding her on the shoulder, and he lowers her to the floor. Her palm raises, and an abrupt flare of energy flows over me, entombing the five of us just as my rescuers breach the room.

Kurtis's gaze widens at my abused body stretched across the table before narrowing on the blade at my neck. His rage penetrates my skin even through the barrier dividing us. The intense blues do a double take when he spots my sister standing by my head. Long lashes blink several times before bouncing back to mine. The group's expressions mirror my mate's as they ogle my twin.

The compulsion to communicate with Kurtis hovers over my PTSD-fogged brain. I want to tell him I regret not entrusting him with my secrets, but it's hopeless with the shield in place—one my sister erected. When did I lose control of everything?

In the gloomy recess of my mind lingers the realism I'm laying here butt-ass naked in front of everybody, but reality seems inconsequential in the big scheme.

Kurtis's fists clench around the lethal weapon at his shoulder, no doubt sighting in Zach to put a round between his eyes. Three loud bangs echo through the great hall as the shock wave generated by the bullets leaving his rifle break the sound barrier, like a miniature version of the sonic boom. But the projectiles never strike their mark. Instead, they lodge in a tight cluster in the boundary, as if hovering in midair.

The steel pressed against my jugular shakes as Zach bursts into a short bout of laughter. "Your human weapon will not affect this shield." He demonstrates his confidence by raising the sharp blade from my neck and lowering it to the table, although he keeps the hilt within reach. Not as confident as he would like everyone to believe.

"I see you've teamed up with the filthy demons, *cagna*," Zach says, directing his disgust at the former queen.

"Oh, they're not with me." Nicki smiles as she eases forward a step; Logan and Bastian move with her. Between them, I glimpse blue tattoos pulsing with low light. *Please lower the shield, Icarus.* "King Darath has personal reasons for being here."

"And those are?"

Jagorach and his team pan out, investigating the shield's perimeter. Zach watches him with curiosity. Underneath his calm facade, he fears the demon. And rightly so, Darath's powers have been expanding for two millennia.

"I'm here for your head, Giordano." Jagorach's heavy, grating tone sends shivers along my already icy skin. The red-eyed devil holds a position behind Zach.

"I have no issue with you, Jagorach," Zachariah says over his shoulder.

"Lu." Nicki's voice snags my attention. "Who is this?" She nods in my sister's direction.

I open my mouth to confess, but the king slams his fist on my broken forearm. Excruciating pain radiates up my limb. I rasp out a cry, arching against the agony.

Kurtis charges the shield, but Liam and Bastian grab him before he reaches it. His canines extend, and his beautiful orbs shift between light cobalt to the wild brown of his animal and back again as he endeavors to remain in command.

After a couple minutes, the boys ease off and the shifter takes several deep breaths—his body tense but in control. Under the fury lies anguish and despair at his failure to protect me.

Uncertain how this cluster will resolve, whether Zach kills me or Logan does when he discovers the truth, I need Kurtis to know how much he means to me, how the strength in his blood kept me alive. Our bond soothed my psyche during the torture when I wished to escape into a darkened hole in my mind and never come out.

I grind my teeth in frustration. The damn shield prevents me from using telepathy, and a verbal declaration would place his life at risk.

Kurtis's voice permeates the room with his will. "You have my mate. Give her to me, and I'll kill you quickly."

Oh no! I shift wide eyes to Zach's shocked expression.

The dining hall doors burst open, and over fifty Guardians file inside; every single one well-armed and dressed for battle. They establish a perimeter around the chamber.

Zach's livid glower lowers. "Your mate? Interesting." His fist closes on my neck. "*Piccola troia.*" You little bitch. "You will pay dearly for that."

He flings my head to the side, and I choke for air. "You are misjudging the situation, shifter."

"My female is covered in blood, shackled to the table and I'm misreading the situation?" Kurtis questions incredulously, his beast heavy in his tone. "I'll give you this warning once and only once, Zach. Release Lucretia or your death will be a slow one. Nothing would grant me greater pleasure than to rip you to pieces."

"You are no match for me, young prince. Besides, once you hear the truth about your precious *mate,* everyone will demand her execution. And need I point out you are surrounded?"

Oh, God. Here it comes.

"Not to interrupt this testosterone-driven bullshit, but I have a question." Nicki waves her hand in the air, and every immortal outside the bubble freezes. Her intense gray regard settles on me. In my periphery, I notice King Darath stealthily moving closer to the shield, unaffected by Nicki's power. "If you were a shifter turned vampire by none other than daddy dearest, how the hell is your sister one of us?"

Icarus' head pops up, also untouched by Nicki's telekinesis, his swirling blue eyes gape at Viessa for several moments before he squeezes them shut. An ominous shadow passes over his face, and the tattoos pulse brighter before he darts back down behind Logan in what I hope is an attempt to lower the damn shield.

"It appears you're ignorant of the full sordid history. Allow me to enlighten you, dear stepsister."

Nicki glances over her shoulder at Icarus and closes her lids for a brief second before twisting to Zach with a quiet sigh. "I would love to hear it, but could you cover Lu up so her mate over here will stop growling?"

"A fair request," he replies calmly before dragging the table runner through my legs and over my abdomen and chest. It offers little warmth, but at least I'm no longer exposing my girl parts to the room.

I arch my neck to peer at my sister, silently imploring her to glance at me. She holds the key to the oppressive cover, and since Icarus is experiencing trouble bringing it down, maybe I can get her coherent enough to lower it.

'*Vi. Can you hear me? Please bring down the shield or Zach will kill me.*' Not even an eyelash flickers. '*Vi. Drop the damn barrier,*' I holler and still nothing. Despair settles in my chest. It's time to deal with the consequences of my actions.

"It would seem Lu only confessed to some of her numerous deceptions."

My body trembles. Kurtis's fists clench and unclench, his breathing ragged. When our eyes lock, his expression takes on a desperate quality, and the blue deepens. Zach is about to ravage the delicate bond between us. Soon those beautiful sapphires will darken with disgust and rage.

"Trez… don't," I plead in a gruff whisper.

"Lucretia turned her twin sister against her will." The delight in his face sickens me.

Nicki's stunned gaze swings to Viessa before dropping to mine. "Is that true, Lu?"

My lids lower in shame. "Yes."

"Why?" Logan asks, and I concentrate on his disappointed frown.

"She… she was dying. I couldn't let that happen." My speech is barely detectable.

"But wait, that is not the best part," the king chortles.

"Fuck you, Zach." I regret the raspy words the moment they leave my lips. He's been conditioning me the last four days to expect punishment for foul language. Sure enough, a dagger appears, from God knows where, and pierces my side. I scream as it cleaves through muscle and tendon before puncturing my spleen. Warm, dark blood pools on the table.

The shifter's roar is deafening. He thrashes against Nicki's telekinesis. All four canines extend once more, and dark claws shoot from his fingertips. He's on the verge.

"Kurtis," I rasp out through clenched teeth, the pain making it challenging to speak. I need my mate, not his beast. "Stay with me." The metamorphosis is immediate. The claws and massive fangs retract, but the creature continues to shimmer over his body.

"How touching," Zach sneers.

"Get to the point, sick bastard," Nicki demands, her luminous stare spotlighting Zach's face.

"I understand where she gets her foul mouth. Someone needs to bring you to heel."

"I'm going to fucking enjoy watching the demon rip your goddamn head off your motherfucking spindly neck, you piece of shit," she whispers with a malevolent grin. Leave it to Nicki to antagonize the enemy. I've always admired her devil may care attitude, even when it escalates the problem.

Blackness swirls in the depths of Zach's sockets, so I'm astonished when he pierces his finger on a fang and runs it along the open wound at my side, sealing it closed.

"Don't want you ruining my Gucci shoes," he whispers before facing Nicki once more. "You've just demonstrated why I am the vampire to lead this nation: self-control. But I digress. Where was I? Oh yes, my dear little *principessa* here told Dimitri where you were as a youngster. In fact, she abandoned her post so he could have his wicked way with you."

I close my lids against the stunned disbelief on Nicki's face, but it's the pained animalistic roar from Logan that signals my doom.

CHAPTER 40

Lucretia

With my heart in my throat, I squint against the brilliant green painting a bullseye on my skull as Logan charges the shield. In her shock, Nicki dropped her telekinetic hold. Close to a century, I've fought alongside this mighty warrior, but his murderous rage was never aimed at me. Death awaits me in the fury-filled stare, and I perceive those massive fangs ripping into my neck and severing my head.

Kurtis and Bastian team up to lunge at the barrier with Logan, and the extraordinary force between the three immortals produces a deep crack down the middle of the shield, but it holds. And for the first time, relief flows through me it's there. Without it, I'd be dead.

Nicki stands frozen, the hurt and betrayal sparking in the grey depths shoot agony through my heart.

'I'm sorry,' I silently mouth the inadequate words and her scrutiny hardens.

Zach grabs the sword off the table and shouts at my twin. "Viessa! Strengthen the cover."

Her hands lift into the air. "No, Vi," I croak. "Don't listen to him. Lower the shield."

That's when I notice Liam. He's not attacking; instead, he inspects my sister. The chocolate stare travels over her with deep regard. What is wrong with him? He glances briefly at me and relief enters his expression for a split second before refocusing on Viessa.

"I will rip your heart from your chest, Lu." Logan pummels the shelter with his bare fists. "I entrusted you with what is mine, and you betrayed me. You betrayed her."

"I'm sorry, my lord. I didn't realize what he was doing." Why am I seeking to reason with the crazed vampire? There is no reasoning with an enraged mate when his inner predator has taken over. If he doesn't listen, maybe I can get through to Nicki. "He gave me no alternative."

"I will fucking kill you." He continues to rage, redoubling his efforts. Yup. He's beyond rational thinking.

"Logan..."

"No." He rounds on his female. "She allowed him to hurt you. She must pay."

"And she will, but you need to cool down. You are no good to me like this."

Holy crap. Her fearlessness and confidence in their bond are unbelievable.

"She's correct, brother. We should step back and figure out another approach."

"No. We've damaged it," Kurtis argues. "Let's continue..." Before he can finish, the fissure above my head seals, like a zipper on a raincoat.

No. No. No. Damn it, Vi.

"Oh my, what a predicament," Zachariah taunts. "Guardians, slay these vile creatures."

Our team spins into a defensive posture, their backs to each other, weapons drawn and at the ready. Not one Guardian circling the dining hall steps forward, and Nicki smiles in gratitude. They weren't here to support the current ruler. They showed up to reinforce their queen.

When Zach realizes he no longer possesses the security of the Guardians, he strides to my side. "Sedric, unchain Lu. Thaddeus, grab Vi, it's time we depart."

Movement catches my attention, and I peer over my arm. Liam stepped up to the shield near my sister. What's he doing?

"Viessa." His low rasp snags my sister's awareness. She blinks several times before swinging her head towards him. "That's it, sweetness, concentrate on me." The blank haze inhabiting Viessa's mind most of her life clears in an instant as she inspects the werewolf king up and down.

"Ignore him, Vi or Lu dies," Zach warns.

Viessa disregards his command. Her concentration never wavers from the wolf.

"Can you do something for me, beautiful?" His voice is like a lover's caress even to me, and I'm stunned when my twin nods, advancing a step in his direction. Liam smiles. "That's my girl. Lower the shield and come to me."

Vi's heart rate elevates, her soft pants rasp through parted lips. Holy crap. I am experiencing my twin's responses, and she desires him.

"Liam James Scott?" Her inquiry is husky from seldom use.

Zach marches over to Vi and snatches her by the arm before Thaddeus has a chance. The werewolf erupts in a rough growl, his irises flashing pale blue. "Did you understand me, *cagna pazza?*"

"Get your filthy hands off her," I croak out in a gruff whisper as I struggle against the chains. despite the paralyzing pain and Sedric's relentless grip on my ankles.

Vi flicks her wrist, the shield splits down the middle, and both sides collapse, melting into the floor.

Bedlam erupts.

The demons charge Zach, overpowering him and forcing him to his knees before he can trace away.

The stoic Guardians surrounding the room surge forward, engage Sedric and Thaddeus, decapitateing them in a matter of seconds.

The raw, aching flesh on my wrists sizzles under the silver. Bone grinds against bone in my forearm and femur as I endeavor to locate my sister. Liam has her pinned behind him with one arm enclosing her waist, the other gripping a sword, ready to defend her with his life. She peeks around his shoulder and blesses me with a quick smile. A smile. Something so commonplace, but for her, a rare and magnificent sight. I don't get the chance to bask in Viessa's transformation when Logan advances. My heart stops. Death fills his gaze.

Instead of fear consuming me, I regard my executioner with acceptance. The guilt and dishonor have eaten away at my soul for far too long, and I'm relieved it's finally over. No more secrets to conceal. No more burying my emotions beneath an icy wall of indifference. My mate and Liam will look after my sister and keep her safe.

Kurtis.

Tears blur the vision of death's stare charging me. I regret we didn't enjoy more time together. Our relationship just started to blossom despite the obstacles. The shifter pierced my soul, tore down my walls with relentless tenacity. Now I'll never get the chance to experience the sting of his bite or the fusion of his mental link.

"No! Stop!" Kurtis's broad muscular back fills my view as he blocks Logan's path, and I'm startled when Nicki and Bastian move beside him.

Do they guard me? Why?

"My love. I am just as furious as you, but we need to learn the whole story before we pass judgment. She will stand trial for her crimes against the Vampire Nation and council."

"I do not give a good goddamn about the laws," he snarls low. "She brought him straight to you. Abandoned her post I—I assigned her. Allowed him to violate you." Even though Logan wants to rip me apart, my heart breaks at the pain and misery running through the violence. He's right. I deserve his sword.

Large hands enclosed in leather brush against my wrists, breaking the silver chains. Beautiful blue orbs, identical to his son's, pierce through the haze of agony. Slowly King Ruse lowers my arms to my sides, and I bite my cheek to keep from crying out.

"King Scott, your shirt." At the sharp command, Liam removes his t-shirt and tosses it to Cipher. Viessa ogles the exposed beauty of the werewolf's back before boldly reaching out and caressing his spine. Liam sucks in a gasp, his muscles twitching at her touch.

King Ruse eases me into a seated position before gently guiding my fractured arm through the wide sleeve. The soft fabric pools around my hips and the warmth from Liam's body alleviates the shivering.

"Get the hell out of my way." Logan fights against Bastian and Kurtis with Nicki right in the middle, her palms planted firmly on his chest. "I fucking trusted you, Lu." His hatred causes my throat to convulse as I attempt to swallow.

With no strength left, I can't even hold myself upright. Cipher's searing grip on my shoulders steadies me. "Let him through," I croak out, calling for an end to this. "I deserve his wrath."

"We each own a part to play in the destiny which unfolds and guides our existence." Through the screen of backs before me, I glimpse the Oracle, the harmonious melody of his voice soothes the trembling even further.

"What are you suggesting, priest?" Kurtis asks.

"Lu played her role, voluntarily or not, in shaping my lady's future. Without her contempt for her father, her anger motivating her intentions,

Nicole's destiny would have altered. She would never have developed into the prophesied halfling to rule the Vampire Nation and create peace in our world."

"Well, that's one way to fucking look at it," Nicki mutters before her sharp regard turns on the Oracle. "You foresaw Lu's actions and did nothing."

"I foresee many things, my lady, but if I interfere, the consequences are severe. One day the gods will demand payment for defying them and rescuing your soul from the depths of purgatory."

Nicki's eyes widen. "What price, Icarus? Tell me, and I'll pay it."

The Oracle smiles with affection. "Please consider, Lucretia's actions, no matter how abhorrent, were necessary."

The Oracle's comments obtain the desired effect. Through my mate's massive arm, I watch Logan's fangs retreat, the brilliant light recede. Nicki immediately wraps her arms around his midriff. My commander peers at me a second longer, jaw clenched before sheathing his swords, enclosing his female in his embrace, and burying his face in her neck.

"You do not recognize the destruction you've done following this halfling bitch. She will destroy millennia of progress in the Vampire Nation," Zach shouts from his kneeling position between the massive demons.

"Could someone shut him the fuck up?" Nicki growls over her shoulder just as King Darath produces a roll of duct tape.

At Nicki's raised brows, he tears off a strip and slaps it over Zach's mouth. "Duct tape is the devil's favorite tool."

I'd snort if I had the energy.

With Logan somewhat under control, Kurtis turns and steps between my spread thighs. He nods to his father, and the warmth from the king's palms disappears. When I fall sideways, my mate clasps my neck to steady me. So many concerns rush through him. Fury, hurt, regret, failure, and sorrow. All directed at me? The acute emotions make it challenging to ascertain, and in my weakened state, nigh impossible.

"Why aren't you healing?"

"Injected with silver." Kurtis's face tightens with violence.

"He shredded her back," Cipher says in a low growl.

"Did he..."

"No," I answer, knowing what he was about to ask. "You arrived just in time."

"Jagorach." Intense sapphire irises bore into mine as he calls out to the demon king. "Exact your revenge or I fucking will."

"Mrmph! mmmrpph mmmrrrmph..."

Zachariah's muffled pleas around the tape stutter to a gurgle. I peek over my shoulder to witness King Darath running a massive serrated blade along the vampire's neck, his fist clutched in Zach's hair. My mentor struggles against his captors, disbelief and horror forever engraved in his expression as blood squirts from his jugular before gushing down his body.

In ancient Latin, the demon verbalizes his vengeance as he gleefully saws through tendons, muscles, and bone with slow jagged slices, prolonging the vampire's death. "*Et hoc actum est, fili peccata patris componat. Ego et puer ultionis in corde meo uxorem. Et vindicate volnere Lucretiae extractum ad Nicole.*" *With this act, the son pays for the sins of the father. I avenge my wife and child. I exact retribution for Nicole and Lucretia.*

When Zach's head drops to the stone floor with a satisfying splat, relief eases the muscles in my chest. The bastard can never trouble me or anyone ever again.

"Look at me," Kurtis orders and I don't want to, but I do. The beautiful eyes compel me to produce a different answer for my sins, one I can't offer. "Tell me it's not true, and I'll believe you."

Tremors vibrate through my body. "I can't." I breathe, silently pleading with him to understand.

"Perhaps now is not the best time, son."

He ignores his father, and the cobalt stare turns frigid. "How could you?"

The outrage in his expression fractures my heart. Granted, the allegations against me are severe, but he didn't ask why, or if I had cause. I've done horrible things for which I am not proud. Ones forced upon me, but Kurtis's response hurts worse than all the pain and suffering Zach put me through. It doesn't matter his loathing is justified.

I lower my shame-filled eyes and solicit the one being in this room I hope will come to my rescue. Before I open my mouth, Icarus is at my side, and Kurtis shifts backward, drawing his hurt and anger with him.

"I need to drain the poison from your body," the Oracle explains before presenting a knife from his robe pocket.

At my nod, he slices the inside of my forearm from elbow to wrist. I hiss against the pain. As I observe the dark red blood—laced with swirling rivers of silver—flow from the open wound to saturate the table before spilling onto the floor at Icarus' feet, I pray he takes it all. I have nothing left. Kurtis despises me, Viessa is finally safe, my career as a Guardian is over, and Nicki and the council will demand my death.

After several minutes my vision dims, and what little strength I had oozes from my body to congeal like stagnant waste.

CHAPTER 41

Kurtis

Deep down, where I feared to investigate, a gut-wrenching dread existed. I'd refused to examine it or acknowledge it was there. Nicki recruited me to discover Lu's secrets, and I let my lust overshadow my intuitions, Nicki's instincts—hell, even my beast couldn't accept its mate did anything wrong.

Lucretia Bramen's whole existence is an endless list of heinous sins, and it sickens me. She colluded with King Dimitri. Escorted the fucker to her front door and did nothing while he abused and violated his own daughter.

A weighted bowling ball of rage and disgust sit on my chest, crushing my sternum. How could she look the other way while Dimitri molested her? Lu was the child's last line of defense against the evil bastard.

There are certain situations I condone, like her turning her sister to avert her death. It's against council law, but I understand the rationale. She's family. I would most likely do the same. But this? This I can't disregard or accept or even fucking comprehend. All I notice is the female who betrayed my best friend in the vilest manner.

Icarus stated Lu played a role in Nicki's rise against King Giordano. Meaning if Dimitri hadn't found her, she never would've had the motivation or desire to slay him, and the evil son of a bitch would still be in power. But does that justify what she did?

As the blood leaks from Lu's arm, my beast stirs, but my outrage and confusion keep it at bay. My father catches her by the shoulders again before she tumbles off the table, a harsh glare shoots my direction. I ignore him and twist to face the woman I failed.

"I'm so sorry, Nicki. I let the bond cloud my judgment. It kept me from seeing her true self."

"Kurtis. Nothing is black and white." She turns from her mate's embrace to scowl at me, her lips set in disapproval. Of me? What the hell? "Logan's fury and betrayal towards Lu I understand, but what perplexes me is how swift you are to judge your mate without learning all the facts."

"What facts?" The numbness fades, and righteous anger takes its place. "The fact she turned her sister against her will? Let everyone believe she was a natural-born vampire? Or how about the one where she relayed your location to Dimitri, then left her post when he demanded access to you? It was her responsibility to protect you. What type of person does nothing while someone violates a child?" My voice swells in outrage as I recite each sin.

"Enough!" My father's bellow startles me, and I glance in his direction. Lu's chin rests against her chest. The dank, tangled tresses curtain her face, and the last visage of energy diminishes with the pints of her life essence oozing from her veins. The sole factor keeping her upright is my dad's hands on her shoulders. "Your mate needs you. If you don't get your head out of your ass and feed her, I will."

A part of me is horrified by the atrocities Lu's body endured these past four days, and I crave to scoop her up in my arms and provide her comfort and blood to repair her wounds. But then I peer at Nicole and visualize the brutalities she suffered as a defenseless teenage mortal.

"Don't—want—his," Lu whispers through the shroud of hair.

Her rejection fuels my resentment, and I clench my jaw. What right does she have to be angry or upset with me? When my dad lifts his wrist to her lips, my beast trembles in possessive outrage. *Mine.* I tense, readying to wrench his arm away and replace it with my own. Instead, I spin on my heel and head for the exit.

"What the fuck is wrong with you?" Nicki blocks my progress to the doors. "Are you really gonna allow your dad to feed your mate?"

"What is wrong with *you*?" My whisper is generous with my animal. It's filled with doubt, anger, and betrayal. "She served you up on a silver platter. How can you not crave to rip her throat out?"

"You want me to rip your mate's throat out?" she asks with stunned disbelief.

"No!" I bellow and seize her shoulders, giving her a slight shake. "Of course not." When Logan steps forward, she lifts a hand to halt him, never taking her concerned stare from mine. "Because of her, you suffered horribly at the mercy of your father for years. She fooled us all. How can you not demand her death?"

Nicki gently lays both palms on my chest, her eyes soften. "You didn't fail me, Kurtis, and neither did Logan. The ones who failed me were my mother, for abandoning me, and my father. Now he's dead, and my past with him." She exhales, her expression willing me to understand. "I've learned something over the years; even good people do bad things for righteous reasons. That's gonna be in a song I write one day."

"Nothing could justify what she's done," I hiss in agony.

"Are you sure?" Her soft murmur causes doubt to nip at my conscience. What lengths would I go to protect my siblings or my father? Would I sacrifice a friend for them? A child?

"I'm not certain about anything anymore. If you'd asked me yesterday if she was capable of this, I would've said not a snowball's chance in hell. How can you be so blasé about this?"

"Because I had my suspicions of her involvement with Dimitri since the battle. And even though I was shocked to hear it out loud, I've had time to come to terms with it."

"You knew all along?" I gape.

"You knew, Nicole?" Logan's stunned expression mirrors my own.

"Empath, remember?"

"Sorry to interrupt," Bastian says, joining our little circle. "Once Lu is restored, we must detain her in a cell until the council assembles. They will determine the punishment for her crimes."

A sharp spasm flutters inside my heart at the rulers demanding Lu's death. No matter how furious and disillusioned I am with my mate's actions, I do not wish her dead. In truth, I couldn't survive in a world where she didn't exist. I'll plead her case. Hell, I'll threaten the council with a shifter withdrawal if they insist on her execution. And if all else fails, abduct her reluctant ass and shackle her to my bed until I can come up with a plan to overturn the verdict. My beast would tolerate no less.

"You are correct, brother. Her future is in the council's control," Logan agrees, knowing full well half of the representatives are in this room.

"Kurtis?" Liam saunters over with Lu's twin following in his wake. My gut clenches. In appearance they are identical, but the frenzied expression in Viessa's eyes sets her apart. "Don't turn your back on Lu. She needs you now more than ever."

"You're mistaken, my friend. Lucretia never needed me, or anyone for that matter." I can't control the bitter sadness in my voice. If she had trusted me even a little, we wouldn't be here.

"We all need help in our lives, Kurtis, whether we own up to it or not," Nicki says, and I glance down to realize I still retain a firm grip on her shoulders. I drop my hold and ease back a step, maintaining the visual of my mate feeding from my father behind me.

"At times, the assistance arrives from a source we never imagined." Icarus walks around me to join the little semi-circle facing me. "In such a pivotal moment, we make a choice: to fight and perhaps die, or flee to fight another day."

An uneasy ripple passes through me as I frown at the allies I regard as my closest friends. "What is this? An intervention?"

"I get it," Nicki says. "You're angry with her for not informing you about her sister or the part she played in my past, but did you stop to consider she had a legit reason we know nothing about? Don't turn your back on the only mate you'll ever receive. It will destroy you."

It's destroying me now.

"While I appreciate this," I wave around the group, "Lucretia's the one in trouble here. Yes, she is my female, and no matter how furious I am with her, or how horrific her crimes, I'll do everything in my power to keep her alive." Warmth fills my chest at their loyalty and caring, but it can't eclipse the hurt and betrayal lighting up my entrails like a live wire. "I—I cannot, however, complete the bond, even if it were permissible. I'm not certain I could ever accept her as my mate and queen."

Holy Christ!

The pain those words cause almost double me over in agony, and I gasp to catch my breath. In this moment, I finally realize I'm knee-deep in my own self-righteous bullshit. Once again, I can't see past my hurt and betrayal. My notion of right and wrong. Black and white. When Zach abducted Lu, I immediately assumed the worst of her. It was Liam who'd believed in my woman when I didn't, who questioned the circumstances.

Here I am once again condemning her, and it's my friends, the ones she wronged, who are insisting I hear her side. Instead of judging her, I should have concluded she had a legitimate reason.

"Your time has run out, my lord," Icarus whispers. "The Guardian decided for you, aided by those she wounded. It is you who will endure the consequences of your actions and hurtful words. It is you who will live with unjustly condemning your female."

Panic surges through me, and I whirl around to face my father's disappointment. "What have I done?" I gape in horror at the sole residual left of my mate—the dark, precious blood dripping from the wooden table.

Lucretia vanished.

CHAPTER 42

Lucretia

I awaken like someone injected me with pure adrenaline. I bolt upright, panting, heart galloping, my fingers twisting in the sheets. Disoriented, my eyes dart around the room, struggling to take in everything at once.

Each evening I wake the same way: not knowing where I am. Over the past month, I've slept in a strange bed every day, a different motel, a new town. Being away from the organized chaos of the castle, the boisterous camaraderie of my fellow Guardians is a hideous existence.

Forced into hiding like an ordinary human for fear our enemies will use me as leverage against Nicki as Zach did, my admiration for my queen doubled over these past few weeks. How she endured this for years boggles my mind.

I toss my legs over the side of the bed and stand, moving like an old woman. My leather pants creak as I teeter before gripping the back of the chair next to me. I grimace at my haggard appearance in the wall mirror.

King Ruse's powerful blood healed my injuries and restored my strength enough for me to teleport away, but I haven't fed since. In the month I've gone underground like some damn leper, I've lost considerable weight. The ability to glamor a human has no appeal. Mortal blood wouldn't sustain me for long, anyhow. I need my mate's, and the odds of that happening are slim to never.

If I don't feed soon, my body will weaken to the point of death. With no strength to fight, or even close the damn curtains against the killing sun, I'm as good as dead. But maybe that would be preferable.

I rub at the permanent ache in my chest as my thoughts shift to my mate. I was angry, devastated he never questioned why. Still am. His initial reaction was to defend Nicole and condemn me. My heart shattered into a million pieces sitting there while my blood pooled around me. His own father stood by me and nourished me when his son refused.

What astonished me were the words Nicki whispered in my brain. *'He's hurting, Lu. He doesn't mean the things he's saying. You both require time and separation. We'll distract him. Once you're healed enough to teleport, leave. I'll be in touch. Your only other option is a silver-lined cell for the next month and with everything you've been through in the last four days you need to get the hell out of here.'*

She couldn't be more wrong. Kurtis meant every word. The shifter prince can never see past the things I did, no matter the reasons. I've always felt there was no real future for us, but I didn't comprehend how utterly broken I'd be when it ended. His lack of faith in me pierced my soul. A silver dagger through my heart would be preferable to this chronic torment.

But with all the lies I told, and the activities I performed to protect my sister, can I blame him for his reaction? Would I have behaved any differently if our positions were reversed? I'd like to think I would. If for no other reason than the bond.

I'm linked to Kurtis for the rest of his life, but he never completed his end. Was it for my safety or because deep down, the thought of mating a vampire is abhorrent? The shifter's disgust and anger rang loud and clear that night in the dining hall. He declared he could never accept me as his mate or queen, and it solidified what I'd already experienced from him. Even if Nicki hadn't ordered me to take off, I would have anyway—no matter the repercussions.

Any day, I will face the council and answer for my transgressions. A part of me longs for death. It would be favorable to this eternal suffering without my strong, handsome soldier. And based on Liam's reaction to my sister, I no longer need to worry about my twin.

My phone vibrates on the Formica table, and my heartbeat skips. One individual has my burner number: Nicki. My hand trembles as I pick it up. '*Out of time. Get ur ass home, council meeting conference room midnight tomorrow. Don't make me track you down.*'

If there were an ounce of grit inside me, I would stroll into the sun at daybreak and finish it. A fitting conclusion to years of misery, but at least it would be on my terms, not at the council's order.

One thought keeps me from ending my existence—the chance to see my love once more. I'm anticipating the council will summon him to testify, which permits me an opportunity to bask in his gorgeous face, glory in his commanding presence, and smell his intoxicating scent before they demand my execution.

'*I'll be there.*' I text back, sealing my fate.

* * *

Instead of teleporting directly to the conference room, I drop quietly into the inner courtyard, requiring a few minutes in the tranquil beauty of the gardens. In my absence, spring finally arrived at the castle. Most of the snows melted, and the trees and bushes budded.

This is where Kurtis first confronted me, swore to discover my secrets. It seems like a century ago. I squeeze my eyes shut and visualize his impassioned stare as he growled low. The desire and fear had spiked my heart rate.

"Angel?"

At the deep husky voice behind me, my lids snap open and I stiffen. God, I am depleted; I didn't hear him walk into the garden. My vampire cries out for her mate, but I don't turn. I can't bear to witness the disgust and fury blazing from his eyes.

The heat from his body penetrates my t-shirt as he steps closer. Dizziness fogs my brain as his alluring aroma fills my senses. My fangs ache, starved for him.

"Look at me."

His command sends a tremor through my limbs but I shake my head, my long braid swishing back and forth across my protruding spine.

I'm startled when he strolls around to confront me. I expected him to insist I obey. I drop my gaze. Let him state his peace, but I don't deserve to look him in the eye. I am nothing but a lowly vampire who broke countless laws, betrayed her own queen, and is about to meet her death. I can't even claim the status of a Guardian anymore. Kurtis is a future king. What a damn fool I was to believe we had a chance.

"Christ, you've lost so much weight. When was the last time you fed?"

"It does not matter. The end will arrive soon enough. If you don't mind, I would appreciate a few minutes alone before I face my executioners." I keep my hands clasped behind me and contemplate his enormous boots.

Rough fingers gently clasp my chin and raise my gaze to his. "Forgive me."

I'm stunned, not merely by the words but by his haggard appearance. The blonde hair curls over his forehead and ears in an unruly but sexy manner. Dark circles shadow the tormented stare, and the blue are no longer the vibrant hue of the sky at midday.

I wasn't the only one suffering from our separation. Even after everything, my mind screams to soothe his sorrow. Is it selfish to want his last thoughts of me laden with pleasant, loving memories?

"You have nothing to apologize for, mate. It is I who should atone." The energy to raise my palm to his cheek is draining, but I force my limb to obey. His lids close briefly at my touch, and he leans into the caress. "I dragged you into the lies and deceit of my life. You are a fierce and noble male. One day you will be king and marry a beautiful shifter worthy to rule by your side."

Kurtis grips the back of my neck and draws me closer. "No, angel. It is I who needs absolution. I failed you. Condemned you without even offering to learn your reasons." The bitterness and sorrow in his harsh whisper pull at my heart.

When he goes down to one knee, I gasp in stunned disbelief. "What are you doing?"

"Lucretia Luna Bramen, I love you more than anything. I care not why you did what you did. All I know is my world is a living hell without you. I understand vampires don't go the traditional route of marriage, but shifters do. Marry me. Become my mate. Rule at my side."

"Are you crazy?" I hiss in dismay and blink the tears threatening to run unchecked.

"Yes. For you." He seizes my left hand, and the most beautiful, princess-cut blue diamond, the color of his eyes slides over my ring finger. "Say yes."

"No," I whisper harshly and step away. The weight of the band is like a vicious vice around my bruised and bleeding heart. "I'm about to face some severe charges which will no doubt precede my execution. I'll not end my life contaminating your good name."

Kurtis rises to his feet with gradual effortless grace for such a huge man. "You think I give a rat's ass about my reputation?"

"You should. You're the next king, damn it," I grate out through gritted teeth.

"And you will be their queen." His glare blazes with determined intent.

I growl. How can I dissuade him from this course? "No, Kurtis, I won't. Even if this trial wasn't hanging over my head, my future uncertain, I am a vampire."

He smirks, and my hollow stomach flutters. "I'm well aware."

"This is not funny. Your people will never accept me as their queen."

"I can't lie. There'll be an adjustment. But they will grow to worship you as much as I do. My father already does." His grin broadens, and I want to howl in frustration.

The shifter is not getting it. All this is a moot point. The council decides my fate in the next few minutes, and at the very least, they could condemn me to incarceration for a century or more. His stubborn ass is wrecking my attempt to finish this lovingly. As much as it pains me to harm him further, the situation calls for a little tough love. Before we leave this garden, I must convince my mate I have no deep feelings for him. Because if I'm not sentenced to death, he's the type who would wait, no matter how long it took.

"Kurtis, even if you weren't the future shifter king, I could never wed you." At the questioning lift of his brow, I allow icy indifference to settle over my expression and utter the words to crush both our hearts. "You're my mate, and we've had incredible sex, but why would you ever think I love you?"

His blue scrutiny drills into mine as he takes a menacing step towards me. I hold my ground. "No more lies between us," he growls before his mouth descends, plundering my lips with possessive intent.

The heat from Kurtis buffets my chest. He surrounds me. Overwhelms me. His presence sucks all the oxygen from the crisp air, and my head swims with his citrus and pine scent. I crave to fall under his spell and forget everything.

No. Protect him.

I delve deep and uncover the fortitude to drag my lips from his, but I'm too depleted to break his embrace. "Let me go, Kurtis." Meaning more than just my body.

His response is a rough growl. "Never." The anguish in his tone is visceral, and it cuts through me, leaves me raw. I allow none of it to show until my gaze lands on the rapid pulse in his neck. My stomach cramps with a violent hunger, drawing my muscles taut and circulating adrenaline through my bloodstream. A sudden pain shoots through my gums as dormant fangs descend.

Just a little nip to get through this trial.

Fuck, his fragrance ignites my senses. I lick my lips, anticipating his sweet, potent blood quenching my raging thirst. Kurtis's low rumble vibrates my chest, tightening my nipples.

"Feed, angel. Let me nourish you as I should have done before."

Even in the first few weeks of my existence as a vampire, I never struggled against such an urgent yearning to assuage my parched throat with his rich, powerful essence. When my tongue runs along the skin over his vein, and my nails dig into his shoulders, realization dawns.

If I were to give in to the demands of my body, any objective to spare him would vanish. It would prove I need him despite my words and abating my hunger would solidify his determination to wait for me.

I refuse to condemn my mate to a lonely existence, pining for a female imprisoned for centuries. The vision of his dismal future gives me the fortitude to pull away. I stumble back several steps and harden my resolve.

With shaking hands, I slide the beautiful ring from my finger and tenderly lay it upon the concrete bench to my right. My soul splinters. "Get it through that thick skull of yours; I don't love you. Find yourself a nice little shifter to warm your bed and forget I exist."

His low growl skates anxiety straight up my spine. I allow myself to drink in his savage appearance a second longer, before tracing away to the conference room.

I'd much rather endure the council's verdict than Kurtis's wrath.

CHAPTER 43

Lucretia

Once I materialize in the spacious conference room I head straight for my queen, but before I can even sink to one knee, Logan traces behind me and slaps silver shackles around my wrists at my back. I hiss against the burn but refuse to lower my gaze.

"The other council members are being plied with booze, so we have a few minutes." The powerful halfling steps to me, her gray orbs hard. "They are under the assumption you were imprisoned in the dungeon these past few weeks—not roaming the world, hence the shackles."

I nod in understanding, but nerves quiver in my gut. As Nicki is fond of saying: shit's about to get real.

"Logan will secure you to the wall. You'll have an opportunity to plead your case, but keep your mouth shut until you're called upon. Clear?" Her anger ignites the gray, and I swallow.

"Yes, my queen."

Her laugh holds no humor. "Lu, I don't believe I've ever been your queen."

My heart aches at her remark. She is mistaken. Nicole Giordano was more a leader to me than Dimitri during the hundred years I served under him.

I wince as my former commander jerks me towards the back wall, his rough treatment a potent reminder of his anger and hatred. My psyche plummets to the days of torture Zach put me through, but I stubbornly shove the relentless nightmare away.

"Logan, I'm...."

"Hold your tongue," he interrupts harshly. "I have no desire to listen to your apologies. Save it for the council."

He shoves me against the stone and clamps the cuffs to a circular hook in the wall at my waist. I deserve his contempt. Not only did I betray his trust, but I also aided Dimitri in hurting his mate. No matter my reasons, the warrior will never forgive me for my actions. I see it in his brilliant emerald regard.

King Ruse ducks through the door and Logan steps aside. A vivid blue eye winks, and I frown. Does he assume I'm innocent of these charges? He's in for a rude awakening.

Behind him, the colossal demon shoots me a perfunctory glance before heading to his place at the long oval table in the center. Is he being sworn in tonight? Who would have guessed the devil would occupy a seat on the Council of Unity?

Alex's mother, Queen Svaldana, saunters in and sits across from Cipher. A tender look passes between the two, and I can't help but envy their devotion to each other throughout the centuries. What misery they underwent to keep their love secret. Although at this stage, it's not a mystery anymore.

When a glint of red grabs my attention, I gape in disbelief as Queen Oresha strolls through the door like she owns the place. The succubus's sexy body is draped in maroon leather, her long crimson hair unbound and tumbling around her shoulders and waist. Jilaya sided with Dimitri in the famous battle and yet here she is, bold enough to be in the same room with Nicki and Logan.

My queen walks right up to her, and I tense, waiting for the fists to fly, but when the two women shake hands, my jaw drops. What the fuck? Did hell freeze over in the past month? If Syn Grayflame comes through the door, I might suspect I've entered an alternate universe.

Instead, Priestess Tanagra sashays through the threshold dressed in a forest-green gown flowing to the floor with an empire waist braided in gold. Shimmering bangles snake around each bicep, matching the golden sandals peeking beneath the hem with each stride. She looks like she stepped from a Roman palace back in the era of Caesar.

Nicki greets her warmly, but it's the demon king who watches the little priestess. His eerie ruby stare unashamedly devours her from head to toe. If he's not careful, his look will set her elegant gown on fire.

The last to enter are Liam and Icarus, followed closely by my sister. My heart skips a beat at her appearance. She's wearing jeans, a pink sweater, and black boots. She appears... normal. The thick curls glisten with health as they undulate across her back with each step. Somber eyes skim the room, but when they settle on mine, I perceive her fear and anxiety. The clenched jaw and fingers wringing together at her waist are a dead giveaway to my twin's inner anarchy.

Many times over the last month, I tried connecting with Vi telepathically, but she never responded. Is it because she did not wish to speak to me, or because her mind is so muddled, she's powerless to identify if it's me or one of the million other voices in her head?

When she emits a rough mewling sound, the werewolf king turns and grabs her arm. In an instant, her demeanor changes like the snap of a light switch. The frantic expression softens, the amber clears, and she smiles up at him.

Holy cow. Liam is her calming force. Her security blanket, if you will. His touch eases the turmoil in her mind. The big wolf leans down and whispers in her ear before lowering her into a chair set against the wall. He reaches under his blue western button-down and removes a gold necklace, handing it to Viessa. She clutches it with desperation and nods.

Icarus murmurs a few words to her, but Vi glares at him. Resentment and hatred brighten her regard and he backs away. How odd. She doesn't even know the priest, why is she so furious with him?

When Nicole takes her place at the table, Logan moves to a monitor on the wall and flicks it on before sauntering back to me. Syn's strange visage slowly emerges. Silver irises immediately pinpoint Nicki and a sneer lifts his lips. His pointy ears twitch with his emotions; Syn is strikingly beautiful. Too bad he's a power-hungry, evil son of a bitch.

"Thank you all for gathering here tonight," Queen Giordano begins. "It appears you're too cowardly to show your face in person, Grayflame. I would love five minutes of your time." Nicki's malicious grin causes the hairs at my nape to stand at attention. I peer over at Logan, and his lips twitch to hold in a smirk.

"Only five? I would enjoy hours, Halfling." The silver leer hardens to ice as they travel Nicole's length with hatred. A low growl rumbles from Logan's chest.

"Might we proceed with the meeting, my lady," Icarus scolds gently from her right.

"Let's do it," she responds, her glare never leaving the monitor. "We have several items to discuss and vote on tonight, so we will try to get through them as quickly as possible." Her finger swipes at the tablet resting on her palm. "Sebastian emailed you all the agenda. Our first item is to commence with the vote to swear me in as vampire queen."

"All those in favor?" Icarus asks, and everybody at the table responds yes. "All those opposed?"

Syn's resounding "No" echoes through the chamber and Nicki grins. "It appears you're outvoted, Synie."

I almost snort at the indignation on Grayflame's face at her nickname. A tremendous battle with the dark fae is coming. I'm saddened I won't be around to take part.

Icarus performs a hasty coronation and it's finished. Nicole Giordano is finally the vampire queen. Little by little, she is fulfilling the prophecy, and I've never been prouder of who she's become.

"Next order, adding King Jagorach Darath as a council representative," Nicki announces before she suddenly grips the edge of the table. Her head slumps forward, the auburn tresses concealing her face.

Logan is at her side in a millisecond. "Nicole?"

"Mayhap the halfling is too fragile to lead the Vampire Nation."

The taunt lifts Nicki's regard. Her overly bright scrutiny lands on Grayflame before she straightens and places a palm on Logan's chest. After a brisk nod, he returns to stand next to me.

"Even if I were near death, I'd stomp your ass, Syn."

"All those in favor of adding Jagorach Darath to the council respond yea," Icarus says, doing his best to mediate.

At the unanimous decision, the demon doesn't crack a smile.

"You've read and understood the bylaws, King Darath?" Nicki asks, and I note her skin appears paler.

The red-eyed demon scrutinizes her. "Yes."

"And you agree before this council to abide by those laws?"

"Yes."

"I'm unable to tell if you're excited or angry, King Darath," Kleora says with a teasing grin.

He pins her with a torrid stare. "When I am excited, peach, you will know it."

Her pointed ears twitch at his response. "Mmm, sight to behold, I am sure."

By the arching of Jagorach's brow, he's startled by the blatant suggestiveness in the land nymph's tone.

This is better than any soap opera.

"Anyway…" Nicki interrupts. "The last point left to confirm your seat is a blood oath. Archaic I realize, but it seals the deal."

Icarus hands my queen a parchment filled with red thumbprints next to signatures. She pierces her pad with a fang, plants it on the paper, adds her autograph, and shoves it down the table to the demon. His enormous fangs descend to pierce his flesh before pressing it into the surface below Nicki's. The scarlet irises fasten on Kleora as he slowly licks the blood away and scrawls his signature.

Geez. Get a room.

"Welcome to the Council of Unity, Queen Nicole Tiana Giordano, and King Jagorach Darath," Icarus announces.

The throb in my shoulders is becoming unbearable, but I don't dare move. I've had enough silver burning my skin to last a lifetime. The atrophied muscles in my legs tremble, and I'm uncertain my limbs will support me for much longer.

A peek at my sister reveals she's still clutching the necklace, her gaze glued to Liam. '*Vi? Can you hear me?*' Her stare darts my direction before beelining it back to the male who owns her rapt concentration.

"Yes," she says out loud, grabbing the attention of everyone in the room. She doesn't seem to care. Maybe my earlier notion that Viessa can't communicate telepathically with all the other noise in her brain is true after all.

"Let's move on to the next order of business," the halfling queen announces, demanding everyone's attentiveness.

I tune out the meeting and fixate on Vi. My sister is the person I treasure the most in this world. My twin, the other half of my spirit, no matter our differences. '*I hope you realize how much I love you.*'

"Yes. Yes. I know," she answers out loud again.

The werewolf king frowns and rises from his chair. "She's fine, Liam," Nicki interjects with a raised hand. "We require you here." He nods and relaxes back.

'*The people in this room will reveal shocking details about me. I did appalling things to protect you, to keep you safe. Although, as it turns out, I didn't do such a great job did I? Dimitri found you, then Zach.*' Her fingers tighten around the jewelry at the mention of Nicki's father, but she nods. "*Did Dimitri hurt you, Vi?*"

"Yes," she hisses, and my heart constricts.

'*I'm so sorry. No matter how hard I struggled, I neglected to protect you.*' A silent tear courses down my cheek. Since I can't wipe it away, I lower my head to conceal it.

"No. You couldn't."

A strange sensation settles inside me at her words, like a black hole. My stomach is hollow and not just from hunger. My heart spasms and throbs with each painful beat. I lock my knees to keep from collapsing.

I failed my twin. She was defenseless. Innocent. '*I hope one day you can forgive me.*' She shakes her head and part of me withers.

Viessa blames me for everything, and I can't fault her. I dragged her into the vampire world, to an eternity of psychological chaos, without the sun's warmth, or food for enjoyment. I forced her to survive in darkness and isolation, imprisoned in an institution by her own twin.

The saddest part, the one ripping my soul in two: I did not shield her against my enemies. She suffered at Dimitri's hands and most recently, Zach's—all because I didn't trust those around me. Logan or Bastian would have welcomed her in and sheltered her. Deep down, I realize it to be true.

I foolishly believed I could control every situation on my own. It was my burden to bear, after all. She was my responsibility, mine to shelter. A lie I told myself. I wonder if I kept her a secret for selfless reasons, or to preserve my own hide. Maybe a little of both?

I gladly embrace whatever punishment this council decides.

CHAPTER 44

Kurtis

When will she ever learn to trust? Here in the garden, I craved to tackle her to the ground and kiss her until she ceased being so goddamn stubborn and acknowledged there is more than sex or a biological bond between us.

I've never encountered anyone this good at putting up a facade of ambiguity as if nothing I said affected her in the slightest, and I was in the military. The female ties me into knots. She flips me on my axis, and I can't even trust my own responses. One minute I need to be as far from her as possible, then I'm craving her more than my next breath.

Nicki summoned me as a material witness in Lu's case. In a few minutes, I'll stroll into the conference room and plead with the council members for her life. Why the hell did she come back? She'd been safe. Her damn sense of honor and pride wouldn't allow her to shirk her responsibilities, her duty, even if it costs her head.

What will I do if they vote for her execution? No way I'll convince her to trace away with me. Once again, I seriously envy the vampire's ability to teleport.

Lucretia Bramen is mine, and I'd give up my kingdom, my life, my family, to keep her alive. At my marriage offer, despair and hope flashed in her eyes even as she shut down emotionally. She loves me. She just refuses to acknowledge it out of a messed-up belief she's saving me.

"How are you holding up?"

I turn to Bastian, leaning against the doorway to the great hall, arms crossed over his chest. Since Logan's already in the meeting, there was no need for his presence. "I'd like to get this shit over."

He tilts his head, scrutinizing me. "You wish to protect her after everything she has done?"

"Of course. She's my fated female."

"I hate to break it to you, Ruse, but the mating bond makes you weak. It transforms you. You say and do things you would not typically do."

His sneer raises my hackles. "Isn't the little valkyrie your one true mate?"

He shrugs. "Biologically, yes. It does not mean I must give up my way of life or a part of myself for her. I will perform my duty; find her, bond with her, then return her to her family. Beyond that, no other relationship exists."

I chuckle. "You haven't found Alex yet, Bastian." His low growl proves he's pissed the little redhead keeps slipping from his grasp. "You've spent no significant time in her presence. My man, you are in for a rude awakening, and I hope I'm around to watch it happen."

Bright blue flickers with resentment. "No female will acquire control over me. Mark my words." He thrusts away from the doorway and walks straight towards me with long, angry strides. "My goal is to fulfill my vow to the queen by locating Alex, mating her to restore her mind, then dumping the fiery redhead with her mother. By the next evening, a new sub's moans of ecstasy will fill my ears."

"What is your deal with women, Sebastian?"

Bastian growls. "I do not..." He stops short, angles his head as if listening. "They are ready for you, shifter. Good luck. You are going to need it."

*   *   *

Striding through the door, the first thing I zero in on is Lucretia. Her haggard appearance shocks me once more, and it appears as if she's standing by sheer will alone. The silver cuffs agitate the beast, but Nicki warned me they would be unavoidable.

She doesn't even bother to raise her head, defeat written in every line of her gorgeous body. *Don't give up on me yet, angel. I'll figure out a way to salvage this.*

The second factor drawing me is Lu's doppelgänger; identical but as diverse as night and day mentally. Viessa's perched on the edge of a wooden armchair with a gold chain clutched in her fists, her upper torso swaying back and forth, and her contemplation glued to Liam.

"Please be seated Kurtis, we are almost ready for you," Nicki says, waving at the vacant chair next to Lu's sister. Unease settles in my chest at the frenzied expression on Viessa's face, but she doesn't even acknowledge my presence.

Bizarrely, this female captivates me. A protective spark flares from the beast, pulling me to this vampire in a way I can't explain. It finally dawns on me why Liam felt a connection to Lu. These two females are more than mere sisters. They are identical twins, linked physically and psychologically in a manner I will never understand. This is what drove my friend crazy; knowing Lucretia was my mate while battling to contain his beast's instincts.

I glance over at the wolf, watching me, and I nod my understanding. His shoulders relax.

"Okay, before we proceed to Lucretia's trial, I would like to bring one further vote to the table." Nicki swipes her finger across the tablet, and I scowl at her paleness.

Something is off with her, but what? I rotate my gaze to Logan, and he's scrutinizing his mate with a deep line between his brows. Maybe she's stressed with everything on her plate? But Nicki's faced more formidable issues than this in the past without batting an eye.

"The council has collected thousands of petitions over the years to reform the statute regarding different species mating." Nicki eases back into her chair. "It's antiquated and quite frankly, ludicrous. Everyone here knows we don't choose our mates. Not like humans. Fate and whatever gods you believe in, manipulate our genetics or biology or whatever you prefer to call it, and to condemn a being to an eternity of misery because it goes against the law this council established in fear and ignorance is asinine."

My heart rate trips. If the council passes this legislation, it's one less charge against Lu, allowing us free rein to mate and wed. What amazes me is why Nicki is presenting this. With the Guardian's transgressions against her, you'd expect she would do everything in her power to see Lu either dead or imprisoned for centuries.

"What about all the tales of deformed offspring from these unions? Do we want half breeds with untold abilities? We do not fully comprehend what they would be capable of, or if they would be mentally unstable," Priestess Tanagra voices gently, her sad regard flicking to Viessa.

"That's indeed what they are, peach, rumors." King Darath interjects. "Even though it's a rarity, over the past two millennia, couples from divergent species gave birth to normal, healthy offspring. As Queen Giordano eloquently stated, we do not choose our fated ones. Children born from these unions receive one parent's abilities. It is uncommon for them to be gifted with both."

Icarus rises from his seat, and all eyes shift in his direction. "It is not up to the Council of Unity to govern destinies. The gods predetermine every individual's fate. We must have faith the universe will balance the power. By approving this initiative, we accept the first steps towards an abiding unity, and fulfilling the prophecy."

"Thank you, Icarus, for your insight. I second Queen Giordano's proposal and motion for us to proceed forward with a vote," Arra says, hope sparking in her expressive face.

The valkyrie and my father loved each other for centuries. This referendum would finally release them to complete their bond and be together publicly. But until Dad retires, I'm not sure how readily our people will welcome a valkyrie as queen, probably about as eagerly as they would accept a vampire.

I peer over at my female chained to the wall, her head lowered, revealing nothing.

"All those in favor of revising the law to allow fate to determine our mates, acknowledge yea or nay. I say yes."

Surprisingly, the only ones opposed are Jilaya and Syn. My heart soars. I am now free to give Lu my bite and complete our bond. Desire rolls through me at the prospect, but I quickly squelch it. Her future is still uncertain. Will the council, many I consider friends, condemn her to death?

"I would like to make a formal announcement before the Guardian's trial begins if I may." My father rises, his frame towering over the seated occupants.

"Of course, King Ruse. The floor is yours," Nicki responds.

"How many more interruptions must we endure," Syn growls from the monitor. "I have a kingdom to run."

"You can terrorize your people later, Synie, so shut it." Nicki's eye spark with light before they dim and swing back to my father. "Ignore the jackass, Cipher. Please proceed."

"I would like to announce, amid these witnesses, I am stepping down as ruler."

Shock tenses the tendons in my body. What the hell is he doing? I expected this wouldn't take place until I reached my third century, as per our custom. When his proud regard lands on me, I push to my feet.

"I appoint my son, Kurtis Joseph Ruse, Shape-shifter King effective immediately, and bequeath him my seat on this council."

Fuck me.

I stepped into this room expecting to plead Lu's case and either kidnap her or walk out of here with her after being pardoned, *not* crowned king. My father unwittingly derailed my plans.

"My son has our soldiers and people's absolute support. They will follow him as they followed me."

I tilt my head at my father's peculiar regard and remarks. He's seeking to express something without declaring it out loud. Does he mean if I move against the council to save Lu, our Sentinels will rally behind me?

For the first time in months, a lightness enters my soul. The knowledge I receive the unconditional support of my people, no matter what I decide, means more to me than I envisioned. A feral grin lifts my lips, and as I regard my father, a similar smile graces his visage.

You cunning son of a bitch.

"Do you accept the role of Shifter King, Kurtis Ruse?" Icarus asks.

"You bet your ass I do," I say, and my father's laughter warms my heart.

CHAPTER 45

Lucretia

Nerves shot, my body jerks in response to the sudden boom of thunder. A raging storm couldn't be more suitable for this occasion. I no longer experience the burn of the cuffs as they shift on my wrists, my energy depleted to the extent it's gone numb. How I'm still standing is a miracle.

Kurtis is king. I watch with pride as Icarus performs the impromptu coronation and the blood oath as he's sworn in as a council member. My mate will be a phenomenal ruler, and even though this thickens the barrier between us, I couldn't be happier for him.

Kurtis assumes his dad's seat, and the sinfully sexy shifter winks at Arra before easing into the chair next to my sister. The petite valkyrie bites her lip as a blush graces her pale cheeks. One hurdle left in their way: Arra's queendom, and with Alex still MIA, who knows how long before she's able to step down and openly be with Cipher.

"Can we get this goddamn trial underway now?" Grayflame whines from the monitor.

"Yes. Let's study the charges brought against Lu." Nicki swipes her finger over the tablet, and a file shows up on the screen next to the dark fae's image.

Good. God. As I scan the list sealing my doom, another round of thunder shakes the rafters.

"The first allegation, breaking the law for mating a shifter, I presume we can nix after our latest vote. Any objections?" When no one responds, Nicki swipes her finger down the screen, and the charge disappears. Just like that. "For the unlawful act of turning her sister, Viessa Bramen, against her will, we'll attempt to get Viessa's side after we hear from Lu." She swivels her chair and fixes me with her sharp scrutiny. "In your own words, please inform us why you defied council legislation and turned your sister."

My throat convulses with the desire to swallow, but with no fluid passing through my system, it's like struggling to gulp down dirt. I peek at my twin, but her head's lowered, her fists cling to the necklace as she sways. The longer she's in here, the further her psyche deteriorates.

"My…" The word is an unintelligible croak, so I clear my throat and start again. "Viessa was born with a cerebral anomaly. The majority of the time, she was unaware what day, or even what year it was. From the moment she could crawl, she required constant supervision for fear she would injure herself." Liam watches my sister with a scowl. "At eight years old, she tried to walk off a cliff, and I expect it was more because her mind was someplace else, not because she wished to die." I transfer my weight to keep my legs from falling asleep; performing a face plant right now wouldn't benefit my cause.

"At thirteen, immortal hunters murdered our parents, and Vi became my sole responsibility." Sure as hell not going to mention I was a lady of the night. No doubt they would include it on my list of transgressions. "And making certain she didn't harm herself, or others became exceedingly challenging, but she's my twin, and I love her more than anything. I'd hoped when she shifted on her eighteenth birthday, she…"

"Hold on a damn minute," Grayflame interrupts. "You were a shifter? How the hell did you become a vampire?"

"Old news, Syn. Dimitri tortured, raped, and turned her." Arra dismisses him with a wave. The low rumbles from Kurtis, Liam, and Cipher quiet the office, and grant me the fortitude to continue.

"Viessa never achieved the ability to shift, and her mind deteriorated significantly. I can't estimate how many instances I prevented her from injuring herself, until one night, after our twenty-fourth birthday, I arrived home to discover she'd—she'd sliced open both wrists." Tears burn at the memory of Vi lying in the middle of our bedroom floor. Blood splattered the walls and furniture as if she'd danced around, happily flinging her life essence before collapsing.

"I panicked. We're connected, and deep down I knew my sister didn't deliberately set out to kill herself. At that point, I'd only been a vampire for three years, but I was desperate. My one option was to change her."

Utter silence meets my statement. Tears of sympathy pool in Arra's somber stare and understanding fill Nicki's.

"So, would you say you kept your sister alive against her will?" my queen asks.

"No. I would not. What she did was an accident."

"It's a marvel it even worked," Kleora says. "Down through history, stories of immortals with the strength to turn another immortal never existed. Now we have two such cases. Yours and Viessa's. I'm not nearly as ancient as King Darath here; therefore, he might provide further insight on the subject." She blinks and swings her forest-green observation on the demon.

"I can count on one hand the times it was attempted over the last two millennia," he confirms. "It was never successful. Based on the obvious mental instability, do we pursue Viessa's rendition of events?" Jagorach asks.

"By the look of her, it would be an unproductive effort, and serve to stress her further," Kurtis interjects, and a murmur of agreement rounds the table.

My lids close briefly. The thought of upsetting my sister stirred my vampire's protectiveness.

"Let's vote." Syn leans towards the screen. "We all realize the penalty for turning a human, or in this case another immortal, is a death sentence."

"Yes," Kurtis agrees. "But do we charge Lu for doing so against her sister's will? The law is precise, and it sounds to me like Viessa had no knowledge she was dying. So, it begs the question; if she'd been coherent, would she have permitted the change to preserve her own life? And would any of us, with the ability, do no less to save a loved one?"

I suck in a hard gasp.

"All those in favor of charging Lucretia Bramen with unlawfully turning Viessa against her will?" The council members answer Nicki's query with silence, and I exhale my captured breath in a rush. "All those opposed?" A resounding music of yea's circles the table, even a begrudging affirmative from Syn.

Christ. One regulation left. Granted, it's a doozy.

"Before Lucretia gives us her side of the report concerning the charge of treason, I would like to point out I was *not* the queen yet."

What the hell? Is she my defense lawyer? If anyone possesses a right to demand my head, it's Nicki.

"Ms. Bramen, in your own words, explain to the council why you disclosed Nicole's location to King Giordano, and why you abandoned your post as her Guardian?" Icarus asks.

Nicki's stalwart scrutiny penetrates my soul even as Logan's low rumble banishes the numbness from my limbs. Judgment has arrived. I refuse to make excuses for what I did.

"I chose my sister over my queen," I state simply.

"To be clear, I was not your queen at the time, was I?"

"No, but you were the prophesied one, and I was your Guardian. My actions are grounds for sedition."

"Are they?" Kurtis says in an ardent undertone. "Lucretia was being dutiful to the current ruler, not seeking to overthrow him. Can a levy of sedition hold?"

"A valid objective, my lord." The Oracle nods before turning those strange blue orbs my direction. "Explain what you mean by you chose your sister over Nicole, my child." Icarus tips his head with interest.

"Dimitri discovered I had a twin and snatched her from the institute where I'd placed her. After he'd roughed her up, he showed me pictures and threatened to rape and kill her if I didn't help him."

"Sounds like him," Nicki murmurs bitterly.

"You should have fucking come to me," Logan snarls next to me.

"And do what, commander?" Anger ignites energy into my limbs, and I jerk forward, ignoring the sizzle of my flesh. "Risk my sister's life? Expose you and Sebastian to Dimitri?" Fire kindles behind my eyes.

"No!" At Viessa's piercing scream, I twirl towards my twin, ending the fierce stare-off between us. She thumps her fist against her skull. "No. No. No. Not this child. Not this child." Liam runs to her side, Icarus right on his heels. He sinks to one knee before her, and the second he clasps her wrist to save her from hurting herself further, the ranting ceases.

"Look at me, sweetness." The werewolf's purr relaxes Viessa's tense shoulders, and I sense my twin's instant arousal as my own. It's darkly passionate, assertive, and compelling.

Amber raises to stare into Liam's whiskey irises, her smile fills with promise and determination. "One day, werewolf, you'll belong to me. I'll own your heart, body, and soul. At my command, you'll show me tremendous pleasure, and I will reward you in kind."

The entire room stills in bemused disbelief. Not only at the power and conviction in Viessa's voice but the blatant sexual dominance of her words. Liam's jaw hardens, the Alpha objecting to the apparent authority in her tone, even as his gaze wanders to her mouth.

My sister shocks me further when she grasps the back of his neck and yanks him forward until her lips brush his ear. "It pleases me to have you on your knees before me, king." Her statement is hardly a whisper, but the immortals in the room hear it.

The werewolf jerks backward, standing abruptly, his face a mask of displeasure and confusion. If my sister seeks to dominate this Alpha, she has a long, arduous road ahead. Liam will not submit. His wolf would never tolerate it.

“Is the lovefest over?” the dark fae growls from the screen. “I’d like to get on with the final fucking vote.”

“God, you’re an impatient son of a bitch, Syn.” Kleora’s furious retort has Darath throwing his head back and laughing. The demon’s humor widens her enchanted green eyes.

“Everyone, resume your seats,” Nicki demands, having never surrendered her own. With the group’s full attention once more, she gestures to me. “Would you like to add anything else in your defense, Lu?”

“Yes. I’m not making excuses for what I did, but I did not understand…” my voice wobbles. “I should’ve investigated what he sought from you. But to be honest…”

“Lucretia.” My gaze darts to my mate. “Whatever you’re about to say,” he warns darkly, “rethink it.”

I ignore him. “Even if I’d known, my decision wouldn’t have been any different. I chose my twin over you, my future queen, and I deserve any punishment the council determines.”

Kurtis strikes the table, and Nicki sighs with frustration. “Then I suppose your fate rests in the representative’s hands.” She rotates her chair back to the group. “Let’s vote.”

"Might I remind everyone of Lucretia's years of exemplary service to the Vampire Nation." Kurtis leans his elbows on the gleaming surface, scrutinizing the leaders. "How she remained by your side during the battle with Dimitri, when two members on this council stood against you. Or the fact she never revealed our intentions or your location to Zach even after four days of torture."

While it melts me to hear my male plead my case, it's a moot point. The beings in this room already made up their minds.

"Your comments are duly noted, King Ruse," Nicki says.

I blink several times at the title. Wow, it just sunk in. My mate is now the shifter king.

"All those in support of sentencing Lucretia Bramen on the charge of treason?" The Oracle asks.

Four members: Kleora, Syn, Jilaya, and Darath, respond. Hope flickers to life, but I tamp it down.

"All those in favor of dropping the charges?" Kurtis, Arra, Liam, and Nicole reply.

Hell's bells. A damn tie. Now my destiny lies with the priest.

"Icarus?" Nicki questions with a lifted brow. "What's your vote?"

"I am afraid I must excuse myself from the tally."

"What? Why?" Kurtis demands.

The nagging suspicion in my mind clears, and it strikes me like a punch to the gut; Zach hinted at it for days.

"I'll tell you why." I grind out between clenched teeth. "The almighty High Priest Oracle is our father."

The room erupts.

CHAPTER 46

Lucretia

“Everyone shut the fuck up!” Nicki shouts at the group standing and arguing around the table.

The second the words escaped my mouth, a few condemned me a liar. Some turned to Icarus for verification. He neither confirmed nor denied the accusations. Instead, he remained serene amidst the chaos with his hands clasped at his waist, his eerie blue eyes boiling with a fervor I couldn’t decipher.

Once the room quiets down, Nicole indicates with a wave for everyone to sit back down. Kurtis and Liam look shell-shocked, as does Logan, who keeps blinking at me like I’m a strange creature he’s never seen before. In fact, everybody’s stares bounce between me, Vi, and the priest.

"Care to dispute Lu's claim, Icarus?" Nicki asks.

"No, my lady. My daughter speaks the truth."

I inhale sharply at hearing him admit it.

"How?" Cipher requests.

"Once every five centuries, the gods appoint a High Priest Oracle to father the next Seer. The selected species is always human. I was unaware they chose a shifter."

"What the hell do you mean?" the queen demands. "And please don't try the whole *I did not have sexual relations with that woman* bullshit."

"I am uncertain to what you refer, but an Oracle has a carnal appetite similar to other beings, just not during the conception of the next Prophet."

"Oh, God. Are my ears bleeding?" Nicki whines. "It's like listening to your father discuss sex. Get to the point, please."

I frown at the slight tremor in Nicki's hand as she drives it through her hair. My queen is unwell and seeking to disguise it.

"The gods determine the beneficiary of the Oracle's divine seed. I had no knowledge of the female during procreation."

"Hold on. Back the bus up. Are you claiming you didn't have sex with their mother? That it was an immaculate conception?" Nicki asks.

"So, what? You jacked off into a cup, and the gods inseminated a random human?" Liam inquires with a slight grin. "Where's the fun in that?"

"Not precisely, but for your understanding, we will use your analogy."

"Then what?" Arra questions with keen interest.

"At the child's third birthday, they reveal the location to the Oracle, and we retrieve the toddler to start their training."

"Did you reject us because there were two instead of one?" I don't even try to mask the derision in my voice. If he'd been a part of our lives, Viessa's life would've been so much more—not normal, but meaningful. Revered by all immortals

"No, my child. They never divulged your location. I searched for you for decades. It never dawned on me you would be anything other than a mortal." Icarus eases a step towards me, his expression beseeching me to understand. "When I met you for the first time after the great battle with Dimitri, I sensed our relationship, but you displayed no characteristics or abilities of an Oracle. Your presence puzzled me. After seeing Viessa, I understood."

With stiff movements, he reaches out, as if to caress my cheek. I jerk away until my back hits the wall, and the silver cuffs dig into my flesh. The sorrow in his expression irritates me.

"You are both my children, and while you possess unique abilities, your sister is the Oracle. Fate caused you both to suffer. To what conclusion, I cannot guess. Viessa is not mentally unstable. She lacks the proper discipline to manage the visions of past, present, and future. To her, it is like voices shouting from every side."

"Can you make it stop?" Hope fills me that my twin could one day lead a lucid existence. If that's the case, the sacrifices I've made up to this stage were worth it.

"Indeed. It will take quite some time to dismantle the damage. She needs to come with me and train for many years."

"To where, priest?" Liam demands. His body moves, partially blocking Vi. "And for how long?"

"To a holy place, my lord. How rapidly she learns determines the duration of her education."

"Will I be able to see her?" I ask the question burning through the werewolf and myself.

"No. For her safety, she is forbidden contact during training."

"Thank you for sharing." King Grayflame's sneering voice from the monitor breaks the tension. "But can we get back to this meeting? You all hug it out and kumbaya later."

Nicki snorts at Syn's sarcasm. "He's right. Let's bring this to a conclusion."

Once the group is seated, the queen tips her head to Icarus. “Now that we understand Lu and Viessa’s divinity, does anyone care to switch their vote?”

When Priestess Tanagra raises her palm, my heart nearly pounds out of my chest. Oh, my God. It’s a five to three majority in my favor.

“I have no wish to condemn an Oracle’s offspring, whether or not she’s gifted,” Kleora announces.

“That settles it. The council withdraws the charges against Lu.” Nicki waves her fingers, and the shackles release.

A sob begs to emerge as my arms drop to my sides, and I sink back against the wall to keep from collapsing on the stone floor.

It’s over. I can’t believe I’m walking away a free woman with my head still attached.

“However,” Nicki’s compelling voice freezes everyone mid-rise. When their butts lower to their seats once more, she flicks Kurtis a glance. His lids widen briefly before zeroing in on mine. Apprehension and sorrow mar his attractive face.

Oh, God. Now what?

Nicki swivels in her chair to stare up at me. “In light of your decisions; the lies, the subterfuge, and the turmoil they generated within the Vampire Nation, I have no alternative but to discharge you from your duties as a Guardian and excommunicate you from vampire society."

I gape at her for several moments, impotent to process her meaning. When my brain finally catches up, everything inside me solidifies with horror. "Please, my lady." For the first time in my existence, I openly beg as tears well. "Do not take away who I am. I've already had an identity stolen, please don't steal this from me. Who am I if not a Guardian?"

"You will need to figure it out, Lu. I'm sorry, but as queen, your actions demand no less."

Shaky breaths whoosh from my lungs as I attempt to hold the weeping at bay. My insides quake and tremble in shock. The council spared my life today, but at what cost? Being excommunicated from the Nation means no vampire territory will welcome me. Where will I go? What will I do? For over a century, my universe revolved around being a Guardian.

"The meeting is adjourned," Icarus announces.

"Thank fuck." Syn sighs with exacerbation before his glittering irises land on Nicki with a grin. "I'll be seeing you, halfling."

"Not if I see you first, Synie." She touches the tablet, and Grayflame's silver gaze disappears.

All attention shifts my direction, and my cheeks blaze with humiliation. Too weakened to trace, I have no means to evade the sympathetic glances.

"Angel." At Kurtis's dark, husky tone, the burning in my gut intensifies. "Come with me. Let me feed you before you collapse."

"I don't—I—can't." I have no concept what I'm struggling to say. My shell-shocked, blood-deprived brain refuses to form complete sentences. Deep down, where I refuse to study, I need him.

Cipher steps between us. "What are your intentions with Lucretia, son?"

"She's my mate, as you well know, Father."

"And beyond that?" Why is he pressing him?

"I've already asked her to marry me."

Oh shit. I can't believe he admitted it in front of all these witnesses.

"Kurtis." Nicki's stunned voice addresses her friend. Cipher slides to the right, and I get a clear view as Nicki lays her palm on the new king's chest. Even in my weakened state, my vampire seethes.

"You are a king. How readily do you think your people will accept a vampire as their queen? Even an excommunicated one."

He lifts her hand, kissing her knuckles. "I appreciate your concern, but Lucretia and I will figure it out together."

Oooh, burn. Kurtis basically told her it's none of her goddamn business. Well, maybe he didn't mean it as harsh, but I can pretend.

Her pale lips twitch as she faces me. "I hate it had to go down this way, Lu. As a queen, you..." Her words cut off abruptly as she sways on her feet. My mate reaches out to steady her, but Logan has her in his arms in a second.

"Baby, what is wrong?" His troubled scrutiny scans her body for any injuries.

"I'm not sure," she whispers, gazing up at the warrior she sacrificed her life to save. "But I've felt like shit for the last few days."

"Why the hell did you not inform me?" The fierce Guardian scoops her up before gently setting her butt on the conference table. "Icarus."

The priest steps over, tenderly laying his fingers on her forehead. "No fever."

"She's not sick." All eyes rotate to my sister, shocked to witness her amber irises swirling with magma. Liam winces at the death grip on his bicep.

"Do you recognize what's wrong with her, Vi?" I ask, her tumultuous stare freaking me out a little.

"Yes. The queen carries a vampire in her belly."

CHAPTER 47

Lucretia

Nicki's terrified expression is almost comical, and it's in complete contrast to the shit-eating grin spreading over Logan's face.

"Holy fuck! I'm pregnant? How—how can that be?"

Logan laughs. "Sex, my love. Lots and lots of sex."

A pretty blush steals over her pale cheeks. "Yes. I know how it works, smartass, but I didn't expect it would happen this fast." Her troubled gaze pleads with his. "We've barely had any time together."

The warrior's smile fades. "Are you not happy?"

"I'm just—I am not ready." It's printed all over her face; she's petrified.

Hurt darkens the green regard. “Do you not want children?”

Whoa. They should discuss this in private.

Nicki’s expression shuts down. “Logan, I’m well aware of how my future plays out, it’s written in the damn prophecy.”

That answer couldn’t be vaguer.

The warrior considers her for several minutes. To her credit, she doesn’t even fidget under his keen scrutiny. Then without a word, he lifts her in his arms and strides out the door.

“Well, I guess we can check another box off the prophecy list,” Kleora remarks with a smile.

“Indeed, Priestess.” Icarus grins. “The first natural-born vampire to walk in the sun.”

Sebastian stomps in and heads straight for Jilaya and the land nymph. “My Ladies. Are you ready to depart?”

“I will transport Priestess Tanagra wherever she needs to go,” Jagorach interjects.

“If you assume I am an easy conquest, King Darath, think again.” With a wicked grin, she places her hand on Bastian’s shoulder, and the three of them disappear.

The demon smirks at the land nymph’s daring, then winks at Kurtis before vanishing himself. I’m too exhausted to ponder what that meant. Every bone in my body is gradually crumbling even as fire rushes through my muscles, shrieking for sustenance. Tracing away is out of the question, but I can't lean against this wall forever trying to pretend it's not holding me up.

I need to speak with my twin. "Vi?" The heaviness in my chest eases when she looks directly at me, but I'm flummoxed on what to say. For years our conversations were mostly one-sided.

Liam reaches down and helps her to her feet. His influence once again centers her enough to respond. "I love you, Lu. You did the best you could. It wasn't your fault." Deadly amber swivel to the Oracle. "You carry all the blame, *Father*."

Icarus' eyes widen. "Apologies, my child. I searched for you for decades."

Viessa's expression turns manic. Her violent emotions slam into me like a gale-force wind, and I clutch the stones to keep from toppling over. "Then, I condemn the gods," she suddenly shouts, and I gasp at her daring. "Dimitri found me. Zach located me. Why not you?"

"Vi..."

"Sweetness," Liam and I begin at the same moment, unsettled by the venom in her tone.

She ignores us. "Do you have any notion the misery I suffered? Of course you don't. They trained you to control the visions, the voices. You've lived a life revered by immortals, while I've endured mental and physical torture my whole existence." Viessa takes a stride toward Icarus, the rage lighting up her irises, highlighting the blue tattoos on his astonished face. "Now, you wish to take me away from the one being that soothes my mind and spirit."

"You speak of King Scott?" The little priest's regard lands briefly on the werewolf's protective posture towards my twin.

"Yes," she grates out between clenched teeth. "He is mine, and I will not allow you to separate us." I gape at my sister. The complete authority in her manner floors me. This is a side of her I've never witnessed. To be honest, she's a little scary.

"I am sorry, my daughter. It is forbidden for Oracles to mate. I can eliminate the bond."

"What? Not a snowball's chance in hell," Liam chimes in, his face a mask of fury.

One second Icarus is standing before us, the next he's sailing through the air, slamming into the stone wall across the office.

"Viessa!" The werewolf king grabs my sister's outstretched arm in fear as the Oracle rises from the floor with little effort and straightens his garment.

Holy crap. Zach was right. My twin is powerful *and* livid, not a stable combination.

"My child, you are out of control, and require isolation and training."

"Oh, you haven't seen anything yet," she growls back.

The huge werewolf steps in front of Vi. His expression pleads with the priest. "Please, allow us a minute, Icarus. Let me talk to her alone."

"No, my lord. Your actions will produce further hurt. I apologize."

And just like that, my sister and the Oracle vanish.

"No!" Liam bellows and twists in a frantic circle, unable to accept she's gone. His tortured gaze flickers to the ice blue of his fierce wolf.

"Liam…" Kurtis takes a step in his direction.

"Don't." He snarls while holding out his hand to stop his friend. "I have to get the fuck out of here." And with that, the devastated werewolf king stalks from the room.

Blackness circles my vision. "Mate." His saddened regard immediately finds mine. "Please, I need you."

In two strides, he sweeps past his bewildered father and picks me up like Logan did with Nicki. "Sebastian will be back in a few minutes to escort you and Arra home, Dad," he says over his shoulder as we exit.

With the last morsel of strength, I drape my arms around his shoulders, and before his foot touches the first step of the imposing staircase, I'm licking and suckling on his skin above his vein. Consumed by bloodlust, the incidents of the past hour vanish from my mind.

He groans and my fangs descend. "Wait until we are in my chamber."

His demand has me clenching my fists to abate the thirst. If I could teleport, I'd be devouring his force right this second.

"Hurry."

What seems like an eternity later—but was mere minutes with the enormous shifter's long strides taking the stairs three at a time—he kicks his bedroom door closed. The plush mattress hits my spine, and his hips wedge between my thighs.

"Drink, angel," he commands. "I require you strong to withstand my bite."

My heart squeezes tight at him marking me. These gut-wrenching, cosmic emotions for my mate aren't just a biological connection. This is real, raw, and a little scary. I've never loved before, and it's a strange phenomenon.

When I don't instantly comply, he lifts his head. "Make no mistake, Lucretia. Before this night is through, you will bear my mark and complete our mating."

It's what I've wanted more than anything. More than the burning thirst for his blood, but he's taking an enormous risk bonding with a vampire—one banished from her own people.

"Why, Kurtis? Why would a king wish to mate a warrior who can offer him nothing? Who is nothing?" My voice is weak.

He considers me with an enigmatic expression, as though seeking to peer into my soul. "You are mine. My everything. You grant me my life because, without you, I am the one who is nothing." His lips press lightly against my own, and I swallow back a sigh. "I will not allow you to belittle my queen."

"Nicki was right. Do—do you truly believe your people can accept a vampire?" I whisper distractedly as he rains kisses down my neck.

"In time, they will grow to cherish you as much as I do." He raises his head, his stare penetrating as he brackets my skull. "Tell me honestly, angel, do you love me?"

The uncertainty in the proud Alpha shatters the last remnants of my wall. My next remarks will seal his future and mine, but I can deny my passions for him no longer. "God, help us, yes." Just saying the words out loud lifts the burden weighing down my spirit. His smile lights my world and expels the darkness that's followed me since the day my parents died. "But perhaps we need to keep our union secret from your people, for now. Give them a chance to become used to the new law before you spring a vampire mate on them."

"No more secrets. No more hiding." The low grumble vibrates my breasts, teasing my nipples.

"Then allow me space. Time to figure out who I am. I'm no longer a Guardian, and I must discover my place in the world once more."

With a frustrated grunt, Kurtis rises to his knees, drawing me with him. When my butt rests on his bent thighs, my legs wrapped around his hips, his determined stare devours me.

"No. Your place is with me. I can tell you precisely who you are. You were a shifter who lost her parents at a young age in an extremely wild time in history, and who sacrificed herself to provide for her unstable twin." He reaches behind me and with slow movements separates each snarl and tangle in my mass of hair. "You survived being turned into a vampire against your will and defied everything to preserve your family. You became the first female Guardian through arduous work and commitment. You are the daughter of an Oracle." Cobalt irises darken with emotions as he spreads my tresses over my shoulders. "It is I who does not deserve you."

My frame trembles. Not merely with weakness, but in the conviction of his comments. I've never looked back over my life in such a manner. To me, it was always one shit show after another I sought to lie and cheat my way through. The shame I felt having to debase my body to survive forced me to loathe who I was. But to hear Kurtis, it was noble of me.

I shake my head, refusing to trust what he's claiming. I sacrificed Nicki's childhood, her innocence to protect my twin. My actions were not heroic.

"Yes. Lucretia, understand me. I will not permit you thinking so lowly of yourself. You are everything I could ever wish. In a mate. In a queen. In the mother of our future children. Allow me to devote every minute of my life proving it to you."

Tears blur my vision, and my breath catches. How could this male love me so much after all I've done? As I gaze deep into the alluring depths, one thing becomes transparent: I either accept the things he's declaring or harden my heart and run away from the love of a lifetime. The beliefs drilled into my skull for over a century will not be easy to discard, but for this fierce Alpha King, I must try. For my own sanity, I must try.

"All I can pledge is I will endeavor to do my best." Anxiety presses against my chest; it won't be sufficient. Please let it be enough.

"That is all I ask." His smile releases the dam and tears stream down my cheeks. "Aw, baby." Gentle fingers smooth the moisture away.

The ability to hold my head up becomes more than I can manage, and I sink my forehead to his.

"Are we finished with all these silly emotions, cause if I don't feed in the next few seconds, it won't matter."

He chuckles, palming the back of my skull. "Drink, angel. Restore your strength."

CHAPTER 48

Lucretia

A new frenzy of emotions explode inside me. Kurtis's sweet, powerful blood restores my strength, and I no longer care if this is foolish or dangerous. I need this magnificent creature like I've never needed anything.

His arms tighten, offering comfort and security. Desire zings through my body akin to an electrical current lighting me from the inside out. My aching nipples brush against his sculpted chest with each breath while the sublime essence that is my mate quenches my hunger.

How did I presume to run away from this male? He is my everything. My fists clench in his longer tresses as I recall the heartache and misery the night he refused to offer his blood. I can't fault him for his attitude. The allegations against me were severe, and I can hardly imagine the turmoil inside this fierce soldier's brain. My actions tested his sense of right and wrong. The unbreakable tie to Nicki warred against the demands of his beast and the mate bond. It's a miracle he didn't scrub his hands of me altogether.

"That's it, angel," Kurtis purrs low, affected by the sexual ritual of my bite. A broad hand slides up and down my back in encouragement and the other grips my ass, dragging my wet core against his firmness. "Take what you need."

Heat spirals through my frame, causing my stupid leather pants to become stifling. The male's blood provides the much-needed sustenance to the tissues and muscles, plumping them with moisture and strength. Energy builds, and I shamelessly grind my aching center against him.

Since talking would require dislodging from his neck, I use telepathy. '*Need you inside me, mate.*'

His arms constrict briefly before they reach between us and rip open the button and zipper on my leathers. With ease, he lifts my legs to one side, quickly dispensing with my pants and thong before settling my back on the mattress, careful not to dislodge my fangs.

Without preamble, he opens his trousers and his thick length spears into me. My muffled cry fills the room, and I clutch him tighter. The pleasure-pain shoots me over the edge and with that one deep thrust my body bursts, convulsing around his hardness.

"God, I love how you grip my cock when you come," Kurtis growls with approval and sets a steady, inexorable pace.

This is my happy place; my mate drilling into me, his essence cascading down my throat before spiraling through every artery and vein. After a couple of minutes, sated on his blood, I lick the wounds closed before kissing my way to his mouth. Kurtis whips my shirt and bra off, grasps my skull in both palms before taking over the kiss.

Forceful thrusts drive me to the threshold once more, but it's the demand for his mark, to belong to him entirely, that overwhelms me. This male, this king, is mine, and I crave to become his. Forever.

I ease back and peer into the fascinating blue depths. "Make me yours."

At my command, his beast shifts. Hardened muscles enlarge, cerulean irises darken to whiskey. Enchantment blended with anxiety stirs as all four enormous tusks descend. Holy shit. Kurtis could rip an immortal's head clean off with those things. Will the agony of his bite prove too much?

"Easy, angel." His speech grates out around his canines. "The pain is brief." His head tilts, breathing harshly as the cinnamon gaze of his predator scrutinizes me.

Hell's bells, he's scary, but determination spears through my gut. I would suffer anything to become his. Hell, if I could endure four days of torture from Zach, I can surely tolerate a few minutes of extreme discomfort from my mate to complete our bond, to make us one.

At my nod, his beast's powerful growl cascades over my torso and my insides tighten around him in response. His fullness leaves me, and in the next second, he's flipped me onto my hands and knees and is moving over me to plunge deep once more.

In a purely instinctual act, I sweep my hair over one shoulder and ease my head to the side, exposing my vulnerable neck. Apprehension spears through me as I wait in this submissive posture for my mate to claim me. His harsh animalistic breath at my back escalates my fear, but I remain steady.

Instead of leaning over and latching on, Kurtis's lean hips begin a smooth glide through my slick core. Anxiety builds, but I'm more turned on than I've ever been. I want, need, crave his bite. To experience his canines sinking into skin and muscle at the same moment his cock thrusts within me.

Little breathy whimpers escape my swollen lips at the glorious friction of his girth sliding along my sensitive flesh, and I shove back demanding more.

When his fingers reach around and rub at my throbbing clit everything tightens and builds anew. His other palm moves up my rib cage to clasp my neck, drawing me against his torso. The trembling escalates, and I grip fistfuls of the bedspread to keep from splintering into a million fragments.

"You. Are. Mine," Kurtis says in a possessive growl as firm fingers stretch my neck farther to the side. "From this moment forward, we are one. One mind. One heart. One soul. Forever."

Tears blur my vision as I recite the ritual to unite us for all eternity. "I am yours, as you are mine. From this moment forward, we are one. One mind. One heart. One soul. Forever."

"I love you, Lucretia Luna Bramen."

"And I you, Kurtis Joseph Ruse."

His hips drive deep at the same second the massive canines sink into the muscle between my neck and shoulder. Intense pain bursts through the area and I cry out, instinctively seeking to pull away from the jaws latched on to me, but the shifter's firm grasp and his powerful bite restrain me as he continues to pump his hips aggressively.

After a few minutes, the sharp agony eases, and the transcendent burn I'm addicted to spreads down my breasts, over my abdomen, straight to the throbbing bundle of nerves Kurtis gently caresses.

My moan is rough and needy, and my mate answers with a grunt of approval, altering the angle of his thrusts. The head of his cock hits the sweet spot inside, and I shatter. My scream bounces off the walls as pleasure spreads over my body in scalding waves of lava. My focus narrows and my senses take over as small fireworks explode throughout my core.

The harshness of my mate's ragged gasps, his constant growls vibrating my shoulder and collar have me arching toward the excessive flame from his big powerful torso. The fingers around my neck flex with an affectionate caress. I purr, rubbing my head against his like a cat.

Raw, turbulent emotions slam through me. Lust. Possessiveness. Aggression. Love. The desire to dominate and protect. Kurtis's violent passions and the heavy build of his climax fuels mine once more. I shift against him, calling for more of—I'm uncertain what until his jaws clamp down with a slight shake to hold me immobile. The pain, fused with his masculine dominance, sends me flying over the pinnacle again. Kurtis's bellow is muffled as his scalding seed saturates my insides and his bulky arms tighten like a gratifying vice.

Holy crap. My mate's baser, beast-like emotions ramped up everything tenfold. I glory in his need to conquer me, to claim me with his bite, but also his eagerness to bring me pleasure. Add in the profound love and pride consuming him at finally claiming his female brings tears to my eyes.

His canines ease from my tender flesh with excruciating slowness, and I suppress a cry, already sensing his agitation over causing me injury. The huge male collapses on his back before gently gathering me to his heart.

"I fucking love you, angel."

"I love fucking you, mate," I smirk and kiss his chest, draping my thigh over his muscled legs. He chuckles and draws me tight, running the pads of his fingers over the permanent evidence of his claim.

I never dreamed I'd belong to a mighty king. Me. A lowly shifter turned vampire, former Guardian, excommunicated from her own species, and the prospective queen of his people. The thought of revealing our link has needles of worry stabbing the back of my neck.

"Um, Kurtis. I still maintain we should delay announcing our mating." His instant anger pushes against my scalp. "Just until they grow used to the new law, and their new king. Maybe with time, they will become more welcoming of a different species as their queen."

"Is your concern truly for my people, or yourself?" His cool tone accelerates my heart rate.

"A little of both," I answer honestly. No point in lying, he would detect it in a heartbeat. "After everything, grant me a chance to figure out my place now that I'm no longer a Guardian or tolerated in any vampire territory." Just uttering the words out loud dims my spirit.

"Lucretia, you are my fated female. Whether you're a vampire, shifter, or hell, a demon, you will wear my mark proudly." Kurtis shifts our position. His broad shoulders hover above me as his determined gaze pins me in place. "We are one. It would not matter if the entire world turned against us, as long as we have each other."

An emotion akin to happiness bubbles below the surface. Could he be right?

"I won't lie, troublesome days stretch ahead, and it will take time for my people to understand there is no one better suited to be their queen than the proud, ferociously loyal, and courageous warrior before me." Hard knuckles caress my cheek. Blue eyes glisten with love, but his worry and uncertainty of my response clinch the contract.

"Okay. No matter what arises, we face it together."

CHAPTER 49

Lucretia

Two months later...

If I'm forced to endure another hostile glare from a shifter bitch, someone's head will roll. After the initial shock, the community took a wait-and-see attitude to our mating. It's the high-ranking females who don't even veil their hostility and outrage at their new ruler choosing a vampire over them. I can't say I condemn them, but get the fuck over it already.

The shifter king presides over endless economic issues, territory disputes, crimes, and whiny demands inside what they refer to as the Assembly Hall, a four-story, thirty-thousand-square-foot log cabin deep in the wilds of Yukon, Canada. Unlike the

Vampire Stronghold in Nunavut, it's accessible by road, including an airstrip, which is how Kurtis traveled here before he mated me.

The Shifter Territory is nearly as vast as the Vampire Nation. Of course, like the vampires, shifters control territories all over the world, and while those regions fall under Kurtis's jurisdiction, respected elders of the king's choosing control the areas.

Before our arrival, my thoughtful mate had electronic shutters installed in the central throne room and somewhat modified the gathering times to allow me to attend before sunset.

In this hostile environment, I keep my senses on full alert. Cipher attends all the sessions for now, but I wouldn't put it past these bitches in heat to plunge a silver dagger through my heart first chance they got. Or steal the colossal rock the king slid back over my finger the minute we departed the castle.

It took some work, but I eventually persuaded him to hold off on a wedding until his people accept me, or at the least stop plotting my demise.

Other than the occasions I'm obliged to meet my queenly duties, I've never been happier. Kurtis has demonstrated his gratitude for eliminating the need for air transportation to oversee his vast territory in prolific and satisfying forms. The Alpha is a pure dominant, and while I get off on submitting, I revel in pushing his buttons every chance I get to experience the burn of his discipline.

And I'm quite in love with Loki. The fierce, proud, enormous furball melts my heart. It grieves me I can't observe his transformation, but Kurtis insists the energy surge would injure me. I'd be more than willing to accept the risk, but my stubborn mate put his foot down. Although I've enjoyed the thrill of running with the beast, experienced the heart-pounding excitement of the hunt, delighted in the lust-filled aftermath of being vigorously taken against a timber, or him granting me the pleasure of his magnificent cock in my mouth after ogling his naked form.

I do miss my responsibilities as a Guardian, but I've secretly appointed myself the king's personal bodyguard. Granted, the gigantic shifter can protect himself, but it gives me purpose. And the only moments I begrudgingly let Kurtis out of my sight is when the sun is at its peak, and I must sleep. More often than not, he rests at my side, watching over me. It's adorable.

I itch at the chance to oversee and train his Sentinels. They appear tough and capable but need to learn to rely on more than brute strength. Unfortunately, they'd just as soon spit in my face, but I'll earn their respect and maybe one day teach them a thing or two about war strategy and cunning. It shocked me to discover my mighty SEAL has not trained his soldiers in his favorite combat method. An issue I hope to resolve.

Nightly when we return to the cabin in B.C., I insist Kurtis trains me in this fascinating discipline and fighting technique, and it provides me the chance to spar with my mate, which always ends with me beneath him, his glorious cock buried deep, his lips branding my soul.

'*Lu,*' I jolt at Nicki's voice in my head, drawing a concerned glance from the king. "*Please bring Kurtis and his father to the throne room ASAP. Events require a family meeting.*'

Family meeting? I doubt the invitation includes me. Am I expected to drop them off and leave? Another slap in the face if that's the case. I tamp down on my pity party and slip into my king's mind. '*Nicole is requesting you and Cipher at the castle for a crucial gathering.*'

He frowns with a nod before catching my hand and rising to his feet. "I apologize, but urgent matters require our attention elsewhere. We must adjourn." He turns to his dad, seated on his left. "You're needed as well, father."

The sexy shifter raises a brow before following us out of the vast hall. "What's going on?"

"Nicki has requested our presence at the castle," Kurtis responds.

"Oh, wonderful. More teleporting," the former king grumbles before planting his huge palm on my shoulder.

I press my lips together to keep from grinning at his dread and trace our trio to my old home. In all fairness, my discomfort matches Cipher's but for different reasons. I haven't seen or spoken to the queen or Logan in months and apprehension eats at my insides at how I'll be received.

The second we materialize in the massive chamber, I let go of the two and step aside as Nicki comes forward and embraces my mate and his father. When she turns those gray eyes my direction, I tense, bracing to trace away if she demands it.

"Thank you for bringing them, Lu. I appreciate it wasn't easy to come here."

I nod. "I will leave you to it." I turn to my male. "Contact me when you're ready to go."

"You have something better to do?" Nicki asks, her brow raised in irritation. "This is a family meeting. As Kurtis's mate, that includes you." Warmth spreads through my chest, but before I can react, a large hand clasps my shoulder. My former commander's bright emerald orbs tighten my gut.

"Nicole ousted you from vampire society as a display of strength, but you are welcome here, Lu. As much as I abhor your actions, I came to terms with your reasons. You suffered enough."

Whoa. What's with the complete turnaround? Last time I was here, Logan wanted my head.

He moves to Nicki, drawing her to his side with a possessive arm around her shoulders.

I stiffen. The slight sound I perceived when we emerged finally registers. My wide gaze zeros in on Nicki's flat stomach, and the rapid heartbeat of their unborn child fills my ears. The future king rests in her belly. The first natural-born vampire with the capability to roam in the daylight and carry forth a modern breed of sun walkers.

Nicki snorts at my expression. "Pretty fucking real, isn't it?"

"Yes, my lady. Pretty fucking real."

A door opens to my right and Liam saunters in looking gorgeous as ever in jeans, cowboy boots, and a dark blue t-shirt. A dusty black Stetson sits on his head. His long strides gobble the distance as he heads straight for me. The closer he gets, the more the flickering lights around the room chase away the shadows under his hat and I'm dismayed at how tired and haggard he appears.

"Hey, Lu." He rasps before stooping to plant a hasty peck on my cheek.

"Hey back," I offer, startled by his affection. "Are you all right?"

He shakes his head. "Have you heard from Viessa by any chance?"

"What do you mean? I understood she was with the priest." Panic spreads through my chest that my sister was abducted once more.

"She is," he all but growls. "But I was hoping she connected with you telepathically."

"Oh. No. I'm sorry. Liam, she's safe with Icarus. She must complete her training."

"I know. And I realize the Oracle is helping her, but—she needs me."

Does she need him? Or does he need her?

"Be patient, bro," Kurtis interjects. "She will come back when ready."

"And if it was Lu? Would you heed your own advice, bro?" Liam shoots down his friend's attempt at comfort with a resentful sneer.

But instead of getting pissed, the shifter king barks out a laugh. "Hell no. But as my best friend you'd offer it anyway."

A slight smile twitches at the edge of Liam's mouth. "Point taken."

When Queen Arra walks through the door with Sebastian, Cipher's expression lights up, and before we can greet the newcomers, he enfolds her in his embrace and devours her lips. There's quite the disparity in height between these two, but Cipher just lifts her against his chest. No matter how hard they worked to keep their love a secret, we all knew, but until this moment they never publicly showed any signs of affection.

I peek at Kurtis to gauge his reaction and am reassured to catch his smile and sense his acceptance.

"Good. We are all here except for Icarus and Viessa, for obvious reasons." Nicki motions for everyone to take a seat on the benches facing the dais. I'm surprised when she doesn't parade up the steps and perch on her throne. Instead, she stands on the main floor before us.

"What's this about, Queen Giordano?" Cipher asks, his mate's hand clasped securely in his.

"Please, can we dispense with the formalities? This is an informal family meeting."

Hearing her repeat it, realizing they include me in this tight circle, causes tears to burn the back of my eyes. Kurtis squeezes my fingers, no doubt sensing my turbulent emotions.

"I will get right to it. Alex is in trouble." At Arra's gasp, Nicki holds up her palm. "Please let me finish, then we can discuss." With apparent reluctance, Arra agrees with a stiff nod. "According to Icarus, Viessa has had a vision. Although with her chaotic brain process, the prediction was a discombobulated mess. The upshot, Alexandria has lost all memory of who or what she is and is living as a human."

"What?" The petite valkyrie bolts from her seat. "If she uses her powers in plain sight, the humans will lock her up and—dissect her. The immortal way of life is in peril."

"I'm well aware, Arra." Sebastian steps forward. Dark circles rim the vivid blue depths. "Thanks to Cipher intervening, I've been working with King Darath to pinpoint her whereabouts, but every time we imagine we are close, the link is blocked." Sapphires harden with determination. "I will recover your daughter. I vow it."

"I mean no disrespect, Mr. Moretti, but... based on your reputation, what are your intentions with Alexandria?" A mother's anxiety deepens the frown lines between her dark brows and compressed lips.

A valid question. As long as I've known Bastian, he's never had a relationship last longer than a week. And I wouldn't even call them relationships, more Dom/Sub interactions. He insists it's because he must take his role as owner and head coach of his BDSM clubs seriously and never lets his subs become attached.

If I were a gambler, I'd bet his attitude and treatment of women goes much deeper. I wonder if his reaction to his valkyrie mate will be any different? Is it conceivable Bastian could drop the barriers around his emotions at her feet?

"My sole intention is her safety. The goal is to get King Darath to restore her memories *without* a mating. But, if that fails, I am Alexandria's only option."

I fear the always-in-control vampire hasn't considered what Alex may want. Does he honestly imagine he possesses the strength to ignore or discard the mate bond?

"Let's concentrate on one thing at a time, shall we?" Nicki interrupts the stare-off between Arra and Bastian. "Our goal tonight is to figure out a way to locate my best friend and strategize how to handle her memory loss once we do. I am open to all suggestions."

I cringe, reflecting on Nicki's missing past. Although if you hear her tell it, she could have gone a thousand fucking years without remembering what her father did to her. Now Alex has lost who and what she is, residing in fear among mortals and believing she is one of them. God, her powers must be frightening.

I scoot closer, seeking my mate's warmth and security. When his thick arm drapes over my shoulders and hauls me against him, I smile. What would my story have been if Kurtis hadn't accepted me? Bleak, dark, and lonely. This male glories in my wicked lusts. Wants to offer me everything and more. I wouldn't care if every female shifter under his command hated my guts or made attempts on my life daily. I would endure anything and proudly stand by his side.

'I love you, mate,' I whisper telepathically, not caring if Nicki hears. Warm fingers caress my arm, causing goosebumps to come alive across my skin. The king and I still suffer many obstacles and pressing issues to deal with among this narrow circle of friends, but there is no mightier perception than to understand your part of a network that watches your back.

Even though my father isn't here, with no inkling when he or my twin returns, I look forward to getting to know Icarus. And my sister. My initial anger towards the Oracle dissolved into happiness soon after the trial. Vi and I are no longer alone. We have a family again—friends who care about us and mates to conquer.

I frown recalling the priest's declaration that Oracles cannot mate. With a mental shrug, I shove that aside to deal with another time. For now, my sister is secure and hopefully mastering the pandemonium in her psyche. Alex is the priority at present.

'Later, I'll demonstrate how much those words please me, angel.'

My insides clench at the erotic promise, and I squeeze his thigh in response. This diverse circle of comrades and my mate are my universe. I will kill, cheat, or lie to protect them. Happiness warms my chest as I finally understand; they would do the same for me.

The future is precarious, holds many challenges and dangers, but together, our odd little band of friends can overcome anything.

I hope.

ABOUT THE AUTHOR

A.R. Vagnetti is a writer of paranormal romance with a splash of erotica. Writing has always been her passion, and her idea of heaven is a rainy day filled with her computer, a steaming mug of coffee, and warm fluffy socks. She draws inspiration from the picturesque shores of Lake Huron in the summer and the wildness of the Arizona desert in the winter. When not immersed in her characters, she enjoys traveling, fishing, and camping with her husband and Labrador.

MORE FROM KYANITE PUBLISHING

With the threat of World War 1 and its technological horrors looming, the heir apparent to the deadliest warrior kingdom, and home to honest-to-god Centaurs, must find a new path for her peoples before they are massacred in the trenches.

Journeying to America, she searches for a future free of death, but will her absence leave the kingdom vulnerable to her conniving siblings?

CPSIA information can be obtained
at www.ICGtesting.com
Printed in the USA
LVHW042057090820
662765LV00027B/796

9 781952 152030